Dora Russell

Footprints in the Snow

A novel

Dora Russell

Footprints in the Snow
A novel

ISBN/EAN: 9783337044435

Printed in Europe, USA, Canada, Australia, Japan

Cover: Foto ©Andreas Hilbeck / pixelio.de

More available books at **www.hansebooks.com**

PRINTS IN THE SNOW
A NOVEL, BY DORA RUSSELL.

FOOTPRINTS IN THE SNOW.

A Novel

BY

DORA RUSSELL

AUTHOR OF "THE MINER'S OATH," "THE VICAR'S GOVERNESS,"
"ANNABEL'S RIVAL," ETC., ETC.

"He prayeth best, who loveth best
All things both great and small ;
For the good God who loveth us,
He made and loves them all."

Stereotyped Edition

LONDON

JOHN AND ROBERT MAXWELL

MILTON HOUSE, ST. BRIDE ST., LUDGATE CIRCUS
AND
SHOE LANE, FLEET STREET, E.C.

CONTENTS.

FOOTPRINTS IN THE SNOW.

CHAPTER I.

ELIZABETH GORDON.

AT WENDELL WEST-HOUSE, in Uplandshire, one bleak, cold December morning in 1871, the hall clock had struck eight, and the unstaying hand of Time had crept on minute after minute until nearly another half-hour was past, when Elizabeth Gordon, the niece of the master of the house, descended the staircase with her usual somewhat stately footsteps.

A handsome woman this Elizabeth; handsome, tall, and dark, and with a face and form that you would have expected to meet in some Roman palace, rather than in the comfortable, well furnished English farm house in which we find her. She moved also with unconscious dignity, sweeping her rich, long skirts down the ordinary stair-carpeting, and across the ordinary oilcloth in the hall, with an air that made her seem unfitted and above, somehow, her present surroundings.

Yet Wendell West-house was her home, and when she entered the breakfast-room, which opened from the hall, one of its occupants, a tawny, half-blind, mastiff dog, rose from its place on the rug, before the blazing fire, and with an affectionate whine welcomed her as a familiar friend.

Then up with her light feet sprang out from a basket, which was also near the fire, a black cat, fixing her gleaming green eyes fearlessly, and with God-given instinct, on the face of *her* friend also. Wonderful judges of character are these creatures that we despise, and alas! how often ill-treat. They can tell who are the noble and tender souls who will never hurt them. They recognise faster than we do (for pleasant and deceitful words deceive not them) the great and the small, the true and the false. Judge, my friends, by the dumb beast's instincts, and you will rarely if ever err. The merciful man is merciful to them. They used to creep to the side of the gifted Burns, and we all know the pleasant stories of the gentle Cowper and his pretty playful hares. But there is no reason to enumerate here how the highest

B

and brightest of our fellow-beings have ever remembered the fact that God gave the breath of life to these creatures also, and that in endowing us with qualities that they do not possess, He confided them to our protecting care. The man who ill-treats his dog will beat his wife—the heartless tormentor of one will surely end by being the heartless tormentor of the other.

An especial friend then was Elizabeth Gordon (whose high, proud nature made her always most gentle and gracious to her inferiors) to every animal that crossed her path. See the black pussy now purring and rubbing her sleek head against Elizabeth's brown velveteen dress, and endeavouring with maternal pride to attract her attention to the last plump little addition to her race, which was reposing in the sound sleep of infancy in the basket before the fire. Mark the half-sightless eyes of the old dog fixed with loving affection on the noble and tender face, which was full of sympathy for it, and for all God's creatures. Elizabeth patted the tawny head, and stroked pussy's glossy fur, and poured some milk into a saucer for her, and then going to the well-spread breakfast table, cut some bread up into small pieces, and proceeding to the window opened it slightly, and looked out upon the snowy scene beyond.

A great snow storm had occurred the day before, and had continued until nightfall. Inches and inches deep lay the beautiful treacherous covering to the earth; whitening the leafless boughs, the fields, the hills, hiding away the frozen roadways, and drifting deep into the hedgesides, in which starved and miserable little birds hopped shiveringly, looking out despondingly on what to them was a foodless world.

Elizabeth Gordon pushed away the snow with her well-shaped hand from the window sill, and then sprinkled the bread that she had cut on it, and closed the window, and presently a little timid flock of winged pensioners came fluttering to the spot to partake of her bounty. The black cat lapping the milk on the rug looked up wickedly and enviously with her green eyes at the sound of the chirping outside. But her desired prey was beyond her reach, and so, after a covetous glance or two, she resumed her legitimate breakfast.

Elizabeth, too, commenced preparing for hers. She made tea in the handsome engraved old-fashioned, silver tea pot, and slightly altered the arrangement of the breakfast table. Everything on this (as indeed everything in the room) spoke of ease and comfort, and the supply of good things was abundant and appetising. Cold game, a ham, home-made bread, and fresh butter, all were there; and presently, on a man's footstep being heard in the hall, Elizabeth rang the bell, and at her summons a neat, fresh-coloured, country maiden appeared, bringing in on a tray a smoking dish of bacon and newly-laid eggs. This dish Elizabeth also arranged on the table to her taste, for she was a woman who loved to make everything pleasant to the eyes ; and as she was settling its position the door opened, and the master of the establishment entered the room.

A homely man enough, to look on at first sight, seemed Mr. Horton, of Wendell West-house. Short, broad-made, and ruddy, his commonplace features were yet redeemed, almost ennobled, when you knew his face well, by the benevolence and kindliness of its whole expression. A sly twinkle of humour, too, lurked in the small but penetrating eyes, and stole down to the corners of the somewhat roughly-cut mouth. A gentleman by nature, if not exactly by birth, was this well endowed farmer, and after being in his company for a little while you could not fail to recognise the fine qualities that only make a true one.

" Well, Uncle," said Elizabeth, turning round with a smile to welcome him ; and Mr. Horton went up to her, and kissed her smooth and oval cheek.

" Well, Lissa, my dear," he said, with kindly affection in his tone and words, " and how are you this cold morning ?"

" Half frozen," answered Lissa, with a little shrug of her fine shoulders ; and then, after patting her uncle on his broad ones, she told him to sit down and commence his breakfast, and the healthy jovial farmer needed no second bidding.

No likeness was there between these two ; none of that subtle family resemblance which shows itself in faces so diverse that the broad distinction of beauty and ugliness lies between them. Elizabeth Gordon was, in fact, no blood relation of Mr. Horton's, but her mother and his late wife had been sisters. A certain difference of class, too, divided them, for Elizabeth's father, Captain Gordon, was a well-born Scottish gentleman, who had fallen in love with, and married, the handsome daughter of a rich farmer, when stationed in her neighbourhood, while her sister had wedded in her own rank and become the wife of Mr. Horton, of Wendell West-house. The sisters, however, had loved each other, and clung to each other in spite of this difference in their husbands' station. This tie was kept up perhaps more closely by the fact that Captain Gordon's relations totally refused to receive or acknowledge his wife. An old, proud, Scottish family, they were furious at his making what they considered so degrading an alliance. The good-natured young soldier, however, was quite contented with his handsome Elizabeth, and when her father died, and she was discovered to have ten thousand pounds for her fortune, he felt even more contented still. This fact, too, softened the feelings of his family towards her, and a reconciliation would probably have taken place between them, but Captain Gordon's young wife did not live to be noticed by her husband's family. She died before she was thirty, out in India, and her last wishes were that her only child, a little daughter, should be intrusted to her sister's kindly care.

The Gordons, however, made an offer at once to the bereaved husband to take charge of the motherless child. This offer Captain Gordon after some hesitation declined. He wrote to his prim maiden sisters in Scotland to tell them of his wife's last request, and informed them also that he should not feel justified in acting against the wishes of the dead. The Misses Gordon were almost as indignant on receiving this letter as they were on first hearing the news of their brother's marriage.

"Malcolm was mad," they said in their sharp voices, "utterly mad to throw away such a chance of redeeming the position of his child. What," they cried in shrill chorus, for there were three of them, "not prefer us as the guardian of his daughter to a low-born English farmer and his wife!" The idea seemed absolutely incredible to the long-descended, middle-aged spinsters, full of their narrow prejudices and home-bred notions, which made their little world seem large to them.

After this, in their letters to their brother out in India, they made no further allusion to his child. The little Elizabeth came to England in the charge of an officer's wife, who had been a friend of her late mother's, and was received at Southampton by the warm-hearted Uplandshire farmer and his comely, affectionate wife.

Mrs Horton had no daughter, and Elizabeth, "Lissa," as she informed her aunt that "Mamma" had always called her, became in a few days as dear to her as her own two stalwart boys. Lissa was one year older than Mrs. Horton's eldest son, and upon the strength of that one year she tyrannized over the boys in her pretty childish way from the age of five, when she arrived at Wendell West-house, for the next ten years without mercy or contradiction. Mr. and Mrs. Horton, in fact, spoilt the lovely little Anglo-Indian girl, who was so imperious in her ways, and yet such a loving high-minded little lady too. She reminded Mrs. Horton of the beautiful Elizabeth who once was the pride of her own early home, and Lissa was unquestionably now allowed (even though another baby-boy was born after her arrival) to be the pride and darling of Wendell West-house.

The boys went to school, and Lissa had a governess; and by-and-by, when she was ten, the news came from India that her father was married again (a General's daughter this time), and the family pride of the Misses Gordon was somewhat comforted by this event. About a year afterwards a son was born of this marriage, and Elizabeth's chance of the scanty and strictly entailed Scottish acres, that the maiden aunts held so sacred, was thus entirely cut off. This seemed to separate Elizabeth completely from her father's family. The son and heir was sent to

Scotland, when his age required his removal from the dangerous climate of India, but Elizabeth never saw her little brother. Then her father died, and his widow came to England, but she made no claim to remove her step-daughter from her aunt's affectionate care. Elizabeth had her mother's fortune of ten thousand pounds, and being thus amply provided for, Mrs. Gordon the second not unwisely thought it best to allow her to remain among her own people.

In the meanwhile Elizabeth had been growing into a lovely girl, and her uncle and aunt were not a little proud of her exceptional beauty. This was exceptional not only from its greatness, but from the rarity (in England at least) of its type. There was an olive tint in the clear skin, and the thick hair that grew low on the broad brow was darker by many shades than is generally seen in this country. She was above the average height also, and her finely developed figure, and the grand outline of her whole physique, made her a strikingly handsome and remarkable looking woman.

When she was not quite seventeen a great loss happened to her (the greatest almost that a beautiful girl like herself could sustain), her good aunt, who had ever acted like a mother to her, died, and Elizabeth was left without womanly love or counsel in the world. Her uncle had always spoilt her, and everything that she said or wished now became law at Wendell West-house. She was too young naturally at first to exercise such uncontrolled sway with great discretion; but still, though she made some enemies, she made many friends. People said that she was a coquette too, and despised the pretensions of one or two excellent young men in her own (or at least her uncle's) station in life, and that such pride was sure to have a fall. Elizabeth, it must be admitted, at this period was not unconscious of her own attractions, and did not find the awkward, sporting young farmers who came to her uncle's house at all to her taste. They were all very well for a little while (and thus probably arose the report of her coquettishness), but she soon grew tired of her many admirers, and at twenty-one had never seen any one whom she could even contemplate marrying. When she was just about this age, however, the farm that Mr. Horton leased changed owners, and from this event new interests and excitements sprang up for Elizabeth's life.

Yet three years had passed since then, and Elizabeth was still unwedded. That this was her own fault most observers would have decided who had seen her at the breakfast table, opposite her uncle, on the snowy December morning in 1871, when this story commences. Young, handsome, and with a good fortune, Elizabeth was a prize that many men were sure to strive for. Her manners were winning, too, and there was a look of sweet trustful happiness on her face, that told of some secret joy which made all the world just then seem bright and pleasant to her.   An air of placid content also was imprinted on Mr. Horton's homely features; and it was evident by every word that they exchanged that the greatest good-will and regard existed between them. No one, in fact, was like Elizabeth in her uncle's eyes, and she repaid his unvarying kindness with real affection.

"And so the Lieutenant left last night?" said Mr. Horton (not without a sly glance at his handsome niece), as he helped himself to his third rasher of bacon.

"Yes," answered Elizabeth softly, and her colour deepened as she spoke. "He would reach Southampton about midnight he expected, and embark at once in one of the Peninsular and Oriental steamers."

"Humph," said the farmer, going on vigorously with his breakfast, "so Sir John told me. Well, he's a fine young fellow, and I hope he'll have a nice cruise, though I can't say China's a station much to my taste."

"Perhaps not," said Elizabeth, thoughtfully, and then she was silent—silent for a moment at least; for the next the door of the room was flung open, and a fine, handsome lad of sixteen rushed in, and with as much noise as was possible seated himself at the breakfast table.

"My dear Hal," said Elizabeth, reprovingly, "need you make all that noise?"

"Noise!" grumbled the boy, rubbing his red hands together, "no wonder a fellow makes a noise when he's starved to death. D'ye know, father, the ice is an inch thick in the water jugs in that sky parlour of mine?"

"It will make you all the hardier," laughed the farmer. "In my young days boys like you didn't know what it was to be cold, and if they dared to grumble, they were rubbed down with snow."

"Oh! of course," said Master Hal incredulously, with his eyes fixed on the ham in the centre of the table. "I say, Lissa, cut me a slice or two thin, will you, for if I try you're sure to say I spoil the look of the ham."

"So you would," said Lissa, rising from her place at the table, after pouring out her cousin his tea, and coming round to cut the ham. "There, child, is that enough for you?" she continued, after carving a plateful to whet his youthful appetite.

"It'll do for the present," replied Hal, commencing operations at once; but Elizabeth went on carving after she had handed her cousin his plate.

"I may as well cut some for the other boys," she said.

"Boys!" said Hal, with his mouth full, "that's cool, you calling us boys! Dick's a nice boy of four and twenty, isn't he?"

"Three and twenty you mean, my dear," said Elizabeth, with conscious superiority.

"Well, three and twenty, then. Do you call that a boy?" asked Hal, going on the same time rapidly consuming his ham.

"You all seem boys to me," replied Elizabeth calmly, laying down her knife and fork after cutting many slices of ham, and then leaving them on the dish. "There, uncle, do you think that will be enough for them?"

"Let them cut for themselves, Lissa, don't you bother about them," said Mr. Horton. "Good morning, Bob," he went on, as his second son, a tall, heavily-built young fellow of twenty-one, now slouched into the breakfast-room. "Well, are you ready for skating this morning, Bob?"

"The pond will have to be brushed first," answered Bob, seating himself at the breakfast-table also. "Good morning, Lissa," he added, looking at his handsome cousin.

"Good morning, Bob," replied Lissa, smiling.

"Is Dick ready yet?" asked the farmer, addressing his second son. "He's always last."

"He won't be long," said Bob, commencing his breakfast; but Mr. Horton, having finished his, now rose from the table.

"You spoil them, Lissa," he said, "waiting for them. In my father's time the breakfast things were carried out as the clock struck nine, and whoever had not finished breakfast by that time got none."

"Manners have improved since then, you see, father," said Hal, looking up from his plate. "Lissa, give me another cup, please?"

"Wait till Dick has some," replied Lissa, inspecting the teapot.

"Oh, bother Dick," said Hal.

"My dear, you must wait," said Elizabeth, with her grand air.

Upon this Master Hal jumped up from the table, and rushing out of the room, went into the hall, and began calling "Dick, Dick," at the top of his voice.

"Oh, that boy!" said Elizabeth, putting her hands to her ears.

"Stop that noise, Hal," cried Mr. Horton, following his offspring, and giving him a good-natured shake of the shoulders, as he passed him in the hall. "Oh, here you are at last, sir," he continued, addressing a tall young man in slippers, who was at that moment descending the staircase.

"What are you making such a confounded din for, Hal?" asked the young man on the stairs, rather crossly, who was Richard Horton, the farmer's eldest son

"Because Lissa won't give me another cup of tea till you come," answered Hal, with perfect candour.

"Well, that's good of Lissa," said Richard Horton, as he

entered the breakfast room; and he advanced to where his cousin was sitting at the table, holding out his hand as he spoke.

"Good morning, and thank you, Lissa," he said.

"But you are a bad boy to be so late," answered Elizabeth, putting her hand for a moment into her cousin's. "Uncle has done his breakfast, you see, Dick."

"Well, I don't mind as long as *you* wait for me," replied young Horton, and he looked at Elizabeth somewhat significantly.

"I am forced to wait," said Elizabeth, with a shrug, and Richard Horton frowned as she spoke.

"No forcing about it," he said, sullenly enough. "If you don't want to stay, you can go."

"My dear, do not be so foolish, and eat your breakfast," said Elizabeth. "Here is your tea, Dick. I assure you I did not mean to offend you."

"You might be civiller to a fellow, I think," said Richard Horton, still rather sullenly.

"Be civil to me, Lissa, and give me another cup of tea, now when you have poured out all the strong for Dick, like a stupid that you are," said Hal.

Elizabeth gave another shrug, and then complied with her young cousin's request, for Harry was her pet among "the boys," as she called them, though her eldest cousin, Richard Horton, could not now justly come under that designation. He was a tall, rather broadly made, handsome young man, with a clear dark skin, black eyebrows, and regular features. He stooped, however, a good deal, which somewhat detracted from the effect of his otherwise fine figure. Bob, the second brother, was also a good-looking, broad-shouldered young fellow, of about twenty-one; and Harry, the youngest, was a singularly handsome lad. A faint family likeness might be dimly discerned in all the three to Elizabeth Gordon. Richard and Harry had the same fine, dark, clear skin that she had, but her expression was totally different to all her cousins. It was at once both more intellectual and sweeter than theirs; and somehow, though she had lived nearly all her life at Wendell West-house, she seemed to belong to a different and more refined class than her cousins did.

"If I get the pond brushed, will you go to skate this morning, Lissa?" said Richard Horton. "The ice is quite safe I'm certain."

"Not this morning, Dick, for I've so much to do," replied Elizabeth.

"What nonsense! What can you have to do?" said Richard.

"Hosts of things," answered Elizabeth, "Letters to write, a new dress to see after, and the servants to scold."

"Oh well, please yourself," said Richard; and he rose from the table, put his hands into his pockets, and went leisurely up to the fire, stationing himself with his back to it, and stood watching Elizabeth, while in her neat, womanly fashion, she locked away the tea-caddy, fed the old mastiff, and made some other little household arrangements.

The two other youths we e by this time in the hall, Harry calling loudly for his boots, and by-and-by Richard followed their example, and Elizabeth was left alone with her dumb friends. Outside she heard the farmer calling and whistling for his dogs, and the old, half-blind mastiff heard him too, and whined significantly to Elizabeth to let him out of the house door to join his master.

"Poor Tory, it's too cold for you," said Elizabeth, patting the big, tawny head, that was nestling against her soft brown dress; yet she did not refuse the old dog's request, but went to the front door of the house and opened it, and Tory walked out stiffly and sedately, as became his years, into the snow.

For a moment or two Elizabeth stood there, looking on the white world around and the leaden sky above, and then, with a soft, low sigh, she closed the door, and going upstairs, went into her own room, which was prettily and tastefully furnished, and where a large fire was burning brightly in the grate.

Elizabeth walked to the mantlepiece, and leant her arms on it, and stood looking thoughtfully into the blazing fire. Then she sighed again—not an unhappy sigh though, but as if her heart were full of some deep and tender emotion. She was thinking of her lover; the favoured lover, who had won Elizabeth's heart, and whom she had parted with but yesterday as his betrothed and promised wife.

CHAPTER II.
ELIZABETH'S LOVERS.

WHO this lover was had better now be told. To do this we must go back three years in Elizabeth's life—back to the days when she was twenty-one, and a bright, spoilt, handsome, wilful girl, who had never seen any one (as she often told herself) that she could even dream of caring for. When she was this age, however, as has been previously mentioned, the large farm that Mr. Horton rented changed owners, and thus Elizabeth found herself surrounded with new interests, new acquaintances, and new friends.

From the front windows of Wendell West-house (which is itself a substantial stone building) you can see through a short vista of trees and fields, the much more imposing edifice of Wendell Hall. This, in the days of Elizabeth's childhood and early girlhood, had been to her the most uninteresting house in the whole neighbourhood. It was then inhabited by her uncle's landlord, Sir Henry Tyrell, Baronet, who was a lonely, solitary, and very peculiar man. Elizabeth used sometimes to wonder if some of the blinds were ever drawn up; and there was an air of "rust and cobwebs," she used to say, about the whole place, that made you melancholy to look at it. The Baronet indeed lived there without "kith or kin," and the few old servants that he had about him were almost as quiet and peculiar as himself.

One day, however, all the blinds were drawn down, and news came to the farm that Sir Henry was dead. He had died as he had lived—in the most unobtrusive manner, but there were some (and among them Mr. Horton) who sincerely regretted their old landlord, and were not sure that they would find such an easy and generous one in his successor. This of course remained to be proved, and scrutinizing glances were plentifully bestowed on the tall, spare, aristocratic-looking man who came to the late Baronet's funeral, and whom it was understood he had appointed as his heir.

This was John Tyrell, his half-cousin, who had lived for years in what he designated as "necessary seclusion" in the country, on a small but certain income, while his wife and family had spent their time grumbling at the enforced quietude of their existence.

It was a great change to them all, therefore, when they came into their new possessions. Lady Tyrell felt that the wearisome days were over when she was for ever politely battling with her husband to obtain more money than she knew he could afford, to endeavour to keep up her own and her daughters' position in the world. The young ladies were delighted at the prospect of living in a large house, and having plenty of amusement, about which there would be no difficulty in paying; and their views on matrimony and dress naturally immediately enlarged. But the greatest change of position by the death of Sir Henry Tyrell came to his young half-cousin and namesake, Henry Tyrell, Sir John's eldest son. This young man, who was then about twenty-three, and who was a good-natured but reckless youth, had been in the deepest disgrace with his father, the prudent and economical John Tyrell, for having, while at Oxford, incurred heavy liabilities which that stern-minded parent assured him that he neither could nor would ever think of paying. Only very dismal prospects lay before him, and the possibility of his return to college after the long vacation was more than doubtful, when the news came of his rich kinsman's decease, and of his father's and his own (ultimate) succession to the title and property. There had been grave and uneasy doubts even as to the title. True, the late Baronet had never openly acknowledged to have formed matrimonial ties, but scandal had frequently whispered that he had formed private ones. John Tyrell, therefore, had always, with the philosophic calmness which he assumed as his chief characteristic, pressed upon his wife and family, on their attempting to lead him into any extravagance on the strength of his expectations, that he had none.

"In the event of Sir Henry's death taking place before my own," he would say, speaking of his cousin the Baronet, "we shall probably only have the pleasure of being introduced to new under-bred relations—the children of some low-born mother. No, my dear"—this was to his wife—"please limit your aspirations, for I fear Lady Tyrell will never be inscribed on your tombstone."

Great rejoicings then took place in the modest household of this prudent gentleman, when it was found that no spurious heir to the house of Tyrell had been presented to the world. The late Sir Henry bequeathed his large estates to his cousin John Tyrell, and the title legally descended to him. He bequeathed also a considerable sum of ready money—some twenty-five thousand pounds—to Harry Tyrell, his cousin's eldest son; which sum, on the event of his death without heirs, was to become the property of Jasper Tyrell, the second son. And thus, the "penniless spendthrift," as his father had often designated his offending offspring Harry, became by one stroke of good fortune independent, and heir beyond his father's control to the fine estates known as Wendell, Seeford, and Scardale, all of which are situated in the county of Uplandshire.

Naturally highly delighted and elated was Harry Tyrell. He paid his debts honourably the moment that he received his late cousin's bequest, and went back to Oxford with the comfortable feeling that he was free from the worst and most galling of annoyances. Then the first Christmas that his family spent at Wendell Hall he came down there, and it was during this visit that he saw Elizabeth Gordon.

This meeting was an event in his life, and also in hers. Though such near neighbours, the social difference between them had up to this time prevented the ladies of the Tyrell family and Elizabeth from forming each other's acquaintance.

The Misses Tyrell, indeed, had noticed at the parish church the handsome, well-dressed woman, who walked up its narrow aisle with a very different mien to anyone they expected to see there, and on making enquiries had heard her story. Still, though her father had been a gentleman, her mother had not been a lady; and considering that she had two sons, Lady Tyrell determined to ignore their beautiful neighbour's existence.

But however much in this case she might have wished it, she could not induce her eldest son on his arrival at the Hall to be equally prudent. There was a splendid pond for skating on Mr. Horton's farm, and a severe frost having set in, the young heir could not hunt, and was strolling about the place one morning with his gun in search of something to shoot, when he heard the sound of laughter and mirth quite close to him. Curious to see from whence it proceeded, he mounted the side of a snow-wreathed hedge, and in the next field beheld the handsomest woman (to his mind) that his eyes had ever rested on.

This was Elizabeth Gordon, who was skating with her three cousins, Richard, Robert, and Hal Horton, and on the head of the young heir appearing over the hedge to survey them, the two younger youths, Robert ank Hal, began to laugh.

Elizabeth, too, looked up with a smile, and on her doing so Harry Tyrell laid down his gun, and leaping over the hedge came upon the ice.

"May I come on?" he said, taking off his hat with his admiring eyes fixed on Elizabeth's face; and she answered (for she knew him by sight) frankly and pleasantly,

"Oh! yes; but you have no skates."

"That is easily remedied," said young Tyrell, now laughing also, and from that day, whenever he was at Wendell, he became Elizabeth's shadow.

In vain did his mother remonstrate with him; in vain his sisters alternately chaffed and lectured him on the subject.

"You girls needn't talk," he told them one day; "I'm my own master now, and Elizabeth's a girl in a thousand—and she doesn't make a fellow feel too sure of getting her either, I can tell you that."

Sir John, as usual, bore the news of his heir's infatuation with dignified philosophy.

"My good creature," he said to his wife, who was bitterly lamenting over "Harry's folly," as she called it, "your son Henry is just the sort of young man to pick a wife up out of some slum or other, and you ought therefore to be thankful if he chooses one from so clean a place as a dairy."

Poor Lady Tyrell, however, did not see this in the same light; but even she and her daughters were forced to admit that it was Harry who ran after Miss Gordon, and not Miss Gordon after Harry.

About this, in fact, there could be no doubt. Young Tyrell made the acquaintance of Mr. Horton, and courted the good-natured farmer and his sons as assiduously as he did Elizabeth. This young lady, however, it must be confessed, received his attentions at first by no means unwillingly. She was flattered, in fact, and not displeased to see the anxious glances that Lady Tyrell bent upon her whenever they met. She liked Harry Tyrell too, who was frank, good-natured, and in love with her; and probably, had the young man had the courage to declare his feelings during the first year of their acquaintance, he would not have been disappointed in his answer. But he did not do this. He returned to college, then he came back to Wendell, then went to college again, still leaving the momentous words unspoken. He was desperately in love with Elizabeth, he told

himself; "awfully far gone you know, dear old fellow," he wrote
to his younger brother, Jasper, at Malta, who was a lieutenant in
the navy; and this young gentleman who had had some experience, and who had gone through various semi-tender partings
at the different stations that he had visited, sent Harry a
word of warning in reply.

"Don't make a fool of yourself, dear Hal," wrote Lieut. Tyrell,
"for *any woman*. They're all very well, you know, and fascinating,
and that sort of thing; but a fellow who loses his head for any
daughter of Eve is an ass. You tell me your enchantress is
wonderfully beautiful, etc. Well, I'll tell you what I think when
I get to Wendell. I expect that the ship will be paid off shortly,"
etc. etc.

The ship was paid off, and Lieut. Tyrell came down one
autumn (just at the end of September) to the new home that he
had never seen. He had been on a three years' cruise, and in
these three years his family circumstances had totally changed.
He had left his father, Mr. John Tyrell, with barely one
thousand a year to live on, and he returned to find him Sir John
Tyrell, Baronet, the owner of a splendid property, and altogether in a completely different station of life.

At first everything was bright at Wendell Hall after his return,
and his good-natured brother Harry was as well pleased as the
rest of his family to see the handsome sailor, whom the three
years' cruise had improved in every way. Then, little by little,
a new feeling sprang up between the brothers, and jealousy, the
subtlest foe that love or friendship has, began to chill and freeze
the old affection which had been undisturbed since boyhood.

The cause of this is not difficult to guess. Jasper Tyrell, with
good-natured superiority, had laughed at Harry when they first
met about his ardent admiration for the "fair farmeress," as he
called Elizabeth Gordon, and then on being introduced to her
had frankly admitted her charms. Still he used to jest Harry
about her, and Harry was well pleased to be the object of such
raillery. This went on for several weeks, and the brothers were
constantly with their beautiful neighbour, and at Jasper's request
Lady Tyrell condescended to call on Elizabeth.

"She would be an excellent match for him," said Sir John,
when his wife consulted him about paying this visit. "My
worthy tenant, Horton, assures me that Miss Gordon was left
ten thousand pounds, and that her fortune has been accumulating
during the last eighteen years Few young officers marry a girl
with such a sum absolutely at her own disposal."

"Still—" hesitated Lady Tyrell.

"My dear, there are always 'stills' and 'buts' to be attached
to everything in this world, and it is best not to permit them to
weigh with us. Miss Gordon's father was a gentleman, and she

herself is a beautiful girl with a good fortune, and I shall be happy to bestow my blessing on my second son."

Sir John smiled sarcastically as he said these last few words, and Lady Tyrell felt very angry with him for doing so.

"It is Harry I was thinking of," she said, in an aggrieved tone.

"Yet you say that Jasper asked you to visit her," retorted Sir John, still smiling. "Well I hope it won't end in their cutting each other's throats about her." And having expressed this amiable wish, Sir John left his wife to suffer her maternal solicitude alone.

CHAPTER III.

ELIZABETH'S ENGAGEMENT.

LADY TYRELL did, nevertheless, after some consideration, determine to call at Wendell West-house, and accompanied by her two daughters, Matilda and Fannie, arrived there one afternoon in considerable state. To her surprise, however, Elizabeth received her with such sweet composure and dignity of manner, that she even impressed Lady Tyrell, who was a woman of feeble mind, with the knowledge that Elizabeth saw no honour or condescension in her ladyship's visit.

"I think that you are acquainted with my sons," said Lady Tyrell, after some faint preparatory attempts at conversation; and Elizabeth answered frankly and pleasantly.

"Yes, I know them both very well, and am pleased to make the acquaintance of their mother and sisters."

At these words the faded blue eyes which had won John Tyrell's heart twenty-seven years ago, by the sweet innocence of their expression (he then thought) opened a little wider than usual, and Lady Tyrell moved uneasily on her chair, unable exactly to make out what course of conversation she should now pursue.

Elizabeth, however, with the easy tact that was natural to her, at once started a subject on which they could all meet on equal grounds.

"Are you fond of reading?" she said, addressing the eldest Miss Tyrell, who smiled and blushed, and answered,

"Oh! yes; of course."

Then Elizabeth, taking advantage of the labours of those who are good-natured and industrious enough to give us the benefit of their cultivated thoughts, and who at least may have the pleasure of reflecting amid their toil that they not only lighten many a weary hour, but frequently afford conversation for those whose brains are less endowed than their own—taking advantage, then, of the work of one of her favourite authors, Elizabeth began a lively conversation on the merits of a book which had recently appeared; and so agreeable did she make herself, that when she courteously offered to lend it to the young ladies, the offer was graciously accepted, and the prospect of a more intimate acquaintance thus opened between the families.

"What do you think of her, mamma?" eagerly asked Matilda Tyrell, the moment that they had left the neat grounds of Wendell West-house.

"I think," answered Lady Tyrell solemnly, "that her manners are extremely self-assured; but I think," she added with some maternal foresight, "that we had better be civil to her for young men are so headstrong, no one can tell what they may do;" and Lady Tyrell sighed.

"But do you really admire her?" said Matilda Tyrell.

"She is what some men call a fine girl," said Lady Tyrell, who was little, slight, and faded; "but I cannot say she is the style I admire."

"She is so dark," said Fanny Tyrell.

"Well, at all events, my dears, we had better be civil to her," again advised Lady Tyrell, and accordingly after this visit the ladies of the Hall were "civil" to Elizabeth. They, in fact, believed that Harry Tyrell would marry her, and as they were powerless to prevent this catastrophe, they wisely determined to make the best of the situation.

"Jasper is getting foolish about her too, I believe," Miss Tyrell confided to her sister after the Lieutenant had been about two months at home, and other eyes—eyes sharpened by jealousy and real affection—began also about this time to fear and dread that this actually was the case.

Harry Tyrell, in fact, awoke all at once to the miserable knowledge that he had a dangerous rival in his brother Jasper. He had tried hard to make Elizabeth Gordon love him, but she had never done so; yet her dark eyes had not met his younger brother's a dozen times, when a new, strange, and instinctive emotion sprang up in her heart.

To do Jasper Tyrell justice he did not seek to create this. He had acknowledged to Harry the first time that he saw her that he had never seen a handsomer woman, and at the beginning of the acquaintance used to chaff his brother about the "lovely Elizabeth." Then he too grew uneasy and reserved on the subject. He had seen a good deal of women, and knew, or thought he knew, their ways, and after a while he came to the conclusion that Miss Gordon was foolish enough to prefer a penniless lieutenant to the rich heir of Wendell Hall.

This might be folly on the part of Elizabeth (and such Jasper admitted it to be), but it was very flattering to the lieutenant, and not unnaturally awoke a corresponding feeling in his heart. Honour, however, and regard for his brother, made him at first hesitate to show this. Then ill-will grew up between the two young men—ill-will, jealousy, and distrust. Harry taunted his brother with trying to win the affections of the girl he had chosen away from him, and Jasper retorted by declaring that he believed they had never been his. He was of warmer temperament than his elder brother, more passionate and excitable; and while Harry was sighing and fuming, Jasper, with his winning, practised tongue, and handsome face, was wooing Elizabeth for her love.

It was a glad, bright hour for her when, beneath the leafless woods of Wendell, she learned that Jasper Tyrell loved her.

She looked up with her dark eyes into his, and made no answer, but that look told as much as many words, and Jasper, as he clasped her to his breast, whispered that she had made him a happy man.

"And poor Hal?" laughed the lieutenant; but Elizabeth's face grew grave, for she knew now what love meant, and could not smile about what she feared would be a very bitter disappointment to Harry Tyrell.

"I hope that he will forget me," she said. "I hope that I have never led him to think—I cared for him."

"Oh, but he did, I assure you," answered the lieutenant, with some triumph; "but he'll get over it. Harry isn't a fellow to break his heart."

"And is Jasper?" said Elizabeth softly, and we may be sure that the ardent young sailor made some very tender reply.

A tall, slim, handsome young man was Jasper Tyrell. His features were regular and sharply cut, and his skin and hair dark; his eyes dark also, and quick and changeful. "He has a hot temper," you decided, after looking for a moment or two at the fine face, and noting the sudden movements, the intense vitality of his whole appearance.

He was highly thought of in his profession, and was considered a brave and rising young officer, though somewhat of a martinet to the men under his command.

He was about twenty-five at the commencement of this story, one year younger than his brother Harry, and one year older than Elzabeth Gordon, and they had known each other a little more than three months when he made this declaration of his love.

He was on the eve of leaving home when he did so, having been appointed to a ship then stationed in the Chinese waters, and for a few days only did they enjoy the happier knowledge of each other's affection; and they agreed between them to keep their engagement a secret until his return to Wendell, which he expected would be in about a year.

This was Elizabeth's proposition, and was made for the sake of Harry Tyrell.

"Let him learn it by degrees, from my manner, Jasper," she said gently. "I wish to have no scene, and hear no words that perhaps I could not fo:get from one whom some day I wish to love as my brother."

Very sweet and low was Elizabeth's voice as she said these words, full of feeling at once tender and true. She loved Jasper so much that his brother was dear to her, and she wished therefore to spare him every possible humiliation and pain; and she had promised herself to act to Harry, after Jasper was gone, in a manner that it would be impossible for him any longer to deceive himself.

Jasper Tyrell gave his consent somewhat unwillingly. He was proud of having won Elizabeth—won her without any of the social advantages which placed his brother in so different a position to himself. Angry feelings, too, had arisen between the brothers, and taunting words had been exchanged—exchanged even in the presence of Elizabeth, and he felt eager to be able to say, "Was I not right? Did I not tell you that you had no chance?"

But Elizabeth, whose womanly feelings were touched with sympathy and compassion at least for one whom she felt had really cared for her, would not allow this; and Jasper at length yielded to her wishes, and their farewell meetings were perhaps sweeter because they were stolen ones.

They had had a long and very tender last interview on the day before the bleak morning in December, when this story of Elizabeth's life begins, and when they parted the sailor felt that she had become more to him than he believed that any woman could have become. One of those solemn betrothments had in fact taken place between them which the soul only recognises, and which cannot be broken by the passing and changeful events and influences of the world. In that inner life, the life shared or unshared which we all possess, there are moments that we never forget—moments which come back time after time, year after year, and whose sweet or bitter remembrance we never ignore. This was one of them for Jasper Tyrell and Elizabeth. Outside the snow was beating on the window panes, and the storm winds sighing and moaning among the bare branches of the leafless trees. Inside the two stood with clasped hands, and eyes full of feeling too intense for words. They were about to part, but they could never be quite separated from each other again. They might meet outwardly as strangers—for amid the shifting scenes and uncertain programme of the world, we know not what parts we may be forced to play—but they never could be strangers any more. Elizabeth the woman saw this more clearly at that moment than Jasper the man, for her finer instincts and more delicate perceptions made things transparent to her that he could but vaguely feel. Still he recognised that she was to him what no other woman had ever been, or could ever be. The "secret sympathy" which we cannot create, and cannot define, was between them, and this invisible tie, which in a greater or lesser degree forms alike our loves and our friendships, was very strange and powerful in the hearts of both.

She stood and watched him after he had left her; watched his tall lithe form disappear amid the hazy twilight of the winter's eve. Above the sky was grey and dusk; around the snow lay thick and soft, and heavy flakes came slowly floating downwards on the already whitened world. Jasper Tyrell stopped for a moment and looked back when he reached the first clump of evergreens in the neat and well-kept approach to the house, and where the broad gravel walk turns, and partly hid it from his view. He saw Elizabeth watching him; saw the dark wistful eyes, the noble tender face; and waving his hand in farewell, with an anxious restless heart he turned away.

CHAPTER IV
THE FOOTPRINTS.

AFTER Mr. Horton had left the break-fast room on the morning when this story commences—on the morning after Lieut. Tyrell's departure from Wendell—he proceeded to the well-kept farmyard at the back of the house, where his oxen were fattening themselves, and in the straw of which his pigs grunted and slept. Everything here, as in the house, spoke of comfortable and easy circumstances. Mr. Horton was not a farmer barely able to meet his rent out of the profits of his land. His wife had had ten thousand pounds, as well as Elizabeth Gordon's mother, and he himself had been left a considerable fortune by his father, so that he was to a great extent independent of bad crops, hard times, and other misfortunes incidental to the tillers of the soil. Mr. Horton was proud of his farming, and somewhat given to boast of his profits. His losses, however, like a wise man, he never disclosed, bearing them philosophically, or good-naturedly expatiating on the uncertainty of human expectations. He was, however, always ready to help those who were less fortunate than himself, and many a poor neighbour had good cause to speak of Mr. Horton in the high terms very generally applied to him. Miss Gordon might be considered "high" by the farmers' wives and daughters around, but Mr. Horton certainly was not. The jovial, cheery man, who loved his pipe and its usual consoling accompaniment, was a welcome guest at every house in the neighbourhood. He was a clever man also, shrewd, and jocular, and for his class well educated and well read. He never contradicted Elizabeth, for he would tell her quizzically that no wise man ever gained anything by thwarting a woman. "My pretty Tyrant" was one of his pet names for his niece, and "Lissa" naturally reigned also over her three young cousins with undisputed sway. They were all, in fact, proud of her beauty, of her long-descended name, and various attractions; and, considering how they spoilt her, Elizabeth was wonderfully unselfish and kind.

For some little time past, Mr. Horton had, however, begun to grow slightly disturbed on the subject of "Lissa's lovers." He had been pleased and quite satisfied when his shrewd small eyes had first perceived that the attentions of Harry Tyrell were sincere and heartfelt. The young heir of Wendell Hall was to his mind a suitable husband for his beautiful niece, and Harry had been encouraged in his visits to Wendell West-house by the kindly farmer. Then Jasper Tyrell appeared on the scene, and the shrewd small eyes perceived also that "Lissa" soon learnt to regard the handsome sailor with very different feelings to his good-natured and wealthy brother. This was not unnaturally a disappointment to Mr. Horton. The best of men are worldly in a greater or lesser degree; and the heir to a fine property, in the eyes of an English farmer, is a very different person to a young officer, however charming the young officer may be. Still Mr. Horton did not interfere. "Lissa knew her own mind best," he thought, with a sigh, and so no word on the subject had been exchanged between them. Yet he was uneasy, and would sometimes wonder what his "poor wife," had she been alive, would have said about it. As his "poor wife" however was not on earth to be consulted, he left matters to take their course, and Jasper Tyrell had been kindly received by Mr. Horton on his visits to Wendell West-house, as well as his elder brother.

But come, let us follow the easy, wealthy farmer on his morning walk through the snow; for after he had surveyed his cattle, inspected his stables, poked his fat grunting pigs with his walking-stick, he whistled for his dogs, and proceeded for a sharp walk over his whitened and deserted fields.

Barely a quarter of a mile lies between the Hall and the farmstead. The Hall, which is a grey, stone, handsome building, stands in a large garden and grounds, which slope down in the front of the house to a little rivulet, which forms at this point a boundary between them and the highway, but the stream this morning was invisible from the drifted snow.

Presently Mr Horton, having crossed several fields (examining his fences as he went), reached the roadway, which runs straight past the front of the Hall and through the land leased by Mr. Horton; Wendell West-house, however, being some little distance from it.

The snow on the road had been trodden apparently by one person before Mr. Horton, who walked briskly along the narrow track till he came in front of the Hall. Here the depth of the snow over the brook which parts the grounds from the road attracted the farmer's attention, for the wind had blown it into a deep drift right across the watercourse, and into the fine holly hedge opposite, which runs along it as far as the grounds of the Hall extend.   Along this hedge, which is a very tall and handsome one, pollard willows also stand at intervals; and with all the intense interest with which living in the country invests trivial things, Mr. Horton stood still to examine the drift, and mentally to measure its depth.

By-and-by he tried practically to do so, for a little farther along the roadway is a rustic bridge over the brook, which leads into the grounds of the Hall, a gap being cut in the holly hedge for this purpose, and in this gap is placed a rustic gateway, which acts as a private entrance to the grounds.

Upon this bridge the farmer stepped briskly, and, plunging his walking-stick into the snow, at the imminent risk of toppling his stout little person into the hidden water beneath, endeavoured to measure the depth of the drift to the best of his means and his ability.

While he was thus employed his dogs—for three had accompanied him on his walk—amused themselves each according to its taste. Tory—the half-blind mastiff—stood solemnly on the road-way waiting for his master, and wondering doubtless what vagary had induced him to trust himself on the slippery and rather unsteady bridge.   Nell—a beautiful setter—plunged into the snow, dashing it about with thorough enjoyment; and Frisk—an impertinent-looking Scotch terrier—began scratching and barking at some object which she had discovered a little further on up the course of the brook,

When the farmer had satisfied himself as to the depth of the drift, he returned to the pathway, and, whistling for his dogs, crossed the road and entered a field at the other side of it, for the purpose of inspecting some sheep which were feeding there.

Tory followed his master into the field gravely, as was his wont; Nell came bounding along, her nose and tail in the air, frightening the timid sheep, for which she was sharply rebuked by the farmer; but Frisk, the terrier, remained by the waterbrook, barking and scratching, and apparently in a state of the most violent excite-ment.

"Frisk, Frisk," called Mr. Horton, but Frisk was deaf to the voice of her master, and so Mr. Horton walked on a few yards, and proceeded to survey his living property.

There is always something touchingly pitiful to me in the patient endurance, and apparent one-mindedness with which a flock of sheep go through the ills of life, If one of bolder spirit than the rest lies down, mark how the others follow. If one begins to nibble the often scanty herbage, the rest nibble after him; if one flies at the approach of a dog, they all fly—nay, I verily believe if one were to sneeze the whole flock would do their best to follow that sternutatory process. The particular flock that Mr. Horton had come to inspect were at the moment of his approach all engaged in the mastication of cut turnips. The grass lay hidden away beneath their feet by the cruel pitiless snow; but the patient, worthy creatures had not been left to perish. Mr. Horton had eaten a good breakfast, and every living thing beneath his hospitable sway had had the opportunity of eating a good breakfast also. But the graceless Nell in her own exuberance of spirits now appeared to interrupt the placid enjoyment of surely the most spiritless inhabitants of earth. One sheep looked up, saw her, and turned to fly, then another, and in a moment the whole flock were careering over the snowy field.

In vain the farmer called his dog to his heel. Nell came repentant and cowed, but the panting sheep huddled and shuddered together at the farthest end of the enclosure. The good-natured farmer, therefore, turned to leave the field, conscious that Nell's continued presence there was causing helpless terror to his one-minded flock; and the handsome setter, seeing his intentions, bounded past her master, dashed out of the field-gate, and ran forward to join the excited little terrier Frisk, who still remained barking and scratching at some object by the side of the brook. Then, as the farmer closed the gate of his field behind him, the half-blind mastiff Tory also walked stiffly on, and joined the other two dogs by the water-course, emitting the moment after he had done so a portentous howl.

This weird cry at once drew Mr. Horton's attention to his dogs, and after securing his gate he proceeded a few yards up the road to see what was disturbing them, and was dismayed to find as he approached near the spot where they were, that Frisk was barking and scratching at the boot and leg of a man.

With a cry the farmer sprang forward; with a cry pushed aside the little dog, and seized the foot of the prostrate man, who was lying head downwards, with his face and chest buried in the snowdrift in the brook.

"Oh! my God!" exclaimed Mr. Horton, as with a vigorous effort he drew the body on the road, and the face and head emerged from the snow. "Oh! my God—my God!" and he knelt down by the stiffened form, and lifted the head and face tenderly on his breast. It was a young face—a familiar face—the sweet boyish face of Harry Tyrell, whom he had seen but yesterday looking so strong and well.

With trembling hands Mr. Horton then proceeded to tear open the waistcoat on the young man's breast; with trembling hands felt for the stilled pulsation of his heart, and chafed his cold and nerveless hands. But it was all in vain. Harry Tyrell was gone.

The young life whose prospects had been so bright, had passed suddenly, unaccountably away. Unaccountably? But what was the red stain on the dead man's linen; what the small blue wound on the dead man's side that now met Mr. Horton's horror-stricken gaze? Harry Tyrell had been shot; shot in the side, and had fallen where he had been stricken, with his head forward into the snowdrift over the brook. There had been no struggle for life; no struggle with the foe who had shed his blood. The farmer looked along the pathway before him; there was but one track here, one man's footprints, Harry's own, which ended on the spot where he had met his tragic fate.

Unutterably shocked, Mr. Horton placed the body once more gently on the snow, and as he did so the old dog drew near, and licked poor Harry's open, powerless hand, and then lifting his head in the air, gave forth another dismal howl in token of his sorrow and regret.

Tears rose in the farmer's eyes as he heard the mournful sound.

"Poor lad! poor boy," said Mr. Horton, rubbing his rough hand over his face; and then starting to his feet he hurried to the homestead to give the alarm, leaving Tory standing guard over the dead man's body.

He encountered his three young sons as he ran towards the house, who were amusing themselves by trying a new pony at the back of the stable-yard, and in breathless accents told his dreadful news.

The greatest excitement at once prevailed. The three young Hortons left their pony to look after itself, and ran forward to the fatal spot. The farm servants and the farmer with pitying and wondering exclamations followed; Mr. Horton calling for brandy in the vain hope of reviving the stricken man, and the alarm was thus spread into the house. Here the maid-servants hurried (each eager to be the first to tell it) to Elizabeth's room, who was standing at that moment with her sweet and noble face pressed against a portrait that she was holding in her hand.

"Jasper," she murmured, "my Jasper," and she kissed the fine forehead and smiling eyes depicted in her photograph with her rosy, tender lips. But her love-dream was rudely broken.

"Miss Gordon, Miss Gordon!" cried an hysterical voice at the door. "Oh, Miss Gordon!" exclaimed another agitated woman.

"What is it?" asked Elizabeth, opening the door in some alarm and surprise at this interruption.

Then the tale was told in several different versions to Elizabeth's shocked and horrified ears. "Master" had found young Mr. Tyrell murdered. His throat was cut, said one. He was riddled with shots, said another. Elizabeth could scarcely believe their frightful stories; and pale, trembling, and afraid, went down into the kitchen, and stood there undecided what to do or what to say.

As she was standing there she saw her eldest cousin Dick approach the house. "Dick, Dick," she said, running out towards him, "What is this they tell me—what about Harry Tyrell?"

"He is shot," answered Dick Horton, who looked pale and excited. "Lissa," he went on in a sort of whisper, "wait for me a minute, I want to show you something." And the next moment he left her and ran into the house.

Sick and pale Elizabeth stood and awaited his return. She was trying to realise what had happened, trying to think how such a thing could happen, and her heart beat fast and painfully; and when in a minute or two Richard Horton came back to her, she put her hand into his with a choking sob.

"Oh! Dick, how dreadful," she said, "how dreadful—who can have done it?"

"Who?" answered Dick, with some emotion, and he crushed her hand in his, "I can well guess who—I am sure who did it."

"But who, Dick?" asked Elizabeth, fixing her eyes with intense eagerness on her cousin's excited face.

"Jasper," said Richard Horton, darkly, almost vindictively. "Come with me, Lissa, and I will show you what will hang the fine Lieutenant when it's known."

"Dick!" exclaimed Elizabeth, with deep indignation, wrenching her hand from her cousin's—how dare you utter such a thing —how dare you breathe such hateful words?"

"Come with me, and I will prove them," answered Richard Horton, and he put his arm through Elizabeth's, and half led her, half dragged her on.

As they proceeded across the fields, by the shortest way to the road, where the fatal discovery had been made, they saw a group of men approaching them, bearing poor Harry Tyrell's body to the farmstead. With some delicacy of feeling Dick Horton drew Elizabeth into a cattle shed near, until Mr. Horton, his two younger sons, and his farm-servants, carrying the poor dead lad's corpse laid on a gate, and decently covered with a coat, and with the old dog walking beside it, had passed them; and then once more with hasty, hurried steps, Richard Horton dragged Elzabeth on.

"To think of him doing such a thing," muttered Dick as they went; "to think of him shooting his own brother—it's about you, Lissa, as sure as there is a God in Heaven, it's about you!"

"Hush," said Elizabeth, sternly; "hush, Richard Horton. How do you know, boy—how dare you lay such a thing to *his* charge."

"By *his* footprints in the snow," replied Richard, eagerly.

"You know what a small, slim foot he has, and how proud he's of it.   Well, when the others were lifting poor Harry up, and talking about him, I noticed a footprint different to all the others around, and I looked back and I looked forward.   It was on the little bridge to the Hall grounds, and a broad footstep (another man's) was there too; but the slim, narrow footprint had crossed the bridge, and entered the grounds, for I looked over the gateway and saw them, and they go up on the other side of the holly hedge to the place where Harry was shot."

"You saw this?" gasped Elizabeth.

"I saw it, but I did not tell the others, for I wanted to be *sure* —and I wanted to tell you first."

"But how can you know—how can you tell—a dozen men might have slim slight feet?"

"I'll tell you how I can tell," answered Dick.   "Look here—this is what I went into the house for—this is one of the Lieutenan t's boots;" and he produced a man's boot from his coat pocket as he spoke.   "Do you remember when he came on Sunday, when it was so wet?   He asked me then to lend him a pair of dry shoes, and he left his boots in my room, and forgot them when he went away;—and as certain as there is a God above us," added Dick after a moment's pause, "the man whose foot would fit these boots shot Harry Tyrell."

Elizabeth moaned and put her hand to her head.   "No, no," she said, "it cannot be."

"But it is," said young Horton, positively.   "Look Lissa, look here—here his footprints begin;" for the cousins had now reached the roadway, and as Richard opened the field-gate for Elizabeth to leave it, he pointed to a narrow footprint on the road upon the snow.   But here there were many others.   The farmers, and the farm-servants—broad, hobnailed impressions these—then the three young Hortons', Richard, Robert, and Harry's; but still distinct, a narrow, slim footstep, met Elizabeth's horror-stricken gaze.

The cousins were all alone now.   The men who had come with Mr. Horton to the fatal spot were carrying the corpse or following it.   The boys also had gone towards home with their father, and the alarm had not had time to spread further in the neighbourhood.   So all alone Elizabeth and Richard Horton walked on; Elizabeth's eyes fixed, fascinated on the snow; fascinated on the narrow footprints which here and there, again and again, were visible.

At last they reached the little rustic bridge; the bridge where the farmer had measured the depth of the snow-drift, and here they followed the footprints still.

"Look," said Richard, pointing to them; "look—and here's another—a broad one—but here's the Lieutenant's;" and he put the narrow boot he carried into the narrow impression in the snow upon the bridge.

"Come on," said Elizabeth wildly, and she pushed open the rustic gate, and the next moment she and her cousin were in the grounds of the Hall.

Here there were no other footprints but the narrow straight ones. These were in two distinct lines—one line advancing and the other returning.

"Measure for yourself," said Richard Horton, and he put Jasper Tyrell's boot into Elizabeth's quivering hand.

She knelt down as he did so, or rather she fell on her knees upon the snow, and put the boot into one of the clearly and sharply defined impressions before her. There was no mistake. The foot that had worn the boot in her hand was the foot that had passed up and down behind the holly hedge ; that had passed on the previous night, after darkness had set in, for only then had it ceased snowing, and not a flake apparently had fallen after these two distinct lines of footprints had been made.

Without a word Elizabeth rose ; without a word ran swiftly forward the few yards that were between the bridge and the spot where, on the other side of the hedge, poor Harry had been found. Then, when she reached it, she stopped, and the footprints stopped here, too.

"It was here," said Richard Horton, who had followed her. "Ay, this is the place—he must have shot him through the hedge."

No word from Elizabeth ! Ghastly, almost grey, she stood, now looking on the snow which here was a good deal trampled ; now on the hedge, where the snow had either been pushed or had fallen away."

"What's that ! Look there !" cried Richard Horton the next moment, pale with excitement, springing forward and eagerly clutching some white object (but a different white) lying on the snow ; lying almost at their feet. He lifted it, looked at it, examined it, and then with a stern smile handed it to Elizabeth. It was a handkerchief—a man's handkerchief, and in one corner was Jasper Tyrell's name, marked by Elizabeth's hand, and with Elizabeth's own dark hair.

"There is no doubt now," said Richard Horton.

As he spoke Elizabeth turned and looked at him ; looked at him so wildly, and with such terrible despair written on her face, that the young man's heart was touched with pity.

"Do not grieve about it, Lissa," he said, laying his hand on her arm ; but with a cry Elizabeth fell once more on her knees, and with eager, passionate, trembling hands, began to efface the impressions of the footprints in the snow.

"Don't do that, Lissa ! You shan't do that," said Richard,

seizing her roughly by the shoulder as he spoke   "Let him hang for what he's done."

"Dick! Dick!" cried Elizabeth, imploringly, twining her arms round her cousin's knees, "Don't tell——! Oh! never tell. I am to blame! I alone! If you kill Jasper Tyrell you will kill me!"

"Nonsense," said Richard Horton.

"It is not nonsense," urged Elizabeth, with passionate accents, "for if they quarrelled it was about me.   Swear to me, Dick—swear by the God who is above us that you will never betray him."

"I won't swear anything of the sort," answered Richard, gloomily.   "A fine thing indeed, to let a murderer escape ; perhaps you would even marry him ? "

"Never, never," cried Elizabeth, still with her arms tight round her cousin's knees. "Dick, keep Jasper's secret and I will never marry him.   Never, I swear it to you."

"Will you swear it, on your soul ?" said Richard Horton, looking down on his beautiful cousin's agonised face with half-averted eyes.   "Swear it as you hope to be saved ? "

"I swear it," said Elizabeth, solemnly, "I will never marry Jasper Tyrell."

Richard Horton made no answer to this, but still stood looking at her—looking at her as if uncertain how to act, and Elizabeth continued her piteous entreaties.

"Richard," she said, "dear Dick, promise me. I will never marry him. I will do anything you ask—anything—if you will never breathe this to a human soul."

"Very well," said Dick slowly.   He was moved apparently by his cousin's words ; but the next minute he caught her hand in his.

"Remember," he said, "I may ask my price for this secret some day, and you will have to pay it."

"I will," said Elizabeth. "Do not fear me—whatever you ask I promise to give you."

"All right," answered Dick Horton, and he dropped Eizabeth's hand.   Then she rose to her feet, and after secreting the handkerchief marked with Jasper Tyrell's name in her dress, began again with eager, half-frantic hands to endeavour to efface each impression of the narrow footprints in the snow.

"Help me, Dick," she said, in broken accents, "help me," and with a half-contemptuous movement Dick Horton kicked some snow on one of the footprints at his feet.

As he did so, and as Elizabeth went on with her self-imposed task, now kneeling, now standing, so as better to accomplish it, a soft snow-flake fell on the crown of dark hair bound round her uncovered head, and the next moment another followed.

"There," said Richard, who had noticed them, "you need not go on.   It's begun to snow, and that will hide the footprints better than you can."

As he spoke, Elizabeth, who was kneeling, looked up with her dark eyes to the leaden sky, and slowly, too, lifted her arms, her face full of impassioned and unspoken prayer. She was asking for the snow—the snow that would hide her lover's fatal footprints, and, as if in answer to her unuttered cry, a minute later hail and snow intermixed came pattering on her head.

"It's going to be a sharp shower," said Dick. " Come, Elizabeth, get up and come home."

" Let me watch it," answered Elizabeth, slowly, still looking heavenward. "Let me feel it—let me see it—it will hide them, Dick—hide them for ever."

"Yes, but come home," urged the young man. "Come, dear Lissa," and he helped her to her feet, and then drew her arm through his.

"There is no one but us, only us two, Dick," went on Elizabeth in the same vague manner that she had spoken before—"only us"—and she clung to her cousin and shuddered as she did so.

"Yes, Lissa," said Richard, and he led her down the path behind the holly hedge; led her over tho narrow, half-effaced footprints—the footprints that each moment grew less and less visible beneath the falling snow. "Come, child," he went on protectingly, when they reached the little bridge, and Lissa turned and looked back on the fading tracks, "no one will see them now."

"No one but God," said Elizabeth, and with another shudder she went away.

____

CHAPTER V.

SIR JOHN TYRELL.

WITH a very sorrowful heart Mr. Horton had desired his farm servants to bear poor Harry Tyrell's body to the homestead; but with a yet more sorrowful heart, when they reached it, did he remember that it was now his duty to break the terrible news to the parent of the poor murdered youth.

He was on good terms with his landlord, Sir John Tyrell, for Sir John was a just man and glad to recognise all good qualities in those around him. He also appreciated the fact that Mr. Horton was a rich man—rich at least for his station, and ready and willing to improve the land that he leased and paid for with such agreeable regularity. Mr. Horton was, in fact, Sir John's favourite tenant, and the well-born, stately gentleman had ever a pleasant word ready when he met the ruddy, genial farmer. They were not akin outwardly, but there was a real and instinctive liking between them.

"That man is a gentleman at heart," thought the landlord. "Sir John is a jolly good fellow when you get through his crust," decided the farmer; and this mutual appreciation made each a pleasant companion to the other.

Full of grief then was Mr. Horton, not only at the tragic end of his young favourite, Harry Tyrell, but at the grievous news that he was now bound to convey to Sir John.

He moaned as they bore by his direction the young man's body into the dining-room at Wendell West-house; moaned when he saw them straighten the limbs of the poor dead lad, and draw down the blinds in outward token of mourning and sorrow. The farmer's heart was very sad within him, and tears stood in his small, kindly grey eyes, and fell (though he tried to dash them away with his rough hand) on the calm, white, almost smiling face of his landlord's eldest son.

"Who can have done it!" groaned the farmer for the twentieth time since the fatal discovery. "Who can have shot the happy, bright young lad?"

"Sir John'll ha' 'tectives down from Lundon I reckon, and we'll ha' him hung yet," said one of the men who had borne the body in, and these words made Mr. Horton see that his duty was at once immediate and imperative.

"His father should know," he said, with another groan. "His father must know;" and he seized his hat, and pulled it over his brows, and set out on his dismal errand.

The heavy snow which had begun to fall on Elizabeth Gordon's head, as she endeavoured to efface the footprints behind the holly hedge, fell now on his as he went on, but it never struck the simple farmer that the snow would blot out the murderer's track. Over the fields he went; over the fields, and on the roadway, when he reached it, he encountered Elizabeth and his son Richard—Elizabeth clinging to her cousin's arm, with her face so white and so grievously altered that Mr. Horton was utterly shocked by her appearance.

"Lissa—my darling," he said, tenderly. "Lissa, why did you come here?" And he put his hand on her shoulder as he spoke.

"Take me home, uncle, take me home," moaned Elizabeth; and the farmer without a word put her other arm (one was through Dick's) in his, and together they dragged her nerveless, half-paralysed form through the snowy fields. She felt quite benumbed by the sudden shock, and with difficulty they succeeded in getting her to the homestead. Then, when they reached the house, she crept up to her own room, and sat down, asking to be left alone—"quite, quite alone." And after Mr. Horton had insisted on her swallowing some wine, he yielded to her wishes, conscious that she was suffering more than she cared that they should see.

When every one had left her, with a suppressed moan Elizabeth put her hand into the bosom of her dress and drew out the handkerchief—the fatal evidence of Jasper's guilt. But a few days before his departure she had bought the set to which this handkerchief belonged, as a parting gift to her betrothed, and some loving jests had been exchanged between them because Elizabeth had insisted on marking his name and crest on them with her hair. With trembling fingers she now examined her handiwork, and recognised that this very handkerchief that she now held was the first of the set that she had marked, for she had made a slight mistake in the crest, which Jasper had smilingly detected and asked her to correct in the rest. As with fascinated eyes she had gazed at the narrow footprints in the snow, so now with fascinated eyes she looked at the error in the crest—at the damning evidence against the man whom she passionately loved.

Yet could she believe it—believe that Jasper, her bright, handsome Jasper, could have a murderer's heart! "Oh! that I had died before it," moaned Elizabeth in her bitter grief. "Oh! that I were dead rather than know this."

She tried to think how it could have happened; tried to remember if anything in his mode had shown vindictiveness or bitterness during their parting interview on the day before. When could the brothers have quarrelled? What taunting words could they have exchanged before Jasper would stain his hands with his brother's blood? But let us leave Elizabeth at this miserable time; leave her with her terrible fear, her dread, her painful doubts, her torturing love. Unchanged at least in one thing, she loved him still. Cruel and wicked he might be, but "Many waters cannot quench love, neither can the floods drown it;" and in this dark hour Elizabeth was true to the one great passion of her life.

*　　*　　*　　*　　*　　*　　*

Meanwhile Mr. Horton, full of sadness, had reached the Hall, had rung the door-bell, and had been ushered into the library, which was a room used almost exclusively by Sir John.

The Baronet, however, was not in it when the farmer entered, but a few minutes later Sir John, urbane and with outstretched hand, appeared, greeting Mr. Horton cordially, whose usually ruddy cheeks had by this time turned bluish-coloured from the painful prospect before him.

"Ah! Mr. Horton," said Sir John, "and how are you this snowy morning? Not much farming going on to-day, I should think, or anything particularly new, eh!"

Sir John Tyrell had a fine face, fine skinned and fine featured, and with a grave expression, lit occasionally by gleams of dry humour, arising from a keen appreciation of others' follies and his own. He was a quiet man, but in his quiet way he knew the human heart, and judged men forbearingly, knowing that he shared, and therefore could sympathise with, the frailties of his race. His wife was peculiarly unsuited to him ; but he had married her for beauty, and therefore never blamed or reproached her for her want of mental capacity.

"I chose the shell without examining the kernel," he would tell himself, "therefore I only am to blame if the shell is hollow." And in this philosophical vein he regarded all the ills and joys of life. Jasper was his favourite child, for his pluck and gallantry when a boy, and the character for bravery that he had acquired as a man, pleased his father's pride, or "vanity" Sir John designated it; while his good looks and taking manners were also agreeable to his father's feelings.

Poor Harry had always been considered the black sheep of his family by this calm, even-minded gentleman. Harry had got into debt (a thing Sir John abhorred). Harry was wayward, slightly infirm of purpose, lacking the decision of character, the Baronet thought, which constituted one of the necessary elements to form a worthy or reliable man. At the same time he did justice to his sweetness of temper, his absence of self-appreciation, and general amiability.

"Harry will make an excellent country gentleman," Sir John once said of his eldest son, after his own accession to the Wendell property, "for it is a position in life where brains are by no means essential," and he smiled, pleased with his own remark, after he had made it.

Alas, the poor lad, who would have made an "excellent country gentleman," was now lying cold and still in the farmer's dining-room; and Sir John's intelligent eyes discovered in a moment, after his first salutation to Mr. Horton was over, that there was something unusual in his tenant's manner.

"Any news?" said Sir John, looking curiously at the farmer's usual ruddy face, which was now working strangely, while one of his large, rough hands was clasped nervously on the back of a chair standing near him.

"Yes, Sir John," answered Mr. Horton, huskily, "sad news —terrible news, sir—" and he drew out his red silk handkerchief, and wiped his brow as he spoke.

"I hope that nothing has happened in your family?" said Sir John courteously. "I hope that Miss Gordon and your sons—" and he paused.

"Lissa and the lads are well," said the farmer; and then almost with a sob he added, "but, oh! Sir John, I wish all were —poor Mr. Harry—your poor son—."

"What has happened to Harry?" asked Sir John, and his finely tinted skin flushed faintly.

"He's dead!" answered Mr. Horton, now fairly breaking down, "the fine lad—the noble young fellow is lying dead, Sir John, this moment at my house. And not only dead, sir," he added excitedly ; "not only dead, but he's lying foully murdered by some scoundrel's hand."

"Dead ! murdered !" echoed Sir John, and his face grew quite pale.

"Ay, sir, as sure as I'm standing here. He's lying"—and the kindly farmer heaved a sob—"lying, as I said, at West-house—and I found him this morning a few yards up the road, past the little gate into your own grounds."

"And—he—was—dead ?" faltered Sir John.

"Dead ! Ay, dead sure enough," answered Mr. Horton, sorrowfully. "He was lying head downwards in the heavy snow-drift, over the brook; and he'd lain there no doubt since the bloody villain who shot him took his life."

"But how do you mean ?" asked Sir John, with some excitement in his manner, arising from the natural emotion he was repressing. "How can you tell that he has met—with foul play ?"

"There's a wound in the poor lad's side, Sir John—a bullet wound, that tells the tale; he's been shot, sir, by some villain lying in ambush—aye, to be sure, I never thought of it—no doubt lying behind the holly hedge."

"Then there must be traces in the snow," said Sir John, looking quickly up. "Come, Mr. Horton, let us go at once and examine the spot."

"Yes, Sir John," answered the farmer ; and together the two men left the room, crossing the hall, and leaving the house by the front entrance, which opens on a stone terrace, from which you descend into the garden and grounds.

Here everything lay covered with inches of untrodden snow. The smooth gravel walks, the greenhouses and fernhouses, the pond in the centre, round which the leafless willows grew, and the duckhouse at one side of it, were all white and chill. Above, the sky was grey and heavy, while the snowflakes fell fast and thick on Sir John and Mr. Horton as they walked straight through the gardens, straight through the grounds, and straight to the tall holly hedge which serves as a boundary from the road.

They soon reached it, and in a moment both saw through the thin covering that the fast-falling snow had already made, that here there had been many footprints—a track, in fact, from the little gateway to the fatal spot where, on the opposite side of the hedge, the farmer had discovered the body of Harry Tyrell.

"There's been a lot of them," cried Mr. Horton, looking down at the effaced footprints ; at the evidently trampled on and been trodden snow. "See, Sir John, there's been more villains here at work than one."

"Was he robbed ?" asked Sir John, in a low, pained tone.

"By George, I never looked !" answered the farmer, vehemently. "I was so upset, sir, so horror-struck, that I never thought of putting my hand into the poor lad's pockets."

"And it was here?" said Sir John, examining the hedge, and the snow. "Here?"

"Just here," said Mr. Horton. "Just at the other side o' the hedge. The dogs, poor dumb beasts, sighted him first. I couldn't think what they were barking and howling at. And when I came up poor Mr. Harry was lying head downwards, as I said, in the snowdrift over there—just his feet and legs to be seen."

"My poor boy," muttered Sir John, and he turned away his head to hide the tears which rose unbidden to his eyes. The next moment he had conquered his weakness, and began steadily examining the fast-fading foot-tracks in the snow.

"Here is a woman's footprint," he said at length, "a woman's small footprint!" And he pointed to one small impression close to the hedge.

"A woman's!" repeated the farmer. "Ay, sure it will be Lissa's—my poor niece, Sir John, Lissa Gordon; for when the news came she ran down with the lads, and no doubt she's been here to see if she could make this foul business out. She's terribly cut up—terribly, poor lass, for I met Dick half carrying her home, and went back with her before I came here."

"She knew poor Harry well, did she not?" asked Sir John, thoughtfully.

"Yes, yes," said Mr. Horton, shaking his head. "In fact, Sir John——" and then the farmer paused.

"Was he her lover?" went on Sir John, looking in his tenant's face.

"Well, sir, it's hard to say what's what when women folks are concerned," answered the farmer, moving his body with an embarrassed air. "At one time I thought it was all right between them—and though, perhaps, I shouldn't say it to you, who are my landlord and a gentleman, and all that, still nothing would have given me such joy, for I loved the poor lad with my whole heart."

"Well?" asked Sir John, as with a heavy sigh Mr. Horton once more paused.

"Then your other son, sir, Mr. Jasper, the Lieutenant, came home," continued the famer, "and from that time somehow—I don't know how it was—but Lissa did not seem so kind with Mr. Harry—perhaps they quarrelled—or, perhaps——"

"She liked Jasper best," said Sir John, slowly. "You know that he started last night, Mr. Horton, in time to catch the Peninsular and Oriental boat *en route* for China. By this time I fear he will have left England—otherwise he should be telegraphed for at once."

"It's a sorrowful business," said the farmer, shaking his head very mournfully. "But won't you come now, Sir John, and see the poor lad lying yonder—in his last sleep?"

"Yes," answered Sir John; and then together as they had come to the scene of Harry's murder, so now together they returned down the narrow pathway behind the holly hedge, crossing the little rustic bridge; and having reached the roadway proceeded almost in silence along it until they came to the fields which lead direct to Wendell West-house.

As they approached this dwelling place, Sir John's face began to work painfully; his even temperament was strangely stirred, for the remembrance of Harry's mother—the weak and once pretty woman he had loved and won twenty-seven years ago, and whom for more than twenty years at least he had learnt to regard with placid indifference—now rose to his mind.

"What would she say? What would she think?" he was mentally cogitating. Lady Tyrell had, in fact, worshipped this eldest son—her first born, her darling. Harry had no faults in the mother's eyes; none to the narrow heart where the maternal instinct had overwhelmed every other feeling and desire. Through all his troubles and follies this fond friend had clung to him, and she had often resented as a mother the decisions which, as a wife, she ought to have respected and yielded to. If Sir John's wishes were opposed to Harry's, Sir John to her mind was in error; and this was the woman, this the mother, who was to learn that her young son's life-blood lay cold and curdled by a murderer's hand.

Sir John's stoicism was more outward than real. To a responsive nature this man's heart would have echoed back every loving and noble thought. But he had never met one. His wife, his sons, his daughters, were all of an inferior and more commonplace organisation than his own. He had wrapped himself therefore in the calm, smiling philosophy which gently derideth all things, and hid away from observers whom he despised the real tenderness and nobility of his heart.

When therefore his eyes fell on the sweet, placid face of his dead son; the face that looked so young, so peaceful, so at rest, Sir John's assumed indifference utterly gave way, and a heavy tear or two fell on the dead youth's unruffled brow.

"My poor boy," murmured Sir John; "My poor, poor boy."

The sturdy farmer standing near gave a sympathetic groan at this natural outbreak.

"It's a mournful sight, Sir John," he said, and he held out his honest hand, and took in it the fine white one of his well-born landlord.

"Yes," answered Sir John, struggling hard to suppress his emotion, and then almost with a sob he muttered beneath his bitten writhing lips—

D

"His poor mother—how can I tell her?"

"Ay, ay," said the farmer, and his eyes too filled at the idea of the mother's certain misery. Both these manly hearts felt more for the woman's coming pain than their own. Sir John remembered her pride and joy at that moment when she had first shown him her baby's face; when as a fair young wife she had first uncovered the little red and tiny morsel, nestling on her breast, which seemed so sweet and lovely to her eyes. Long years had passed since then—years on his part of placid indifference, on hers of feeble discontent. Between these two there was only the outward bond of marriage, for there was no soul union to bind them; none of the fine ties which blend and make two lives into a happier fuller one. Sir John was always kind to his wife, always considerate to her, but even her feeble instincts recognised his secret want of sympathy and love.

To her boy then she had clung with extraordinary fondness. Other children had come, but none had ever been to her what her first-born was; and the generous, light-hearted young fellow had repaid his mother's devotion in his usual sweet and somewhat careless fashion. Poor Harry Tyrell! His light sins might easily be forgiven, but his kindly, good nature could not easily be forgotten by those who had known him and loved him best. Ever ready to oblige every one, and to forgive and forget all small social wrongs, he had done little harm, if he had done little good, on his brief life journey.

Strange, then, that to this sunny-hearted youth had come so sudden and tragic an end. He was one of those who usually wed early, live to a good old age, and sit in the winter-time of life with their grandchildren prattling on their knee. Such was the career which Sir John, with conscious superiority, had prophesied for his eldest son. Now, it was all ended; all the placid foreshadowing of a long life; all the mother's fond hopes; all the young man's bright dreams of love. Shot by a murderer's hand he lay there; shot for some secret grudge, some hidden motive, for the only one natural, that of robbery, had certainly not been the temptation to the crime. In his waistcoat pocket was Lady Tyrell's last birthday gift, an expensive watch; in his note-book two or three bank notes, and some loose gold and silver about his dress, all untouched.

These painful details Sir John and the farmer discovered with sinking hearts, with vague uneasiness and distrust.

"Who could have done it?" they asked each other, but more by startled inquiring looks than words.

Harry had not dined at home the night before, Sir John told Mr. Horton, but his absence had created no surprise or alarm to his family, as he frequently did not appear at the family dinner table. They had dined earlier than usual, to suit Jasper, who had started by train in time to reach Southampton about midnight when he expected to embark almost immediately on board one of the Peninsular and Oriental boats *en route* for China. This was all Sir John knew. When he had last seen Harry alive it was about four o'clock on the previous day, just as it was turning dusk, when he had noticed him from the library windows cross the grounds in the direction of the stables and outhouses, and he had never seen him again till he saw him now lying cold and still in death. Mystery was thus added to the young man's untimely end; mystery which Sir John felt it his duty alike as a magistrate and a father to endeavour to dispel. He therefore arranged with Mr. Horton before he left West-house to telegraph to London for detectives, and offered a large reward for the discovery of the murderer of his son. But the worse was yet to come. Lady Tyrell was still to hear that the young object of her pride and love had passed away from her, and, with faltering steps and bitter lips, her husband proceeded back to the Hall to fulfil this most painful task. The kindly farmer accompanied him on his way, wringing his hands when they reached the front entrance of the Hall with the truest sympathy and pity, and then hurried, by Sir John's wish, to the nearest station to telegraph for the police.

Then, with a sinking heart, Sir John entered his stately home, and, as he crossed the hall, his wife, who had been watching for him, came out of the breakfast-room, with a disturbed and anxious look imprinted on her face.

"John," she said, in her usual querulous tone, "I'm uneasy about Harry. Do you know he has not slept at home, and he has never been in the whole morning?"

At these words Sir John's pale face grew paler, and with a sudden movement of intense pity he took the hand of his wife.

"Come in here, Eleanor," he said, in a broken voice, drawing her into the library, which he knew would probably be empty; "come in here my poor, poor child."

He had not spoken to her thus for years, and Lady Tyrell looked up with vague alarm into his face at his unwonted tenderness.

"Nothing has happened?" she asked quickly. "Nothing, surely, to—Harry?"

"May God help you," answered Sir John, with a choking sob; "may God help you, my poor girl, for Harry is—"

He could not speak the word. The look of startled horror on Lady Tyrell's face paralysed his tongue, while with fierce and passionate force she grasped her husband's arm.

"What!" she cried, "*What!*"

"Let me comfort you," said Sir John. "My dear, my dear," and he would have pressed her to his breast; but the tigress deprived of her young was not fiercer now than this wretched mother.

"Tell me," she choked forth, pushing her husband back. "Tell me, *what have you done?*"

"I—I have done nothing," said Sir John. "Except poor lad, perhaps not been very kind to him, for Eleanor—my poor Eleanor —our boy is dead."

* * * * * * *

For years afterwards Lady Tyrell's shriek at this announcement haunted Sir John. It was the shriek of departing reason; the shriek followed by long days, long months of hapless apathy, of fantastic fancies, of bewildered helpless pain. The poor lady's feeble mind was in fact overthrown by the sudden shock, and the evening that saw her young son carried lifeless to his home, saw the unfortunate mother raving and tossing in a madwoman's dreams.

CHAPTER VI

DICK HORTON'S PRICE.

ELIZABETH GORDON was very ill after Harry Tyrell's sudden death. Ill during the painful inquiry that followed; during the Coroner's inquest adjourned, and re-adjourned, as fresh hopes arose that some new light would be thrown to discover the murderer or murderers of the dead.

The whole country around was roused into indignation by the fatal catastrophe. Harry Tyrell had been popular; popular among the sporting young squires of his own age; among the ladies who had ignored his foolish admiration for Elizabeth Gordon, and who naturally saw in him a young man eligible, agreeable, and goodlooking. His mother's pitiable condition, too, when it came to be known, excited the utmost compassion. Poor Lady Tyrell (like Harry) had made few enemies, and her amiable qualities were now extolled and commented on, and her sufferings and sorrow almost universally sympathised with and deplored.

But all this sympathy, all this commiseration, availed nothing to unravel the mystery which hung over Harry Tyrell's untimely end. Sir John offered a large sum to endeavour to discover it, but all in vain. One man, indeed, was arrested on suspicion, a tramp who had been seen lingering about the neighbourhood under somewhat dubious circumstances on the night of the murder, and Richard Horton carried this piece of information up to Elizabeth Gordon's sick room, as he had previously carried the details of the adjourned and re-adjourned inquest.

This news not unnaturally excited the most miserable feelings in Elizabeth's already miserable heart.

"Oh! what shall we do, Dick? What shall we do?" she cried, wringing her hands. "If they were to try this poor man—if they were to find him guilty—"

"Perhaps you would let him be hanged, Lissa," said Richard Horton, somewhat scornfully," to save your fine Lieutenant's neck?"

Lissa did not answer for a moment, and then she said in a low, very determined tone,

"No, Dick, I would not let an innocent man die; but I would die rather than betray Jasper."

Her voice faltered, and dwelt on that name with unutterable fondness still, and Dick Horton's brow darkened as he heard it.

"What," he said, indignantly, "can you care for a fellow like him—a fellow who—"

"Hush!" said Lissa, interrupting him; and she rose and put her hand over her cousin's mouth. "Hush, Richard. Remember, you swore never to breathe what—we fear—"

"What we *know*, I should say," sneered Richard.

"You swore, at least, never to breathe it," went on Elizabeth, "and I shall hold you to your word."

"There was a condition attached, though," said Richard Horton significantly; "don't forget that, Lissa."

"I have not forgotten it. I can never forget that miserable hour," answered Elizabeth, and her head fell on her breast as she spoke with an air of utter despondency.

She was indeed tired of life. The hideous secret that she had to carry about with her; the terrible knowledge that the man she loved was utterly unworthy of that love; and the yet more terrible knowledge that she loved him still; that life would be utterly weary without him, had destroyed all hope of future happiness in her heart; and her uncle and cousins were alike shocked and pained by the change in her appearance; by her listless apathy and hopeless ways.

She had received a letter from Jasper Tyrell on the evening of the day that Harry Tyrell's body had been found. It had been written in the tidal train, and posted at Southampton, after the boat had started, by a friend to whom he had intrusted it.

Full of loving words was this epistle, full of the tenderness that Jasper unquestionably felt for her. But on one passage Elizabeth's tear-stained eyes had a hundred times dwelt since its arrival with shuddering pain.

"I have done what I did not care to do, to win you, my Lissa," wrote Jasper, "so you must pay me in love. With you by me I shall forget every one, and everything but *you*."

Had his conscience touched him already then, Elizabeth thought, or had it been some fatal accident which in a moment of weakness he had tried to hide, that had destroyed his brother's life? To this hope Elizabeth often clung. The brothers might have quarrelled—Jasper, in passion or mischance, might have shot him—but how account for the position of Harry's body when found? how for the double line of narrow footprints in the snow behind the holly-hedge?

These footprints rose up ghastly in Elizabeth's dreams—rose condemningly, damningly, to her waking sense. She could not forget them, and even if she had been able to do so, Dick Horton was always by her side to remind her that they once had undoubtedly existed.

The snow lay long after the heavy fall which took place before and after the murder, but the snow melted at length, and so the footprints passed away for ever, only leaving their traces always in Elizabeth's heart. No shadow of suspicion, however, was cast on Jasper Tyrell's name. At the inquest Sir John stated that his second son had started for China the night of his eldest son's death, but as this intended journey was well-known beforehand in the neighbourhood, it excited neither remark nor conjecture. Nothing condemnatory either could be brought home to the unfortunate tramp who had been arrested, and whose greatest crime appeared to be his poverty, and who, therefore, was most unlikely to have missed the opportunity of robbing his victim if he had been such, and the man after various examinations was discharged; Sir John Tyrell, with a certain characteristic generosity which belonged to him, providing him with necessaries at the time of his release, and work on his estate afterwards, as some compensation for his unjust incarceration.

So Harry Tyrell's death remained a mystery, and after awhile ceased to be spoken of, passing out of men's minds as all events do as time goes on. In his immediate circle, of course, this change did not come quickly. At the Hall Lady Tyrell, with her flickering, light-blue, reasonless eyes, wandered about in an upper storey especially set apart for her use and that of her trained attendants. Downstairs the girls, who at first had watched and nursed their afflicted mother unceasingly, now began to grow a little weary of the task, and of the seclusion in which they necessarily had lived since their brother's tragic end. Sir John outwardly was almost the same. He sat in his library, he rode and walked as was his wont; but he shuddered sometimes when a shriek from the guarded invalid upstairs reached his ears, and painfully reminded him of the tragedy that had happened in his household.

At the farm the shadow of Harry Tyrell's death, too, lingered on the threshold. The jovial farmer walked for many a day afterwards with a heavier step and a clouded brow. Richard Horton looked older and more determined since he had carried the terrible secret about with him; and Elizabeth Gordon was a changed and altered woman from the time of the fatal discovery.

It was said in the neighbourhood that she was heart-broken at Harry Tyrell's death. People believed that she had been engaged to him, and had never lifted her head since the terrible blow which had struck her love and her pride alike into the dust. She heard this report, but she never contradicted it. "What matter was it?" she told Dick, who had repeated it to her; but if she did not deny it her cousin did.

It was a confounded lie, Dick Horton told his companions. Lissa had neither been engaged to one brother nor the other, though both of them had admired her, and perhaps had wanted to be engaged for anything he knew.

Dick's manner to Elizabeth had also greatly altered since they had become bound together by this terrible alliance. Formerly Elizabeth in her grand way had regarded her young cousin as a mere boy to be patronised or petted as best suited her humour. Now, Richard Horton exercised a strange and fearful power over her mind. He held Jasper's life in his hands she told herself when startled by Richard's strange and unaccustomed ways, which she dared not now either resent or quarrel with.

One of her first acts after recovering from the bodily illness which had struck her down on the day that the murder was discovered, had been to write to Jasper Tyrell renouncing him for ever. In this letter, which she addressed to the ship that he had been appointed to in the Chinese waters, she gave no reason why she broke her engagement; no hint of the dreadful cause that compelled her to part with him.

"I can never marry you, Jasper," she wrote, "never, never; but I shall never forget you, or cease to remember the last happy days of my life. *I can have none now.* I loved you then, and I love you still, but not less surely we must part for ever."

In such miserable words she gave him up, knowing that this was part of the price that she must pay to purchase her cousin's silence. He had questioned her, indeed, on the subject, and Elizabeth had read unspoken menace in his manner when he had approached it. She told him, therefore, what she had done, and Richard answered in few but emphatic words.

"It was quite time, Lissa," he said, and there was something in his face as he spoke that made Elizabeth shiver and turn pale.

Thus things went on for a time, and the bleak winter months passed away, and another letter, reproachful and passionate, came to Elizabeth from Jasper Tyrell. He had received her letter, he wrote, with the utmost astonishment, and the most bitter disappointment and pain.

"I do not pretend to understand you," he added, "for if you still profess to love me, you certainly show it in a very strange and unaccountable manner. But I cannot, will not, believe that your decision is irrevocable. I have received a letter from my father also by this mail, urging me to relinquish my profession, and return to Wendell, but this under the present circumstances I shall certainly not do. If you persist in your determination I will, on the ship being paid off, make a lengthened tour through Europe. Wendell without you, and haunted also by another unhappy memory, would be too unendurable."

This letter was lying open on Elizabeth's desk one soft spring morning, just about four months after poor Harry Tyrell's death, while she herself was sitting by it, writing an answer with a very sore and troubled heart.

"Do not come back, Jasper," she had written on the note-sheet lying before her; "stay away years and years—"

She paused after she had written these words, and leant her head wearily and sorrowfully on her hand. "Poor Jasper," she was thinking, "my poor Jasper—"

One of woman's sweetest qualifications at least, if not one of her highest, is the way that she clings to the miserable and unfortunate. The wretched murderer lying in his cell, the horror and scorn of all men, has generally one pitiful and loving visitor. This is the wife. Wronged, perhaps, in her tenderest feelings—wounded, betrayed, and shamed—she yet creeps to the dreary prison; yet mingles her tears and prayers with the con-demned and crime-stained man.

It was this feeling of womanly compassion and forgiveness to the sufferer and the sinner that was now swelling in Elizabeth's heart. He had no one to comfort him, she thought, no one to confide in, no one to sooth his remorse and pain. In some sudden moment of misguided passion, she believed now that he had spilt her brother's blood, and she felt that an unsummoned dreadful guest must ever be haunting and stealing to his side. Remorse—terrible remorse—would never leave him, she felt sure; and with passionate prayers and tears she had often asked forgiveness for him from One whom she knew would not judge him as men judge, but weigh him in the truer balance of Almighty and All-seeing Justice.

At this moment, then, when her bosom was heaving, and her eyes were filling with the intense pity and sorrowful forgiveness and love that she felt for Jasper Tyrell, the door of the breakfast-room where she was sitting writing her letter was opened by one of the maids, and Jasper Tyrell's sisters were announced.

This was the first visit they had paid to the farm since their brother's death, and was paid by the express wish of Sir John. Mr. Horton's kindly sympathy, and his unaffected sorrow at the loss of his young favourite, Harry Tyrell, had been noticed by the Baronet's observing thoughtful eyes, even in the midst of his own sincere and heartfelt grief. He respected and liked his tenant also, and he had been touched by the accounts of Miss Gordon's changed appearance, and evident depression since the death of his son. "The poor girl probably loved him," thought the Baronet, and it seemed a sort of respect to his memory to treat her now with every possible attention and kinduess.

So he had requested his daughters to visit her, and not unwillingly (feminine curiosity being somewhat largely developed in their minds) the young ladies had complied.

The room that they were ushered into was the one where, four months previously, on the bleak, snowy, December morning, just before Harry's body had been found, that Elizabeth, her uncle, and cousins were seated at breakfast. It looked such a bright, warm, comfortable, home-like room then. Elizabeth, smiling, gracious, and happy, was the central figure; then came the jovial, cheery, red-cheeked farmer; then the three good-looking lads, and lastly the grave old mastiff, that shortly afterwards was to take his part in the discovery of the yet unknown tragedy enacted on the snowy roadway.

Now when the Misses Tyrell entered everything seemed changed. Elizabeth, pale, thin, and drooping, scarcely looked the same woman who then had jested with her cousins, kissed her uncle, and fondled the old dog. Her face had now a grey, set look of suppressed anxiety painful to contemplate, and the room lacked somehow the pretty, tidy, little daily adornments that come so naturally from a happy woman's hand. Even the old dog had a depressed air, for with the wonderful heaven-given instinct that these creatures possess, he seemed to feel that his mistress was sad, and therefore that it would ill-beseem him to indulge in any demonstrative liveliness.

The two Tyrell's were good-looking girls. That is, they had smooth, white and pink skins, light and abundant hair, and fairly regular features. Their usual expression in company was a mild, amiable simper, intended to express great sweetness of disposition, unfailing good temper, and a perfect absence of all malice and uncharitableness. This expression Matilda and Fannie Tyrell generally assumed in public, but on any captivating little piece of scandal being repeated in their presence, it was apt to brighten into something more lively and real, and at home they sometimes indulged in frowns and sulks. They were, however, as girls go, tolerably good natured and agreeable, and they met Elizabeth Gordon with some cordiality and kindness of manner, for they were naturally struck by the great change in her appearance, which they naturally also did not ascribe to its real cause.

Elizabeth rose, grave, gentle, and dignified, to receive them, and after they had exchanged greetings with her, the two young ladies sat down, Matilda Tyrell not far from the desk on which her brother Jasper's open letter lay.

The usual remarks on the weather having commenced, Miss Tyrell's eyes fell on the familiar handwriting, which she instantly recognised. She could not read the words exactly, but the sight of the letter distracted her attention from the conversation, and she replied to one or two sentences rather adrift.   After, however, they had been about five minutes in the room, young Richard Horton entered it, and while talking to Matilda Tyrell his eyes also fell on the Lieutenant's open letter.   A deep scarlet flush spread to his very brows at the sight of it, and after a moment's hesitation he advanced to the desk and took it in his hand.

This action Elizabeth instantly remarked, and, rising hastily, she approached him.

"That is my letter, Richard," she said.

"So I see," he answered, brusquely, almost rudely, and he threw the letter down on the desk, and the next minute without another word walked straight out of the room, closing the door behind him with much unnecessary violence.

As he did so Elizabeth folded her letter, and placed it, and the one in reply, that she had barely commenced writing when her visitors arrived, together into her desk, and then with as much calmness as she could summon she continued her conversation with the Misses Tyrell.   Matilda's innocent-looking blue eyes, however, looked sharp for a moment or two, for she had seen the by-play between the cousins, and guessed at once that Richard Horton was angry at her brother writing to Elizabeth Gordon.   Like all of us, however, who generally see more than we appear to do, Matilda made no sign, but presently began discussing the relative merits of two different kinds of fancy work.   Their work-baskets are indeed most useful to a certain class of young women, for who can believe that evil could be wrought by the white, supple fingers, apparently so busily engaged in the ravelling or unravelling of silks and wools!   Experience perhaps has taught us that other webs are sometimes spun by these delicate spiders—webs in which they often mesh the too trustful and nobler of their kind.   The eldest Miss Tyrell, however, was by no means a deep schemer.   A fly of ordinary abilities would not have walked unknowingly into *her* meshes.   She was one of those women, in fact, who with every wish and intention to be artful, show the intention.   This is by no means an uncommon error, and honest and ingenuous eyes often look on smilingly at the little play that these small actresses so transparently perform.

"Papa wishes Jasper to return to England at once now," said Miss Tyrell, anxious to hear how far Elizabeth was in her brother's confidence.

"That is only natural," replied Elizabeth with a burning blush spreading over her smooth skin, and with a slight huskiness in her usual clear tones.

"Yes, now of course," went on Miss Tyrell, "after—our sad loss."

"Sad indeed," said Elizabeth, and her dark eyes grew dim.

"Papa thinks Jasper should be at home," continued Miss Tyrell, her pink skin turned a little pinker, "he is the eldest son now—after poor Harry's death," and his sister's eyes also filled as she mentioned her hapless young brother's name.

"It must have been a terrible grief to you all," said Elizabeth, summoning all her nerve and courage to her aid, and she was a woman who on an emergency possessed this power. "And Lady Tyrell—I trust that she is a little better now?"

"Poor Mamma is still a great invalid, I am sorry to say," replied Miss Tyrell. "You see the shock was so great. But I trust with care—and of course everything that we can do—everything that Papa can do is done. We rarely leave her."

This had been quite true once; quite true when first the dismal tidings of her son's death had shattered the poor lady's reason, and clouded and lost in imaginary and fanciful wrongs the memory of his tragic fate. But like many good intentions—many soul-sworn resolutions, both Sir John's and his daughters' attentions to the afflicted woman had cooled with time. They could do her no good, they said. It was terribly painful to see her, Sir John had mentally decided; so they had all three returned by degrees to their ordinary home life. The girls received visits and paid them; wore white tulle ties, and began to think of curtailing the depth of their crape; while Sir John led his usual placid and philosophical life. Occasionally he saw the distracted mother of his murdered son, and as he had always been gentle and forbearing to her, he was gentle and forbearing now. She knew him sometimes, and sometimes fancied that he was some one else. It was very painful, as Sir John said, and he was a man who avoided pain on principle, so he kept generally out of the sight of his wife.

"As time goes on," said Elizabeth gently, "I trust that she may become more reconciled."

"Oh! yes," answered Miss Tyrell, rising, "we all hope that. But come, Fannie," she continued, addressing her younger sister, "we are preventing Miss Gordon from going on with her letters." And she offered her hand to Elizabeth in farewell as she spoke.

Elizabeth took it courteously, and accompanied the sisters to the house door, where she parted with them; the young ladies politely saying that they would be glad to see Elizabeth at the Hall.

After they were gone Elizabeth returned to the breakfast room, and sat down again with another weary sigh at her desk, and once more drew forth Jasper Tyrell's letter of reproach and love; reading it again—reading it as women read and re-read the letters of the man they love. While thus employed the door of the room opened, and Richard Horton, with a dark, sullen, and determined expression of countenance, came in, and after fastening the door behind him approached Elizabeth.

"Look, Lissa, I'll have no more of this," he said, laying his hand with some force on Elizabeth's shoulder. "I won't have you writing to that—you know what. I won't have letters from Jasper Tyrell coming here, and I won't have you answering them. I tell you this once and for all."

"It is only a letter to say good-bye, Richard," said Elizabeth, looking almost timidly up, for she was ever afraid to provoke her cousin. "You know I wrote to him—it was only natural he should answer my letter—"

"He'd better keep away from here, that's all, I can tell him," said Richard darkly. "I would not answer for myself, I know that, if my eyes fell on his smooth, self-satisfied face."

"But, Richard, you promised never—*never*—don't you remember, dear Dick—to betray him?" And Elizabeth looked up with her sweet beseeching eyes into young Richard's face.

"Ay, but I said I might ask my price," answered Horton sullenly, and dropping his eyes as he spoke; dropping them perhaps with some self shame, "and I'm going to do it now, Elizabeth—"

"Well, Richard?" asked Elizabeth, still looking at the dark agitated face of her cousin.

"Can't you guess it?" replied Richard Horton, with much emotion, clasping Elizabeth's hand with sudden passion. "Haven't you known that before those fellows—before the Tyrells ever came near, that I loved you —ay, Lissa, loved you well?" and the young man's voice broke and grew hoarse with the violence of his feelings.

Elizabeth's large eyes opened wider at this announcement, in utter astonishment.

"I never dreamt of such a thing," she said. "Richard, you are mad."

"No, I am not mad," answered young Horton vehemently, "or perhaps I am—driven mad by your beauty, by your coldness. Oh! Lissa," he went on—and he came nearer to her, seizing both her hands, and fixing his eyes with passionate earnestness on her face—"have you never guessed what I have gone through —never guessed what I felt when those Tyrells came here? Playing fast and loose with you, as I know they did. Don't tell me not," he continued, raising his voice, as Lissa rose from her seat, and tried to draw away her hands from his fierce grasp, "*for I know they did.* You flung over your cousin—your mother's sister's child—for them—for two strangers—two fine gentlemen who were trying to pass their time."

"You are mistaken," said Elizabeth, gravely and bravely, "neither poor Harry Tyrell or Jasper were amusing themselves, to my misfortune, with me. Harry never asked me to be his wife, but I fear he liked me too well—and I was engaged to Jasper, before the unhappy night—"

"When he murdered his brother," said Richard Horton bitterly.

"My God!" said Elizabeth, looking round with sudden fear, "Richard, do not—do not say that—speaking so loudly, too. Take care, for God's sake, what you say!"

"What do I care!" answered Richard Horton recklessly. "If you don't care for me, I care for nothing—they may hang him if they like."

"But I do care for you, Dick," said Elizabeth, with a white and eager face. "I do indeed, dear Dick. As you say, you are the son of my dear, dear aunt—the son of my mother's sister, so how can you but be dear to me—very dear, Dick, but of course not as—"

"You liked Jasper Tyrell, I presume?" sneered Richard Horton.

"I—I—was to be his wife," faltered Elizabeth, full of fear lest she should provoke any further outbreak on the part of Richard. "I—of course felt differently—"

With an angry gesture Richard Horton turned away as Elizabeth paused, and with hasty unequal steps he crossed the room; Elizabeth's frightened eyes following him as he went. He stood for a moment looking out of the window, and then he came back to her side, flinging himself down on his knees before her, and clasping her dress in his hands.

"Elizabeth—Lissa—" he said, in a broken voice, "listen to me. You cannot marry this man now—you cannot marry Jasper Tyrell—"

"I shall never marry him," said Elizabeth, gently laying her hand on her cousin's shoulder. "Get up, dear boy, I have promised you, and you need not fear."

"Then marry me," said Richard, looking up eagerly in Elizabeth's face. "Marry me and his secret is safe. If you were mine I would do anything—anything, Lissa. If you won't be, I don't care what happens. See, Lissa, you hold his life and mine in your hands."

"But, Dick," said Elizabeth, and her face grew white and red by turns, and her breath came short, "how can I—I—who—" And she covered her face with her hand.

"I will try to make you happy, Lissa," urged Richard. "I will indeed. Oh! if you only knew how I love you, dear." And he rose, and would have clasped Elizabeth to his breast, but she pushed him away.

"No, no, don't," she said, "don't. I have no heart to give you, Dick, and you would not surely wish me to marry you without that."

As Elizabeth said this, a look of bitter disappointment and passionate anger passed over Richard Horton's face.

"Well," he said, sullenly and darkly, "with or without heart, you know the terms now on which I will keep Jasper Tyrell's secret. I told you I should ask a price some day, didn't I? You know it now then. If you wish to save his life, you will have to marry me—ay, even if you hate me, Elizabeth." And with these ominous words he turned and left her.

CHAPTER VII.
A VAIN APPEAL.

FOR some minutes after Richard Horton had gone, Elizabeth sat utterly stunned and panic-stricken at this new danger which had arisen for Jasper Tyrell. Of all her cousins she liked Richard the least, for from boyhood his temper had been sullen and exacting, and no thought of his love for her had ever before crossed her imagination. She could scarcely realize it even now; yet what woman could mistake his looks, his words, in the brief interview which had just passed between them?

"You know the terms now," she kept repeating to herself; to her bewildered, terrified self; "the terms on which I will keep Jasper Tyrell's secret." What if she refused these terms? And yet to marry Richard—Richard Horton, her cousin—her boy cousin, whom she could never love!

At last a faint hope arose in her mind that she could influence him to give up this mad—to her, utterly impossible idea. "I will see him; I will beg on my knees," thought poor Elizabeth. "Oh! why was I born—oh! why was I ever born to be so miserable as I am now!"

She watched for an opportunity, therefore, to see Richard Horton alone, but the young man did not appear as usual at the family dinner-hour, and Elizabeth was told by Robert (the second brother) that Dick was gone to Mitchin, which is a small country town about two miles from Wendal.

"How did he go?" asked Mr. Horton on hearing this.

"He rode Winny, father," replied Robert Horton, and nothing more was sa d on the subject; the farmer inquiring, with affectionate solicitude, after dinner was over, about Elizabeth's health.

"How pale you are, my girl," he said, laying his hand kindly on his niece's arm. "What do you say, Lissa, to going for a change somewhere? We want a little holiday both of us, don't we? Suppose we pack np, and are off to Scotland for a fortnight, and leave Dick to look after the farm?"

"You are very good, uncle," said Elizabeth, and she looked at her uncle fondly. "Oh! if I could but trust this faithful friend," she thought. Lay her weary head on his shoulder, and tell him her weary burden. "But no, no, none must know—none but—"

And, she shuddered, remembering Richard Horton, and the price that he had asked for this ghastly secret.

"Well, will you go, then?" asked Mr. Horton, cheerily, and Elizabeth smiled a wintry smile in answer.

"We can think it over, she said." "Dick, perhaps, and the boys would not care to be left."

"Dick be hanged!" answered the farmer, promptly. Dick to him was by no means a very important personage, we may be sure, and he did not therefore see why Elizabeth should allude to him.

"Well, we will see," again said Elizabeth, wearily, and then she changed the conversation, leaving the farmer disturbed and uneasy about her altered appearance and manner.

When the evening came she left the house, and started for a walk in the direction where she expected that she would meet Richard Horton returning from Mitchin. It was one of those fair nights when the year is fresh and young; but the green fields, flecked here and there with sweet primroses, and the glorious verdure of the new born-leaves and grasses awoke no pleasing emotions in Elizabeth's saddened heart. Nay, she groaned aloud as she looked on the holiday garb all nature wore, contrasting its brightness and beauty with her own heavy and gloomy thoughts.

She could see, as she walked on the spot where her uncle had found poor Harry Tyrell—could see the dark holly hedge, the hedge behind which she had prayed for Jasper's life on the bleak December morning when all her sweet hopes of life and happiness had passed away. There, too, she had promised— "But no, no, it could not be. He will listen to reason," she told herself; and with some hope in her heart, at least for this, she watched and waited for her cousin.

Presently she heard the tramp of his horse's feet coming quickly along the roadway; quickly past the grounds of the Hall, and on to the spot where Elizabeth stood by the gate of one of the fields that he must cross before he reached the homestead.

There, when he saw her, he checked his horse sharply, and pulled up, a strange flush on his face the while, and a strange light in his dark, rather deeply sunken eyes.

"Well, Lissa," he said, "I didn't expect to see you."

"I came on the chance of meeting you," answered Elizabeth, in her grave, sweet voice. "I want to talk to you, Dick." And then looking at the mare her cousin rode, which was a very handsome one, and had been bought especially for Elizabeth's use, she patted its neck, while the docile creature whinnied and moved its head caressingly at her touch.

"How hard you have ridden her, Dick!" went on Elizabeth, rather reproachfully.

"Nonsense, we've had a sharp trot, that's all," answered. Richard. "But I may as well give her a rest now, so I'll walk home with you, Lissa;" and suiting his action to his words, the young man dismounted, and putting his arm through the bridle rein, thus led his horse and walked by Elizabeth's side.

They entered the field together, and together in silence proceeded a few steps down the narrow path at one side of it, Elizabeth trying to frame her thoughts into words that she hoped would have some influence and weight with her cousin. When they reached about the middle of the field she paused, and said nervously and uncomfortably, pointing at the wild blue hyacinths which were growing thickly and luxuriantly in the hedge-side near them: "How pretty those are, Dick? Do you think you could get me some?"

"Hold Winny, and I will," answered Dick; and Elizabeth took the bridle in her hand, while the young man strode over the ditch, and proceeded to gather the flowers that Elizabeth had asked for.

While he was thus employed, she made up her mind.

"Dick," she began, "I met you on purpose to-night—I met you to talk over—what we talked of this morning—to ask you here, where no one can overhear us, never again to renew the foolish words—about marrying me—that you spoke this morning."

Richard, who was pulling the flowers, looked up as Elizabeth said this, and then jumped back over the ditch on to the pathway again.

"Oh!" he said, doggedly, "so that's what you came for. was it? Well, then, Lissa, you might have spared yourself the trouble. What I said this morning I mean to keep to; so there are your flowers for you, and now we may as well be walking on."

Mechanically Elizabeth held out her hand for the hyacinths, and then said, earnestly.

"But you must listen to me, Dick. Do you know what a mad thing you ask? What happiness can come of a marriage when my consent could only be rung from me by such a threat as yours?"

"It's not an idle threat, I can tell you," answered Richard Horton, raising his voice. "What I said I would do, I will do. If you don't marry me you will hang Jasper Tyrell."

Richard said this loudly and excitedly, for he had been drinking at Mitchin, and Elizabeth's heart died within her at his words and tone.

"My dear Richard," she said appealingly, and she put her hand on the young man's arm, and the blue flowers that he had gathered for her dropped unheedingly from her grasp as she did so.

"Not very dear, it seems," said Richard roughly.

"Yes, yes, dear in one way," continued Elizabeth; "dear as I told you that you were this morning—too dear for me to allow you to do what will ruin your whole life.   Dick," she went on, urgently, "listen to me at least for a moment; listen to a woman older and more experienced than yourself.   You are young and good-looking.   Many girls would be proud and glad to marry you.   Marry some young girl who will love you, who will watch for you, and wait for you—to whom the very sound of your footstep will be sweet."

As Elizabeth spoke thus, with her beautiful dark eyes fixed on her cousin's face, and her noble and finely cut features lit with the intensity of her feelings, she had never looked more dangerously attractive to Richard Horton.

"You, too, listen to me," he said, with his eyes fixed eagerly and passionately upon her. "Do you know what you are, Elizabeth?   You talk of young girls—what are young girls to me? What beside you—a lovely, perfect woman like you?   Bah!" he added, "all the young girls on earth—all their love and their devotion, or whatever folly you talk about, would not make up for one moment to me, for the right to kiss your lips!"

"Oh! hush, hush, Richard," said Elizabeth.

"No, I will not hush," he went on determinedly.   "I love you, and I mean to marry you.   Nothing you can say, Lissa, will move me—nothing will change me.   If you will marry me, Jasper Tyrell's secret is safe.   If not—"

"Give me time at least," prayed Elizabeth, putting out her hand, "let me think—"

"Give me your answer to-morrow then," said Richard Horton. "Let it be yes or no—life or death—mind, Lissa, I'll stand no foolery."

With a shuddering sigh Elizabeth turned away; with a shuddering sigh moved slowly onward, Richard Horton and the mare following her, and in total silence the cousins reached Wendell West-house, leaving the blue flowers lying on the path where they had fallen from Elizabeth's hand.

CHAPTER VIII.

A BETROTHAL.

ONCE or twice during our life-time, to most of us, I suppose, come moments and days which, if they were prolonged, would produce madness or death? I write not of course of those happily constituted beings whose coldness, indifference, or self-esteem supplies them with a soothing balm wherewith to heal their wounds.   But what about the sensitive, the generous-hearted, and the proud? What about those whom cruel words can cut deeper than a knife, and who shrink inwardly with horror from the world-struggle that perhaps their circumstances force them to encounter? These will understand what I mean; will understand what Elizabeth Gordon suffered during the night on which she was left to decide Jasper Tyrell's fate and her own.

Quite alone all through the long hours she sat; quite silent all through the night, until the early dawn stole in at the windows and the new day was born. Then she fell on her knees and prayed—prayed with all the passionate force of her nature—that she might be given strength to save Jasper Tyrell. She was a woman who would have died for him with a smile—died for him, aye, how gladly—but this was a sacrifice worse than death. To marry Richard—her cousin Richard—a youth whom she could never love—nay, whom she must ever despise, for wringing so fearful a price from her, for the sake of his own passionate and selfish love.

But the price must be paid, she decided; so pale and cold, she lay down at last, dressed as she was, on the bed, and through sheer fatigue fell into a restless and uneasy slumber. Then she awoke, rose, bathed her face, and looked at her watch. It was past eight o'clock she found, and she heard the boys and the farmer downstairs, and presently descended, and went into the breakfast-room, where they were waiting for her to make the tea.

"My dear," said Mr. Horton, the moment that he looked at her, "what is the matter?"

"Nothing, uncle, nothing," said Lissa: and with trembling hands she went on performing her usual duties. She saw (though she never looked up) that Richard Horton was present; saw his hands when he took his cup from hers; and if she had looked in his face she would have seen one even more agitated than her own. Now pale, now flushed, with blood-shot eyes and shaking hands, the young man sat, utterly unable to swallow any breakfast, and feeling as the unhappy wretch must feel who awaits the sentence yet unuttered by the Judge's lips.

At last, one after the other, they all went out, and Richard Horton and Elizabeth were left alone. Then with shamed eyes and faltering tongue he approached her.

"Lissa," he said, "put an end to this—has it to be yes or no?"

As he thus addressed her, Elizabeth raised her dark sad eyes to his face, and answered slowly and coldly, for she had decided on the very words that she should use.

"Richard," she said, "you have asked a price, and I will pay it, but on you, remember, rests all the responsibility, and all the blame, for forcing on what can only be an unhappy marriage."

"No," he answered, grasping her hand. "no, Lissa, you will learn to love me; you will come to love me, I am certain, I am sure."

"Do not deceive yourself," went on Elizabeth, "for I never shall."

"Yes, yes," said Richard Horton, eagerly, "in time I know you will. Wait, and it will come," and he drew Elizabeth to him, and kissed her cold pale face.

No blush rose to her cheek at his touch; none as he went on with his frantic, eager loving words. Her beautiful face might have been carved in cold, grey stone for any sign of emotion that she showed, and at last he angrily pushed her away.

"Aye," he said, "you hate me, do you—take care you don't make me hate you too, Lissa."

"Would to God you did," said Elizabeth, in answer to this outburst.

"Well, hate or not," went on Richard, with a rude oath, "I'll marry you, so you may as well make the best of me—and if you're a wise woman you will, Lissa."

And she was to marry this man, thought Elizabeth; to marry this rough, rude, unmannerly youth, who dared to speak to her thus, dared to advise her, to order her at his will! For a moment her temper rose in rebellion at this early tyranny; but the next she checked it.

"For his sake," she whispered, "for his sake!" And so for Jasper Tyrell's sake she bore her cousin's insolence; bore with his violence of one minute, his scarcely less odious penitence the next. Oh, these were miserable days—very, very miserable days. For any woman to marry a man she does not love must be a cruel trial, but when there is not only no love, but no respect, no esteem, and worse still, love for another man, surely as Elizabeth often thought, it is more cruel than death, more bitter than the grave.

No one was more astonished at the announcement of Elizabeth's engagement to his son than the farmer. The good man would not believe his ears when he was first told of it, and insisted that the two were inventing some joke at his expense. He could not understand it. Could not understand the bride elect's pale cheeks, her heavy, listless steps. He remembered her mother—the blithe, bright Elizabeth—when she was about to wed her young soldier lover; remembered the sweet flush on her face, the lovelight in her eyes. His own comely wife, too, had come a blushing, smiling, happy bride to his arms. But here was Lissa—Lissa, his darling girl, about to become his daughter, looking as if her grave-clothes were being manufactured instead of her wedding dress!

He urged her to say if she were happy at the prospect before her; urged her to confide in him, even though naturally he was pleased that "Dick," as he called his son, had done so well for himself. To these inquiries Elizabeth had one reply.

"I am going to marry him, uncle," she used to say, with her

wintry smile; and the honest farmer could extract no other word.
In his perplexity he even hinted some of his astonishment to his
landlord, Sir John, and that grave thoughtful gentleman pondered
gravely and thoughtfully over his tenant's words.

"And she is going to marry this cub," he thought; "probably
then for some reason known only to herself;" and a vision of his
two sons—of the dead Harry, and the living Jasper, crossed his
mind uneasily as he mused.

But whatever people might think or say, the fact remained
the same. Elizabeth Gordon, who had held her head so high,
was about to marry her cousin, young Richard Horton, and her
friends and neighbours were rather pleased than otherwise that
she had come down off her pedestal, and was at last to become
the wife of a tenant farmer after all.

Richard Horton's excitement, his miserable frantic jealousy,
his passionate outbursts, his disappointment at her continued
coldness as time went on, were pitiable to behold. "The young
man has lost his head," people said, "as well as his heart."

Indeed he acted the part almost of a madman on many occasions, and lived in a perpetual fever lest his shrinking victim
should escape him in the end. He was always urging and entreat-
ing Elizabeth to fix a day for their marriage, and at last she coldly
consented to do so; this promise being wrung from her as her
first promise had been—by threats and dread.

"Do you mean to marry me or not, Lissa?" asked Richard
Horton, when July had come, and weeks and months of mutual
torment had gone on between them. "For I'm not always going
to be put off," he added sullenly.

"What hurry is there?" asked Elizabeth.

"Perhaps you don't wish to keep your promise at all," retorted
Horton, "but in that case, mind, I won't keep mine."

"I do mean to keep my promise," said Elizabeth; and before
the interview was ended the day was fixed when this unmatched
couple were to become man and wife.

At the Hall the girls heard the news with the greatest surprise.
Matilda's meek but really acute eyes had noted her brother
Jasper's manner, as well as poor Harry's before his tragic fate,
about the "fair Elizabeth," as Jasper sometimes in the earlier
days of their aquantance used to call her, and Matilda was a girl
who in general drew her conclusions very sagely. The Misses
Tyrell not unnaturally had always looked down on the young
Horton's with the utmost contempt. Matilda, therefore, could
not understand, as she said in sisterly confidence to Fannie, why
Miss Gordon had not at least waited to "try for Jasper."

"Perhaps she has written to him," suggested Fannie, "and he
has shown her that he means nothing. You know you saw a
letter in his hand-writing lying on her desk, did you not?"

"So I did!" said Matilda. "You have just hit it, I believe, Fannie. She has written to him, no doubt. Well, we ought to be thankful that we shall not be connected with the family of a farmer at any rate. Yes, no doubt, in pique at Jasper, she has accepted this elegant young gentleman."

Thus, as is often done, Miss Tyrell decided on the reason for an act that she could not understand. But it mattered very little to Elizabeth what the young ladies at the Hall thought, or what the small world around her thought of her conduct. We must still have some little interest in life, some little hope, at least, of brighter days, when what "people will say" adds to our troubles. Elizabeth had no such hope, no such interest now. The sacrifice she was about to make was to her a complete one, and all her coming life lay shrouded in darkness before her.

Thus, then, the days and nights stole on; the days and nights, each of which, as it faded into the past, drew her nearer to the future, from whose contemplation she shrank with ever increasing dread.

Once more—but once, she tried to avert her coming fate. It was on a summer eve, a Sunday eve, near the end of July, and she and Richard Horton were walking together in one of the farmer's cornfields; the tall, fast-ripening grain waving and stirring the while in the pleasant breeze. Elizabeth never went to church now; never had entered a church since she had promised to marry her cousin. To her mind the vows she then had agreed to make were an insult to the God in whom she believed, and who had made this tie from the beginning as a blessing and not as a curse to His creatures. How could she kneel down and pray—pray for her future husband as happier maidens can do? It was a sin, she knew, that she was about to commit—a sin to save Jasper Tyrell, and she dared not now ask God's blessing on her present or coming life.

But this evening—this holy, peaceful evening-tide, when all the world seemed at rest around them—made Elizabeth look heaven-ward with a strange, yearning hope. Richard Horton too, apparently, was touched and softened, and he spoke more gently to Elizabeth than was his wont, dropping for a while the imperious air of ownership which it was now generally his pleasure to assume.

"It's only for a little while, Dick, after all," said Elizabeth, with her now habitual sad smile, on the young man making some remarks on the inequalities of life.

"Ay," answered young Richard, "but a little while of torment or joy—"

Elizabeth looked at his face as he said this; at the sullen, handsome face, which just at that moment wore a gentler and more thoughtful look than usual, and she timidly put her hand through his arm.

"Dick," she said, do you ever think of the hour that we must all meet?"

"What do you mean?" he asked sharply.

"When it will be all over," went on Elizabeth, in her gentle, ringing voice, "all our love, all our hate—when the good we have done and the evil will alike come back?   Oh! Dick, will you wish in that hour—"

"Hush!" said Richard Horton, interrupting her with sudden vehemence.   "Hush, Lissa!" and he laid a burning hand on the small one resting on his arm.

"Nay, I will not hush," continued Elizabeth, earnestly.   "For something bids me speak.   Dick, will you wish in that hour that you had not forced me to be your wife?"

As Elizabeth asked this question, the young man dropped her arm from his, and clasped his hand over his face.

"Why do you say that now—when it is so near?" he said, hoarsely.

"Because it is never too late to repent," urged Elizabeth. "Because, Dick, we are both doing a deadly sin—I the greatest, perhaps, in taking a false vow before the altar of God."

For a minute Richard Horton was silent; for a minute perhaps a struggle took place in his passionate, wayward heart, and the powers of good and evil held conflict for the young man's soul. Then, almost with a cry, he fiercely seized Elizabeth's hand.

"Look, Elizabeth," he said, while the veins swelled about his throat and neck, and his face grew darkly crimson, "there is no turning back for me.   If hell is the price I have to pay for you, I'll pay it.   Nothing shall snatch you from me now—nothing, I swear it, in heaven or earth!"

"You have my promise," said Elizabeth, slowly, a moment or two after this outbreak, and then the cousins walked on together through the pleasant fields, and bounteous ripening crops.   But the quiet peace of the Sabbath night was gone.   The evil passions of man had swept away the serene beauty that fell from heaven, and Elizabeth saw no more the lovely hues and tints— the golden glories and the purple streaks shed by the setting sun. But she looked at that sun, sinking in the west; looked at the great orb of light, and knew that before it rose on another Sabbath morning it would rise on her wedding day.

CHAPTER IX.
ELIZABETH'S MARRIAGE.

IT was a bright morning when Elizabeth rose on her marriage day, bright, hot, and shining, but before nine o'clock heavy clouds rose to the eastward, and came driving up before the wind; while distant, ominous peals of thunder rolled at intervals, as if in warning of the coming storm.

They were to be married at ten, and by ten the heavens were black with clouds, and great drops of rain came pouring upon the earth, while the lightning seemed to rend the sky, flashing with extraordinary brilliance over the darkened world.

In the midst of this terrible storm, Elizabeth, with a pale set face, dressed in her wedding garments, stood waiting for some abatement of it in the dining-room of Wendell West-house. It was the same room into which they had borne the corpse of young Harry Tyrell on the morning that his murder was discovered, and from that miserable event had sprung indirectly the miserable marriage that was about to be solemnised in the House of God.

The church at Wendell is a grey old building, grey, time-worn, simple, and antique. Up its venerable walls the ivy creeps and flourishes, and among the moss-grown tombstones that surround it stand ancient trees, that have budded and leafed, and budded and leafed, while the mouldering inhabitants of the graves below played and prattled as children in the sun.

In these old trees a colony of rooks are settled, and have built their nests, and cawed and cawed through long years of possession. Elizabeth had gone to this church when a little child; her mother had been married there to her handsome soldier lover; her aunt, Mr. Horton's wife, lay sleeping outside beneath the green grass mound, at the head of which was a simple stone, recalling her simple virtues. A hundred early and hallowed recollections, in fact, for Elizabeth, were connected with this sacred spot, and now she was about to be married there; about to utter her false vows before the face of God and man.

Hers was not the only pale face though that morning in the dining-room of Wendell Farm. The ruddy farmer had a scared look as the ill-omened thunder broke with crashing peals over the house, and the fire seemed literally, in the language of Scripture, to run along the ground. The bridegroom's usually brown, bronzed skin looked absolutely pallid in the dim light, and his brow was damp and clammy. But neither the terrors of heaven nor the reproaches of his own heart for a moment changed him from his purpose, and with a resolute and determined expression he stood watching the storm, holding his watch impatiently in his hand.

"It's no use waiting for it," he said at last. "Come, Lissa, we'll be there in five minutes, and the rain won't do you any harm."

"But the lightning will startle the horses, Dick," said Mr. Horton, uneasily. "It's not safe to have them out. Wait for half an hour, and it will surely be off by that time. I've sent a message to Mr. Hay, and he knows we're coming as soon as we can."

"It's getting lighter," answered Dick. "I'll go round to the stables and see if they are getting the horses put in."

Just then the whole room grew ablaze, and a tremendous crashing peal overhead seemed to shake the house to its very foundations.

"My God!" ejaculated the farmer, and for the first time during the storm a faint cry broke from Elizabeth's pale lips.

"It has struck one of the outhouses I believe," said Dick Horton, coolly pausing at the door-way. "Ay, that flash has done some mischief."

"My dear," said Mr. Horton, advancing to his niece, "give it up for to day. There is no one but ourselves to consult, and old Hay won't say a word. You are shaken and frightened, Elizabeth; it's absurd, Dick, for you to attempt to get married in a storm like this."

At these words the young man's face grew dark as the thunder-clouds above.

"What folly, father," he said, also advancing towards the pale bride. "Lissa, you won't disappoint me, will you?" he added, touching her hand. "You won't let a thunderstorm, surely, put off our wedding-day?"

"It's so dreadful, Dick," answered Lissa, piteously.

"It'll be off directly," he went on. "See, it's really lighter. Come, Lissa, may I tell them to put the horses into the carriage?"

"I have promised," murmured the unhappy Elizabeth; and Dick gave a glad low cry at her words.

"Yes," he said, and he kissed her cheek; "You are a brave girl, Lissa—my own brave girl;" and the farmer looking on saw the shudder that passed through the bride's frame at the bridegroom's caress.

"I'll have the carriage round in a minute," continued Dick, and he left the room, and as he did so Mr. Horton went forward and closed the door after him.

"Elizabeth," he said, earnestly, returning to his niece, and taking her cold hand in his," before it is too late, tell me, my dear, do you really wish to marry your cousin Richard?"

At this unexpected question Elizabeth's firmness for a moment gave way, and she fell on her uncle's neck, who drew her kindly to his breast.

"Tell me, my dear," he said, "for you have no mother, no aunt now to trust in, and from first to last I've been uncomfortable about this matter. What power has Dick got over you, Lissa? Tell your old uncle, my dear, for who knows but the hand of God sent this storm as a warning to us all?"

These words at once recalled Elizabeth to herself.

"No, uncle," she said, quickly lifting her head, "I am marrying Dick from my own free will. Nothing compels me— he has no power—what power could he have?"

As Elizabeth said this hastily and eagerly, the farmer released her with a sigh.

"Well, you know best, my dear," he said, "but when I wedded my poor Ann, she didn't look at me as you did at Dick just now, when I kissed her cheek."

"I was afraid—of the storm," answered Elizabeth; and Mr. Horton had nothing else to do but accept her explanation; and a few moments afterwards the carriage which was to convey them to the church drove round to the front entrance of the house.

Mr. Hay, the venerable incumbent of the parish, had received notice of their approach, and was ready waiting for them when they reached the grey old church. It was almost quite dark in the interior of it, for the dim yellow light outside shone dimly indeed through the narrow windows, in the thick time-worn walls, and added not a little to the solemn effect of the solemn ceremony which a few minutes later began.

He was an old, old man, this priest who wedded them; an old, grey, worthy venerable man. Nearly fifty years he had lived at Wendal, and had baptised, married, and prayed for nearly all its inhabitants, and had buried many, "Oh, how many!" he sometimes thought, of its dead. He had never been married, and lived quite alone, except for an old housekeeper, nearly as old and as venerable as himself, at the Parsonage—that pleasant spot near the church, with its well cared for, old-fashioned garden in front, and its fruitful orchard at the back, in the proceeds of which many a young scamp of Wendell shared, as well as its meek and unsuspecting owner.

Dorothy, the housekeeper, indeed had her suspicions, but the old woman was somewhat blind, and never had succeeded in capturing any of the knowing urchins, who were well acquainted with her habits, and knew when her after-dinner nap was sure to come on.

Thus in this peaceful fashion, year after year, the good old clergyman had lived on. Who knows—perhaps some dead romance, some faded memory of his youth was cherished still, and not always, maybe, had he so serenely trod the paths of life? Be this as it may, long years had passed and gone since any disturbing element had crossed the old man's way. He rose early, and could be seen working in his garden before eight, reaping the fruits of his temperate and virtuous life in his ruddy healthful cheek, his clear and placid eye, his firm and almost youthful step.

With pleasant words he greeted Elizabeth then, when, amid the darkness and the storm, she stood before him on her wedding-day. "She must not be afraid," the old man said, and patted her shoulder with his kindly hand. "God directs the storm, you know, my dear," he added, not unnaturally ascribing

Elizabeth's pale stricken face to her dread of the yet warring elements around her.

Then, a minute or two later, her uncle led her .to the altar, and the ceremony began. The words so solemn, so holy, so sacred, when pledged between two who love each other, two whose hearts silently respond, and who know there is no lie on their lips, were uttered by Elizabeth with faltering tongue, witb shamed and miserable heart.

"Oh! that I were dead—that I were dead," she thought, as she knelt there; as she put her cold hand in Richard Horton's, as he placed the holy symbol of marriage on her finger, binding her to cleave to him only as long as they two should live!

Then the priest blessed them, praying that "Almighty God, who at the beginning did create our first parents, Adam and Eve, and did sanctify and join them together in marriage, pour upon you the riches of His grace, sanctify and bless you, that ye may please Him both in body and soul, and live together in holy love unto your lives' end. Amen."

But no Amen came from Elizabeth's white lips; none from her hopeless and unhappy heart.

CHAPTER X.

THE BRIDE AND BRIDEGROOM.

A MONTH after the great thunderstorm, which remained memorable at Wendell from its severity, and from the serious accident that occurred during its continuance to the stables at the Hall, which were struck by the lightning, and two valuable horses of Sir John's were killed, whilst a groom who was standing near was rendered insensible, and was recovered with considerable difficulty—a month after this storm, then, memorable also in the village as the wedding-day of Elizabeth Gordon, the bridegroom and the bride returned to the homestead.

Great preparations had been made in honour of this event by Master Hal; or at least he had contemplated making great preparations, but with the best intentions (like us all) some of his intended decorations proved signal failures. To begin with, he insisted on erecting a triumphal arch of evergreens at the entrance gate of Wendell West-house. The foundation of its frail structure was composed of card-board, and thin laths of wood, at which Master Hal toiled many days in an outhouse before he disclosed his design to his brother Bob and the farmer. Bob, with all the dignity of very early manhood, ridiculed Hal's idea, and spoke disrespectfully of "such trumpery" as he designated the work of the energetic boy. The good-natured farmer however entered into the scheme, and Hal's ever-green arch was raised after considerable difficulty.

"If there's a wind in the night it will be down," prophesied Bob.

"There won't be a wind," affirmed Hal, with venturesome confidence.

But alas! in the night the wind and the storm arose, and Hal in his attic room at the top of the house heard the sound thereof, with a sinking heart. Scarcely then had daylight stolen on the world, when the boy arose and hurried out to discover the fate of his leafy architecture. One glance told the tale. The arch lay toppled from its eminence over the gate, having fallen forward into the avenue, though still attached by the sides to the wooden pillars on which the gate was hung.

For a moment Hal stood dismayed; then the indomitable spirit of resistance to the strokes of adverse fortune, which make all men and women great, rose in the boy's heart, and with energetic industry Master Hal set to work to repair in secret the damage that had happened to his handiwork.

Silently he procured a ladder; silently raised his arch, on a yet more precarious footing than the first time, and when Bob strolled down after breakfast to the spot (having also heard the sound of the wind in the night), Hal with calm assumption of innocence and ease pointed out his superior knowledge of the durability of his erection.

"You said it would be down," said Hal; and Bob taking advantage of his usual taciturnity whistled, made no remark and went away, leaving Hal, however, undoubtedly the master of the situation. But though outwardly he might show no sign, inwardly Master Hal was trembling throughout the day, and when the afternoon came, and the hour nearly arrived for the expected returning of the bridegroom and the bride, he was considerably relieved to find that his arch was still standing. He therefore hung the hall and rooms with evergreens and flowers according to his taste, and nearly broke his neck, and did ruin a pair of light new trousers in his efforts to place a flag-staff in one of the chimneys. At last four o'clock came, and the carriage started for the newly-married pair to the station, while the farmer wandered somewhat restlessly in the front of the house, now anxiously awaiting their arrival.

"They're coming!" cried Hal presently, who was reconnoitring from an upper window of the house. "Coming!" And he ran to the front door and joined his father.

Coming—but they came not; and a minute or two having passed, Hal unable to restrain his impatience ran down the avenue to discover the cause of their delay.

This the instant he came in sight of the carriage was but too evident. One of the wheels in entering the gate had touched the evergreen arch, and the whole structure had at once swayed and

fallen forward, firstly on the coachman's head, nearly blinding him
with the blow, then on the horses, thus naturally completely ter-
rifying them. But this unfortunately was not all. Hal's arch,
repaired by ropes and twine, remained an insuperable barrier in
its present prostrate condition to the advance of the horses and
carriage, for when Hal arrived on the scene it had fallen over the
horses' heads, and was thus nearly choking them in their efforts
to proceed forward.

Hal ran at once to the rescue, seizing the horses' heads, and
speaking to them in his familiar voice to quiet their alarm; while,
with angry exclamations, Richard Horton, the bridegroom, sprang
out of the carriage.

"What's all this tom-foolery, Hal?" he asked, passionately,
when his eyes fell on his younger brother. "Is this any of your
doing?   By Jove, if it is I'll thrash you within an inch of your
life."

"Never mind, Dick," said Lissa's voice. "Is that you, Hal?
Come, Dick, no harm is done after all."

"Confound it!" went on Dick, struggling with the ropes, the
card-board, and the prickly holly, of all of which there appeared
an avalance upon them.   "Did ever you know of such a stupid
trick? Get me a knife, boy—well, this exceeds everything!"

But now the farmer, alarmed also at their delay, arrived, and
with a good tempered laugh at the accident proceeded with his
big knife to cut through the ropes of Master Hal's arch, and
clear away the *débris* amid such pleasant jokes and kindly talk,
that Richard Horton was forced by shame to smooth his ruffled
brow. Then Mr. Horton came to the car iage door, and lifting
Lissa out, kissed her cheek with the greatest affection as he did
so.

"Welcome home, my dear," he said, "thrice welcome" (this
was with another kiss). "Hal was determined to give you a
surprise, you see," he added, smiling. "Well, well! the boy
did it out of his love for you, my dear, so you mustn't scold
him."

"Of course not, dear uncle," answered Lissa; and when the
farmer heard her voice he looked in her face, and somehow he
sighed as he did so.

"Come," he said the next minute, "Master Hal, since you
have chosen to do all this mischief, you had better be sharp and
undo it as fast as you can—and you come to the house with me,
my dear," he added to Lissa, "and leave the lads and John"
(this was the coachman) "to look after the carriage and
luggage.

"Yes, uncle," said Lissa, and she put her arm through her
uncle's and walked with him up the familiar avenue, through
the familiar flower-beds, and into the house that she had lived

in since she was a happy little child. The servants came into
the hall to speak to her; the cook, who had grown grey, stout,
and red in the service of her aunt and uncle, and who had remembered Lissa since she was a lively laughing girl of twelve,
looked also into the bride's face as her uncle had done, and
sighed too, and shook her head as she did so.

"I don't like the looks of her," she confided to one of her
fellows in the kitchen a few minutes later. "She looks more
like a widow than a bride to my mind—ay, ay, no doubt her
heart is buried in young Mr. Tyrell's bloody grave."

Such indeed was the general impression in the neighbourhood;
for Lissa Gordon had been a changed woman, as every one knew,
since the young Squire was carried a corpse into her uncle's
house. Conscious now, however, that remarks would probably
be made on her appearance on her first return home, Lissa tried
to smile, and did speak kindly to every one in answer to their
welcoming words. But a heavy heart or a light one is hard to
hide. Lissa's lips might smile, but her eyes had a sad far-away
look impossible to describe, but which we have all seen in faces
showing outwardly in faint reflection the grief or care that lurks
below.

"And you had a nice journey, my dear?" said the farmer,
bustling about, and offering his niece (now his daughter-in-law)
wine and other refreshments.

"Yes, the weather was so fine," answered Lissa; and then
after a few more words she asked leave to retire to her own room.

"I'm a little tired," she said; but she felt in fact that she
could scarcely any longer control the choking emotions that were
swelling in her heart.

When she reached her old room—the room where she had been
so happy and so miserable, tears—that she could not suppress—
sprang into her eyes, and fell fast and hot down her cheeks.
Not long, however, was she allowed to indulge alone in her
reflections, whatever they might be, for, with scarcely a rap at the
door, a few minutes later Richard Horton entered the apartment,
and when his eyes fell on Lissa's wet and tear-stained face, the
cloud already on his brow darkened considerably.

"What is the matter? What are you crying for?" he asked,
sharply.

"I'm a little upset by coming home, Dick, that is all," answered Lissa, meekly, almost guiltily; and she rose, dried her eyes,
and affected to busy herself about the arrangement of the toilet,
while Dick took two hasty turns across the room.

"Look, Lissa," he said at length, excitedly, "this is a nice
way to welcome a man home, isn't it?—crying and groaning as
you are now, and letting them all see downstairs, deuce take it!
that you wish yourself unmarried again."

"Nonsense, Richard," said Lissa, gently, in answer to this outbreak, "why do you imagine such things? I am sure no one thinks—"

"Don't they though!" answered Dick, darkly and doggedly, "I see it in their faces—and besides, any one can see it in yours."

And Dick threw himself on a chair, and covered his face with his hand.

As he did so, Lissa crossed the room, and laid her hand on her husband's shoulder.

"Richard," she said, with unconscious pathos in her ringing voice, "do not, please, act thus. Our marriage was a mistake, and I told you so; but let us try now—I at least mean to try now—not to make the mistake greater than it is."

For a moment Richard Horton was silent, and then with irrepressible passionate emotion he turned his head round so that it rested against Lissa's hand.

"Oh! if you could but learn to love me," he murmured, and he eagerly kissed the slender fingers lying on his shoulder.

A feeling of pity thrilled through Elizabeth's heart at these words.

"Perhaps in time, Dick," she said softly; and she stooped down and kissed Richard's burning brow. "How hot your head is," she went on the next minute. "Does it ache, Dick?"

"Ache! I should think so," answered Richard Horton, "it's always aching."

"Poor boy!" said Elizabeth, pityingly.

But the wayward humour of the young man was offended by what she meant only for kindly words.

"Why do you treat me and talk to me like that?" he said, angrily. "Poor boy indeed! I'm not a boy, and I'm not going to be treated like one. I'm your husband, though you sometimes seem to forget it, Elizabeth!"

"I never forget it, Richard," answered Lissa, coldly; and muttering and grumbling, Dick Horton left the room, only, however, to return a few minutes later, for with exacting tyranny he never allowed her to spend half-an-hour alone in peace.

It was a miserable life that lay before these two; miserable from many causes, but mostly so from the passionate love that Richard Horton felt for Elizabeth—love that he was bitterly conscious was totally unreturned.

This continual disappointment made him jealous and tyrannical in the extreme. In vain Lissa was gentle, kind, and considerate to him always, for he knew and felt all the while that her heart was utterly cold to him, and that only a sense of duty made her bear with his temper, his exacting love, his outbreaks, which seemed almost to partake of hatred at times, so bitterly did he resent the knowledge that he could not win her love though he had forced her to become his wife.

They had not been at home many days, when the farmer's shrewd eyes were opened to the fact (which he had before suspected) that for some cause or other Elizabeth had married her cousin against every wish and feeling of her heart. He saw (though he made no sign) the weary look in her eyes when Dick was present; saw her expression brighten when he left the room, and darken when the loud voice and heavy footstep again drew near. It was in fact the very reverse of the loving wife—the wife that perhaps Dick Horton might have won, if he had not conceived the mad and unsuitable passion for his cousin, which she had warned him could only end in a miserable marriage for them both.

The two young brothers, even, Bob and Hal, saw it was not all right between the married pair.

"When I have the misfortune to get married," quoth Hal to Bob one day, some disagreement having occurred a short while before in their presence between Elizabeth and Dick, "I wonder if the happy female will look at me with the same concentrated essence of disgust which was depicted in Lissa's face just now when she regarded our amiable brother."

"Dick's a sulky fellow," answered Bob, who was of a practical turn of mind, "and I can't conceive why Lissa was ever such a fool as to marry him."

"The ways of women," replied Hal, "are ever unaccountable. Some day, my dear Bob, no doubt some woman will be fool enough to marry you."

Bob laughed good-naturedly at this sally, and the subject was dropped, but not the less did the brothers and the farmer continue to marvel at the strange cause which had bound together two so utterly unsuitable to each other as were Elizabeth and her husband.

Thus as this marriage had been inauspicious from the first, unblessed by mutual love, unhallowed by faith, or truth, or honour, as time went on the dark cloud over-head grew darker, and Richard Horton found that solemn vows when forced from unwilling lips may be kept outwardly, and yet lack the subtle secret sweetness which forms really their happiness and joy.

CHAPTER XI.
SIR JOHN'S VISIT.

AFTER Elizabeth had been some weeks at home, Sir John Tyrell called upon the bride. The courteous gentleman paid this visit from two motives, one of which was that he wished to show every attention and kindness to his neighbour and tenant, Mr. Horton, and another that he had some curiosity to become personally acquainted with Elizabeth, admiring her as every man of taste admires a beautiful woman, and interested in her for the sake of the hapless young son that he had lost.

Elizabeth was in her garden cutting roses, when the tall, thin form of Sir John appeared approaching up the avenue of Wendell West-house, and she at once advanced to meet him.

"My uncle is in the house, Sir John," she said, as the Baronet took off his hat and bowed low before her, with all the grave politeness which became his fine face and appearance so well.

"But I have not come to see my friend, Mr. Horton, to-day," answered Sir John, with a smile, "but to claim my privilege as a near neighbour and call upon you."

Elizabeth blushed, and a strange emotion stirred in her heart at these words, for between Sir John and Jasper Tyrell there was a strong family likeness: though, good-looking as Jasper was, he lacked a certain grace of manner that pervaded every action and word of Sir John.

"How your roses bloom here!" said the Baronet, his eyes fixed the while on Elizabeth's handsome face. He was thinking of his sons. wondering and musing as was his wont on all passing scenes, and Elizabeth moved uneasily under the gaze of the bright yet soft dark eyes, which judged so wisely and gently of his fellow beings.

"Yes," she said, "we have some rather good kinds—but of course at the Hall—"

"We have none half so good, I can assure you. I shall beg a few of yours when I go, to take—to my poor invalid."

Sir John's voice faltered a little when he made this allusion to his wife, and Elizabeth looked at him with increasing interest.

"How is Lady Tyrell?" she asked, feelingly.

Sir John shook his head.

"She is a child," he said, gravely and sadly; "weak alike in body and mind. The blow was too heavy for poor Harry's mother to bear."

"No wonder," said Elizabeth, with agitation that she tried to hide from her companion's discerning eyes. "It was too—dreadful—"

"And the mystery that surrounds it," went on Sir John, "the inexplicable mystery—it is this that continually disturbs me. I would give many years of my life to be able to discover Harry's murderer."

As Sir John said this, Elizabeth's varying colour, her clenched and quivering hands, were all perceived by Sir John, who, however, with well-bred ease appeared perfectly unconscious of them.

"Shall we go in?" said Elizabeth, with a nervous effort to change the conversation.

"I shall be pleased to do so," replied Sir John, and he followed Elizabeth into the house.

She led him in her agitation into the dining-room, the door of which happened to be standing open, forgetting as she did so that the last time Sir John had entered it had been to view the corpse of his murdered son. Sir John, however, looked round the room and recognised it with a sigh.

"He was carried in here, was he not?" he asked of Elizabeth in a low sad tone.

"Yes," said Elizabeth. "Oh! Sir John, pardon me—I—I forgot."

"Nay," replied Sir John gently, "there is no reason why you should not bring me here. I cannot understand that shrinking from allusions or memorials of a grievous fact *we know*. My boy was murdered; why should I not then enter the room in which your uncle's kindly hand first bore him, poor lad, after he had met his tragic and, to me, most mysterious fate."

"Still—" faltered Elizabeth.

"You fear it might pain me, but it does not," went on Sir John. "It is the mystery—the miserable mystery—as I said before, for any cause for this crime that I have so continually before me. I had his note-book and his watch in my hand the other day, poor fellow, for they lie in my desk, and it ever strikes me anew when I see them. They were the one temptation that any one could have to take his life—the one temptation at least known to me." Sir John paused before he spoke the last few words, for Elizabeth's almost uncontrollable emotion while he was speaking of Harry's watch and money caused suddenly a strange suspicion to enter his mind. Did this beautiful woman know more than he knew? he thought. Was all this agitation caused by the mention of the dead youth's belongings—facts that she had known for months—or was there something hidden—something beyond? Sir John thought a moment or two while Elizabeth sank back into an arm-chair with her face from the light; and then in his even tones the Baronet intentionally continued the conversation.

"Yet who could have any motive?" he said. "His brother—the one person benefited apparently by his death—had started on his journey, in all probability hours before it occurred; for my belief is that Harry had been returning home late at night, intending to enter the grounds by the little gate-way in the holly hedge, when he was shot. But to mention Jasper is preposterous. Jasper would have given his life for his brother, and I fear is but too brave and careless in risking his own."

"Yes," said Elizabeth's trembling voice, though she could scarcely force the brief monosyllable from her white lips.

"I am indeed in a state of grave anxiety and uneasiness," continued Sir John, "about Jasper. He has been struck by fever, and the doctor of his ship telegraphs to me—"

When Sir John had proceeded thus far, a gasping moan fell on his ears, and rising hastily he went to the side of the arm-chair on which Elizabeth was seated, and one glance at her death-like face told him that she had fainted.

Quietly, but promptly, he at once wheeled the arm-chair to one of the windows, and having opened it, he seized a vase standing near with flowers in it, and after flinging them out, he sprinkled Elizabeth's face with some of the water in which they had been.   Then, as Elizabeth showed no sign of life or revival, he rang the bell of the room loudly for assistance, and in a minute or two a frightened maid-servant appeared.

"Miss Gordon—Mrs. Horton I mean—has fainted," said Sir John, calmly.   "Will you bring some brandy?   Is Mr. Horton in the house?"

"Oh! yes, sir—Oh! dear!" cried the red-cheeked damsel, and she ran away, returning in a minute or two with the brandy; the alarmed farmer, who had been enjoying his pipe in the breakfast-room, following her with scared and frightened looks.

"Sir John!" he exclaimed, on seeing his landlord. "Lissa, my darling," and he ran to Elizabeth's side, "what is the matter?"

"Do not be alarmed," said Sir John, "she has fainted.   Give me a glass, my good girl," he went on, addressing the maid-servant, "and the brandy," and having procured these he forced a little of the spirit between Elizabeth's white lips, while he directed them to bathe her hands and face with cold water.

Presently, with gasping sighs, Elizabeth began to revive, and when she first opened her eyes she glanced with a frightened, startled, appealing look at Sir John, who bent over her and gently pressed her hand.

"Do not be frightened," he said, "you will be quite right in a minute or two.   It is the great heat of to-day that has upset you."

"It is hot," said the farmer, rising and wiping the dew from his red brow with his red handkerchief. "But Lissa isn't a girl to faint.   Did anything put her out, Sir John? Or what was it?"

"Oh! nothing," answered the well-bred gentleman, with almost justifiable prevarication. "We were talking of—yes, to be sure, we were talking of your roses.   I must beg a few slips of you this autumn, Mr. Horton, for you have some splendid plants.   A crimson one—I forget the name, though Mrs. Horton was good enough to tell it me.   Ah!" (this was to Elizabeth) "I see you are better now, so I think I must take my leave, as I am sure it will not do you good to talk.   You must keep quite quiet, and if you will allow me I will do myself the honour of calling to ask how you are to-morrow, for I blame myself for keeping you so long out in the sun to-day, talking of your roses."

As Sir John spoke, Elizabeth looked at him with a glance he could not misunderstand. It was a silent appeal to his honour, to his gentlemanly feeling, almost to his mercy; and Sir John answered with a reassuring and sympathetic smile.

"I am sorry to say that my son Jasper is not very well, Mr. Horton," he said the next moment, in his usual calm tones. "He has—or rather I hope he has had—a slight attack of fever, but there is no danger the doctor telegraphs to me."

Faint as she still was, the colour rose to Elizabeth's very brows as Sir John said this, for she knew at once that he guessed her secret—that he had fathomed her love for Jasper Tyrell.

"It is a trying climate," continued Sir John, "but he has promised me to obtain sick-leave at once, and I propose to meet him, probably in Paris, before the winter. Good-bye, Mrs. Horton," and he once more pressed Elizabeth's hand, who looked at him with unconscious gratitude for his parting and considerate words.

The farmer went out with Sir John and just when Elizabeth was thinking of trying to walk to her own room, for she was still trembling and shaking in every limb, Dick Horton rushed in, and ran eagerly and excitedly up to where Elizabeth was still sitting.

"Lissa!" he said, "Lissa, what is this? They tell me you have been very ill? What is the matter—what has happened?"

"Nothing, Dick," answered Elizabeth, with a faint smile, "the heat made me faint, that is all."

"But are you sure?" and he knelt down beside her, kissing her hand and pressing it passionately to his cheeks and lips.

"Yes, Dick," answered Elizabeth gently, and she put her slender fingers through his thick dark hair. "Poor Dick—" she half-murmured. She was thinking how he wasted his love—his passionate, adoring, jealous love, all on a woman who gave him nothing—to whom the very name of danger to another man seemed to stop the life-blood surging through her heart.

"Let me help you upstairs," said Dick, and Elizabeth put her arm wearily through his, and together they left the room; Dick attending so gently and kindly to her comforts, that he left Elizabeth bitterly self-reproachful and unhappy.

"Poor boy!" she said many a time to herself during the afternoon, as she lay in her darkened room, and was supposed to be taking rest after her fainting attack. "Why cannot I learn to love him—why cannot I banish an unworthy idol from my heart?"

Yet the day did not pass without an outbreak of passionate anger on the part of Dick, when he heard accidentally that Sir John had been present when Elizabeth was taken ill.

"So," he said, addressing her, with ill-suppressed fury lighting his dark eyes, "you had Sir John Tyrell here this afternoon, though you did not condescend to inform me of his visit?"

"I thought you knew, Dick," answered Elizabeth.

"And may I ask," went on Dick, with gathering passion, "what conversation took place between you that you thought it necessary to faint?"

"We talked of many things," said Elizabeth slowly. "It was the heat that made me faint."

"No doubt," sneered Dick, "and perhaps the news that Lieutenant Tyrell was ill, which my father tells me is the case."

"Hush, hush, Dick," answered Elizabeth, "how can you be so foolish—so mad?"

"You try me too far, Elizabeth," went on Dick, darkly, and then with a muttered curse he left the room, leaving Elizabeth alone with her bitter reflections.

He was even yet more indignant the next morning, when he came into the house about twelve o'clock for something that he wanted, and found Sir John sitting in the breakfast-room with the farmer and Elizabeth. Sir John had called to inquire how she was, and was not displeased to find his tenant at home as well as Elizabeth, as he naturally shrank from any more exciting conversation between them. Of one thing he was now convinced, namely, that Elizabeth had loved Jasper and not Harry—yet how came her marriage with this cub?

Sir John had thought over this problem many a time since Elizabeth's sudden attack of yesterday, and some painful doubts—some undefined dread—were lurking, against his will, in his mind this morning, and he resolved to seek to fathom the mystery of Harry's death no more.

"If she knows anything she is not a woman to betray it," he decided, and his conversation therefore had been on the most ordinary topics, when Richard opened the door of the room, and came in, scarcely even replying to the pleasant but somewhat stately words with which Sir John greeted him.

The well-bred gentleman opened his clear large eyes a little wider as the ill-bred youth, with sullen brow and impatient gestures, kicked about the furniture, and finally kicked the old dog Tory, which was lying at Elizabeth's feet, as a means of venting his ill-temper, calling forth by this action a well-merited rebuke both from Sir John and Elizabeth.

As the old dog howled and crept under Elizabeth's chair for protection, Sir John rose, bent down, and patted its tawny head.

"These faithful friends I think, young sir," he said, addressing Richard Horton with some sharpness, "deserve better treatment from our hands than cruel and unjustifiable blows."

"Cursed old brute," muttered Dick, "he's always in the way—he should be hanged."

"For shame, Dick," said Elizabeth, with heightened colour, "to say such a thing! Poor Tory—dear old dog."

"He is a noble creature," said Sir John, as Tory emerged from his retreat, and leant his head lovingly on Elizabeth's knee. "Ah, Mrs. Horton," he added with a smile, "I see he knows his friends."

"I like all animals," said Elizabeth.

"I can believe that," went on Sir John, "it is, indeed, extraordinary what wonderful sagacity they display in the choice of their friends. I am a great believer in the good opinion of animals."

"Ay, the dumb beasts are not to be humbugged," said the farmer, laughing.

"Though we talking animals are," answered Sir John, smiling.

"Well, good day, Mrs. Horton," he continued, preparing to leave, and then he took Elizabeth's hand.

"I am glad to see you well again," he said, and after a slight bow to Dick, he left the room, the farmer following him to the hall door.

Scarcely was he gone when the full storm of Dick's passion burst forth.

"What is that confounded, overbearing old fellow doing here again, Elizabeth?" he said, loudly. "I won't have it—do you hear, I won't have it."

"You had better speak to your father, then," answered Elizabeth coldly, "it is his house—and Sir John is his friend."

"Friend!" sneered Dick, "not he. He's too fine a gentleman to be friends with any of us—and if he comes dangling here after you, I can tell him—"

"You forget yourself," said Elizabeth, "utterly forget yourself. If you have no respect for me, show some at least to Sir John's position and age."

"Confound him," went on Dick, passionately, "with his insolence—finding fault with me, indeed!"

"You deserved it, most justly deserved it, for kicking Tory."

"Did I," shouted Dick, "then I'll show you I'll thrash Tory, or kick him blind if I choose!" And he seized a heavy whip lying on the table as he spoke, and advanced to where poor Tory had lain peacefully down again. But before the lash could fall Elizabeth sprang forward, and received its stinging cut on both her outstretched arms, a broad red weal rising on one of her white wrists a moment later.

"Strike me, but not the old dog," she said.

Then, as Dick's eyes fell on the red line on her wrist, sudden shame and repentance seized him.

"I did not mean to do that," he said, flinging the whip on the floor, "Elizabeth—Lissa—I did not mean to hurt you."

"I do not think you did, Dick," answered Elizabeth.

"I did not, God is my witness," went on Dick, pale with emotion. "Will you forgive me—Lissa, forgive me—"

"Do not strike Tory again then, Dick," said Elizabeth, and the young man, with fond and eager words, promised to obey her; promised never to be angry with her any more.

"Very well," said Elizabeth; but she sighed, for she knew that in all probability before the red line on her wrist would fade that Dick would forget his good resolutions and promises alike.

CHAPTER XII.
"I FLED AND CRIED OUT DEATH!"

IN spite of Richard's objections Sir John Tyrell grew more intimate with the Hortons; the farmer indeed sharply rebuking his son on one occasion when he made some unpleasant comments on their landlord's visits.

"Dick, my boy," he said, "when I put off my shoes you can wear them, you know, and be master here; but that time's not come, and as long as I've a house over my head Sir John shall be an honoured and welcome guest under its roof—and if that doesn't please you, well, you can find a home of your own."

Never before had such words been addressed by the good-natured farmer to any of his children, and this added not a little to Dick's hatred and jealousy of the whole Tyrell family. But though deeply indignant at the rebuke, Dick yet loved and honoured his father, whose genial sunny nature, and considerate kindness to every one around him, not only was such a contrast to Dick's own character, but could not fail to endear him to his entire household. If any one was in trouble at Wendell West-house, they came to the "Master." He had a humorous sly way of softening asperities, and soothing word-wounds with his pleasant tongue. In their convivial hours—for the farmer it must be admitted did sometimes endorse the sentiment—

> There are five reasons why men drink:
> Good wine, a friend, because I'm dry,
> Or lest I should be by-and-by,
> Or any other reason why:

—in these hours, then, the difference of his disposition to that of his eldest son was never more strikingly evident.

The "good wine" made the farmer even yet more genial, hospitable, and generous than his wont; while under its influence Dick grew first captious and unpleasant, then quarrelsome, unmanageable, and violent.

Elizabeth used to dread the arrival in these days of a neighbour of their own class, knowing that the visit was almost sure to end in a stormy scene with Dick after the guest's departure. He used to ride constantly into Mitchin too, and would return flushed and excited, filling Elizabeth's heart with dread that in some unguarded moment he might utter words that he could never recall.

What angered Dick excessively was that Sir John Tyrell always treated him with the same good-natured superiority with which he treated his two younger brothers. After the scene about kicking Tory, Dick encountered his landlord with sullen eye and brow, but the easy courteous gentleman utterly ignored the fact that any unpleasantness had ever passed between them.

In vain Dick gave short curt answers to the Baronet's placid, smiling, and indifferent words. Sir John would not have condescended to have quarrelled with this "young cub," as he privately designated Dick; and Dick knew that it was so, and felt that he was no match for their well-bred landlord.

Before his father, however, after the rebuke that the farmer had given him, Dick did put some curb on his temper and dislike. Sir John, when the shooting season came on, frequently invited the farmer to accompany him for a day's sport, and perhaps Dick was not quite indifferent to the privilege of roaming over the well-stocked preserves of which Sir John was the owner.

By the Baronet's wish his daughters had called on Elizabeth after her marriage, but though she returned their visit, she quietly declined any further intimacy with the ladies of the Tyrell family.

"It is better not, dear uncle," she said (for she still called the farmer by the old name). "It is different with Sir John—he is a man of larger mind and higher aims than these young ladies, and besides I believe he truly likes you, and therefore his society is pleasant to us both. But I am sure the others do not really care to know us, and am sure in that case we do not care for knowing them."

"Settle it as you like, dear," said the farmer, who had not been without his ambition to see Lissa dine at the "Hall;" and so Lissa settled it. Sir John was a welcome and honoured guest whenever he appeared at the homestead, and Lissa and the Misses Tyrell exchanged friendly bows when they met, but their intimacy after her marriage advanced no further. Lissa was conscious that she had forfeited her former position to a certain extent by marrying Dick Horton, and the Misses Tyrell no longer had any motive for being "civil" to the girl that they feared at one time their brother was going to make his wife; and thus by mutual consent their intercourse almost entirely ceased.

Of Jasper, as the autumn advanced, Lissa heard at intervals from Sir John, but only by a few casual words, always spoken in the farmer's presence. Sir John indeed had determined after the morning when she had fainted on hearing of his illness, to approach the mysterious connection of his son with Elizabeth no more. His keen and observing eyes had convinced him that there was a mystery, but what that mystery was he left time and chance to unravel, for he feared to bring further sorrow or misery upon her by endeavouring to fathom it.   He liked, respected, and admired Elizabeth, and he would gladly have seen her the wife of his son; and now, when that tie could not be, he liked, admired, and respected her still.

So the autumn glided away—a miserable autumn for Elizabeth, and apparently anything but a happy one for Richard Horton. He still loved Elizabeth, resenting with jealous and unreasonable anger every word or look that she bestowed on any one else. His temper, indeed, utterly embittered her life, and rendered the tie that bound her to him doubly distasteful and trying to bear.

As far as she could, however, she hid her grievances from the farmer.   She could not bear to overshadow his bright cheery life with her troubles, and Mr. Horton lived pretty much under the delusion that "Dick was a bit bad-tempered, poor lad, but a right good fellow at the core."

The end of September came, bright, breezy, and healthy, on the high-lying lands of Uplandshire, and many a day the sturdy farmer and the slim delicate gentleman, followed by their game-keepers (at least Sir John followed by his gamekeeper, and the farmer by a sharp lad on the farm who acted occasionally in that capacity) tramped together in quest of partridges over the stubbles, from which the newly-reaped corn had been gathered in bounteous harvest.

Dick sometimes accompanied his father on these expeditions and sometimes not.

"Bring your boys with you," Sir John would often good-naturedly say, when he was in the humour; but it was merely to please the farmer that he asked them, whose sterling good sense and genuineness made him so pleasant a companion to the thoughtful and somewhat exclusive Sir John. He preferred him, in fact, to the generality of his fellow squires, with their narrow notions, and their talk of quarter sessions, where they inflicted severe sentences for the theft of a hen or a pigeon, and believed that the whole prosperity of England lay in the up-holding of their order, and in the protection of their land.

There was another reason also why Sir John shrank from any great intimacy with his fellows.   Lady Tyrell's mental affliction continued unabated, and Sir John scarcely cared that the sound of mirth or feasting should reach the ears of the unhappy mother of his murdered son.   The sharp cries too, that some-times rang through the Hall from the guarded upper storey, were not fit for the ears of strangers to hear; and so the Baronet lived mostly with his books, smilingly saying that their learned society pleased him better than that of most of his neighbours.

But he liked **Mr. Horton** and Elizabeth, and one evening towards the close of September, having invited the farmer to accompany him on the following day to an outlying farm on a raid against the partridges, he added, turning to Elizabeth—

"Why don't you come with us, Mrs. Horton?   There is some fine country about Scardale which I do not suppose you have ever seen?"

" 'Spose Lissa drives over in her pony chaise and brings us some lunch in the middle of the day," suggested Mr. Horton. "How would you like that, my dear?"

"Very much, uncle," answered Lissa, and so they settled it; Lissa ordering various delicacies to be prepared for the coming repast in honour of Sir John.

When Dick heard of the expedition, and that Lissa was going, he at once said that if she went he would go also.

"Shall I drive you over, then?" asked Elizabeth, "or will you start in the morning with uncle?"

Dick at first was undecided on this point, but finally arranged to go with his father; and Lissa therefore left Wendell about one o'clock on the following day alone, intending to meet Sir John, her uncle, and Dick about two, as it is nearly an hour's drive from the farmstead to Scardale, where they were shooting.

It was a bright, beautiful, autumn day, and as Lissa drove along the pleasant country lanes, the fresh breeze the while blowing on her clear brown skin, some of her old bloom stole back into her oval cheeks, and added not a little to the picturesque beauty of her whole appearance.

Presently she came to a wilder country, where the Scar creeps on its somewhat sluggish course through steep banks wooded thickly almost to the river edge. Here, in sheltered nooks, sat solitary patient fishers, watching intently for their finny prey; while sturdy urchins also indulged after their kind in piscatorial sport, fishing in the pools and creeks, for minnows, tadpoles, and the like; their glass bottles standing by their sides ready to enclose the expected victims of their skill.

It was a pleasant scene—the brambles ripening in the woods and hedges; the whirr of the pheasant as he rose startled from his leafy covert at the sound of Elizabeth's carriage-wheels, his burnished plumage glittering in the sun; while the brown hares and rabbits peeped from the ferny undergrowth or ran scampering across the roadway, which in many places is cut through the woods; glimpses of the winding Scar being visible from certain points of the drive almost the whole way.

The spot where Elizabeth had agreed to meet Sir John and her uncle, is named in the common parlance of the country-side, "Rob's Nook." Who "Rob" had been is accounted for by various traditions, most of which are no doubt, like many other

famous histories, entire fabrications.   However, we must suppose
that "Rob" had existed, whether in the capacity of robber, free-
booter, or saint remains considerably shrouded by the mists of
time.   At all events "Rob" had left his "Nook;" a pleasant
spot where the willows droop and sweep into the placid waters
of the Scar, hiding the approach to a natural cave formed partly
by the overhanging river bank, in which it is supposed that
"Rob" had either lived or died.

Above this cave, on the hill-side, is a patch of the finest and
greenest grass, which is a favourite rendezvous for pic-nics and
other rural festivities, in the neighbourhood, and it was here that
Elizabeth proposed to spread her luncheon for Sir John and her
uncle.

She left the pony carriage, therefore, on the drive, which is
some little distance in the woods above "Rob's Nook," and after
securing the pony, went down the almost precipitous bank
towards the river, followed by her servant carrying the hamper,
and finally reached the green patch above the cave.

Here she found, already waiting her arrival, a smart groom of
Sir John's, who had received orders to ride over to "Rob's
Nook," bringing as an offering to Elizabeth a basket of cham-
pagne and grapes from the Baronet.

Elizabeth herself had brought various delicacies, so that when
the sportsmen appeared on the scene, a most appetizing and
tempting repast lay spread out before them on the snowy cloth,
with its bright border of green verdure, and the pleasant rippling
sound of the river gliding below to add to their enjoyment.

Sir John threw himself on the grass at Elizabeth's side, at
which Dick frowned; the farmer rushed at the pigeon-pie; Sir
John's servant carved the chickens and tongue, and drew the
champagne corks, so that every one presently was very busily
employed.   The sportsmen were hungry; the clear exhilarating
air had brightened Elizabeth's usually dulled spirit, and given a
rare bloom to her cheeks, and a light to her beautiful eyes.   As
for Mr. Horton, his spirits rose to exuberance.   Merry were
his jests, and gay and lighthearted his words—so much so that
Sir John, who was his junior by ten years, looked on with
amused astonishment, wondering how a heart could continue
young so long.

Dick as usual grew captious and disagreeable after he had
imbibed various glasses of champagne.

"How long are you going to stay, Elizabeth?" he said.

"Stay!" she answered, "It was agreed that I was to drive
Sir John and uncle home, you know—my going depends on
you all."

"Then I've to go in the dog-cart with the servants, I suppose?"
went on Dick, sullenly.

The dog-cart was Sir John's, which Dick might have considered himself honoured by driving in, and in which they had all three come, but Dick was in one of those humours when everything is at fault.

"Have I to go in the dog-cart?" reiterated Dick.

"Of course you have," answered Sir John, with a light laugh, who had overheard him. "You see, Mr. Richard, age has some privileges, and Mr. Horton and myself mean to avail ourselves of ours."

"Oh, all right!" said Dick, roughly, shrugging his shoulders, "but I suppose we may have a few more braces before we go?"

"Yes—but we must not keep you long," went on Sir John, turning to Elizabeth.

"Oh, I will walk up the woods," said Elizabeth, rising, with a smile, "and will take my pony some bread. Do not hurry for me, Sir John."

The three gentlemen and Elizabeth then left the servants to the enjoyment of the repast spread out on the grass, and proceeded together part of the way through the woods; the sportsmen leaving Elizabeth at a certain point, and diverging towards the open fields.

Elizabeth gave her pony the bread, and then led him to a spot in the woods, that she had observed as she came down, where a spring of clear water bubbled from some jutting rocks, and glided on to the river below.

The pony drank the water, and peacefully cropped the long reedy grass around, while Elizabeth leant thoughtfully against the trunk of one of the old moss-grown trees, listening almost unconsciously to the clear cheéry notes of a robin, which, with all the boldness of its race, hopped from twig to twig upon a fallen branch lying quite near her. Then a big bee came droning and humming above her head, and as the breeze stole through the trees, a faded leaf or two floated down; while below she heard the ripple of the Scar stealing over its pebbly bed. But everything else seemed still. The cool, clear, luminous air, the whispering river, and the robin's note, all conduced to the peaceful, dreamy sensation which such scenes produce, and presently Elizabeth sat down, leaning her head against the tree, and closing her eyes to the outward world around her.

But suddenly as she sat, there rang through the air a cry—a human cry, loud, and full of some mortal terror or grief, striking dread into the listener's heart, and causing Elizabeth to spring hastily to her feet, and to hurry down to where she had left the servants sitting on the grass above the cave.

The alarm had startled them also. Sir John's servant was on his feet, a curious look of interest in his face; the farm youth was rising, and as Elizabeth ran towards them, she caught a glimpse of Sir John himself running quickly up the narrow path along the river side to the spot where they were.

Hastily Elizabeth went to meet him, and breathlessly Sir John told his news.

"Your uncle has had an accident," he said. "James, which is the brandy? Give it to me, and you men follow me at once. Come, Mrs. Horton," he went on, "take my arm. We shall be with him in a minute, and I trust and pray that it is not very serious."

"How did it happen?" gasped Elizabeth.

"I can scarcely explain," answered Sir John, and he led Elizabeth hastily on—led her from the wood into a field; then towards a hedge, at the other side of it, while the men followed, talking and wondering as they went.

"Can you get through here?" said Sir John, pointing to the entangled hawthorn and brambles which composed the fence before them. Elizabeth bowed her head, too sick and trembling with apprehension to speak, and was assisted through the hedge by Sir John and the servants. Then, when she raised her eyes at the other side of it, she saw her uncle lying on the ground, and Dick holding up his head and breast in his arms.

"Father, speak to me!" cried Dick, in tones of bitter agony and fear, as they drew near to them. "Father, don't you know me—father—father!"

"What is it, Dick?" said Elizabeth, running up to them, and putting her hand on Dick's shoulder. "How did it happen? What is the matter?"

Then Dick turned his face round; his white terror-stricken face, and gasped out—

"I did it—the trigger of the gun caught in the hedge! Oh! God, have mercy—God, have mercy, and don't let him die!"

At this moment Sir John approached, laying his hand kindly but authoritatively on young Horton's shoulder.

"Let my servant hold him," he said, "while I pour some brandy into his mouth. You are trembling so that you cannot fail to disturb him." And with a groan—a moan of despair rather, Dick gave way, and Sir John's servant took his place.

The brandy seemed to revive the apparently insensible farmer, who presently opened his eyes, and looked wildly round, while Lissa tenderly clasped his hand.

"Uncle, darling uncle," she said, "are you better? You know me, don't you, uncle?"

At these words Mr. Horton seemed to gasp for breath, while Sir John, with an uneasy glance, laid his hand on his pulse, and then beckoned to his gamekeeper.

"Take the horse from the dog-cart," he said, hurriedly, "and inquire at the ale-house for the nearest doctor, and then ride for your life in search of him, and bring him here at once—remember, it is a matter of life or death," he added in an emphatic whisper.

The man ran hastily to obey his master's command, and Dick, who had thrown himself on the ground, lifted his head as he heard the sound of his departing footsteps.

"Where has he gone? he asked, hoarsely.

"For the doctor," said Elizabeth, looking round to answer her husband's question; and then at the sight of Dick's white grief-stricken face, Elizabeth rose and went towards him.

"Come beside father, dear Dick," she said. "Come, he will like to see you."

"There's a curse on my hand," muttered Dick, "the curse of blood."

"Nay, Dick, come," urged Elizabeth; and so he went back to his father's side, while Elizabeth bent over, and kissed her uncle's clammy brow.

At her touch the farmer again opened his eyes, and this time they fell on Sir John, who was kneeling near, and holding one of his hands.

"Sir John—" he said, in a changed and hollow voice, and then he looked at Elizabeth, "be kind to my girl after I am gone."

"O God! O God!" groaned Dick, clasping his hand over his face.

His father heard his voice of anguish, and through the gathering mists and numbness of death, groped his hand feebly forth to take his son's.

"My lad—it was an accident—" he faltered out. "Sir John—you will prove the accident—and—and—don't grieve, Dick—I am an old man—I am going to your mother—" And with these words the farmer died.

CHAPTER XIII.
THE RICH MAN'S WORD.

THERE was scarcely a dry eye amongst those who carried back his body to the homestead, and related to the weeping women there how, with a cry of insufferable anguish, Dick had flung himself on his father's corpse after his death, refusing to be comforted, and calling on God to take him away from misery which was greater than he could bear.

Dick's heart-rending grief was indeed piteous to behold.

"Father! father!" he had cried in vain, after the good man's soul was gone. "Father, say one word—*only one*—" Alas, none came. The gentle, genial spirit of the farmer had received a sudden summons, for the ghastly gunshot wound, inflicted unintentionally by Dick's careless hand, had left no hope of his life from the first, his spine being fatally injured, and his death occurring probably painlessly, and almost immediately from the shock that his system had received.

When Sir John saw that life was fled, his first thoughts were for Elizabeth, but with streaming eyes and trembling hand she pointed to Dick's convulsed face.

"Try to comfort Dick," she wept forth. "Try, Sir John, to comfort poor, poor Dick."

Then Sir John endeavoured to comply with her request, saying what consoling words he could to the miserable young man writhing beside his father's corpse; putting his hand kindly through his arm, and trying to raise him to his feet. But Dick shrank back from the Baronet's gentle touch.

"No, no," he said, shudderingly. "I want no kindness—I want nothing from you."

"Nay," answered Sir John, "do not say that. There are times, young man, when we all need kindness—and I wish to be your friend."

But sullenly and silently Dick repulsed this offer, and then Elizabeth went up to him, kneeling down by his side, and laying her hands on his shoulder and arm.

"Let me alone," said Dick "what do you all care—?"

"Oh! Dick, you know I care," said Elizabeth. "Dick," she whispered, "do not add to my despair in this miserable hour."

"Yours! you who have never loved me!" cried the unhappy Dick, pushing her away,—"you who have brought this curse upon my hand."

"No, no," said Elizabeth, clinging to him. "Let me comfort you now at least, Dick—let me love you now—"

As Elizabeth said this, Dick's head fell forward, and Elizabeth put her arms round his neck.

"Get up and come home, dear," she said, tenderly, for the young man's frantic grief was so evidently sincere that her heart was deeply touched. "Sir John will see after our dear father—but let me take you home."

"Take me away," said Dick, and he rose to his feet, and staggering like a blind man, Elizabeth led him away; Sir John and the servants remaining near Mr. Horton's body until it was carried to the homestead, where the inquest was held on the following day.

At this inquest Sir John proved himself to be the friend that he had told Dick Horton that he wished to be; exonerating him as far as lay in his power from any blame for the unfortunate accident that had cost his father his life. It was well for the young man indeed that the powerful influence of Sir John was used on this occasion, for there were not a few of the free-spoken farmers who composed the twelve men who sat in judgment who had not hesitated to pronounce the word "manslaughter," as applying to Dick's careless handling of his gun, and with whom indignation was mingled with grief when they talked of the sudden and untimely death of their friend and neighbour.

Bnt Sir John, glib of tongue, and high of rank, threw his powerful protection over Richard Horton; explaining how thick and entangled the hedge was where the unfortunate catastrophe occurred; how even he himself had found some difficulty in carrying his weapon safely through it; how a twig had sprung back and caught the trigger of Dick's gun; and how such an accident, however much to be deplored, could have happened to any man.

The farmers rubbed their foreheads, coughed, and of course could not dispute the opinion of their landlord, and an eye-witness also of the unhappy occurrence; and when Dick himself gave evidence, his ghastly looks, his evidently crushing, heart-breaking grief entirely dispelled any previous ill-feeling against him, and a verdict of Accidental Death was unanimously, as indeed most justly, recorded.

So Dick went out of the room free of the guilt of blood-shedding so far as his fellowmen were concerned; but his settled gloom, his passionate and at times overwhelming remorse, was not the less bitter and complete.

He refused to attend his father's funeral, and sullenly refused also all consolation and condolence, alike from Sir John, Elizabeth, and his father's friends or his own.

"Let me alone," he said, and so he sat still and silent, while one after the other the funeral guests assembled; while the sound of strange feet were in the house, and strange voices on the stairs. He heard them carry his father away—the genial happy man who had loved this son as he had loved his others, and been only too fond and forbearing a parent to them all. Oh! it was terrible, terrible! With a moan Dick flung himself on his knees, but not to pray. God was not near this unhappy young man, and earthly comforters were vain in this black hour. He had killed his father, and he cried aloud that the hand was cursed that wrought the deed.

Elizabeth, however, though she was afraid to enter his room, was hovering near it, and when that "exceeding bitter cry" reached her ears, she went softly and unbidden in, and knelt down by Dick's side, putting her hand in his.

"Let us pray, Dick," she said; "pray together."

"Pray!" echoed Dick; "fine prayers we two would make!" And he gave a bitter laugh.

"We have sinned," said Elizabeth, "but we have sorrowed. God will hear us I am sure, dear Dick, if we ask comfort and forgiveness together from Him now."

"No," answered Dick, starting to his feet, "I'm not going to begin to whine now. Do you see this hand, Elizabeth?" he went on darkly, holding out his right hand. "There's blood on it—I've killed my best friend, and the curse of blood is on my soul."

In this wild and desperate mood Dick continued for many days, and then he settled down into a continued and deliberate fit of hard drinking. In vain Elizabeth remonstrated with him; in vain his brothers; and even when the gentle and venerable clergyman, Mr. Hay, who had christened this young man, ventured to approach the subject, Dick answered him with sullen apathy.

"It helps me to forget, sir," he said, and the old man shook his head.

"Ah, Richard," he said, "drink is but a mocking devil, ensnaring the senses, but to leave them ten times worse than before."

"Mr. Hay," answered Dick, looking with his dark, flushed, sullen face at the gentle priest, "it's easy for those who live and feel like you to preach and pray—but if there is a God," he went on with bitter recklessness, "He has made some of us with sins and passions stronger than He has given us power to resist."

"Nay, nay, Richard," said the good man, eagerly, "there is no such thing! Did you ever try to resist? Did you ever pray for power? God is not our tempter, but our merciful father, slow to anger, and of great kindness."

"I haven't found it so," said Dick, bitterly, and in this unbelieving miserable creed he lived.

But perhaps the strangest change that came upon him after his father's death was that his passionate and devoted love for Elizabeth seemed almost entirely altered. True, he was still jealous of her slightest word; resenting angrily the friendly approaches of Sir John, whose heart was full of pity for Elizabeth, and who could scarcely contain for her sake his disgust and contempt for the unmannerly young man who rejected his kindly efforts, and yet who was so deeply indebted to him; a debt which he appeared entirely to forget and ignore.

He ordered Elizabeth therefore not to have "that man coming here," and Elizabeth was forced with burning blushes and tears to tell Sir John that he had better not call to see her any more.

"My poor girl," said Sir John, when she made this communication, and that was all. But his simple words meant much, and before he took his leave he added a few touching and sincere ones.

"You remember my friend Mr. Horton's last request to me," he said, "when he lay dying, that I should be kind to you? Will you promise me that if the time should ever come that I can be, that you will not forget the wishes of the dead?"

Elizabeth's eyes filled with tears as she recalled her dear uncle's last tender words, and she put a trembling hand into Sir John's. "I will not forget," she said.

But she little guessed that the time was to come when Sir John's kindness and protection was all that she had to rely upon, to save her from sin, or starvation and despair.

CHAPTER XIV

CONSCIENCE.

IN spite of Dick's coldness—nay, Elizabeth sometimes thought his shuddering aversion to her now, she tried to do her duty to him as a faithful wife, in the dark days after his father's death, —she felt, indeed, such intense pity for him that she was ready to forgive all his shortcomings.

"If I had done it," she would say to herself, and shiver at the very thought of what must be Dick's feelings now.

During a sharp attack of illness, which was undoubtedly brought on by his excessive drinking, Elizabeth attended on him with untiring devotion, and by doing so drew even some expression of gratitude for her kindness from the miserable and embittered man.

"You are very kind, Lissa," he said one night, as she was sitting watching him; and Lissa rose, smiled, smoothed his pillow, and gently laid a fresh cold water bandage on his aching burning brow.

As she did so Dick caught her hand in his, and pressed it to his lips.

"Oh! why were you not always like this to me?" he said. "Why did you not love me long ago, Lissa? We might have been so happy then—"

Dick almost whispered the last few words, but Elizabeth heard them.

"We must try to be happy now," she said, gently, "or at least content, Dick."

"No, it cannot be," said Dick, turning restlessly on his bed, "it cannot, cannot be."

"But let us try, Dick," urged Elizabeth; but the young man only moaned and hid his face impatiently away from her.

Still Dick was gentler after this illness, and for a time at least was more temperate in his habits, and Elizabeth began to hope that the dark cloud might pass away from him—nay, might leave him, perhaps, a better and more thoughtful man.

So the autumn crept away, and the early winter came—came heralded in by a snow storm; the first snow which had fallen at Wendell since the fatal storm when Harry Tyrell's body had been found, and when all Elizabeth's bright hopes of happiness were ended.

The sight of the white flakes again floating downwards not unnaturally painfully affected her, and prevented her noticing the dark, gloomy looks with which Dick also regarded the falling snow.

All through the day he drank heavily, and at night had to be half-dragged, half-carried to his room, sinking into a heavy and apparently undisturbed slumber, when he got there ; and after watching him for a little while, Elizabeth, wearied with the emotions of the day, lay down on a couch near, and presently fell into a light sleep.

In the middle of the night however—about midnight—she suddenly awoke. The moon was shining in at the windows, showing each object more distinctly from the reflection of the white surface on the ground outside, and when Elizabeth opened her eyes she had the startled feeling that she had been roused from her sleep by some noise in the room.

Wondering and half afraid she looked up, and even as she did so, a hollow, unnatural voice near her said—

"*Harry Tyrell!*"

It is almost impossible to describe the horror that Elizabeth felt as the name of the unfortunate murdered young man in the dead of night thus sounded in her ears, and a suppressed cry broke from her pale lips, while her face grew white and clammy.

"Are you come back?" went on the same unnatural voice ; and then there was a violent movement, apparently in the bed, and Elizabeth, starting up with a shriek, ran towards it, and then saw Dick distinctly by the moonlight lying with ghastly face and upraised arms as if in some frightful dream.

"Dick! Dick!" she cried, rousing him, and after a while his heavy slumbering senses awoke.

"What is it?" he said, and then he shuddered.

"You were dreaming, I think," said Elizabeth, still terrified. "Have you been dreaming? You were talking in your sleep, Dick."

"Ay—what did I say?" he asked a moment later.

"Oh! some folly," answered poor Elizabeth, "but you startled me." And then she lay down on the couch again ; hiding her head under a coverlet—unable to forget the awful sound of the dead man's name.

Alas! this vision of Dick's was but a beginning of a frightful attack of brain delirium, for again in the middle of the following night Dick began to call aloud on Harry Tyrell's name, and apparently to struggle in the most violent throes with some invisible adversary.

Sick and pale Elizabeth rose and called his brothers, but Dick did not know them, but sat up in the bed and shrieked, and gazed with terror-striken, wide open eyes at a ray of moonlight which crept in between the blind and the window, apostrophising it, as if it were some living, fearful thing.

"Come on!" he cried, waving his arms. "Why do you stand there? Why do you beckon me, Harry Tyrell, to follow you through the snow?"

"He thinks it's Harry Tyrell's ghost," said Hal Horton, in a frightened whisper, in Elizabeth's ear.

"He's got *delirium tremens*," said Bob, more coolly, "we had better send for the doctor, Lissa?"

"No, no, Bob," answered Lissa, shrinkingly, "Let us watch him ourselves—let us keep it a secret between us."

"He was sure to take it," went on Bob, "going on as he's been doing. He drank a bottle of brandy yesterday, I'm certain."

"Let us put in the shutters, and light the gas," said the practical Hal, recovering his presence of mind and natural sharpness. "It's the moonlight on the snow that makes him think of ghosts, for it shone just like this the night after Harry Tyrell was murdered."

"Yes," said Elizabeth, shudderingly, "put in the shutters, Hal; light the gas and the fire; keep out the moon."

"Are you gone?" said Dick, in the same unnatural voice, as Hal dashed in the shutters. "Gone beckoning—beckoning still—" And he sprang out of bed, and endeavoured to leap out of the window, but was forcibly held back by his two young brothers.

His delirium changed in character after the gas and the fire were lit, and he fancied that he was picking grain off the bed, and feeding some tame pheasants which he had kept when he was a boy.

It was easier to manage him when in this mood; and all the rest of the night Elizabeth and the two young Hortons sat up with him; Elizabeth soothing and humouring him as best she could.

He was so exhausted and feeble in the morning that Elizabeth grew alarmed, and dared no longer resist sending for the country doctor near, who, when he arrived, shook his head and tapped his forehead.

"Ah," he said, "brain, brain—an overwrought brain. What has he been taking, Mrs. Horton?"

"Since my poor uncle's death," hesitated Elizabeth, "I fear that poor Dick has been taking too—much—"

"So I thought," said the doctor, shaking his head again, and having all the time a full and complete knowledge of the fact from the gossip in the neighbourhood. "Nervous excitability unduly developed by the over use of stimulants. A sad case, but not uncommon—every excuse in the case of Mr. Richard, too, after the unfortunate accident when his poor father lost his life."

All day Dick continued very ill, but towards night he grew quieter, and when the doctor came in the evening he thought that

the attack was yielding to treatment, and prophesied that Dick
would soon be well.

Elizabeth and Bob agreed to sit up with him, and as the night
wore on Bob grew weary, and slumbered in his chair, but towards
midnight a violent attack of horrors once more seized the unfortunate Dick.

Again Elizabeth heard Harry Tyrell's name shrieked forth in
tones of intense dread and fear; again with starting eyes Dick
seemed writhing with an unseen foe, while great drops of dew
broke out on his ghastly face.

It was "Harry Tyrell! Harry Tyrell!" always, until Elizabeth
grew sick with fear; fancying even that she too saw a pale shadow
in some dark corner of the room, resembling the form of the young
man who had been carried into the dining-room on the morning
that his lifeless body had been found.

"O, Bob!" she said, going up and waking her sleeping brother-
in-law, who started up and rubbed his eyes.

"What is it?" he said.   "I declare I was dreaming—dreaming
of Harry Tyrell's death."

"He is calling on him again," said Elizabeth, shivering and
creeping nearer to Bob.

"Don't beckon, don't beckon any more!" shouted Dick from
the bed.   "I'll come!" And again, as on the previous night, he
sprang up, and again had to be forcibly restrained by his brother
and Elizabeth.

Night after night for nearly a week these dreadful attacks
came on until Elizabeth was utterly worn out with watching,
while a vague dread and suspicion began to creep into her mind.
In the morning, and during the day, Dick was always quieter,
but at night violent paroxysms shook him from limb to limb; and
he invariably addressed the same spectre that he fancied was in
the room.   Then, little by little, his delusions grew less violent,
and gradually yielded to the doctor's treatment, and in about ten
days after his first seizure, Dick, pale, stricken, and changed, was
once more able to appear downstairs.

Sir John Tyrell called to ask how he was during his illness,
and saw with real regret how dreadfully it had told upon Elizabeth.   She was nervous to an alarming extent, and started at
the least noise, and her state left a very painful impression upon
Sir John's mind.

"I join my son in Paris next week," he said, in his quiet
voice.

"Is—is he well?" faltered Elizabeth.

"Not very well, I fancy," answered Sir John.   "I do not
think that he has ever been very well since he went to China."

"No," said Elizabeth, and a choking spasm rose in her throat.
Strange doubts indeed were beginning to oppress and distract

her mind. Why did the memory of Harry Tyrell haunt Dick's disordered brain with such strange pertinacity? Was there any reason other than his father's death, for his settled gloom, his sullen and determinate remorse? These thoughts had recurred again and again to Elizabeth's mind during the dread midnight hours when Dick held his ghastly converse with the dead. His brother Bob, too, had looked at Elizabeth once or twice with uneasy fear in his glance, when Dick repeated and repeated in tones of thrilling horror Harry Tyrell's name, always fancying that he was beckoning to him, or calling on him to follow him through the snow.

At last Bob spoke.

"Lissa," he said, in an awe-struck whisper, "can there be anything in this—can Dick—" And his looks told the rest.

"God knows!" answered Elizabeth, and the two sat still and silent, not uttering even to each other the doubts and fears which involuntary had struck them both.

They never mentioned it again. Dick got better, and came downstairs looking the ghost of his former self, and nervous and irritable to a frightful degree; but apparently he had got a fright about drinking; the doctor indeed, who was himself a little red-faced man with strong alcoholic proclivities, had warned him of its fatal consequences.

"Another such attack, Mr. Richard," he had said, shaking his head as usual when he wished to be very emphatic, "and I dare not contemplate the consequences. Epilepsy, my dear sir, lunacy, idiotcy, death—all might be produced. I do not on principle object to stimulants" (people said the doctor certainly did not); "but when the desire for them is overpowering, unrestrainable in fact to a reasonable quantity, then I say, my young friend, *abstain*. Yours is a case that requires total abstinence—be wise therefore and use it." And having given this advice the doctor left, calling at the nearest ale-house on his road to have a glass of hot brandy and water, as the morning was chill.

One of Dick's great horrors after his illness was to go to bed, and he used to beg and pray them to sit up late, falling asleep many and many a time through pure exhaustion in his chair.

It was difficult to spend the long winter nights, and so Elizabeth proposed whist (though she disliked cards), by way of amusing Dick, and the three elder cousins used to sit and play very sedately and soberly, Hal being the only lively one of the party.

"My belief is," said this boy one night, "that if I were prematurely cut off, that the proverbial ditch-water would be sparkling in comparison to the liveliness of my remaining sorrowing family. Lissa, my dear, if farming gets worse, don't you think Dick and Bob would make their fortunes as mutes? Yes, the undertaking business is certainly open to our family."

Only a very feeble laugh was raised in answer to this sally, and it was no doubt true that the family circle at Wendell farm was now a very dull one. Every day they missed the farmer's cheery good-nature, who, ever ready with his jest and his laugh, had made small grievances seem lighter, and large ones easier to bear. He was gone now, and his honoured name could never even be mentioned in his household. Dick was to be kept quiet and amused, the doctor said, and "father" therefore was a word now never heard at Wendell West-house.

As the anniversary of poor Harry Tyrell's death drew near, Lissa felt a strange but perhaps not unaccountable dread of its approach. Dick since his recovery had had no more frightful dreams or visions apparently, but he often talked still in his restless sleep, and had twice given Elizabeth a terrible fright by walking in it.

Each time when she awoke and missed him, the idea of suicide had occurred to her mind, but on her rousing Bob and Hal, Dick, asleep, with half-open, fixed, expressionless eyes, was discovered once near the door of an unfrequented large attic room in the rear of the house, and another time trying apparently to undo the fastenings of the house door.

Every one in the house remembered what day it was when the pale winter morning dawned at Wendell on the anniversary of Harry's murder. Elizabeth had watched its first beams of light appear with deep emotion, perplexity, and regret, stirring in her heart. She scarcely dared to look at her husband's face, though when she did his knitted brow, his pallor, and restless and excited ways, added not a little to her painful curiosity, to her unsatisfied and anxious doubts.

No one spoke of it at breakfast; no one, until Hal, with boyish carelessness, said—"D'ye know what day this is, Lissa?"

"Yes, yes," said Elizabeth hastily.

"The seventeenth of December," went on Hal. "The day when Harry Tyrell was—"

"No use mentioning disagreeables," said Bob, interrupting the irrepressible boy, for his eyes had fallen on Dick's white and clammy face.

"A great deal of use, I think," continued Master Hal.

"Be silent," said Dick, passionately, "be silent;" and he started up from the breakfast table, and Bob and Lissa looked at each other with one glance of mutual fear as he left the room.

"My belief is," said Hal the next minute, "that Dick knows more than he chooses to tell about the murder. D'ye remember when he had D.T., Lissa, how he always fancied Harry Tyrell's ghost was in the room?"

"You had better take care what you say, I think," said Bob. "You'll have Dick ill again with your folly, if you don't mind. You know he's not the same fellow since poor father's death."

"Well, if I'd had D.T. and I'd been Dick," answered Hal, who always had the last word, "it would have been poor father's ghost, and not Harry Tyrell's that would have haunted me. I don't blame him—nobody can, but for all that I shouldn't like to have the old man's blood upon my hand."

CHAPTER XV
THE ANNIVERSARY.

IT was a fine day this seventeenth of December, in 1872, fine, clear, bright, and frosty, not like the snowy, gloomy one of the year before, made ever memorable at Wendell by the discovery of the body of the murdered heir.

To both Lissa's dismay and Bob's Dick did not return to the house the whole morning after he hastily left the breakfast-table, and when, at Lissa's request, Bob went to seek him, he found that Dick had ordered Winny to be saddled, and had at once ridden from the homestead.

"I wish he mayn't have gone to Mitchin," Bob added, when he imparted this information to Lissa. "If he gets drink there we'll have a fine night of it again."

He never came back all day, and Elizabeth grew so alarmed about him that she entreated Bob, during the afternoon, to ride to Mitchin to seek him, and endeavour to induce him to return home at once; and Bob, who also was very uneasy about him, started at four o'clock.

Five came, six, seven, and the brothers had not come back. Dinner was served at six o'clock, but Hal alone, with unimpaired appetite, partook of that meal.

"I am laying in a stock of strength," he said to Lissa, on helping himself a second time to chicken pie, "for Dick's impending attack of D.T. A fellow can't be expected to hold another fellow down unless he has dined."

"How can you jest about such things, Hal?" said Lissa reproachfully.

"I am not jesting," answered Hal, with imperturbable gravity; "I am preparing myself for an athletic contest with Dick—and that reminds me I think I shall require another glass of beer to keep myself up to the mark."

About nine o'clock Dick and Bob arrived, Dick having decidedly taken too much to drink—"awfully screwed," Bob whispered to Lissa as they came in. Dick could walk, certainly, but his aim and his power of accomplishment were very wide apart.

"Lissa—" he said, "Lissa, my dear," as he staggered into the hall.

"Come in here, Dick," said Lissa, and she led him into the breakfast-room, and presently Dick fell sound asleep in an armchair by the fire.

Though he seemed quiet enough at present, Elizabeth and Bob agreed that they had better sit up with him: but when with some difficulty they got him upstairs, he fell on the bed d essed as he was, in such a heavy slumber, that Bob, after taking off his necktie and his boots, prophesied that he would never move until the morning, and therefore proposed himself to retire to rest.

"Leave your room door open, and a light burning then, Bob," said Lissa, and to this Bob agreed: Elizabeth, meaning to sit up during the night, to watch the sleeping man—in fact, dreading to go to bed, lest in the midnight hours she should again be awakened by his terrible struggles and cries.

She grew more nervous and ill at ease as the time wore on. Eleven o'clock struck, and Dick began to grow restless, moaning occasionally in his sleep, and stirring his arms. Then twelve came. and almost with the last stroke of the clock Dick raised himself up in bed, and slowly. and as if obeying some powerful impulse. rose, still asleep, and with half-opened, fixed, far-away-looking eyes, proceeded steadily to walk out of the room.

Elizabeth sprang to her feet to wake him—then a strange, terrible curiosity rushed into her heart, and seizing the night-lamp, she followed Dick's swift and noiseless steps.

To properly relate what followed perhaps it would be necessary to give a slight idea of the position of the rooms at Wendell West-house To prevent wearisome details, however, I shall content myself by telling that there was a long passage extending from the upper bedrooms to an unused attic room at the rear of the house, which was known in the family as "Grandmamma's store-room."

But it was never opened. "Grandmamma" (Mr. Horton's mother), an old-fashioned dame, had kept here her preserves, her home-made wines and hams, but Mrs. Horton(Lissa's aunt) had never used it, preferring as her store-room a room in a more conveniently situated part of the house than this out-of-the-way, shelving-roofed attic.

The key of it, however, Elizabeth expected, still hung on her household bunch of keys. which generally lay in her work-basket in the breakfast-room. But to her surprise and dismay, as she followed Dick's quick steps, who passed swiftly along the passage between his brother's rooms, and proceeded direct to the door of "Grandmamma's store-room," she saw him put his hand into his pocket and draw out a key, and having fitted it into the lock, he turned it and opened the door.

Again Elizabeth put out her hand to waken him, but again

with sickening dread and curiosity drew back; while Dick, having pulled the key out of the lock after turning it, entered the room, followed by the pale Elizabeth, holding her night-lamp in her hand.

A strange old world place this! Two ancient side-saddles were suspended from the shelving ceiling; short-waisted, antique silk dresses, whose wearers had been in their graves a hundred years, hung here too; and faded bunches of lavender and herbs, of which only the stalks remained, told of the old lady's house-wifely thrift and care. On the shelves were old-fashioned brown jars filled once, no doubt, with preserves and candies, and great baskets for her apples, which had left still a sort of taint and smell of decay in the air.

But it is in vain to describe all "the shreds and patches" with which this room was filled. It was the collection of years, and years, and years. When the farmer was a child and a boy, he had sometimes followed his mother here. *Her* mother's bridal dress was stored away in one of the great oak chests which stood near the walls; and after she was dead "grandmamma's clothes" were carried up, and, with her husband's, now formed part of the contents of the room.

Elizabeth remembered once or twice during her aunt's lifetime being allowed to enter here, and once after her death she had done so. On this occasion Elizabeth (then a young girl) had wanted some dresses to act charades in, and she had then opened one of the oak chests and peeped among the old lady's stores.

To her intense astonishment then, Dick (still asleep) now went up to the very chest she had then opened, and the key of which she remembered leaving in the lock, and bent down, and with a small key, which she now perceived was attached to the door key in his hand, proceeded to open the box.

With wide-staring eyes, and a face pale with excitement, Elizabeth watched what he did next. One after the other Dick took out the contents of the chest, and laid them on the floor. A yellow silk sacque, embroidered with violet flowers and green leaves, came first: then a black silk scarf, and various articles of female attire.

Then came apparently a set of gentlemen's ruffled shirts; a blue swallow-tailed coat, knee-breeches, and silk and woollen stockings of every description. Then a bridal dress—yellow with age, and trimmed at the wrist-bands and breast with fine Mecklin lace, yellow also. One by one Dick took these articles out and laid them on the floor, and then bending down again drew out of the chest a pair of boots—a pair of modern boots, with elastic sides, and made for some man whose feet must have been slim, straight, and small.

What made Elizabeth start, and with difficulty suppress a cry

when she saw these boots? She thought she recognised them—
she thought she knew again the narrow boot—the narrow boot
that Jasper Tyrell had worn, and which she had fitted in the
footprints in the snow, on the fatal morning when Harry's body
had been found.

With the rest of the contents of the box Dick laid down the
boots; and then bending down again, this time drew forth a
pistol—a revolver, and held it in his hand.

At this sight Elizabeth did utter a cry, and seized Dick's arm.
"Dick! Dick!" she cried, "awake! Dick!"

But Dick did not seem to hear her, but stood with his fixed,
half-opened expressionless eyes, handling the pistol as if he
were preparing to fire, and in terror Elizabeth shook his arm
violently.

This awoke him, for he opened his eyes wider, stared round,
while a different expression came into them, though he seemed
at first scarcely to comprehend where he was. Then he grew
deadly pale, and began to tremble violently, and the pistol fell
heavily from his hand on to the floor.

"How did I come here?" he asked.

"You were walking in your sleep," answered Elizabeth, greatly
agitated, "and I followed you here."

"Come away, then," said Dick, with a shudder; "come
away." And he moved forward as if about to quit the store-room.

But with a sudden effort, a sudden spasmodic gesture, Elizabeth stopped him.

"Dick!" she panted out, "Dick!" her arm raised warningly
the while, "tell me the truth! Is this," and she lifted the
weapon from the floor, "is this the pistol with which Harry
Tyrell was shot?"

Dick's eyes fell, and he staggered back as she asked this
question.

"What folly! How do I know?" he said hoarsely. "Come
away."

"No," said Elizabeth, "I will not go," and she looked steadily
in Dick's face, determined now to satisfy her long uncertainty
and doubt. "Dick, speak the truth—was this the pistol with
which you spilt Harry Tyrell's blood?"

As she said this, Dick covered his face with his hand, and
with a groan fell back against the chest.

"Why—why—do—you ask—" he faltered out,—"you know
Jasper—"

"Do not lie any more, Dick," said Elizabeth, in a solemn tone,
interrupting his broken disjointed words. "God's eye saw the
deed, and to Him alone you can now turn for pardon. I have
long doubted you—and His hand led you here to-night—His
voice now bids you clear the fame of an innocent man!"

"Will you betray me?" asked Dick, with some of his old sullen doggedness, looking up into Elizabeth's excited face.

"Never," said Elizabeth, in her ringing tones. "Dick, this has been a mystery, let it remain one—it can never be discovered now. But clear Jasper Tyrell's name—say his hand did not shed his brother's blood."

"God only knows what I've suffered," groaned Dick.

"There is pardon for us all," said Elizabeth earnestly, almost passionately, "if we confess the truth to Him, and seek to blame no other. Oh Dick, tell it to me now, and God will forgive you!"

"No," said Dick gloomily. "He has cursed me—cursed my right hand, for didn't I kill poor father?"

"His mercy is great," urged Elizabeth, "and we can all find it. Seek it now, Dick, by speaking the truth."

"You drove me to it," admitted Dick, " drove me wild by the mad love I felt for you—I couldn't bear to see you marry either of the Tyrells."

"And so you planned Harry's death, and the deceit by which you made me believe Jasper had killed his brother?" said Elizabeth with involuntary bitterness.

"Ay, I may as well tell you all now," answered Dick recklessly, "since you know so much, and you can have me hanged if you like. I'd watched the Tyrells for days, for I never could make out which of them you wanted; and that morning I met Harry Tyrell, and I asked him to come up at five o'clock to see some rats killed by the dogs in the stables. Then, just when it got dusk, I saw Jasper leaving the house, and you standing watching him from the door—and I got mad, and the devil I suppose suddenly put the thought into my head, for I crept upstairs and forced on the Lieutenant's boots, and hid the pistol under my coat, and then ran as best I could across the fields, and went over the little bridge from the road into the Hall grounds, and stood waiting for Harry to come by on his way to the farm."

"And you shot him through the hedge?" asked Elizabeth, breathlessly.

"Yes—he came whistling along the road, for he had come round, as I expected he would, from the back of the Hall, and not by the gardens—and when he came up I fired——"

"And he fell!—did he cry out?—O God!" said Elizabeth, almost overpowered by the horror of the relation.

"He gave just one cry," said Dick, "and fell forward with his head and breast in the snow—he died in a moment, and after it was all over I stole quietly down the hedge—but you saw the footprints—"

"Yes," said Elizabeth, "you meant then to deceive me?"

"I meant to separate you from them both if I could, and I did

it," and Dick gave a kind of ghastly laugh, "though God knows
it's brought me no happiness."

"It could not," said Elizabeth, "it could not. But come, Dick,"
she went on, looking fearfully round, for the tale that she had
heard in this lone place had filled her soul with horror. "Come
back now, and I will put these things away." And she began
hastily to refill the oaken chest.

"Put the pistol at the bottom," said Dick, and Elizabeth
shudderingly obeyed him.

"Did you buy it?" she asked, in a whisper. "When did you
hide it here?"

"I bought it weeks—before—I used it," answered Dick, "and
I hid it here the very night that I—shot Harry Tyrell."

"You took the key of the store-room from my ring, then?"

"Yes, and fastened it and the box key together. If it hadn't
been for this cursed trick of sleep-walking you never would have
found it out."

"Hush, Dick, come away," said Elizabeth, now locking the
chest; and so together she and Dick left the store-room; left
behind them the pistol and the boots—the ghastly records of
Dick's crime, lying amid the old grandmother's faded finery—
the treasured memorials of her youth and love!

Without another word the husband and wife then passed
along the still passage; Elizabeth shading her lamp as they drew
near Robert Horton's door.

"Is he up?" asked Dick, with sudden suspicion.

"No," whispered Elizabeth. "I asked him to keep his door
open, and the light burning, for I was afraid you might be ill
again—he is fast asleep."

When they reached his bed-room, Dick seemed quite overcome,
and sank half-fainting on a chair.

"Get me some brandy," he said.

"Yes," answered Elizabeth, and she ran quickly downstairs
and brought up the brandy, which Dick drank eagerly and
greedily, and then throwing himself on the bed bid Elizabeth
come and sit by him; and when she did so, he grew communicative and talkative under the influence of the stimulant that he
had taken.

"But how did you get the handkerchief, Dick, that you
showed me," asked Elizabeth, "the handkerchief that I have—
Jasper's handkerchief that I marked with my hair?"

"Oh! that was easily enough done," replied Dick, roughly, "I
saw you working at those confounded things, and a day or two
before the Lieutenant left, I met Jack, the lad, with a parcel in
his hand, and when I asked him what it was he said that you
had given it to him to leave at the Hall. So I took it out of his
hand and read the address, to Jasper Tyrell. I guessed what

was inside, so I told Jack to go into the house for something that I wanted, and when he was gone I opened the parcel and saw that I was right. Then I thought I'll take one of the handkerchiefs, and perhaps make her believe something or other about it after he was gone—perhaps about giving it some girl. So I took one, and fastened up the parcel again, and when I showed you the footprints in the snow, I'd dropped it down a moment before without you ever noticing me. But I did it all out of love for you, Lissa," he went on, endeavouring to take her hand, "so you ought to try to comfort me—"

"I pray that God will forgive you, Dick," answered Lissa, in a low voice.

"You needn't begin preaching to a fellow in that tone," said Dick, captiously, and with instant change of humour. "I know what I've done, and I've done it. I am not denying it, am I!"

"No, Dick."

"Then don't preach to me. I say it was you, Lissa, you alone were to blame, you drew me on—you encouraged me. And Dick kept muttering on half incoherently, and then the quantity of spirit that he had swallowed entirely overpowered him, and he fell into a heavy sleep.

With an intense feeling of bitterness swelling in her heart, Elizabeth sat and watched him.

What! her whole life had been sacrificed, her love betrayed, her happiness ruined by the selfish passion of this senseless youth! And Jasper—poor Jasper. All the love that she had felt for him, unchanged still even when she believed him most guilty, came rushing back into her heart at this moment, increasing the loathing and horror with which she must evermore, she knew now, regard the miserable man lying before her.

And yet this man was her husband! "No, no," muttered Elizabeth, as the hateful thought rose before her, "it cannot be —it shall not be. He wrung my promise from me by a cruel lie —he killed poor Harry—he wronged, most shamefully wronged dear Jasper—and I cannot—no I cannot, I will not stay another day under his roof."

As Elizabeth made this resolve, the expression of her face grew calmer, and she rose noiselessly from the bedside determined at once to execute her purpose, and to leave Wendell West-house for ever before another day should dawn.

Quietly and silently she made her preparations. All that she could take away with her she must carry, for in secret she had determined to leave her home, in secret to live, and in secret to die, rather than live another day by the side of Richard Horton.

A few minutes' reflection had convinced her that she must leave nearly everything behind her if she did so. She could not betray Richard, and unless she betrayed him she felt certain that she could not escape his power. He was her husband. He had a right to her; a right that she was sure he would not relinquish as long as he was free from the consequences of his crime—the crime that she must hide, the secret that she must keep, until her cousin, her miserable husband, lay in his grave.

But she must leave him; leave him, cost her what it might, she was determined to do; so silently and noiselessy in the dead of night she made her preparations, arranging in a leather bag in her poor uncle's room, all that she would be able to carry away with her.

She took her jewels, the gifts mostly of her dear uncle and aunt, carefully laying aside those given her by Richard, which she left, with a note that she wrote to him, lying on the dressing-table. A single dress, and a change of linen—a few of Jasper's letters, defaced with bitter tears, sufficed to fill her bag; and these, and about forty pounds in notes and gold which she found in her desk, was all the property with which she started out on the lonely and unknown journey lying before her.

When her other arrangements were finished, she took her pen, and knelt down at her desk, and addressed a few lines to Richard Horton.

"Good-bye, Dick," she wrote, "good-bye for ever—for after what passed between us to-night, it is better for us both that I should never see you any more. Your secret is safe with me, and as long as you live I shall never betray it, and I pray that God in His almighty mercy may forgive you all the evil that you have done. But do not seek to find me, for I will never return to you.

"ELIZABETH."

Then she drew off her wedding ring, and enclosed it in this note, and together with the ornaments that Dick had given her, placed them in his room. She wrote a few farewell lines also to her cousin Robert, going into his bed-room for the purpose of leaving them there, and after she had laid them down, she went softly up to the bed, and looked at her young cousin lying in his placid slumber.

Tears rose in her eyes as she did so. These youths had been as brothers to her almost ever since she could remember any-thing, until Dick's mad passion had begun, and she felt it to be a sort of treachery to leave Robert alone with his miserable brother—his ghastiy secret being certainly suspected by the younger Horton.

But she could not stay, and so, with a light kiss on her sleep-ing cousin's face, she left his room, leaving her note to him lying on a table near.

"I am going to leave Wendell to-night, dear Robert," she had written, "for something has happened which makes it quite impossible that I can stay. Do not be uneasy about me, for I have some money to take with me, and I mean to work for my bread. Be kind to Dick and Harry for my sake, and believe me to remain, dear Robert,

"Your loving cousin,
"ELIZABETH."

Everything was ready now, she thought, everything—but for one moment she went back and looked at Dick; looked at Dick lying on the bed breathing heavily; at his red and swollen face; at his clenched and restless hand, which moved uneasily on the coverlet as she stood and watched him.

"Oh! God forgive him," murmured Elizabeth, and with these last words she turned away.

Then she went down the familiar stairs where she had played and prattled as a child, crossed the hall, and as she did so her light step awoke the old dog Tory, who rose, and came whining and snuffling to her side.

"Poor dog! poor Tory!" whispered Elizabeth, and a sob rose in her throat, and she bent down and kissed the old dog's head.

"Lie down, Tory," she said, "lie down." But the dumb beast looked at her still with his dim but inquiring eyes.

"Lie down," again said Elizabeth, and she patted his head, and then laid her hand upon the door key, and the next moment still and silently had gone out into the still and silent night.

CHAPTER XVI.

FLIGHT.

FROST had made the ground like iron, and the stars shone brightly in the clear, luminous sky, when Elizabeth left her home, and started forth on a journey the end of which she could not foresee.

There is something rather fearful, is there not, to a woman to be out alone beneath the dusky curtain, visible, yet invisible, which steals down upon the world at night? We start at shadows, and the very breeze seems to whisper strange sounds to our unaccustomed ears. Elizabeth was far from being free from these weak but pardonable terrors of her sex. Nerved as she was by her horror of Dick's crime—by her determination to escape for ever from a tie grown so hateful to her heart, that she could no longer endure it—she yet shrank from this desolate walk; and trembled as she went along pursued and haunted by the memory of young Tyrell's tragic death.

She avoided the fields that she had crossed with Dick on the miserable morning when the body had been discovered; but she was forced on reaching the roadway to pass in front of the Hall, and thus of course forced to pass the very place where Harry Tyrell's corpse had lain half buried in the snow.

To her excited imagination as she neared the fatal spot, something seemed to stir behind the holly hedge, and with a kind of cry Elizabeth ran past it; ran panting, trembling on, fearing to look up—dreading to see she knew not what, creating in a hundred shapes the fear and terror that possessed her soul.

She intended to walk to Mitchin, the country town, some three miles or so from Wendell where of late Dick had spent so many riotous days, trying to quench with drink the "still small voice," which yet kept ever whispering in the reveller's ears.   The nearest railway station to Wendell is at this town, and Elizabeth knew that a train passed through it on its way to London about five o'clock in the morning, and by this train she intended to leave Uplandshire most probably for ever.

As she neared the outskirts of the town, heated, trembling, and afraid, she heard footsteps in reality approaching her, and presently a man with a bundle hung on a stick over his shoulder appeared out of the darkness, and passed Elizabeth, pausing the moment after he had done so, thus adding wings to her weary feet as she fled onward, filled with a new and very serious apprehension.

But, thank God! at last the lights of the town were visible, and the weary woman seemed to see in each street lamp a protector, alike from the weird terrors to her of the murder-haunted road, and the rough company, that every moment she was liable to encounter.

One, two, three, four, told the solemn tale of Time, from a church tower, as she entered the main street of the town, and the next moment the gaol clock near chimed its melancholy warning numbers to the weary prisoners lying in their dismal cells. What thoughts—passionate, regretful, miserable thoughts, this gaol clock must have awakened—must ever awaken each passing hour, to the throbbing, panting hearts compelled to listen to its sound!   To one maybe it tells of the fast lessening days of life—the days numbered into hours, passing swiftly away even here, to the doomed wretch condemned to die! To another it speaks of long years; long months, of unrewarded shameful toil; of frustrated plans, of wasted idle hours, counted and repented of now, alas! in vain. To some let us hope it brings relief, telling that the time is drawing near when new life of freedom is at hand, and God's sweet gifts of home and liberty about to be restored to the weary inmates of the prison walls.

To Elizabeth the gaol clock's warning numbers spoke of Dick —of Dick the sullen boy-cousin, the unwelcome lover, the unloved husband, the curse and misery of her life. "Oh! uncle, Oh! aunt," she thought, looking upwards, as if she knew that these dear friends were safe at home with God, "for your sakes I will never betray his secret—but I pray and hope that I may see his face no more."

Just then a drunken woman, crying bitterly and hysterically, passed her.

"What is the matter?" asked Elizabeth.

"Matter?" said the woman turning round her pale soiled face, about which her rough dishevelled hair hung loosely, "matter enough! They've taken my man to-day, and locked him up—locked him up there;" she continued, pointing to the gaol walls, "and they say it's murder. But it is not murder," she went on exc tedly, "it's murder if they hang him. Oh! Jim, Jim!" and she flung herself down in the street, writhing as if in desperate pain.

"Get up, my poor woman," said Elizabeth, gently. "Where is your home?—you had better go to it."

"Home!" shrieked the woman, "I have none. They sold us off—Jim couldn't get work, and that was his sin. But cursed be those who starve the poor—cursed—"

"What's this row about?" said a stern voice in Elizabeth's ear, and the same moment the official hand of a big policeman was laid on her trembling shoulder.

"This poor woman seems to be very ill," said Elizabeth, "what can be done for her?"

"The station-house," answered the man 'armed with brief authority.' And then after eyeing Elizabeth suspiciously, he added, "And what may you be doing out at this time o'night, miss?"

"I am going to catch the five train to London," answered Elizabeth, and she slid some silver into the policeman's hand, "and I shall feel obliged to you if you will direct me to the railway station."

"Oh!" said the mollified official; and the poor drunken soul lying on the pavement looked up also at the magic clink at which the hearts of untold millions thrill.

"Have mercy on me," she sobbed—"don't leave me penniless, lady!"

"She's drunk, madam," said the policeman; "it would be wrong to give her anything—only encouraging her."

These words exasperated the miserable woman to madness, and starting to her feet she sprang at the policeman like a tigress, seizing him by his whiskers, and leaving the marks of her nails in his plump and rosy cheeks.

"You jade!" he cried; but it was all he could do to defend himself, and hopeless of doing any good Elizabeth hurried on, leaving the policeman struggling with the unfortunate creature, who doubtless would speedily find herself locked up in the station-house for assaulting the man of law.

"Some are more miserable even than I am," thought Elizabeth, as she passed hastily along the streets trying to find the railway station. "I should not repine, and yet—Oh! yet—"

It seemed so hard, so bitter. The more she thought of Richard Horton's conduct, the more cruel and wicked did it appear. He had blasted her life, blasted Jasper Tyrell's, and dreadful, most dreadful of all, had shed the blood of the light-hearted and unsuspecting young man, whose sweet careless good-nature might have been supposed to have rendered him safe from the dark, jealous, and stormy passions which unconsciously he had aroused.

But the deed was done. Harry Tyrell lay in his grave, and Jasper and Elizabeth were parted by the miserable marriage vows that she had falsely sworn to save (as she believed) his life. She could not even tell him, if they ever chanced to meet, of the dreadful sacrifice that she had made for his sake, but must remain ever to his mind a perjured woman—an unfaithful wife.

So lonely, wretched and weary, tired with the unaccustomed weight of the bag which she carried, and worn with the horror, the excitement, and the terrors of the night, Elizabeth at last reached the railway station, only to find that it was yet unopened, and to experience again some of the miseries of the homeless and the poor.

Up and down she wandered, afraid to sit on the hard cold steps of the station, which actually seemed inviting to her weary frame, lest some other officious policeman should consider it his duty to inquire what she was doing, though she now was absolutely scarcely able to stand from sheer bodily fatigue.

Presently another would-be traveller approached—a decent woman this, with a worn, wrinkled, yet kindly face, carrying a heavy market basket, and dressed in respectable though rusty black.

She looked at Elizabeth once or twice, and then with the freedom of her class addressed her.

"You'll be for the early train?" she said.

"Yes," answered Elizabeth, glad to have a woman's protection near her, "are you going by it too?"

"Yes, miss," and the woman sighed; "to my daughter's funeral—a fine young woman, and she and her new-born babe are to be buried at ten this morn' at Eastwell."

"Poor thing," said Elizabeth with ready sympathy ; "of what did she die?"

"Well, fever," answered the woman, "that was it. You see her eldest little lad got it and then the babe came, and she took it from him; and she's to be laid in her grave this morning—not twenty-five till Martinmas."

"It's very sad," said Elizabeth softly.

"We're born to trouble, miss," answered the old woman, "and as it's the Lord's will no doubt it's good for us." And in this patient and resigned frame of mind she regarded all earthly troubles.

It was some relief to Elizabeth's overwrought mind to listen to her; to hear how her "man" died after two days' illness of cholera; how her eldest son was a steady thriving, lad, and her youngest a cripple. "The short and simple annals of the poor," are, after all, full of interest to those who view human nature from the broad bias of universal kindred. As this woman is, I might have been; as that poor creature—fallen, degraded, and debased—had I been born in an attic, reared in squalor, and dragged through the mire from my cradle to my grave.

But few of us admit these wholesome truths. Wrapped in our garments of respectability (real or imagined), we shake the dust off our feet, and refuse to admit our relationship—alas! perhaps, were the the garments gone, our close resemblance—to the sinner and the lost.

Vaguely thinking of many things—of what troubles there were to all around her—Elizabeth listened to the decent old woman's talk, and when at last a sleepy official proceeded to open the station, light the gas, and admit the few intended travellers inside, Elizabeth asked leave to take her new companion a second-class ticket, anxious that she might remain so far on her journey by her protecting side.

The woman with honest pride at first demurred.

"Nay, miss," she said, "the third's good enough for the like o' me." But on Elizabeth gently pressing her, she admitted that it had been a "sare time" for her of late, and that the "funeral things," pointing to her basket, had been a heavy drain on her humble resources.

Elizabeth therefore took two second-class tickets, thankfully observing as she did so, that they were distributed by a boy that she had never seen, and not by the ordinary station-master whom she knew by sight, and who therefore might possibly know her.

When the train came puffing into the station, and the usual scene of hurry took place, the wearied night travellers rushing hastily to partake of some trifling refreshment at the bar, during the few minutes' grace that they were allowed, Elizabeth as quickly and quietly as possible got into a second-class compartment, followed by her new friend, and a minute or two later they found themselves driving steadily through the darkness, for the pale winter dawn had not yet begun to shine upon the earth.

They were alone, and Elizabeth was very weary with the excitement and terrors of the night, and she presently fell into a light and disturbed sleep, in which imagery, fanciful and weird, crossed and recrossed her brain, leaving a painful impression on her wakening sense, when she was roused by the slackening of the speed of the train on its approach to another station

"Eh," said her companion with a smile, when she opened her

eyes, "but ye've had a good sleep. I'm glad you've wakened miss, for you and I must part at Eastwell."

"Is that the next station? Is that where your daughter lived?" asked Elizabeth, still half asleep.

"Ay, before the Lord took her," answered the woman; and then she began to draw her little belongings together, and Elizabeth roused herself to speak a few kindly and commiserating words, and forgetting her own probable approaching poverty, pressed a half-sovereign into the hard and work-worn hand.

"Nay—nay—" said the woman, and then she hesitated. What comforts this little sum could bring her, she was thinking, and the lady seemed rich—yet—

"Do take it," urged Elizabeth, and the poor woman sighed, and her fingers closed nervously over the glittering coin.

"You are too good, my lady," she said, "too good."

"You must not say that," said Elizabeth, and she looked up and smiled just as the train stopped at the platform before the station, and a gentleman who was lounging along it, with a railway rug on his arm, and a porter behind him carrying a portmanteau, caught sight of her handsome face, lit by the dim light from the top of the carriage, and coolly paused to examine it.

He was an admirer of beauty this intended traveller—an admirer as some men admire wonderful works of art, and rare pieces of sculpture, and as his cold steady eyes rested on Elizabeth's face, he was struck by its regularity, the nobleness of its expression, its rare and peculiar type.

"I will get in here," he said to the porter, pausing before the door of the carriage in which she was seated.

"But that's second class, sir," said the porter who was following him, touching his cap with all the respect which a liberal tip usually evokes.

"Is it?" answered the gentleman, in a placid well-bred tone, which told of long experience of the world and men. "Ah! it will do very well—it is all the same." And he made a gesture to the porter to open the door, who, with as knowing a smile as he dared to indulge in, complied with his wish, and to Elizabeth's annoyance placed a portmanteau and a leather hat-box inside the carriage.

"I am not disturbing you, I trust?" asked the gentleman, addressing Elizabeth with courtesy, as he followed his luggage, and Elizabeth drew her bag out of the way, while her temporary companion, the old woman, made haste also to get out of it.

"Oh! no," answered Elizabeth coldly; and then she shook the poor widow's hand.

"Good-bye," she said, and that was all. But the woman with freer manners of her class, asked God to bless her, and wished her a safe and happy end to her journey.

"And take care of yourself, my lady," she added, as she stood a moment on the step of the carriage before parting, not without a backward glance at the tall, dark stranger inside, who, with a slightly contemptuous smile which was natural to him curling his thin lips, was watching these strange adieux.

"Oh! yes," said Elizabeth gravely; and then the old woman went away, and the gentleman with quiet ease drew up the carriage window after she was gone.

"With your permission," he said, his dark, hazel eyes fixed steadily the while on Elizabeth's face. "The air is cold in these early hours, is it not?"

"Yes," answered Elizabeth, shyly. She felt half afraid somehow to be left alone with this man, grave and courteous as he seemed to be.

"At least I feel chilly," he went on with a shiver and a shrug. "I've had half an hour's drive to reach the station, and I hate hardships of all sorts;" and he smiled.

A cold cynical smile, which passed over his face somehow without lighting it to warmth, like a sunbeam on the snow. He was good-looking though, with regular features, and dark hair tinged here and there with grey, and he had a slight, well-kept moustache, and looked about forty. But something in his manner—or rather in his expression perhaps—repelled you, and Elizabeth grew uneasy beneath the scrutinizing gaze, which found not good but evil when it was his pleasure to study and judge the motives of his fellow-beings.

"Have you had a long journey?" he next asked coolly.

"Not very," replied Elizabeth, anxious to discourage his questions.

"And London, of course, is your destination?" continued the calm stranger.

"Yes," said Elizabeth, and she blushed and drew down her crape veil.

"Pardon me if I have asked an impertinent question," said the gentleman observing with regret this action. "I assure you I did not mean to annoy you."

"You have not done so," answered Elizabeth gravely.

"I am glad of that. As we are travellers together (temporarily) through this vale of tears, I should regret exceedingly if I were to displease you."

Elizabeth was silent.

"What grubby machines these second-class carriages are;" continued the stranger, looking round. "Do you generally travel in them?"

"No," said Elizabeth.

"How cruel of you to do so to-night, or rather this morning! If I am attacked with rheumatism in this shoulder" (and he touched his left shoulder as he spoke) "from this alarming draught, you alone are to blame."

"I do not understand you," said Elizabeth, haughtily.

"You are the candle, and I am the moth," went on the impertinent stranger. "You know I am sure what lure induced me to enter one of these infernal machines?"

"Indeed I do not."

"A beautiful face," said the stranger. "The lure that tempted Adam in the beginning, and will tempt his sons unto the end."

The cool audacity with which these words were spoken frightened Elizabeth to such an extent, that she determined to leave the carriage at the next station; but with quick penetration her companion had read the changing expression of her face, and immediately altered his manner.

"The morning is breaking," he said, "and unless we have the ill-luck to encounter a fog, we shall have day-light to show us our way before we reach London."

"Yes," said Elizabeth, almost faintly.

"Do you know it well?" went on the stranger.

"Not very—I have been there."

"And I live there—the wilderness of brick and mortar is my home."

Elizabeth acknowledged this piece of information by a cold monosyllable, but her reserve only tended to amuse her travelling companion, and make him the more desirous to break through it; though his manner to her now was not disrespectful, except from his persistence in talking to her, when he plainly saw that she did not wish him to do so.

"She is a married woman," he thought. "The happy fellow will be waiting at King's Cross, I bet a hundred pounds."

But when they reached that Terminus, no happy fellow being visible, his curiosity was yet further aroused, and bending forward just as the train stopped, he read the printed address cut on a brass label on Elizabeth's black leather bag, which until that moment she had utterly forgotten.

"Forgive me," he said in a low tone as Elizabeth turned sharply round and caught him doing so, for she had been speaking to the porter clinging to the window, and desiring him to secure her a cab. "Forgive me, *Miss Gordon*, but I wished so much to know your name. Allow me to be of some assistance to you," he went on. "Here is my servant—can he do anything for you—get your luggage—do anything you want?"

"No, thank you," said Elizabeth, "the porter will get me a cab, and that is all I require."

But the stranger was not to be so easily shaken off. He handed Elizabeth out; he begged leave to be allowed to carry her bag to the cab, and stood at the door of the carriage when she was forced to give the address of the hotel to which she wished to be conveyed.

"The Grosvenor," she said. It was in fact the only hotel she knew, for she and her poor uncle had stayed there once or twice during their rare visits to London.

"The Grosvenor," repeated the stranger slowly. "Ah! then, Long" (this was to his servant), "I may as well go there for breakfast." And as Elizabeth ascended the broad steps of the hotel, she had the annoyance of seeing the stranger's cab drive up at the same moment, and to hear his voice giving some directions, as he followed her up the steps.

CHAPTER XVII.
THE HON. MR. WILMOT.

AFTER Elizabeth was conducted to a private room, and had ordered breakfast, she speedily forgot all about her obtrusive fellow-traveller. The most serious thoughts indeed of her future life forced themselves on her attention, for little as she knew of the want of money, and totally inexperienced as she was about the dire necessity of its possession, she was yet well aware that the small sum that she had brought with her would last a very short time in London.

But what was she to do? She had left her home without a thought of the future, except to escape for ever from the presence of Dick, and by doing this she had perforce left name, fortune, and everything behind her. Only a very desolate life then could lie before her, for a woman's life must ever be desolate who has no home. "What can I do?" thought Elizabeth, and no very satisfactory answer rose in her imagination to this momentous question.

She was not like one of those who are brought up in the hard school of necessity, and drilled by the stern task-master poverty. She had always been well off, and had never known what it was to have no money to buy this or that, or to go here or there at pleasure.

Now this was all ended. She would have to work for her bread, and with a very disconsolate feeling she began thinking how she could best perform this unfamiliar and unwelcome task.

At all events the sooner that she was out of an expensive hotel the better, she decided; and after lying down for an hour, and having bathed her face and otherwise refreshed herself, she determined to go out in search of lodgings, and was leaving the hotel for that purpose, when, beneath the glass vestibule outside, she again encountered her fellow-traveller of the morning, who was lounging there talking to another gentleman.

On seeing Elizabeth he immediately advanced to her side, and after taking off his hat, escorted her down the steps of the hotel.

"I have been anxious to see you," he said, "for I wish to apologize for my rudeness to you this morning in reading the address on your travelling-bag. Will you forgive me, and allow me also to present my name to you?" And he drew out his pocket-book with a smile, and placed a card in Elizabeth's hand.

"Oh! it's no matter," said Elizabeth courteously, but gravely, "and now I must wish you good-morning."

"Can I do nothing for you? Can I call a cab, or make myself useful in any way?" went on the persistent stranger.

"No, thanks—no, indeed," answered Elizabeth, and with a slight bow she turned away, proceeding a short distance down Buckingham Palace Road, and then crossing the platform in front of Victoria station.

With a certain amount of curiosity she then glanced at the card in her hand, on which was written "Edgar Wilmot, 17, Upper Brooke Street."

"I wish that Mr. Wilmot would leave me alone," thought Elizabeth, and she tore the card through, and dropped it as she passed amongst the usual crowd of travellers and porters in front of the station.

But Mr. Wilmot—the Hon. Edgar Wilmot, in reality, though he had chosen to drop that prefix to his name, when he wrote it on a card for Elizabeth's benefit—had no intention of losing sight of the handsomest girl he had seen for years, as he mentally designated Elizabeth.

A little jaded and worn, he yet was an enthusiast—no not enthusiastic, for he had no enthusiasm for any object on the face of the earth, but he was a critical admirer of beauty, and a face like Elizabeth's he regarded as a rare piece of perfection in nature, not lightly to be lost to view; and scarcely had Elizabeth proceeded a step from the hotel when he beckoned to his servant, who was standing near waiting for orders.

"Follow that lady in black, Long, wherever she goes," he said. "Take the address of any house that she enters, and watch if she leaves it." And the man touched his hat and obeyed him; and as Elizabeth went along Wilton Road, crossed Eccleston Square, passed through Warwick Street, and got into Cambridge Street, looking for likely rooms as she went along; so at a discreet distance, whistling and lounging, followed Mr. Wilmot's servant Long, never for one moment removing his eyes from the tall figure in black, that he had been ordered not to lose sight of.

What a dreary business it is seeking for rooms in London, or indeed in any place under the sun! Elizabeth shrank from the bold, hard eyes of one florid woman, to whom she applied, and shivered at the mean, pinched looks of another.

"Are you a single lady?" asked one impudent girl, and on Elizabeth assenting, she slapped the house door in her face.

"Missus doesn't take 'em then," said this saucy young woman; and Elizabeth, accustomed to be treated with courtesy, stood absolutely in dismay on the door-steps at her impertinence.

At last near the lower end of Cambridge Street, she found a house that she thought might possibly suit he . The door indeed was opened by a slovenly maid-se vant, but she said "missus" was in, and ushered Elizabeth up to a well-furnished, though dusty drawing-room.

Here she stayed at least a quarter of an hour, and then the room door was opened by a small, thin woman, with a faded, bluish-tinted, small-featured face; her nose, which was red, having apparently been recently dipped into the flour-jar. By the side of this meagre, eager little face, whose weak, watery, black eyes, had a covetous look somehow, hung a row (four or five on each side) of iron-grey, short, well-oiled curls, while a high ornamental imitation tortoise-shell comb was placed at the back, and a greasy brown satin bow completed her head-gear.

"Me maid has informed me ye're in want of a temporary home, me dear," she said, with an elaborate curtsey, as she entered, "and I'm sure as ye are so young and so handsome, ye couldn't meet with a better than the one which by a mere chonce I'm at this moment in a position to offer ye."

"What are your terms?" said Elizabeth, somewhat embarrassed at this gushing address. "And what rooms have you vacant?"

"Ah! it isn't about terms now ye're talking the first minit ye've put yer foot in me house! Sure now we'll leave them particulars to another time. But I'm thinking how pleasant it is for ye—so pleasant for a young lady loike yerself to have a home offered in a clorgyman's family. Yes, me husband's a minister in the Church of England. The Rev. Michael O'Shee, to be sure he is now, and no other; and if ye can give proper references, and pay a reasonable sum for the accommodation I give ye, I'll be proud to receive ye as a friend under me roof."

"I have no references in London," said Elizabeth, colouring. "I'm from the country and shall only be here for a short time— but I will pay for the rooms a month in advance if you choose."

"Sure now ye couldn't have a better reference than that! Well, then, me dear, I'm so plased with yer looks, that I'll let ye have the rooms a complate bargain—thirty shillings a week, and no extras to spake of. There, what do you think of that! And I may tell ye," added this gushing Irish lady, while an indescribable expression between a leer and a smile stole over her faded face, "that though Mr. O'Shee me husband's a clorgyman, he ain't prim."

Subsequently Elizabeth found that the Rev. Michael O'Shee was certainly not prim; but as it was, though she was by no means captivated either by Mrs. O'Shee's appearance or manner, she was glad to arrange to have what appeared to be a respectable roof over her head. She was weary, too, of wandering amongst the endless streets of stucco-fronted houses, the very door-steps and knockers of which appeared to her to be of the same monotonous pattern. She therefore settled with Mrs. O'Shee (after some further conversation with the accommodating clergyman's lady) that during the afternoon she was to come and take up her residence in Cambridge Street; leaving as a deposit in Mrs. O'Shee's hands one month's rent for the rooms.

As she quitted the house, and stood a moment on the door-step talking to her future landlady, who had followed her to the door, Long, Mr. Wilmot's servant passed just while Mrs. O'Shee was exclaiming—

"Indeed, me dear, it's just as if Providence had directed ye to find a happy home under me roof!"

CHAPTER XVIII.

A WOLF.

ELIZABETH went to her new home during the afternoon, and found everything arranged for her reception. Mrs. O'Shee, in a Swiss black velvet body, and a faded violet "frock," as she called it, received her as a visitor, and began enlarging at once on her own and "me husband's" merits, and the demerits of the race of the female servants at that period in the metropolis.

"Sure now, in Dublin, where me father lived in great stoyle— and good right he had, poor man, with his ancient family to do so, only his revenue was incompetent to cover his expenses—well, then, in Dublin, as I was telling ye, excellent female servants were to be had for a mere troifle, while here, if ye'll beleeve it, for twelve pounds a year, I carn't get a girl totally unfit for her place to remain with me!"

"It must be very awkward," said Elizabeth.

"Indeed, now it is, and no mistake," replied Mrs. O'Shee. "There's my daughter now, Mrs. Pheasant—sure, her husband, Dr. Pheasant, is one of the finest physicians in the town. Why, she's giving her twenty pounds a paice to her maids, I can tell ye! As I say to her, 'Ah! me dear, it's well to be married to a rich man.' But her poor father here, me husband, Mr. O'Shee, is only a poor clorgyman, and so I must just do as best I can."

How bad that was Elizabeth presently learnt. The very day of her arrival a tremendous battle occurred between her landlady and the slovenly, though rather pretty girl, who had first admitted her.

Strong language was exchanged between the combatants; Mrs. O'Shee piously hoping that Mary would be rewarded according to her misdeeds, and Mary retorting that if Mrs. O'Shee got *her* due, she would be hanged.

"Ye're a viper, Mary, and I've nourished ye," screamed Mrs. O'Shee.

"Nourished me! Poor nourishment I've got then," cried Mary. "I would have starved, and you too, if you didn't lay hands on what ye've no business to."

"Mary, leeve the house, I command ye," said Mrs. O'Shee, recovering her dignity. "Leeve this minit, or I'll call in a policeman."

"Don't believe you dare," replied Mary, tauntingly. "And as for leaving the house, I'll only be too glad to leave if you will pay me my wages. Now, there, I tell you *that*."

Some difficulty appeared to exist regarding this settlement, for Mary, with her eyes red with weeping, brought up the greasy ill-cooked chops, when Elizabeth's dinner-hour came. The above altercation between the mistress and the maid having taken place on the first landing, Elizabeth had had the annoyance of hearing every word that was spoken, and began to have serious doubts about the great respectability which Mrs. O'Shee so constantly proclaimed. During dinner Mary, having forgotten some customary appendage to the table, when Elizabeth asked for it, declared herself "so flustered with the goings on in this house," that her head was "just turned."

"And I'm sure, miss, you'd better look to yourself and your things," went on the girl, "for I can't in my conscience-like help giving you a hint. Things are not as they should be here." And after giving this dark warning, Mary caught up a tray and vanished, leaving Elizabeth feeling anything but comfortable.

She felt so lonely, desolate, and miserable, too, and the untidy and dirty appearance of the house on nearer inspection (though the furniture was good) unconsciously added to her depression.

At last she went to bed, after being worried and annoyed by several visits from Mrs. O'Shee. "Jest to see how ye're getting on," she would say, as she peeped in her eager little face, absolutely without even rapping at the door.

During the night her experience of her new home was not more agreeable, and several discomforts, incidental to lodging-houses, disturbed her exceedingly. But worn and weary she at last sank into a deep sleep; and when the hazy, yellow London dawn broke into her little bed-room, she at first could scarcely realise where she was. Then, remembrance and thought, bitter and miserable, we may be sure, came back to her, and with a weary sigh she rose, knowing that she must begin to-day the painful task of trying to find some way to win her daily bread.

Some who will read these pages may, perhaps, have done so, and will, therefore, understand the dreary experience that Elizabeth gained during the next few days of her life. It seems so easy to say, "I will get something to do," and it is in reality so difficult to accomplish. The truth is that this is an age when a severe training is required and necessa y for almost every possible way of earning a livelihood. Thus women unused and unprepared for the position must ever find the greatest difficulty in obtaining a situation, and Elizabeth was no exception to this rule.

When, indeed, after lightly partaking of the untempting breakfast that Mrs. O'Shee herself spread before her, informing her "that viper Mary was gone," she started out on her unwelcome errand, and after consulting several papers, fixed on two register offices to apply to, one in Edgware Road, and the other in Berner Street, she found that at each she was totally unsuccessful.

She had decided that she was best suited to be a lady's companion; but the pleasant, sad-faced young woman who was presiding over the register-office in Berner Street, told her that it was quite useless even to put her name down for such a situation, as they were not to be got.

"We have had one lady, who wishes to be a companion, and who can ill-afford to wait, on our books more than six months," added this young person, who seemed a sort of female clerk in the office. "But would you not take a governess's situation ? "

"Perhaps I might," said Elizabeth dubiously.

"Where were you last ? " inquired the female clerk, and when she heard that Elizabeth had never been out in the world before, she shook her head.

"I fear no lady will think of you then," she said ; "but if you wish I will just put your name down, and we can see what we can do; but I cannot promise you anything." And so Elizabeth paid her fee, and tu ned away very much disheartened.

The register-office in the Edgware Road, where she next applied, was kept by a very different person to the quiet young clerk who superintended the one in Berner Street. Elizabeth's reason for applying here was that she had seen an advertisement from this office (the one in Edgware Road) in that morning's *Times*, for a lady required by a widower to chaperon his two young daughters, and travel with them abroad.

She therefore entered this office, where she found already waiting to see Mrs. Lessbrook, the principal, a faded, broken-down-looking lady, with a pale face, and but shabby garments wherewith to shelter her from the chill and cold.

Presently a bustling, red-faced, showy woman appeared, and sat down at the desk in the centre of the room, with an air of consequential authority.

"Which of you ladies is first ? " she asked, wiping her mouth in a manner highly suggestive of recent refreshment.

"Ah! you, ma'am" (this was to the faded lady, who now came forward). "Five shillings, then, is the fee, please, if your name is not previously on the books, which I think it is not."

The poor applicant drew out a shabby purse at these words, and laid the five shillings meekly on the desk.

"Thank you," said Mrs. Lessbrook, pocketing the money. "Now, ma'am, what can I do for you?"

"There was an advertisement from you, I think," said the faded lady, "in this morning's *Times*, about a gentleman who wants a chaperon for his two daughters—"

Mrs. Lessbrook held up her hands at these words with an amused smile.

"Well," she said, "you ladies all run after the widowers, I think. Do you know that advertisement was only inserted yesterday, and I have had already thirty applications. But, oh!" she added, looking at the poor woman before her, and shaking her head, "you woudn't do at all. This gentleman wants a showy, fine-looking woman—well-dressed—a lady in fact."

The faded face before her turned scarlet, but dire necessity overcoming pride, perhaps, she answered in a faltering tone,

"You see, I thought, as I was well-born—my father having been a clergyman—that I might have some chance."

"Oh! we've plenty of clergymen's daughters," said Mrs. Lessbrook carelessly. "But this gentleman wants really an attractive woman. You see, he gives such a high salary—eighty guineas, that he naturally expects something for it. Oh! no, you would not suit." And so, with a weary sigh, the poor would-be chaperon turned away.

Elizabeth had been an unwilling listener to this conversation, and as the drooping, faded figure passed out of the office Mrs. Lessbrook beckoned to her to approach the desk; eyeing and valuing, as women only eye and value, the handsome dress and rich seal-skin of her new applicant.

"Five shillings, if you please, madam," she said, "for your name to be entered on the books. Thank you," she added, as Elizabeth complied with her request. "Now, what can I do for you?"

"I also saw the advertisement that the lady who has just gone out spoke of," answered Elizabeth, her rich colour flushing to her face.

"What, the widower again!" exclaimed Mrs. Lessbrook, laughing. "Well, you, perhaps,"—and she looked scrutinisingly at Elizabeth's handsome face and fine figure,—"might do."

"Where have you been previously?" she then said. "And what references can you give?"

"I fear I have no references," faltered Elizabeth.

"No references!" eehoed Mrs. Lessbrook ın astonishment. "Then how *can* you expect—how *can* you apply for such a situation? This Mr. Tomkins, a wealthy Manchester gentleman, requires, of course, the highest references. He said, indeed, that he would prefer a lady from a titled family. Oh! to think of such a thing is absurd."

"Then have you any other situation vacant?" asked Elizabeth, gaining courage.

"None unless you have references," replied Mrs. Lessbrook, in a tone of severe virtue. "My office is of the highest respectability, and even before accomplishments, which are so essential now-a-days, I esteem *character*. I can have nothing to do with any one whose pa·t cannot bear the strictest investigations."

Could Elizabeth for a moment have raised the veil which hid the past of this most scrupulous lady, she would have seen a dusky drama, in which figured a performer, then bearing another name, but whose deeds no doubt are recorded in the awful Book of Truth against the highly respectable principal of the register-office for governesses and companions in Edgware Road. As, however, Divine eyesight is denied to us mortals, and we but behold thing; in heaven and things on earth "through a glass darkly," Elizabeth felt almost overwhelmed at the idea that *her past* was too miserable, and too blood-stained with guilty knowledge of her husband's crime, for her ever to face investigation of any kind; and so with trembling feet, and a bowed head, she left the presence of seeming virtue, and went out once more forlorn into the stranger-filled streets.

These were her first attempts to obtain employment in London, but she made many others, with like (though varied) ill-success. She was, in fact, totally unfit for the life that she was trying to begin; and at every register-office—even at one conducted under the superintendence of a truly benevolent lady—her want of references was (and justly) a complete stumbling block in her path.

It was in returning from one of these fruitless, and to her eminently painful efforts, that she again encountered Mr. Wilmot. She had been nearly a week in town when this happened, enduring as best she could the increasing discomforts of Mrs. O'Shee's establishment, and the bitter experience of finding herself alone and friendless in the world. As she entered Cambridge Street on this occasion, and was wearily proceeding to her rooms, her eyes suddenly fell on the tall spare form of her recent railway travelling-companion, who was then only a few yards distant from her. She tried to avoid his notice, but Mr Wilmot's acute hazel eyes had already recognised her, and he at once advanced to meet her.

She did not look up as she encountered him, but Mr. Wilmot

was not a man to be debarred from doing what he wished by trifles.

"Good morning," he said, "I am glad that I have met you."

"Good morning," answered Elizabeth, and would have passed on.

"Pardon me," continued Mr. Wilmot, "but there is something to interest you, is there not, in this paper, if you have not seen it?" And he drew as he spoke a copy of the *Times* from the pocket of his overcoat.

"What is it?" asked Elizabeth, with a beating heart.

"I cannot mistake the description, I think," continued Mr. Wilmot smiling. "No, *Miss Gordon*, there are few faces that. would answer to this," and he opened the paper, and pointing to a paragraph that it contained, held it towards Elizabeth.

It was headed "One Hundred Pounds Reward," and proceeded as follows :—

"A young married lady, having left her home in Uplandshire, on the 17th of the present month, the above reward will be given to any one who can offer sufficient information to lead to the discovery of her present residence. She is tall, straight, and well-formed, with thick dark hair worn plaited across her head, and falling low on her neck at the back. Her complexion is clear and dark, and her features singularly regular. Her eyes are large, dark, and brilliant, and she has a small light brown mole on her left wrist, and small shell-shaped ears, in which she generally wears heavy gold pendants, of foreign workmanship, in the design of an urn. She is about twenty-five years of age, and is supposed to have worn a black silk dress, and a long seal-skin jacket trimmed with a lighter fur when she left her home; and to have a black leather travelling-bag with her, on the brass plate of which is engraved her maiden name '*Elizabeth Gordon.*' Any person or persons who can give the required information are requested to call at Messrs. Bell and Barclay's, Gray's Inn, where they will receive the above reward."

"Well," said Mr. Wilmot, watching with an amused smile Elizabeth's changing colour and trembling hands as she read this paragraph, "shall I honestly earn a hundred pounds, and give the required information to Messrs. Bell and Barclay?"

"You do not know my address, sir," said Elizabeth quickly and indignantly looking up into his face.

"Do I not?" answered Mr. Wilmot still smiling. "I trust, Miss Gordon, you are in comfortable quarters at Mrs. O'Shee's, number——, Cambridge Street?"

"Then," said Elizabeth yet more indignantly, "you must have followed me?"

"I plead guilty," replied Mr. Wilmot. "Here is my excuse," and he laid his hand lightly on the paragraph in the paper containing Elizabeth's description.   "What man of taste would allow such a beautiful picture to pass away from his sight?"

For a moment Elizabeth was silent, and then she said in a voice of some emotion—

"Mr. Wilmot, I am alone in the world—I have no one to protect me—do you mean to tell them where I am?"

"My dear lady, for what do you take me? No, no, certainly not. For reasons best known to yourself you have left your home, and I presume your husband—but I shall not even ask you his name, though I could easily get what information I like by a visit to Gray's Inn. But I will not pay that visit. I shall only ask to be allowed the honour of the acquantance of—shall I say *Miss Gordon?*"

"But this woman," said Elizabeth nervously, "this Mrs. O'Shee, may see this advertisement—"

"She may, certainly, but it is not likely. The *Times* is not a paper generally read by her class.

"Still if she did—"

"Change your rooms then," said Mr. Wilmot quickly, "and that will prevent all danger.   I know some very nice ones—people who may be depended upon; and if you please I shall be proud to recommend them to your notice?"

"You are very good—"

"Nay," and the cold smile played again over Mr. Wilmot's cold lips, "I am only good to myself, for if you take these rooms, I shall again know where to find you."

These words recalled Elizabeth's almost scattered senses.

"You are very good." she said again, "but perhaps I had be..   where I am."

Mr. Wilmot looked at her curiously with his acute calm eyes.

"You mean to leave without telling me?"

"What if I did?" began Elizabeth; and then remembering her miserable position, she went on piteously, "Mr. Wilmot, if you are a gentleman, you will not molest or annoy a defenceless woman."

"No," he answered, "I will neither molest nor annoy you— but in return will you trust in me a little?"

"If you like," said Elizabeth falteringly. "But, Mr. Wilmot, it is better I should not see you—it is better that we should never meet."

"Why?"

"There are many reasons," answered Elizabeth earnestly, "ono of which is that I am seeking a situation—another that I am alone in the world."

"The very reason for making an acquaintance."

Elizabeth lifted her eyes sadly to his face, and shook her head

"You know the world," she said, "how apt it is to impute evil how slow to _elieve in good?   I ask you then as an honourable man not to expose me to its unjust suspicions.

"I know the world," answered Mr. Wilmot, slowly, " but I heed it not. The old story Miss—may I say Gordon?—of the man who painted a picture and asked each friend to put a blot on any spot which displeased him, until the whole canvas was destroyed by his various fault-finders, is a true representation of *it*. What is a fault in one person's estimation is a beauty in another's. Thus, if we were to hear the true opinion of friends, we should be all blots—our chief perfections would certainly seem faults to some. No, the world I care to court and live for, is my own pleasure."

"I can scarcely understand any one saying so," said Elizabeth.

"Not saying so, I believe, but you know many I am certain who do it."

"Perhaps," and Elizabeth's thoughts went back to Dick's selfish passion—to her own wasted and embittered life.

"Don't take me for a monster of iniquity though, pray," went on Mr. Wilmot with a light laugh, "because I am honest enough to tell you that when I want a thing I try to get it. It is every man's creed, Miss Gordon, only I profess it."

"But,"   said Elizabeth hesitatingly and blushing, "our keeping up our acquaintance with each other could do no good. I am a married woman as you know ; I am poor and unhappy."

"Yet you see I wish to keep your acquaintance, so I try for it,"   answered Mr. Wilmot with another smile. "But see,"   he added, quietly attracting Elizabeth's attention to a policeman who was attentively observing them, "yon man in blue with his official eye fixed on the tall, straight form described in the *Times*. The advertisement has no doubt been read in Scotland Yard this morning by many an anxious would-be winner of the hundred pounds. Let us circumvent this especial one though. Allow me to walk quietly by your side until we reach your rooms, and then permit me to enter the house with you, as if we both belonged to it? This will throw the fellow off the scent, for, believe me, he fancies that he is on the right track now."

Elizabeth looked at the policeman, and then at Mr Wilmot. The man was watching them, no doubt, and Elizabeth's heart sank within her at the prospect of discovery—at the dread of once more seeing Richard Horton.

"Come with me," she said faintly, and Mr. Wilmot quietly walked down the street by her side, saying in the coolest and easiest tone imaginable just as they passed the policeman.

"But it will be a horrid sell won't it, if it turns out to be scarlatina? It plays the very deuce you know with young children."

CHAPTER XIX.

IN SHEEP'S CLOTHING.

"THAT wasn't bad, was it?" he said with cool satisfaction at his own audacity, as they reached Mrs. O'Shee's door. "The man in blue believes no doubt at this moment, that we were speaking of some dear little Tommy or Johnny, sent to cheer our earthly pilgrimage with his enlivening screams."

Elizabeth did not speak. She was afraid and ashamed, and silently led the way upstairs to the drawing-room, the door having been opened by a dreadful old charwoman, with a huge rusty black bonnet on her head, Mrs. O'Shee having been yet unable to meet with a domestic to suit her after Mary's departure.

"This is a nice room," said Mr. Wilmot, calmly surveying Elizabeth's sitting-room after he had entered it.

"It looks so, perhaps," answered Elizabeth, "but it is not. They are most untidy people who have the house."

"Who are they?" asked Mr. Wilmot.

"The landlady says her husband is a clergyman, but—"

"Of course he is not. However, that is easily found out What is his name?"

"The Rev. Michael O'Shee."

"The Rev. Michael O'Shee," wrote Mr. Wilmot in his pocketbook. "I shall look the reverend gentleman up when I get to my rooms. I wonder if this same Michael belongs to the angelic host, or is of the dragon's crew, that the first Michael is supposed to have kicked out of heaven?"

"I think at all events that they are very strange people."

"There are a good many strange people in this neighbourhood. But what about this advertisement? I presume you don't wish any one to win the promised reward?"

"No, no, certainly not."

"Yet there is the greatest possible danger of some one doing so, if you go out dressed as you are into the streets. We may have check-mated one policeman, but how do we know that the lynx-eyes of another may not be cast upon you to-morrow?"

"What can I do?" said Elizabeth wearily, sitting down, and covering her face with her hand.

"I would say let me go and buy you some golden dye of the chemist at the corner of the street, only I cannot make up my mind to ask you to destroy the lovely hue of your hair. But I tell you what you can do—change your dress, and wear your hair differently. And, best of all, don't go out for the next week or so."

"But I must—I must seek employment."

"Pardon me—don't think me rude, but can I lend you any money? I will do so with the greatest possible pleasure."

"No, no," said Elizabeth starting up. "I have enough, quite enough—but I thank you."

"Pray don't. I only meant that having left your home, you might not foresee that you would require as much as no doubt you will, if you are seeking employment fit for a lady in this busy wilderness. Do not misunderstand me—I do not mean anything rude, but I mean can I do anything for you—can I help you in any way?"

"I fear not," said Elizabeth sadly, "but I thank you for your kindness."

"Then I will take my leave," said Mr. Wilmot, rising, for having gained his end, and obtained an entrance into Elizabeth's rooms, he was too acute to pay a long visit there. "Take my advice," he went on, "and don't go out for a day or two at least, and if I hear of any more inquiries I will let you know." And then, with characteristic coolness, he bowed and took his departure, leaving Elizabeth a prey to the most cruel anxiety.

From her melancholy reflections, however, she was speedily aroused by a visit from her landlady.

"Sure your friend is a foine tall man, me dear," said Mrs. O'Shee, having intruded herself into the room on the pretext of seeing if Elizabeth's fire were good. "He remoinds me of me own brother now—Capt. Fard of the Dublin Militia. Handsome Jack, the gurls used to call him in me young days, and they were dying in hundreds for luve of him, I can tell ye!"

"Indeed!" said Elizabeth.

"And hadn't he a woife of his own, the sly fellow, all the time too!" laughed Mrs. O'Shee "But he was the living image of the gintleman that's jest left ye; for I said to Mr. O'Shee as he passed the dining-room windows, 'Sure there's Jack's ghost, if iver a ghost was in a living body!'"

"He is almost a stranger to me," said Elizabeth coldly.

"Well, thin, I hope he won't remain one, for young people want amusing, and I think ye're but dull yerself at times, me dear?"

"I am in London on very serious business," answered Elizabeth.

"Whoy not consult Mr. O'Shee, thin? Though I say it meself who shouldn't, he's a clever man, though not so sharp as his neighbours. But for a troifing consideration he'll wind up yer affairs for ye in no time, so that ye'll not know them again yerself when ye see them."

Elizabeth could not help laughing at this, and at the grotesque little figure before her.

"And if it's a little dinner ye're wanting to entertain this gintleman with at ony time now ye've nothing to do but to give me the money, and I'll git it for ye. Ye've not a bad appetite

yerself, me dear, as I said to Mr. O'Shee, when yer dinner came
down yesterday. But I loike to see that—it's a good sign when
the mate doesn't git stale in the house."

In Mrs. O'Shee's there certainly did not seem any fear of such
an accident. Elizabeth was amazed when her week's bill came up
at the quantity of butcher's meat she appeared to have consumed.
A leg of mutton had totally disappeared after being served up
once, "for a tiresome little curly black dog," Mrs. O'Shee,
declared, had snatched it out of the pantry window before she
could turn herself round. Many visits the little curly dog had
apparently paid to the pantry window since; and it was only
the shrinking dread of going again among utter strangers, and
the idea that it would only be for a short time, that induced
Elizabeth to put up with the intense discomforts of Mrs. O'Shee's
apartments.

What annoyed her most was the constant intrusion into her
rooms by this prying Irishwoman. She always seemed to be
watching everything, and there was an uneasy shifty look in her
glance that was not very comfortable to encounter.

The Rev. Michael, Elizabeth never beheld, but on every
occasion Mrs. O'Shee appealed to his name. He was the lay
figure on which she hung her various ideas. It was "sure as Mr.
O'Shee was just saying," or "me husband now thinks" this or
that.

Mr. O'Shee was good enough to prophesy then that "yer
friend, the foine tall gentleman, the living image of me brother
Jack he is," would soon be back; and Elizabeth's annoyance,
therefore, was intense when, on the following afternoon, just as
the early winter evening was gathering in, Mrs. O'Shee herself
threw open the drawing-room door, and with a delighted air
announced Mr. Wilmot.

"Don't frown on me so dreadfully, please," said that gentleman, advancing towards Elizabeth, who was sitting moodily
brooding by the fire, and whose expression when she saw him
could not have been very gratifying to her visitor. "I would
not have come so soon, unless I had something to tell you."

"What is it?" said Elizabeth, rising, and with something of
her old grand manner pointing to a chair.

"It's been horribly cold to-day, hasn't it?" said Mr. Wilmot,
smiling.

"Yes," answered Elizabeth, wondering if he had come to
discuss the weather.

"I am a kind of walking barometer," went on Mr. Wilmot,
"every change of atmosphere affects me. Pardon me," he added,
and he suddenly rose and opened the room door, and discovered
as he did so, Mrs. O'Shee kneeling outside with her ear to the
key-hole!

For a moment the convicted listener was speechless, Mr.
Wilmot looking down upon her with a grim smile; but the next
her comical assurance returned.

"Sure I'd just popped down on me knees and was saying me
prayers," said Mrs. O'Shee, "as well I moight, seeing it's too
soon to light the gas, and begin ony useful employment."

"Pray allow me to assist you to rise, madam," said Mr.
Wilmot, "and conduct you to some more convenient spot to
conclude your devotions."

"Ah! now ye're very obliging, sir," replied Mrs. O'Shee,
skipping to her feet with the assistance of the hand that Mr.
Wilmot extended to her. "Sure, as I told me young friend here,
ye're the living image of me dear brother—a tall, foine, handsome
man he was, just loike yerself, and all the ladies in luve with him
wherever he went."

"I have not his happy experience then, madam," said Mr.
Wilmot, gravely.

"Ah, it's just shy ye are on yer own mirits," answered the
wretched little woman, simpering and giggling. "A fair lady ye
know, not far from us at this minit, thinks so, too, I'll be
bound."

"Perhaps I may be shy," replied Mr. Wilmot with unmoved
countenance, "but pray, do not allow me to interrupt your
twilight devotions any longer. I shall have much pleasure in
seeing you go downstairs."

"And so I shall, thin," said Mrs. O'Shee. "Me poor husband,
indeed, will be wondering what's detaining me here," and with
a little nod the unabashed lady disappeared.

"After all," said Mr. Wilmot, shutting the door, and returning to the spot where Elizabeth was standing, "the human
countenance is a sad tale-teller. Mrs. O'Shee opened the door
for me, and I instantly detected that she would listen to our
conversation."

"It is disgraceful," answered Elizabeth.

"It would have been annoying certainly if she had overheard
what I came to say," went on Mr. Wilmot, "for I regret to
tell you that I bring bad news."

<hr>

CHAPTER XX.
A THIEF IN THE HOUSE.

As Mr. Wilmot said these words, Elizabeth turned deadly faint
and pale, and leant her hand upon the table for support.

"What!" she said, "they have not surely—"

"My dear lady, no," said Mr. Wilmot, quickly, "it's nothing
dreadful—do not alarm yourself, I pray?"

"What have you heard, then?" asked Elizabeth, slightly
recovering herself.

"But this—you remember our meeting yesterday our friend in blue, and my warning you that he was taking notes of your appearance?"

"Yes."

"Well, when I left your rooms, I again encountered our blue-bottle, and the fellow had the assurance to address me."

"What did he say?" asked Elizabeth hastily.

"'Sir,' he said, 'Excuse me, but that lady you were with—'What lady?' I inquired, and I flatter myself that I looked perfectly innocent. 'The tall lady in black with a seal-skin jacket,' went on the man in blue, 'with whom you went into No.——, Cambridge Street.'"

"He must have watched us, then," said Elizabeth.

"No doubt. 'The lady in black,' I repeated after him, to go on with our conversation, 'why, that's my wife.'"

"How dare you say such a thing, Mr. Wilmot?" interrupted Elizabeth indignantly.

"You must forgive me, but I said it to spare you annoyance, for the fellow's face fell, and his manner changed instantly after this announcement. 'Oh! I beg your pardon, sir,' he said, 'but you see there's bills out, and a reward offered for the discovery of some lady who has left her home, and I fancied the lady that you were with answered exactly to her printed description.'"

Elizabeth here gave a restless movement, and sighed deeply.

"Well," continued Mr. Wilmot, calmly, "upon this I smiled, well-pleased, in the fellow's face. 'It can't be my wife at any rate,' I said, 'for she has not left her home, but is with me in London for a short visit; so I fear, my good friend, you won't earn your reward this time.'"

"And he believed you?" asked Elizabeth, her face flushing deeply.

"I hope he believed me," answered Mr. Wilmot, "But now, if my fair wife will pardon my saying so, you see the situation is serious."

Elizabeth looked angrily up at this.

"There is not a policeman in London at this minute I've no doubt," went on Mr. Wilmot, quietly, "whose eyes are not greedily searching for the 'tall figure in black,' and the 'seal-skin jacket trimmed with a lighter fur;' so that if you really wish to escape detection, you must use disguise and wear a very thick veil indeed, over the 'singularly regular features,' and the 'large dark eyes,'" And Mr. Wilmot smiled his peculiar smile as he concluded his sentence.

"It is a miserable position—I do not know what to do," said Elizabeth despondingly.

"Well, for one thing, change your dress; for another, deign to accept from your humble servant this wig of golden curls, which the hair-dresser assured me is arranged in the first fashion."

And Mr. Wilmot drew a parcel from his pocket as he spoke, and presented it to Elizabeth.

"What is it?" she said

"A wig," he answered, with affected gravity. "I asked for a young head of hair suitable to a beautiful face, so you must not despise it."

Elizabeth pushed the parcel away with a weary gesture.

"No, but truly," said Mr. Wilmot earnestly, "you must assume some disguise. I have taken another liberty—I have ordered to be sent to your rooms a waterproof dress, which will, I believe, completely change your appearance."

"Well, that might do something," said Elizabeth, rising. "You must allow me to pay for this dress—how much am I in your debt?"

"Not for the world!" exclaimed Mr. Wilmot eagerly; but Elizabeth had already left the room, going into her bed-room, which was through the drawing-room, for the purpose of opening her black leather bag, in which she kept her purse.

She did so, and put her hand in the dark, on the place where she expected to find it, and to her horror it was not there! "It must have slipped further down," she thought the next minute, and she carried her bag into the sitting-room, which was partly lit by the fire-light.

"Will you light the gas?" she said to Mr. Wilmot. "I have mislaid my purse."

He at once obeyed her, and Elizabeth again opened her bag, plunging her hand here and there, amongst the contents, but all to no purpose, for the purse was gone!

"It must have been stolen," said Elizabeth, sharply, pale with fear and excitement. "I saw it before I went out yesterday—it had fifteen pounds in it—I am sure it was there."

"Permit me to look at the lock of the bag," said Mr. Wilmot.

"Yes," he went on, after he had carefully examined it, "this lock has been trifled with—various keys apparently tried in it. Our good friend, Mrs. O'Shee, is no doubt the richer by fifteen pounds since yesterday morning. But I trust this loss will be no serious inconvenience to you?"

"But it is—it will," said Elizabeth nervously. How serious she did not tell him, but she knew that her whole worldly wealth now consisted of ten pounds, if this money were lost. She had put these two last five pound notes at the very bottom of her bag, among the few letters that she had carried from home; and these two notes, with trembling hands, she now produced from their resting place, and as Mr. Wilmot's eyes marked her ill-concealed agitation, a sinister smile stole over his hard and selfish mouth.

"What do I owe you?" said Elizabeth.

"Nothing," answered Mr. Wilmot, briefly. "But don't you think that we owe our friend Mrs. O'Shee something? Suppose we have her up, and tell her of your loss while I am here?"

"Very well," said Elizabeth, and so Mr. Wilmot rang the bell and presently Mrs. O'Shee appeared at the door; her face turning deadly pale the moment that her eyes fell on the open bag.

"Mrs. O'Shee, my purse has been taken from this bag," said Elizabeth. "I am certain it was here yesterday morning."

"Yer purse!" repeated Mrs. O'Shee, in very tremulous accents. "Taken from yer bag—and in me house!"

"Yes, I am certain," said Elizabeth sharply. "It was a brown seal-skin purse. I had it in my hand yesterday morning, before I started for Regent Street, for I opened it then to take out ten shillings to pay for my journey."

"Thin it just slipped out of yer moind now, but ye've put it into yer pocket, and yer pocket's been picked," said Mrs. O'Shee, recovering her colour and her courage. "Did ye go in one of them busses? As I say to Mr. O'Shee, all the thieves in London travel in them, I belave."

"Do you ever honour them, Mrs. O'Shee." asked Mr. Wilmot, his acute eyes fixed steadily on her face the while, and the little woman writhed and twisted uneasily under his gaze.

"Sure, thin, I do sometimes," answered Mrs. O'Shee, "for what can a poor clorgyman's wife do—for the clorgy have so many calls."

"No doubt—charitable and otherwise. So your husband is in the Church, Mrs. O'Shee?"

"The worse luck!" answered the little Irishwoman.

"He should see that the clergy list is mended then," went on Mr. Wilmot, "for his name appeareth not in its pages."

"Not me husband's name in the clorgy list!" exclaimed Mrs. O'Shee, holding up her hands. "Oh! me dear sir, you must have seen an erroneous edition!"

"No doubt. And now about this purse, Mrs. O'Shee. It would be as well, wouldn't it, to send for a policeman?"

"Oh! ye mustn't think of such a thing, me dear sir," said Mrs. O'Shee in real alarm "Jest thing of the scandal—the police in a clorgyman's house! Oh! me poor husband would faint at the soight of one. If me young friend here has really lost the money, well, I'd rather replace it—at least some of it, than let any discredit fall on me house."

"Well, see how much you can raise," said Mr Wilmot coolly, "while I consult this lady about sending for a policeman." And at these words Mrs. O'Shee ran out of the room in a flutter.

"A policeman wouldn't do, you know," said Mr. Wilmot, in a low tone to Elizabeth, as soon as he had closed the door behind the landlady's retreating figure. "But take what she brings— she stole the purse—about that there's no possible doubt."

"I think so, too," answered Elizabeth.

"I don't think, I'm sure. The little devil deserves to go to Newgate, but for our own purposes we must let her escape."

"Yes, but I cannot stay here."

"Would it not be wise for the present?" said Mr. Wilmot.

"This woman can be bribed or intimidated—she has fairly committed herself in our eyes, and is not likely to court the attention of the police just now."

At this moment Mrs. O'Shee rushed back into the room holding a little china casket in her hand.

"Look, me dear, this is me money-box," she said opening it. "All I have on the arth—and it's little indeed—I keep locked away here. What have ye lost did ye say?"

"Fifteen pounds," replied Elizabeth.

"Fifteen pounds!" repeated Mrs. O'Shee, casting up her eyes. "Sure in all the wide world I haven't such a sum of me own!"

"That I believe," said Mr. Wilmot laconically.

"Ah! ye belave me, thin?" said the little woman, turning sharply round and looking at him.

"With reservations," replied Mr. Wilmot.

"Well, it's true for ye, thin! Look, me dear," she continued, addressing Elizabeth, here are all me little savins. Seven golden sovereigns—so I ask ye—with every wish for ye to have back yer own, which of us can best spare the coin?"

"I can ill spare it at any rate," said Elizabeth.

"Well, thin, I'll tell ye what I'll do now," went on Mrs O'Shee. "I'll keep ye free of charge for a fortnight? Will that content ye? It's an offer I wouldn't make to a livin' soul but yerself, only I'm that fond of ye, I look upon ye as me own choild."

"Would you not rather have the money back, Miss Gordon?" asked Mr. Wilmot.

"I do not know what to say," answered Elizabeth.

"I've no doubt in me own moind," said Mrs. O'Shee, "that yer pocket was picked. Still, as ye've had this loss in me house, I will do what I say—make no charge for these iligant rooms for a whole fortnight; and if that doesn't content ye I really cannot tell ye what will!"

"I shall consider about it," said Elizabeth. "I will tell you what I have decided upon to-morrow."

"Do thin, me dear, and I'll lave ye now to consult with yer friend!" And with a relieved smile on her covetous little face, and a flourish of her miserable little hand, Mrs. O'Shee left the room.

"Leave the door open, Mrs O'Shee," called Mr. Wilmot after her, "so that we may have the honour of seeing you, if the spirit of devotion should again come over you,"

"Ah! it's me saying me prayers, ye're thinking of!" laughed

the Irishwoman, looking back with a roguish leer in her faded eyes. "Sure, ye remoind me of me brother Jack! 'Ah!' he used to say, 'ye ladies pray enough for us all;' and the handsome rogue niver his troubled himself with bending his knees."

"Really," said Mr. Wilmot repressively; and then as Mrs. O'Shee disappeared, he went on. "That is a strange specimen of humanity, is it not, Miss Gordon? She lies without reason— she steals without art."

"She is a dreadful woman," said Elizabeth.

"She is a mistake," said Mr. Wilmot, "for she lacks the qualities of a successful rogue. She is a bungler, with just a touch of native humour to add to her eccentricities. "But," he continued gravely, "take my advice, and for the present remain with her. For her own sake she will keep quiet—and you want quietness."

"Yes."

"Don't pay her for her rooms, of course. She knows well enough that we know that she has stolen the money, and that very knowledge will keep her from further depredations. I noticed," he went on, "that you have removed the plate from your bag, on which your name was engraved?"

"Yes, I did it the second day that I was in London."

"The day after you came here? Ah, but still the sharp twinkling eyes of the old woman downstairs, no doubt, had read it. Where did you put it when you took it off?"

"In my bag—the only place I have that would lock."

"But my lady's pilfering fingers have been in the bag, you see. Is it there now?"

Elizbeth looked, and then drew the engraved brass plate out, and handed it to Mr. Wilmot.

"Let me have this," he said, "and I will pitch it into the Serpentine as I cross the Park."

"Thank you; but will it not trouble you to do so?"

"Not in the least But now I will take my leave. So you won't even look at my golden wig?"

"No, no."

"'The golden locks of Anna,'" said Mr. Wilmot scoffingly, pocketing his parcel.

"And about this waterproof—this dress," said Elizabeth, rising, and lifting up one of her last five pound notes, "how much was it?"

"It was one pound," answered Mr. Wilmot, smiling.

"Then—" said Elizabeth, offering him a note.

"But I have no change."

"You can get change," continued Elizabeth.

"Very well," said Mr. Wilmot, and he took the note, and then offered his hand to Elizabeth. May I bring the change to-morrow?" he asked.

"Oh, any time," replied Elizabeth; and Mr. Wilmot smiled again, for he had thus got leave to pay another visit to Elizabeth.

He closed the door behind him as he left the room, and having proceeded downstairs, rapped gently at the sitting-room door, which opened into the passage, and in a moment the sharp, eager face of Mrs. O'Shee appeared.

"Madam," he said in a whisper into the woman's ear. "I should like to have a few minutes' conversation with you this evening, at eighto'clock, if you will so far oblige me, in the adjoiningsquare ? "

Mrs. O'Shee turned pale. "Ye don't mane now," she said. "Ye are not going to git me into any trouble surely now are ye—if it's about—"

"*It is something to your advantage,*" answered Mr. Wilmot, in an emphatic whisper, and Mrs. O'Shee looked into his face and nodded her head.

"Sure I'll be there," she said; and then without another word Mr. Wilmot went away.

CHAPTER XXI.

AN OLD FRIEND.

"Come unto me, all ye that labour and are heavy laden and I will give you rest."

These words were spoken on a Sunday night, a few days after the foregoing conversation had taken place, in a West-End church, in one of the most aristocratic squares in London. The preacher was a worn, pale man, with a dark, sallow, lined face, irradiated however by a light which sprang from no earthly source. When listening to his simple eloquence, when looking into his solemn, soul-lit eyes, you realized what inspiration meant, and heard, in the words of man, the divine message of God.

But no fiery prophet as of old, lifting up his voice in the wilderness, and pouring forth denunciations of wrath and woe was here. This man of God told not of cities which were to pass away, of pomp to be brought down into the grave, of vengeance when the Lord of Hosts put out his hand, and would not turn it back.

Between him and these ancient messengers stood a divine figure—thorn-crowned, and with bleeding hands and feet, the Saviour of the world, in words of love and pardon, invited through this servant, all to come unto Him.

"Many of you no doubt are weary and heavy laden, my brethren," said the preacher, "for burdens of sin, of circumstance, of age and sorrow, are the lot common unto man. But for these world-wearying diseases, we are given a divine antidote—we are told, 'Come unto me.'"

There was one sorrowful listener at least to these words, whose

burden seemed to her at that moment too heavy for her to bear.
This was Elizabeth. During the last few days indeed she had
given way to the deepest despondency, and again and again
had been tempted to cry out in the pathetic language of scripture, "My soul is weary of my life."

There comes a time to most of us, does there not, when we
feel too tired and disheartened to go on with our earthly journey?
These days of weaknesses—these hours when the soul sickens
at the earth-weight laid upon it—are no doubt common to us all.
But there are natures in which the fibre is so fine, the perceptions so keen, the tragic elements so strong, that the spirit
faints beneath the blows which the more densely constituted
among us learn in time indifferently to bear.

Unused to poverty, unaccustomed to the sharp experience
which dims the eye and fades the cheek of many a sensitive and
well-born woman, Elizabeth had endured each day since her
arrival in London a moral martyrdom. She was growing
absolutely afraid, too, of the cool, calm stranger, Edgar Wilmot;
for only on the day before the evening on which we find her
sitting listening to the earnest almost passionate words of the
preacher in the church at Eaton Square, he had with quiet
deliberation informed her that he had been at the office of
Messrs. Bell and Barclay to make inquiries concerning her.

"I have a confession to make to you," he said, looking at her
intently, during a visit that he had ostensibly paid her to return
the change out of her five pound note; "something that I feel
terribly ashamed of."

"What is it?" asked Elizabeth.

"My interest in you has grown so strong," went on Mr.
Wilmot in his cool way, "that I absolutely invaded yesterday
the dusty precincts of Messrs. Bell and Barclay's chambers in
Gray's Inn."

"You did not surely—" said Elizabeth looking up.

"Betray you? No, no—but it was mean of me I admit. I
wished only to know your real name."

"And did you learn it?" asked Elizabeth with a curling lip.

"I did. I know now that I have the honour of speaking to
Mrs. Richard Horton of Wendell West-house, in Uplandshire."

Elizabeth turned pale and then red. "It was unmanly,
ungentlemanly." she said. "I did not seek your acquaintance—
I have not sought it—you might at least have left me alone."

"I might, I acknowledge," replied Mr. Wilmot, "but you
see I did not. You attracted me as the light attracts the moth,
so I fluttered and fell."

Elizabeth was silent—in act she was too indignant to speak.

"But on my honour I did you no harm," continued Mr.
Wilmot; "nay, I would cut my throat, and it's excessively dear

to me, before I would give you a moment's pain of any sort—
especially before I would betray your whereabouts to Mr.
Richard Horton."

"Oh! don't speak his name," said Elizabeth in a low tone
of horror.

"I will do so no more. You are Miss Gordon to me now, and
always—and I flatter myself I succeeded effectually in throwing
a handful of dust in the face of the very would-be sharp gentleman whom I had the honour of speaking to about you, and who
I understand bears the name of Mr. Barclay."

"What did he say?"

"I sent in my card, and was received with great politeness.
'Sir,' I said, ' I have called because I saw an advertisement in
the *Times* this morning, relating to a young married lady,
who has deserted her home in Uplandshire.'"

"'Exactly,' said the lawyer, rubbing his hands with a
delighted grin, 'a sad case—'"

"'And I wish,' I continued, 'to restore if I can this fugitive
wife to her despairing husband; but I do not wish—you will see
by my card that I am not in a position—to accept the offered
reward.'"

"'Oh ! I'm sure, my dear sir,' replied Mr. Barclay, rubbing
his hands yet more violently; 'Oh! of course, we cannot expect
that a gentleman—quite a gentleman like yourself—would
accept a trifle like this; but if you can give us any information,
it will be gratefully—most gratefully received.'"

"'Well, then,' I said, 'the day before yesterday, I was in
Edinburgh. I was standing looking at Scott's monument—
leaning in fact on the railing outside the enclosure round it,
when a lady passed me.'"

"'Ah, indeed,'" said the lawyer."

"'A lady so remarkably handsome,' I continued, 'that I
turned to look after her—nay, could not resist the temptation of
following her, which I did all along Princess Street, passing her
twice as I did so, and looking into her face.'"

"'Ha, ha, ha !' chuckled Mr. Barclay at this gentlemanly
piece of information, 'quite a case I declare.'"

"'It was,' I answered, with unmoved countenance, 'but
whether the lady did not approve of my too impulsive gallantry,
or whether she saw I was observing her, and wished in her
present fugitive position to escape notice—at all events she
beckoned to the driver of one of the open carriages loitering
about for hire, and in a few minutes, to my great disappointment,
was driven out of my sight.'"

"'But my dear sir,' said the lawyer, fidgeting, and with a
slightly-disappointed air, 'how could you tell she was the lady
our client wishes to discover?'"

" ' She was tall and dark,' I answered, ' with beautiful features, and large, brilliant, and expressive eyes.   She wore a long sealskin jacket, trimmed with a lighter fur, and last, not least—for I am a judge of ears—hers were small and shell-shaped, and in them she wore heavy gold pendants in the design of an urn, evidently of Roman workmanship.' "

" ' Ha ! that looks like business,' said Mr. Barclay.   ' To tell you the truth, Mr. Wilmot, we are employing detectives in this matter, and I believe the husband of the lady would double the reward if he could hear of her whereabouts.' "

" ' Let him look in the land of the Gael, then,' I said, ' for this beautiful woman was no doubt the day before yesterday a visitor to Auld Reekie.   Is the husband a young man ?' "

"Then followed, *Miss Gordon*, what I shall spare you—the story of your parentage, your marriage, and your sudden and mysterious elopement from your home on the night of the seventeenth of December, when I had the pleasure of forming your acquaintance.   Mr. Barclay grew first communicative, and then friendly.   He related the particulars of a visit that—I must for once say the name—Mr. Richard Horton, the husband, and Mr. Robert Horton, the brother-in-law, had paid him about a week ago.   They brought an introduction from an old client of the firm, Sir John Tyrell, of Wendell Hall, who a'so seems to have been interested in your disappearance ; and he was pleased to say that his firm had done business also for my late respected parent, and that therefore he could thoroughly trust me."

"Oh ! they will find me," said Elizabeth, "they will find me !" and she put her hand over her face, deeply agitated at Mr. Wilmot's narration.

"Not if you are wise," said Mr. Wilmot; "not if you will do me the honour to trust in me."

"And Sir John Tyrell—what about Sir John ?" asked Elizabeth.

"He had written to Barclay about you, expressing great interest in your welfare, and this letter these two Hortons had brought with them to town by way of an introduction, I suppose.   I have met Sir John Tyrell," continued Mr. Wilmot.   "I have met him at my brother's place, Langley Park —you know that is the next county to Uplandshire."

"What ! Lord Langley's place ?" asked Elizabeth.

"Yes—the late Lord was what Mr. Barclay called my respected parent, and the present Lord is, of course, my brother. I remember a great deal of talk when I was down there a year ago, about the son of this very Sir John Tyrell having been found murdered.   They said—"

"What ?" asked Elizabeth, in a voice of sharp agony, as Mr.

Wilmot paused for a moment, for his eyes had noted the sudden contraction of her face at his allusion to Harry Tyrell's death.

"More y," went on Mr. Wilmot slowly, for he was thinking what could be the cause of Elizabeth's agitation, "what a good thing it was for Jasper Tyrell, the second son. I know him—a handsome fellow who used to be in the navy. Did you know him?"

"Yes!" faltered Elizabeth; "we were neighbours."

"Ah!" said Mr. Wilmot, more thoughtfully still.

"I—I—knew poor Harry, too," continued Elizabeth, "knew them all. It was a terrible thing."

"Not for Jasper," said Mr Wilmot lightly "But it was never discovered who did it, was it?"

"No," answered Elizabeth, in a low tone, "never."

"Some fellow has cheated the hangman, then. But, confess now, have I done you any harm by my visit to Gray's Inn? Mind, I do not say I should have gone, but will you pardon my curiosity for the sake of all the lies that I have told on your behalf?"

"I—I —have no choice," said Elizabeth. "Only don't betray me, Mr. Wilmot," she went on passionately. "I will throw myself into the river, rather than return to Richard Horton."

"You shall not return to Richard Horton, if I can help it," said Mr. Wilmot emphatically, and then, presently, he took up his hat and went away.

It was after this interview that Elizabeth's spirit felt so utterly crushed and broken down. She dared not go out to seek employment; her money was fast passing away; and, without any fault of her own, she had become almost completely in the power of a bold, daring, and designing man.

"Oh, Jasper! oh, Jasper!" she thought, despondingly, as she sat in the dusk after Mr. Wilmot had left her; and a vague idea entered her unhappy heart. "Shall I die," she thought; "write to him and die—tell him I could not live my life—that my burden was greater than I could bear?"

Aimlessly, unsettled, and wretched, she had wandered out on the following Sunday night, and closely followed by Mrs. O'Shee (who had her order from Mr. Wilmot to that effect), had strolled into the church in Eaton Square, where a well-known and eloquent preacher was telling, in earnest and soul-felt language, a crowded congregation of the gracious promises of God.

"You know, my friends, it is *for ever and ever*," said this preacher, looking upwards in one part of his sermon, his thrilling voice speaking to each listener's heart; "not for years—not for what we esteem a long lifetime, seventy or eighty years, but through an eternity of untold, countless ages to come. Through these your happiness or misery depends now on how you resist the passing temptations of *Time*."

Elizabeth thought of the river as these words reached her ears—of the cold dark river gliding past its embankments, where she had dreamed of ending her misery—where she had thought she would like to die, because her burden seemed too heavy for her to bear.

I will not go on with the passionate and God-inspired arguments with which the good man who was preaching endeavoured that night to win souls from the passing pleasures, the wearing anxieties, and the often bitter miseries of the world. He painted in glowing colours the glories which he almost seemed to see on High. The loftiest ambition, he said, that a man could aspire for was *there*. Then he touched on Death—the inevitable moment to every living thing; the gate to the everlasting life beyond—the turning point for good or evil which could have no end.

Elizabeth covered her face in shame and humiliation as he went on. For the first time she seemed to realize what an awful gulf death was, and how unprepared she had been to cross the dark waters from whence there is no return.

She listened eagerly to each word which fell from the preacher's lips; and when in sweet and touching accents he bid them farewell—praying that the peace which the world giveth not might come to them, and the Light that lightens the darkness through the bitterest storms of Life, Elizabeth bowed her head, and it seemed to her as if some of the Benediction fell upon her—as if the good man's words were heard and answered from on High.

Long she knelt while the large congregation poured past her down the aisles, and then she lifted her head and joined the crowd, her eyes fixed vacantly and indifferently before her. Suddenly, however—in a moment—they fell on the tall, slight figure of a man, who was some little distance in advance of her, and had, indeed, almost reached the entrance of the church when she noticed him. She started and coloured violently as she did so, for there was something familiar to her in the shape of the head, in the crisp, closely cut, brown hair; and as she bent eagerly forward, to obtain a better view of him, the man turned his head, and she saw his face—the familiar, never-to-be-forgotten face of Jasper Tyrell.

***

CHAPTER XXII.
"LOVE'S NOT TIME'S FOOL."

ELIZABETH almost gave a cry when she made this recognition, and the next moment she endeavoured vainly to force her way through the crowd, so as to overtake him. This, however, she found to be anything but an easy undertaking. One stately dowager looked round at her with astonishment as she accidentally pressed

against her arm.   Another aristocratic dame eyed, with unmiti-
gated contempt, her unmannerly efforts to push herself forward ;
and as Elizabeth did so, with her strained eyes fixed on Jasper
Tyrell's retreating form, he vanished from her sight, and, probably,
the next minute, had passed out into the square.

St ll Elizabeth struggled on, though some moments necessarily
elapsed before she could reach the outer door, and just as she
did so, she felt her arm grasped, and turning quickly round, saw
the sharp, little eager face of Mrs. O'Shee by her side.

"Me dear! now it's jest providence thet I saw ye," said the
Irishwoman.   "Sure it's so agreeable to us both to walk home
with each other!   Now that's a foine preacher, don't ye think,
though for my part I loike a discourse on more agreeable subjects."

"Let me go, Mrs. O'Shee," said Elizabeth, impatiently, shaking her arm loose from her landlady's detaining grasp.   "I thought
I saw a friend on before—I wish to go on alone."

"Sure, me dear, I'll not hurt ye though," said Mrs. O'Shee ;
but Elizabeth ran past her, and the next moment was in the
square.

Which way to turn was her next thought, which way ?   Alas !
she must have taken the wrong one, or in the crowd issuing
from the church she must have missed Jasper Tyrell, for vainly
she hurried forward—vainly followed some tall figure that for a
moment, in the dark, she believed was her old lover.   All round
the square she went, breathless, disheartened ; peering into this
face or that, but she could see no Jasper.   He was gone, and
she had been so near him, was her first thought; her next, as
tears of disappointment and pain rose in her eyes, was wiser.
"It is well—it is better," she said beneath her breath ; and
exhausted, faint, and pale, she crept back to her rooms, the
pleasant handsome face of Jasper Tyrell haunting her as she
went.

The next day Mr. Wilmot called again, and though Elizabeth
had requested Mrs. O'Shee to say she was engaged if any one
did so, he was again admitted.

"And so you want to shut your doors on me ?" he said with
some anger in his voice, after his first salutations were over.

"I am not well," answered Elizabeth wearily.   "I am tired—
and—"

"Unhappy ?   Is it not so ?" asked Mr. Wilmot.

"You know part of my history," replied Elizabeth, "and that
is a sufficient answer."

"But I don't want you to be unhappy.   I should like to amuse
and cheer you.   Suppose you come with me to-night and see a
new piece, which is well worth seeing, at the Gaiety ?"

"No, certainly not."

K

"But why?"

"For many reasons—do not ask me,—I will not go."

Mr. Wilmot was silent for a few moments after this, then he said, "Why are you so persistently unkind to me?"

"I do not mean to be so," answered Elizabeth, "but you must see—you must know—"

"That because you are a woman, and I am a man, that we cannot be friends? I neither see nor know it, and I hope some day to convert you to my views."

"Have you heard anything more?" said Elizabeth, anxious to change the conversation.

"Nothing—the advertisement is still in the *Times* though."

Elizabeth sighed deeply, and was silent.

"I came to-day to say good-bye," went on Mr. Wilmot the next moment. "To-morrow, as I suppose you know, being the first day of, probably, rather a dreary new year, the civilized world thinks fit to observe it as a holiday, and I am expected to join an undoubtedly dreary family party at Langley, and to take a present down for the infant heir, whom I naturally love so deeply, for making his appearance in this sublunary scene, and thus cutting me entirely out of all chance of the family inheritance."

"I forgot even that it was New Year's Day," said Elizabeth, with another sigh.

"Well, it is, unhappily, and for the next week or so I shall be out of town. Shall I find you here when I return?"

"I really do not know."

"Well, will you write to me? At least if you are in any trouble, will you let me know? See, I will leave my address." And he drew out a card, wrote a few words in pencil on it, and laid it on the table.

"That will find me," he continued, "and so if these gentlemen from Scotland Yard alarm you—or if, in fact, you have any misadventure, send me one line, and the hour that I get it I will return to town."

"You are very good—but—"

"Please do not say but—when I come back I hope to see much more of you—and don't—will you not quite forget me when I am away?"

"Mr. Wilmot, do not talk thus."

"Very well, you see I obey you in everything—I mean only to live to obey you." And after a few more such speeches, Mr. Wilmot went away, leaving Elizabeth perfectly determined to quit Mrs. O'Shee's house before his return.

"I will go to some attic, rather than stay here," she thought, "I will not have this man coming here. He thinks I am in his power, but when he comes back he shall find me gone."

Then came the miserable consideration of want of means. Elizabeth's funds were very low by this time, and Mr. Wilmot guessed this fact, and therefore made sure that she could not escape. He was a bold, bad, determined man, and Elizabeth's beautiful face had roused a very powerful feeling in his heart. Her very coldness to his advances only piqued his vanity, and he had easily purchased Mrs. O'Shee's connivance. She had orders to let him know all her lodger's movements, and the wretched little Irishwoman was only too glad to obey him. To do her justice, she did not know Elizabeth's real position as he did, but she was grasping, covetous, and very poor. Mr. Wilmot believed, therefore, that he had meshed Elizabeth in a web that she could not break through—but he knew not, and guessed not, of a very deep and overpowering affection, which rendered her alike indifferent to his admiration, and guarded her as securely from such love as his, as if she were sheltered in the happiest home.

He left town, therefore, and Elizabeth breathed more freely after he was gone. She determined to take any situation (even a menial one) to escape entirely from his acquaintance, and put down her name in two register offices; telling the superintendent at both places, that she would accept anything that she would give her.

So, amid trouble, wearing anxiety, and approaching destitution, the new year was born for our beautiful Elizabeth. Oh! these anniversaries! Coming whether we wish them or not—coming in times of joy and times of woe—coming to the lessening circle, to divided lives, to lonely, solitary, and neglected lots! Yet the effort still is made—the sprig of holly perhaps bought, the gala day kept, when all the rest is changed.

Even Mrs. O'Shee made an attempt at festivity to welcome the New Year. She adorned the vases on Elizabeth's mantelpiece with three little sprigs of dusty artificial holly, which apparently had figured for long years in one of her own queer little bonnets. She expatiated on the glories of the New Year's Days when she was a "gurl, in me father's house now," and how they had feasted, danced, and made love until "it was nearly the end of us, I declare," and she finally invited Elizabeth to partake of a slice of beef from "me own table, and a prime one I promise ye it shall be."

Elizabeth, however, declined the proffered hospitality. All alone she sat through the day, her thoughts dwelling with intense regret and longing on the past. That momentary glimpse of Jasper Tyrell's face seemed to have brought everything back to her in more vivid reality. She who was to have been his wife—for whose sake she had accepted a lot more bitter to her than death—had seen him once more; and struggle with the feeling as she might, she longed, oh! how ardently, how passionately, to see him again.

She caught herself watching the faces of the passing strangers in the streets—turning her head eagerly this way and that, as she went on her dreary, bread-seeking journeys. Yet she was conscious that, probably, even if he did see her now, that he would not recognise her, for she dare not go about London without being, as she imagined, completely disguised. She had changed the mode of arranging her hair, wore the waterproof dress, and had discarded her gold earrings, and, indeed, everything that could lead to her identification. She wore also a thick black gauze veil over her face, and altogether her appearance was effectually altered.

Yet a day came—one of those days never again forgotten—when she once more met Jasper Tyrell. She had been to Praed Street, and had returned by the underground railway, and was in the act of delivering up her ticket to the collector at Victoria station, when a cab passed her closely, and in it she saw seated Jasper Tyrell.

"Jasper," she said aloud, on the spur of the moment; "Jasper!" And he looked round, heard his name repeated, and put up his umbrella to indicate to the driver of the cab to stop; and pale, breathless, almost wordless, Elizabeth went to its side.

For a moment he did not know her, but asked, looking at her, "Did you call me? I thought I heard my name?"

"Jasper," said Elizabeth again, and that was all; but the next instant he sprang from the cab, and was by her side.

"Lissa," he said, clasping her hand, "Lissa, you he.e—and *thus?*"

"I wish no one to know me," she faltered. "I wish not to be seen."

"Let me help you into the cab then," he said. "Tell me there what all this means, how I find you here alone."

Without a word Elizabeth obeyed him, and then, as Jasper seated himself by her side, he again clasped her hand.

"Put an end to this mystery, Lissa," he said, "this wretched inexplicable mystery. Why did you leave me, and now why have you left your husband?"

But the long strain on Elizabeth's nerves, the shock of thus unexpectedly meeting him again, and the sight of his beloved face, had completely upset her, and she leant back in the cab, and began sobbing bitterly.

"Hush, hush, for God's sake, hush," said Jasper Tyrell, more alive to appearances than she was. "Do not give way thus, Elizabeth, remember where you are."

"Yes," said Elizabeth faintly, trying to check her overwhelming emotion, "but it came so suddenly, Jasper, seeing you again."

"Then why," asked Jasper Tyrell with sudden vehemence, "why did we ever part?"

Elizabeth gave a deep-drawn, heavy sigh.

"Do not ask me," she said. "I can never tell you—you can never understand—and yet—"

"Elizabeth," said Jasper Tyrell, with some sternness, "when you wrote that letter to me to break off our engagement, I felt there was some mystery behind—a mystery that I now think I have a right to hear the explanation of, however painful that explanation may be. I should not have asked you," he continued quickly, "if you were living with your husband—that would have been enough for me; but I have heard from my father—I have heard the common report in the country about Wendell, that after living some months in apparent unhappiness with the man you married, that without a word to him you left him."

"That is untrue, Jasper," said Elizabeth, lifting up her head, "Richard Horton, at least, knows why I left him, and for ever."

"Then tell me," said Jasper, drawing closer to her. "Tell me, Elizabeth, for you owe me something—months of pain—of passionate regret."

Jasper Tyrell's voice sank almost into a whisper as he said these last few words, fixing as he did so, his dark and beseeching eyes on her face, and Elizabeth gave a kind of piteous cry in answer to his appeal.

"Spare me, Jasper," she said, "spare me! You talk of regret—would that mine had been but regret! Oh! God! your misery was nothing to mine!"

"You loved me still, then?" said Jasper Tyrell, and a shade of triumph passed over his handsome face.

"Loved you!" echoed Elizabeth, and she looked at him, and Jasper Tyrell asked no more.

"Well," he said, "some day you will tell me all. For the present I will torment you with no further questions, except what I suppose you do not wish to keep a secret from me. Where are you living now, Lissa? What means of support have you? For my father wrote to me that you had left fortune, home, everything behind you—therefore, I think, I have a right to ask you—how are you living in London, and with whom?"

"I am very, very poor, Jasper," said Elizabeth, in such sweet and trustful accents that the man by her side grew pale. "I left, as you have heard, everything behind me except the money that I had by me. I brought forty pounds, and fifteen of that has been stolen; and so I am very poor, and I am living at present with a Mrs. O'Shee in Cambridge Street, and I have been there since the eighteenth of last month—the day after I came to London. But I am seeking a situation—I mean to work for my daily bread."

"My poor girl! Oh! my poor girl," said Jasper Tyrell, much affected by this recital.

"What people there are in this place!" went on Elizabeth. "The woman I am with is a dreadful woman—and it is so miserable. Oh! so miserable, Jasper," and Elizabeth's tears began to flow afresh.

"Well, I have found you again," said Jasper Tyrell. "And Lissa—my dear, dear Lissa, all trouble about money will now be over. Take what I have with me now, child." And he put his hand into his pocket.

"I will ask for some when I want it," answered Elizabeth, with a sad smile, pushing back some notes that he held towards her.

"I shall not be afraid to ask you, Jasper—I can take what I want from you."

"I should think so!" said Jasper Tyrell.

"And now, where can I take you? Shall I take you home?"

Elizabeth thought of Mrs. O'Shee—her prying ways, her low and cunning thoughts, and then she answered,

"I would ask you to go to my rooms, Jasper, but the woman is so disagreeable—the—"

"It is no matter," said Jasper Tyrell. "Fix on some other place for me to meet you. Let us meet to-morrow, Lissa?"

"To-morrow—" repeated Elizabeth.

"Yes—and then to-morrow won't be like all the dull weary to-morrows, that week after week, and month after month, I have lately had to look forward to, Lissa. Do you know, child, what you did for me?" continued Jasper Tyrell, his dark handsome face flushing, and his lips quivering as he spoke. "I won't say," he went on with a harsh little laugh "that you broke my heart. Men's hearts are not easily broken—but you made my life intolerable! I tried to forget you—many and many a time I cursed your memory and your name—but your face would come back—haunting me with its beauty, filling me with unendurable pangs of shame, pain, bitter and passionate regret!"

"Oh, Jasper! Jasper!"

"Do you remember, Lissa, the night when we parted?" went on Jasper Tyrell with increasing excitement. "The night when poor Harry was murdered, and you laid your head on my breast, and looked into my face, and I could have sworn—Oh! my God, I did swear, that you would never, never, be anything to another man! And then to hear—to know that you married that cub—even before the year was out—the year that you had promised to wait for me!"

"What must you have thought of me, Jasper!" said Elizabeth, and she timidly laid her hand on his arm.

"Thought of you!" repeated Jasper Tyrell. "I dare not tell you what I thought of you, Lissa—but I swore a solemn oath—"

"And what was that?"

"Never to believe in a woman's word again—never to love one I dare not say now, when once more I feel your hand in mine."

Elizabeth gave a bitter sigh at these words, and would have drawn her hand away, but Jasper held it fast.

"Nay, let it stay," he said. "You can never be to me now what you were, Lissa—but still—but still—"

"Jasper," said Elizabeth, and she raised herself up and looked straight into his face. "I may seem to you a dishonoured and perjured woman—I know I must seem so—but I know in my own heart, and, perhaps, some day, when the secrets of all hearts will be known, you will know also, that to you, at least, I was not one —that to you I was only too true—that for you I sacrificed everything on earth!"

"But how, Lissa? Give me some clue? For God's sake let me understand then your words!"

Elizabeth hesitated, and the dreadful consequences of Jasper's righteous vengeance for his brother's death rushed into her mind.

"I cannot tell you," she said. "And yet will you trust me, Jasper?" she added. "It is so hard that you should think ill of me—so hard not to be believed *by you*."

"I trusted you but too well," answered Jasper Tyrell, with some bitterness. "I believed that you were everything that a woman could be—pure, tender, noble, and good—and what was the end, Lissa? But I will not reproach you for what, I believe, now you have found out to be a fatal error."

"A fatal error, indeed!" said Elizabeth.

"Well, the past is irrecoverable," went on Jasper Tyrell, "the present, Lissa—"

"Yes, Jasper?"

"Seems very sweet to me, somehow," said Jasper Tyrell in a low tone. "What is it about you, Lissa?" he continued, looking at her as he used to look in the bright days at Wendell, when no shadow lay darkly between their love. "No other woman charms me as you do—no other woman seems beautiful to me now."

"Nay, you must not tell me that," answered Lissa, though sudden joy filled her heart at his words. "I scarcely even know how you knew me. I am so much altered, and so much disguised."

"Disguised?"

"Yes—did I not tell you? Oh! Jasper, do you know they have offered a hundred pounds reward to discover me—I am in perpetual fear of being found."

"What! Richard Horton?"

"Yes—I saw the advertisement in the *Times*, and since then I have lived in constant dread—for I would rather die, Jasper, than return to Richard Horton."

Jasper Tyrell made no answer to this. He was, in fact, trying to realize his position—trying to think what it would be best for Elizabeth to do.

"Where are we now, Jasper?" asked Elizabeth presently (the cabman was driving slowly up and down Buckingham Palace Road). "I think I should get out now; it is getting late, is it not?"

"It is only a little past four," answered Jasper Tyrell, looking at his watch. "Where shall I take you to then, Lissa? And where shall I see you again?"

"Do you know the embankment, Jasper, just before you come to Chelsea?" asked Elizabeth. "It is very quiet there—I have sometimes gone there lately—straight up St. George's Road, you know, and if you will meet me there?"

"Very well. To-morrow then, Lissa, and what time?"

"Shall we say four o'clock?"

"Yes that will do. Suppose I meet you in St. George's Road at four—it will be easier to find you there, and then we can walk along the embankment, if you like—and now let me take you home?"

To this Elizabeth made no objections, and so Jasper Tyrell drove her to Mrs. O'Shee's door, which that lady opened herself, and her sharp eyes instantly perceived the tall stranger who was handing Elizabeth from the cab.

"And so ye've had a drive, me dear," she said as she closed the door behind Elizabeth, "and with a friend, too?"

"A very old friend, Mrs. O'Shee," replied Elizabeth, and with a quick light step she ran upstairs.

CHAPTER XXIII.
"TO-MORROW, AND TO-MORROW, AND TO-MORROW."

At first, a great, almost delirious joy possessed Elizabeth after this interview with Jasper Tyrell. Her face was flushed, her heart beat fast, and her head throbbed, as she paced and repaced Mrs. O'Shee's narrow drawing-room. She had seen him again—seen Jasper. She was not quite alone in the world now—she had one friend at least—one who would keep her secret, and who would not leave her to starve amid the vast multitude of strangers around her.

Then suddenly a sort of fear came over her—a fear, however, soon swept away by the overpowering tide of joy.

"We can see each other sometimes," she whispered to her heart, putting away that momentary pang of doubt, "we can be friends"—they who had been lovers once!

She was still in this excited mood when she met him the next

day at the appointed place, and together they walked down St. George's Road; together crossed the quiet square, and presently side by side were wandering by the great river rolling on silently towards the sea.

Of what were they talking? Reader, are there not some from whom it is difficult for you to conceal a thought? Some in whom your mind naturally confides, and whose mind responds to yours as the notes to the skilled musicians' hand? This harmony was then between these two and common-place topics—the faces of the passers-by, the string of barges wending their slow silent way along their watery course, the busy steamers plying their endless trade, and the still winter twilight, stealing with its mist-like mantle over the dark river and the mighty town—all supplied them with conversation, interesting, at least, to them, for in these ordinary words each heard the echo of the other's heart.

Once or twice Jasper Tyrell alluded to the days at Wendell—to little things they both remembered, a meeting, a parting, perhaps, by some gate or stile; but he said nothing of the tragic under-current which had severed their lives—nothing of what had been between them, or nothing of what was yet to come.

He had not, in fact, yet answered this last question in his own mind. He was bewildered by the position in which he found himself, and left the future, therefore, drifting on in the hands. of fate.

Elizabeth told him of Mrs. O"Shee's eccentricities, and of the robbery of her money, but lest it should anger him (for Jasper Tyrell was of quick and jealous temperament) she told him nothing of the annoyance that she had received from Mr. Edgar Wilmot.

This, to say the least, was unwise, for half confidences between near friends are dangerous things. If we love a person we shou'd know their whole lives, or in the mysterious chain of circumstances, in some revolting turn, suddenly we may come upon a broken link !

To lose confidence in one we love is surely among the bitterest of all human ills. "He has deceived me—he has lied to me!" Oh! cruel words. Women are ready to forgive much if they know the truth, but when they turn the lock of some hidden closet—peep by accident or design into some dark place where hang the untold records of Bluebeard's past, and find that one they trusted has not trusted them—Nemesis swiftly overtakes the deceiver, for doubt and cold suspicion steal in to sap the truest, tenderest love.

Alas ! the hapless woman, who leaned with such fond confidence on Jasper Tyrell's arm, looking with her bright and love-lit eyes into his handsome and excited face, as the misty twilight stole around them, had such terrible secrets to conceal that she dared not even think, but wrapped herself for the moment in the

brief delirium of being once more near the only being that she
had ever deeply loved.

This species of forgetfulness will come over us at times, when
the glamour of the present blinds us alike to the coming and the
past.   Elizabeth loved Jasper Tyrell as few men are loved, with a
devoted, tender, passionate love, which nothing—not even the
terrible belief that he had caused his brother's death—had even
changed.

And now she was with him again—now when she knew that he
must thinks she had wronged and deceived him—she who had
endured intolerable pangs of agony, shame, and sorrow, for his
sake !

And as the dark river stole noiselessly on, together they stood
leaning on the railing on the embankment, watching, yet not
watching, the mass of water gliding at their feet. Somehow, silence
had now stolen over them, and the outward converse of the
world had died away on their lips, for they had entered an inner
world—a world where voice is not needed, and into whose .com-
pass none else could come.

In that hour all doubt of her love for him passed away from
Jasper Tyrell's mind, like the snow beneath the thaw. Some
mystery there was, he knew; some terrible secret that had
changed the even current of their lives, and blasted the sweet
hopes that had shone, apparently, so serenely for them, before
the fatal night when he had left Wendell, and their miserable
separation had begun.

"But she loves me," thought Jasper Tyrell, and his heart
throbbed and beat with strange joy and triumph at the thought.
Yet he was the first to rouse himself from the spell which had
stolen over them, and lightly laying his hand on Elizabeth's arm,
he said, "It is growing cold for you here, is it not, Lissa?"

"Is it?" she answered, and she looked up, and put her hand
to her head. She had forgotton all about the cold; all about
where they were—on what spot of this sublunary scene they
were standing, but had been living for the last few minutes in
the golden land, into whose regions we rise only on the wings of
love.

They met several times after this, always at the same place,
and at last, one afternoon, Jasper Tyrell said quite quietlyto her—

"You know this can't go on Lissa?"

She started, and looked into his face at these words.

"What do you mean, Jasper?" she said.

"I mean," answered Jasper, with a certain determination of
manner, which showed he spoke from a determinate purpose,
"that it is time for us to come to some resolution, Lissa, now.
We can't go on, and you must know it, as we are doing now."

Elizabeth turned quite pale as he said this, and leaned for

support against the railings of the embankment, for they were standing near their old trysting-place when he thus addressed her.

"Listen to me," he went on, after a moment's pause, laying his hand on her arm, "and if I say anything to offend you, forgive me—but you have left your husband, you say, for ever?"

"Yes, for ever," answered Elizabeth in a low, firm voice.

"Then that tie is broken," said Jasper Tyrell, "and the old tie, Lissa—the tie that bound you to me is unsevered still?"

"Oh! Jasper," murmured Elizabeth, and she turned her face from him, and her head fell low upon her breast.

"Yes," continued Jasper Tyrell steadily, for you love me, and I love you; and if you will trust your future to me—if you will leave England with me to-morrow, I swear on my honour as a gentleman that the moment I can do so—the moment that you are legally free—I will make you my wife."

No answer came from Elizabeth's white lips at this proposition —no word of assent or dissent—only a quivering broken sigh.

"If I were asking you to leave your home," said Jasper Tyrell; "if, from any feeling of my own, I was asking you to break with friends and fortune, I should be ashamed of my selfishness. But now, Lissa," he went on in low, passionate, and pleading accents, tightening his clasp on her arm which was resting on the railing near them, "now when you are alone in the world—when you have already left what women hold dear, and when you have no future before you but misery and toil, I dare ask you to do this. You were once to be my wife—some day, dear love, my wife you shall be."

As Jasper Tyrell said this, a vague feeling crossed Elizabeth's heart that it was generous of him to trust her thus—generous to make this offer—for she never doubted his word, and that he would keep his promise of making her his wife, if it were possible; and under the influence of this, she turned round and gently put her hand in his.

"It is generous of you, Jasper—" she said, and then she paused.

"I don't know about that, Elizabeth," said Jaspe Tyrell. "I don't know whether it is generous of a man to ask for what he feels he does not care to live without—and that, Lissa, is about what you have brought me to." And he sighed impatiently, adding a moment after, almost under his breath, "for it can never be the same."

Elizabeth caught the sense of the muttered last few words, and gave another deep-drawn sigh.

"Yes, Jasper," she said, "it can never be the same—it can never be."

"Not the same," said Jasper Tyrell. "I won't tell an untruth

about that. But the same or not the same," he added, "I love
you well enough to risk it; and though that cursed marriage
stands in the way—"

"O! don't mention it, Jasper," said Elizabeth with a shudder,

"But we must," answered Jasper Tyrell, with the daring that
was part of his nature. "We must mention it, and hear of it
too, you may be sure, before you are divorced and free to marry
me. In some moment of madness, Elizabeth, you formed this
tie."

"Madness, indeed!" said Elizabeth bitterly.

"But you did do so," went on Jasper Tyrell; "and what is
done, cannot be undone, except by—"

"Only one thing, Jasper," interrupted Elizabeth sadly, "death
only can set me free."

"Nay, dear one!" said Jasper Tyrell.

"Yes, Jasper," went on Elizabeth holding his hand and looking
into his face with her dark and mournful eyes. "Do you think
that I love you too little, that I would drag you down *with me?*
Ah! Jasper, I loved you only too well."

"And yet—"

"And yet I married," said Elizabeth "Yes, Jasper, I married,"
she continued, after a moment's pause, "and thus put a gulf
between us that we cannot cross. You have your life before you,
do you think I would darken it? Do you think I would grieve
your noble father by linking my dishonoured name with yours?"

Jasper Tyrell winced at this allusion to Sir John. He was, in
fact, a proud man, and, to a certain extent, loved the world, and
the world's good name. But the master-passion had now possession of him. He loved Elizabeth, had loved her even when he
tried to hate her; loved her now in spite of her seeming falseness
to her promise to him; in spite of the degrading marriage, which
he justly considered she had lowered herself to form.

"I have counted the cost," he said almost gloomily after
thinking for a few moments. "Don't you think I haven't thought
of my father—and other things before I asked you to cast your
lot with mine. I know it won't be all roses, Lissa," he added with
rather a forced smile, "but we must make the best of it—whatever are our troubles, we will share them together—"

"Oh! Jasper, don't tempt me," pleaded Elizabeth.

"Child, you must be mine!" said Jasper Tyrell impulsively.
"Am I going to lose you again, do you think? No, you are too
dear to me for that—too dear for me to allow anything to come
between us now." And he drew her hand through his arm, and
together, in silence, they walked by the dusky river's edge.

CHAPTER XXIV.

THE STILL SMALL VOICE.

IT is almost impossible to describe the conflicting feelings with which Elizabeth returned to her dreary lodgings after this momentous interview with Jasper Tyrell. She had loved him so much, she had loved him so long, and what now was before her? As Jasper truly had told her, she had already left all that a woman counts most dear—home, the world's good name, and even the means of buying her daily bread.

But on the other hand could she wrong Jasper?—Jasper, Sir John's heir now—a man of fortune and position, and what was *she?*

"Oh! God, help me in my darkness!" prayed Elizabeth, falling upon her knees.

"Help me, Oh! God, help me!"

As she knelt there, lifting her hands and voice in impassioned prayer, some words came back to her memory—the earnest words of the preacher in the church in Eaton Square.

"You know, my friends, it is *for ever and ever*," he had said. "Not for what we esteem a long lifetime, seventy or eighty years, but through an eternity of untold, countless ages to come. Through these your happiness or misery depends now on how you resist the passing temptations of Time."

These words seemed to thrill through Elizabeth's mind—thrill, and then stand out clear and immovable, a warning, like the fiery handwriting on the wall!

What was she about to do? Drag Jasper down in the world's hard judgment; bring an honoured name into a dishonoured court; and stain the very love she bore him by weakly yielding to his prayer? But was this all?

"For ever and ever," said the preacher.

"For ever and ever," repeated Elizabeth; "no, no, it cannot be—Jasper, beloved one, we must part—Jasper, I will bring no sin upon your head—let mine be the shame and the sorrow—Jasper, dear Jasper, I must see you no more."

In such disjointed words, broken by choking sobs, while scalding bitter tears streamed down her pale cheeks, Elizabeth resolved to give up her brief love-dream, and endure poverty, misery, everything, rather than bring disgrace on the man she loved.

We will not follow her through all her mental struggles during the long waking hours that she passed the night after her interview with Jasper Tyrell. Easy it is, Oh! Reader, to say, "I will do right—I will keep in the straight path, however stony it may be"—but do we not cast many a lingering look back to the broad and pleasant one we must leave behind? Another voice whispered in this woman's ears as well as the man of God's. This voice said, "Will Jasper thank you for this sacrifice? You were parted

by a shameful fraud, and your marriage vows wrung from you
by a cruel lie.   Jasper will make you his wife, and will not your
love repay him for everything he loses for your sake?"

Again and again the tempter spoke—and then "the still small
voice."   Elizabeth had given no promise to Jasper Tyrell.   She
had not answered his fond, eager, farewell words.   "You must
be ready the day after to-morrow, Elizabeth," he had said,
"and we will go straight to Paris. I will write to my father from
there—for it is better that he knew everything at once."

"Oh! what shall I do?" thought Elizabeth, wringing her hands.
"Oh! where shall I go?"   Then, suddenly, she remembered Sir
John Tyrell, and her uncle's last words to him, and the Baronet's
kindly offer to help her if ever it were in his power to do so

"I will write to him," she decided.   "I will trust him."   And
having made this resolution, she determined early on the following
morning to leave Cambridge Street, and thus hide herself away
from Jasper Tyrell.

She dare not, in fact, trust herself again to see him, dare not
listen to his half-tender, half-reproachful words, "When I am
dying," thought poor Elizabeth, "I will write and tell him the
truth—tell him that I am not quite such a bad woman as he thinks
me now.   If I am ever so old, if Dick is dead, I will write and tell
him then."

It was a sorrowful consolation at best, though.   What long
years she might live—long years of poverty and dependence—and
Jasper—perhaps he would be married then—another woman's
husband, with children prattling about his knee.   What a pang
darted into Elizabeth's heart at this thought.   Happy with some
one else, while she was wandering about miserable and alone!

For a time her resolution almost faltered under the extreme
bitterness of this idea; and then with a great effort of will, she
still determined to go.   "I must try to do right.   I did wrong
once, to save Jasper, as I thought, and see the bitter misery it
has brought.   Jasper—my Jasper, would that you could read my
heart—that you could know all the pain that I am suffering now."

She wrote a few words of farewell to him on her knees; kissing the lines she wrote; laying her cheeks and lips on them,
because afterwards she knew his hands would touch them.
"Bear my message to him," she whispered, the words that I
cannot write.   Tell him it is because I love him so dearly, that I
must leave him now."

Then, about eleven o'clock in the morning, she summoned Mrs.
O'Shee, and to the dismay of that lady, informed her that she
was going to leave her during the day, and requested her to
make out her bill.

She was not quite penniless now, for Jasper had put some
notes into her hand when he had parted with her the day before,

and had requested her to settle her account with Mrs. O'Shee, who turned pale, and then a dusky red, when Elizabeth told her that she meant to go.

"Ah, now, ye're joking, ye are?" said the Irishwoman. "Sure ye're not going to lave me, who's been jest a mother to ye, and no other. Don't tell me ye're going, me dear, for I fail as if a feather would knock me over, by ye saying it even in jest."

"It is not jest, Mrs. O'Shee," said Elizabeth. "I am going, and at once."

Mrs. O'Shee turned absolutely white.

"Now what will that young man say?" she said eagerly. "That foine, handsome young man, Mr. Wilmot? Sure the last words he said to me was, to watch over ye like me own choild."

"I have nothing to do with Mr. Wilmot, and he has nothing to do with me," answered Elizabeth coldly.

"But he's in luve with ye, me dear, take me word for it; he's in luve with ye, if iver a man was! And sich a foine position of his own, too—a Lord's son—jest think of that—every girl hasn't such a foine chance as that."

"Would you kindly make out your bill, Mrs. O'Shee?" interrupted Elizabeth.

"Well, ye'll lave your address, at least?" urged the landlady, who was really afraid to face Mr. Wilmot without knowing it

"I see no reason for doing so," said Elizabeth; and in spite of Mrs. O'Shee's entreaties, and affected tears, Elizabeth paid her bill (without mentioning the stolen fifteen pounds, which was some consolation to the little Irishwoman), and by twelve o'clock had left Cambridge Street; directing the cabman who conveyed her from thence, to drive to tho District Post Office, in Buckingham Palace Road. There she dismissed him, posted her letter to Jasper Tyrell, and then proceeded on foot (carrying her bag) to a small quiet-looking house in Buckingham Palace Road, where she had observed that rooms were to be let, in returning from one of her weary rambles in search of employment, and through the windows of which she had seen a respectable elderly-looking woman watering some plants.

A young fresh-looking girl, about sixteen, opened the door, and in answer to Elizabeth's inquiries, said that the drawing-room, and two front bed-rooms were to be let.

"Aunts keep the sitting-room downstairs for themselves," said the girl. "But if you will walk in, ma'am, I will call Aunt Jane?"

She did not speak like a Londoner, and her hair and general style of dress were unmistakably countrified. She was, in fact, a Scotch girl, and lived with her two maiden aunts, Miss Jane and Miss Eliza White, who were the joint mistresses of the establishment.

She showed Elizabeth into the sitting-room downstairs, and the air of quiet respectability that prevaded it pleased Elizabeth, and an I made her desirous of engaging the rooms. Everything was shabby, but serviceable and neat. On a little book-shelf, suspended against the drab-papered wall, Elizabeth noticed a large, well-fingered Bible, and in one of the old lady's work-baskets, which was standing on the table, another Bible, open, and turned down at some favourite passage, attracted her attention.

She had not much time, however. to make observations, for presently the door opened, and a g ey-complexioned, prim, sor owful-looking woman, of some fifty-five years of age, came into the room, making a demure and respectful curtsey to Eliza-beth as she did so.

"You have some rooms to let, I believe?" said Elizabeth.

"We have, nia am," answered the woman, "a drawing-room and two bed-rooms."

"I shall only want one bed-room," said Elizabeth.

"Would you please to look over them," said Miss Jane White (for this was the elder of the two sisters); aud on Elizabeth assenting, she led the way up a very narrow pair of stairs, carpeted with neat, though shabby carpeting.

The rooms upstairs were like the room downstairs, quite unlike the generality of London lodgings. All the furniture was large, old-fashioned, and heavy. No attempt was made at decoration of any sort, but, on the other hand, everything was neat, clean and serviceable. The hangings of the beds were of white dimity, and old-fashioned, like the rest; the reason for which Miss White presently explained.

"Our things are all old, you see, miss," she said, turning down one of the beds with some pride, so that Elizabeth might see its spotless purity, "for they belonged to father and grandfather before us. We are farmer's daughters, and not used to London ways—but th'ngs change," added Miss White with a sigh.

"They will suit very well, I think," said Elizabeth; and as the price was not exorbitant, she agreed to take the rooms. But with a dusky blush dyeing her grey skin, Miss White put on an air of hesitation.

"Is there anything else?" asked Elizabeth, reading these signs on the woman's face.

"Only, ma'am, about a reference," said Miss White, now turn-ing literally scarlet. "You see in London—" and then she paused, utterly unable to complete her sentence.

Elizabeth, too, blushed, and for a moment hesitated. Then she acted on the resolution that she had made in the morning, to trust to the generosity and nobleness of Sir John Tyrell.

"Sir John Tyrell will be my reference," she said, as com-posedly as she could. "Sir John and Lady Tyrell of Wendell

Hall in Uplandshire. I will write to him to-night, for Lady Tyrell is an invalid; and I can go to an hotel until you have received his answer, if that will be satisfactory?"

But the name of Sir John Tyrell was, apparently, quite sufficient. Miss White begged the lady to stay where she was without going to an hotel, if it were more convenient for her to do so, and was profuse in her apologies for even asking for a reference.

"But you see in London—" she said again; and Elizabeth quite agreed with her on the necessity of being particular.

So, in an hour after leaving Cambridge Street, Elizabeth was settled with this quiet family. She heard all their simple history before the day was over; heard how their father had been a tenant farmer, who had died without leaving any provision for them, and how their only other sister had married during his lifetime a clerk to some wine merchant in the City, and how he had died also, leaving his wife poorly provided for. This sister now kept a register-office, for governesses and companions, in Conduit Street, and contrived to earn a decent living for herself and her only child by doing so; and Elizabeth's landladies, being forced to work for their own living after their father's death, had, by her advice, come to London, and started the lodging-house in which Elizabeth found them.

They had done pretty well, Miss White said, with a sigh, but she by no means spoke in raptures of her success in her new occupation. The other sister, Miss Eliza, was apparently affected with a perpetual cold in her head. Her nose was always red, and the rims of her eyes watery. "Poor Eliza had had a disappointment," Miss Jane informed Elizabeth, and she was always using her pocket-handkerchief in consequence. But it is a shame to laugh at this poor, forlorn, old woman. Who knows—perhaps her pangs had been very bitter, her disappointment very keen. At all events Miss Jane always spoke of her with affectionate pity, and Miss Eliza's eccentricities and ill-tempers were always excused.

Elizabeth wrote her letter to Sir John Tyrell, and the Misses White received an answer by return of post, which both the ladies pronounced to be more than satisfactory. But perhaps, it were better to tell what Elizabeth wrote to her old friend at Wendell Hall.

"My dear Sir John," she began, "Forgive me for addressing this letter to you, but I feel that I can trust in your generosity and honour, and I remember also my dear uncle's last words to you, and your kindly promise to help me if you could. Dear Sir John, you know that I have left Wendell, but you do not know the reason, and that I cannot tell you; but I shall never return. I came to London, meaning to endeavour to obtain a situation as a governess or companion, but this I find I cannot do, nor

L

even obtain respectable lodgings, without giving a proper reference, and I therefore now write to you, to ask you if you will be good enough to act as one for me. If you will write a few lines to the people who keep this house (whose address I enclose) to say that you have known my family for some time, it will be quite sufficient. They seem quiet respectable women, and I should like to remain here until I find a more permanent home.

"I have met your son here—at first by accident—but it is better for us both that we should not meet again. I therefore trust you will not mention to him nor any one else, that you have heard from me, nor tell him where I am living now.

"I trust that Lady Tyrell is better, and with perfect confidence that this letter will be a secret between us, I remain, dear Sir John, yours very truly,

"Elizabeth Gordon.

"P. S.—You will see that I have again assumed my maiden name, which please address me by.

"E. G."

Sir John's answer to this appeal was characteristic. To the Misses White he wrote as follows :—

"Sir John Tyrell presents his compliments to the Misses White, and begs to inform them that he has known Miss Gordon and her family intimately for many years, and can assure the Misses White of their great respectability."

His letter to Elizabeth was much longer, and touched her inexpressibly by its generosity and kindness.

"My dear Young Lady," he wrote, "Your letter which I have just received has, to a certain extent, at least, relieved the anxiety which I, among your other friends here, have felt about your fate since you left Wendell. I will not allude to the no doubt powerful cause which induced you to leave your home. That it must have been uncongenial to you I can understand; but (pardon an old friend) you ran a terrible risk in going alone and unprotected to London; and I am only too pleased that you have now trusted in me, and remembered your kind uncle's last request, and you must allow me in future to act really as a friend to you.

"Jasper was down at Christmas, and was much shocked when he heard of your disappearance. He asked many questions about you, but I suppose I need not tell you that I shall keep your secret from him, and all others, as long as you wish me to do so. I enclose a cheque for £50, which please honour me by accepting; and will you believe also that nothing will give me more pleasure than to be of any future service to you ? I trust that you are in good health, and I remain

"Yours faithfully,

"JOHN TYRELL.

"P. S.—My poor wife is no better. She did not know Jasper

when she saw him. My daughters are well. Pray let me hear from time to time of your welfare.

"J. T."

This letter was an inexpressible relief to Elizabeth. In the first place it assured her of a comfortable, quiet, respectable home for the present, for the Misses White were delighted to have the friend of a baronet under their roof, and paid Elizabeth every possible attention. Then Sir John's enclosure relieved her from any immediate necessity of going about seeking employment, and thus running a chance at any time of ·recognition and discovery.

So she wrote a very grateful letter to the kindly Baronet, telling him this, and acknowledging, in touching words, her sense of his generosity and honour. She asked also after the unhappy Richard Horton, and begged Sir John to tell her if any change took place at Wendell West-house. She said nothing in this second letter of Jasper Tyrell, but a faint and rather sorrowful smile stole over Sir John's finely cut lips as he read it. He was a man, in fact, who looked below the surface of events, and he guessed (or fancied that he guessed) that the cause of Elizabeth leaving her home was in some way or other connected with his son.

CHAPTER XXV.
JASPER'S DISCOVERY.

In the meanwhile, Jasper Tyrell had received the farewell letter that Elizabeth had sent him, with bitter disappointment and anger. He did not do so until late on the day that she posted it, for he was detained by some business connected with a friend, until the very time that she had agreed to meet him for the last time (as he expected) in St. George's Road. He went there about three o'clock, expecting to see her, and waited impatiently more than an hour. Then he determined to go to Cambridge Street, to see what had detained her, and on reaching Mrs. O'Shee's door, found a handsome cab standing before it.

After some delay, and after he had rung twice, it was opened in answer to his summons by Mrs. O'Shee herself, who either was, or appeared to be, in tears; and when Jasper inquired for Miss Gordon, the landlady broke into a decided whimper.

"How can I tell you, sir?" she said. "She's gone—left me who have been jest a mother to her, without a word!" And she gave another whimper.

"What do I understand by this?" asked Jasper Tyrell sharply. "Gone, do you say? Do you mean she is out?"

"No, gone for iver," replied Mrs. O'Shee, wiping her eyes with a soiled little rag that she extracted from her dress pocket.

"But what do you mean?" said Jasper Tyrell. "Did she

settle her account with you—did she say she was not coming
back?''

''As sure as I'm livin', though I can scarcely tell whether I am
or I'm not, I'm in such a fluster,'' answered Mrs. O'Shee, ''she's
gone! And as for settling—well, I can't exactly say she didn't
—but she couldn't pay me for me luve, as I said to Mr. O'Shee—''

''Woman!'' said Jasper Tyrell, sternly, interrupting her, ''I
don't believe a word you are saying. I will have your house
searched. I am certain that this lady would not have left it
without telling me.''

At these words Mrs. O'Shee gave vent to a shrill scream of
horror, and as she did so a tall, gentlemanly-looking man came
down the staircase of the house, and entered the passage where
Jasper and Mrs. O'Shee were.

On seeing him Mrs. O'Shee instantly ran forward, and would
have seized his hand, but the gentleman, who was no other than
Mr. Edgar Wilmot, coolly drew back.

''D'ye hear what he's saying?'' cried Mrs. O'Shee appealing
to him. ''Mr. Wilmot, I ask yerself now, how can he blame
me? I'm as innocent as an unborn babe! Mr. Wilmot knows
Miss Gordon, too, sir,'' she continued, again addressing Jasper,
''and he'll tell ye how she's given us all the slip, and gone off,
nobody knows where to.''

At these words Jasper Tyrell looked at Mr. Wilmot, who
bowed gravely.

''I think I have the pleasure of speaking to Mr. Tyrell?'' he
said. ''I remember meeting you once at my brother's place,
Langley Hall.''

Jasper bowed also.

''Did you know—Miss Gordon?'' he asked rather huskily.

''I had that honour,'' replied Mr. Wilmot, with just a per-
ceptible tinge of scorn in his tone, ''at least the lady who here
bore that name.''

Jasper's brown handsome face turned a dusky red at this, and
then grew pale.

''What do you mean?'' he asked. ''What do you know about
her?''

Mr. Wilmot gave a cold smile at these questions.

''I might retort,'' he said, ''what right have you to ask—but I
will not, Mr. Tyrell. I have known Miss Gordon well since she
has been in town, and she has done me the honour of passing as
my wife while she has been in this house.''

''What!'' said Jasper Tyrell, in a fierce under-tone.

''This person will answer for the truth of my assertion,'' continued Mr. Wilmot, with an evil gleam in his hazel eyes, turning
to Mrs. O'Shee. ''She will tell you I visited her here—how she
walked openly in the streets with me, and how, by her own

request, I told a policeman who was making inquiries about her (for you know her story, I conclude) that she was my wife.''

"Sure I thought ye were married as fast as the church could tie ye!" ejaculated Mrs. O'Shee, eager to propitiate Mr. Wilmot. "As I said to O'Shee, and as foine a young couple they are, as the sun iver shone on.''

With a violent effort, Jasper Tyrell endeavoured to hide the terrible emotion that was cutting him to the heart.

"This is a strange story, Mr. Wilmot,'' he said, haughtily. "This lady—Miss Gordon, was a neighbour of ours at home—pardon me if I can scarcely credit such monstrous words.''

Mr. Wilmot airily shrugged his shoulders.

"Women do strange things, Mr. Tyrell,'' he said, "when they leave their homes. Will you believe me if I whisper her real name in your ear?''

"Well?'' asked Jasper Tyrell.

"Mrs. Richard Horton,'' replied Mr. Wilmot, with a smile. "The fai lady did me the honour to confide in me her whole history, and, apparently, by your emotion, she has been equally complaisant to you—and then you see has left us both in the lurch—'' And Mr. Wilmot gave another shrug of his shoulders.

"I cannot doubt your word—'' began Jasper Tyrell, and then he paused. "Good God! could this be true?'' he was thinking. "Then what was she—the vile woman, that twice he had meant to make his wife?''

"How—did you first see her?'' he asked, hoarsely, the next minute.

"In the train,'' answered Mr. Wilmot, with perfect frankness. "I travelled with her up to town, the night on which she eloped from her home—and since then—''

"It is enough,'' said Jasper Tyrell. "Good evening,'' and with a pale set face and bitten lips, he turned and left the house, clenching his hands when he got into the street, and cursing Elizabeth in the bitterness of his heart.

"I've been a madman,'' he muttered, "the dupe of a vile woman—and I believed in her—I loved her—fool that I have been!''

With another cold smile Mr. Wilmot watched him take his departure from Mrs. O'Shee's door, and then he turned to that lady.

"So my fair friend had another admirer it seems?'' he said, sneeringly. "How was it, Mrs. O'Shee, that you did not inform me of the fact?''

"Because I didn't know it,'' replied the Irishwoman, boldly. "Because the gintleman that's jest gone niver set his foot within me doors. She used to go out in the afternoons lately to walk, she told me, and then she moight see him but he-e he has niver been.''

"When did she first tell you that she was going to leave?" asked Mr. Wilmot.

"Only this morning now, and not a hint did she give me before!" truthfully affirmed Mrs. O'Shee, "and the minit she was gone I sat down and wrote ye the news—but of course ye would git me letter too late—"

"You mean I have not got your letter at all," brusquely interrupted Mr. Wilmot. " I left Langley this morning, and drove direct here as soon as I arrived in town. It is an unaccountable story," he added, musingly. If I hadn't seen Tyrell's face, I would have believed that she had gone off with him—but no—the fellow was too deeply cut for that. He is probably an old lover, and she has seen him somewhere, and is hiding herself from both. But, my lady," he thought, vindictively, "you will be a clever woman if you can hide yourself from the London detectives and *from me*."

"Did I tell ye she went in a cab, now?" suggested Mrs. O'Shee.

"What was the number? You surely took the number?" asked Mr. Wilmot sharply.

"Sure, I jest didn't thin," replied Mrs. O'Shee. "I was that put out, as I said to O'Shee—"

"Fool!" muttered Mr. Wilmot, without ceremony; and then he proceeded to interrogate her on the smallest particulars of Elizabeth's departure, and finally left the house, leaving the little woman exceedingly indignant with him.

"O'Shee," she said, entering the dining-room after he was gone, where a miserable little creature, in rusty black, was crouching over the small poor fire in the grate, "if ye'd the heart of a man—but ye haven't—ye wouldn't have sat there, and heard me abused as I've been this day!"

"It's your own business," replied the miserable creature in black.

"Yes, it's me business, O'Shee, and your business, too, I'm thinking, to keep a roof over me head!" replied Mrs. O'Shee, much exasperated." Who feeds ye?" she went on, indignantly. "And clothes ye? Meself, and no other. But I'll give ye yer due," she added, "and the very next lodgers I git, I'll not take as much as a spoonful of gravy from their table to help ye!"

This threat quite subdued Mr. O'Shee, who was fond of good living, and who existed principally on Mrs. O'Shee's lodgers, and he therefore humbled himself before his better-half.

"If you had called me," he said, "I would have come."

"Called ye!" echoed Mrs. O'Shee, with a shriek of derision, "I belave ye, O'Shee, now that the inemy's gone! But," she added, quoting unconsciously, "yer no better than a coward!"

And having expressed this opinion of her husband's prowess, she shook her bony fist at him, and left the Revd. Michael to his solitary reflections.

In the meanwhile, Jasper Tyrell, full of indignation, jealousy, and bitter scorn, both for Elizabeth and himself, had returned to his hotel, where he found Elizabeth's brief letter awaiting him.

These words, over which the poor woman had wept and prayed, however, only seemed to add to his indignation.

"Hypocrite!" he said bitterly, flinging the note into the fire after he had read it, "to write thus, and to me—to me whom twice she has duped and fooled!"

And yet he could not understand the story. He would have sacrificed so much for her—he loved her so much. It seemed impossible to believe her guilty, and yet could he disbelieve the direct evidence of his own senses? She had told this man her story—she had passed as his wife—and with a bitter curse Jasper Tyrell swore he would put her away from his heart for ever.

So, while he was calling down imprecations on her head, and endeavouring, amid reckless mirth, to forget her beautiful tender face, Elizabeth was kneeling by her little white-robed bed, at the Misses White's, praying that all good might come, and all peace and happiness to Jasper Tyrell. She had left him, but she seemed to be near him still—they were parted, but between these two the mysterious link of love remained unbroken—and in spite of the hatred that swelled in Jasper Tyrell's heart at the very recollection of her name, he could not, do what he would, forget the memory of Lissa Gordon.

Very quietly the next few weeks glided away in the little old-fashioned house in Buckingham Palace Road, where Elizabeth had found a temporary refuge. The four women who were its sole inhabitants got on very well, and six weeks passed, and Elizabeth had never crossed the street door from the time that she had first entered by it. She thus escaped a vigorous search which Mr. Wilmot had determinately entered upon, for he had vowed that he would find Elizabeth, and had offered privately another hundred pounds to the police for her discovery. They found the cabman who had driven her to the District Post Office but there she was entirely lost sight of. They little guessed how near she was to them, as she sat in her small drawing-room, looking often out wistfully through its misty panes!

She was not, however, idle during this quiet time. She had in fact, resolved to try to be a governess, and for that purpose she studied and practised very industriously. She had had a fair education and played well, and she asked Miss White to hire her a piano, and for hours each day the melodies of Mendelssohn or of some of her other favourite composers could have been heard by any listener in the street below. But there was nothing uncommon in this, and so Elizabeth lived on unmolested, and grew fond of the kindly old maids, who were delighted with their quiet lodger, and would sometimes invite her to honour them by coming down and having a cup of tea in their own parlour.

Elizabeth did not deceive them as to her circumstances, but as far as she could told them the truth. She told them that her father had been an officer, and her uncle a farmer, and that she lived with the latter until he died, and that, by-and-by, she meant to go out into the world to earn her daily bread. The Misses White believed that her uncle's death had caused this change in her circumstances, and were too delicate and kindly to ask any questions. As for the young girl, Lucy White, the niece of the maiden ladies, she positively adored Elizabeth, and declared that she was the most beautiful and sweetest lady that she had ever seen. Elizabeth began to teach her music when she was there, and thus won the young girl's entire gratitude. In fact there was peace in the house, and under the influence of a glass of hot whiskey toddy, which Miss Jane informed Elizabeth that "dear father always took," and which she considered wholesome for "Eliza," poor Eliza one evening confided to Elizabeth the history of her disappointment.

He had been the minister of the parish where they lived, and young and comely, by his poor lady-love's description, and at one time had no doubt intended to lead Miss Eliza to the holy state of matrimony. But a rich gay widow came between them, and the minister was false, and poor Eliza forsaken.

There was almost something ludicrous to hear the poor old woman, with her grey head, and pinched, blue-tinted face, and watery eyes, relating the loves of her youth. Miss Lucy, who was young and innocent, confided to Elizabeth that she thought that "Aunt Eliza was daft; " but Elizabeth, having had sufferings of her own, took a more lenient view of the case, and tried to sympathise with and comfort the forsaken Eliza.

After Elizabeth had been with them about five weeks, she was introduced to Mrs. Perkins, the widowed sister who kept the register office for governesses in Conduit Street, and who had been left no wealth to speak of by the defunct Perkins, but a very fine boy, then about twelve years of age. This child was the pride of not only Mrs. Perkins (which was justifiable) but of the two maiden aunts, who doated on this youthful scion of their house, and spent many pennies weekly on the purchase of "sweets" and other luxuries for his benefit.

Mrs. Perkins was as grey and worn-looking as her sisters, though she had attained the honours of matrimony, which they had not. Her face was lined and sorrowful, and told a story of many cares, but she had a kindly heart, and gladly promised to

interest herself in trying to procure a good situation as governess
for Elizabeth.

"Having such references as Sir John and Lady Tyrell will go
a great way," she told Elizabeth; "city folks like to be connected with titled people in ever so small a way." And she
gave rather a grim chuckle as she imparted this observation on
humanity.

A fortnight later she called at the house in Buckingham Palace
Road for the express purpose of seeing Elizabeth. She had
heard of a situation likely to suit her, she thought, and when
Elizabeth heard the particulars of it she thought so also.

It was to educate the two younger daughters of a Major
Dalziel, a retired military officer, who lived at a village called
Hazelhurst, in the county of Midlandshire.

"They seem quite gentlefolks," Mrs. Perkins told Elizabeth.
"The Major is up in town himself to look for a governess,
and his eldest daughter, who's as pretty a young girl as I ever
saw."

Truly sorry as the Misses White were to lose Elizabeth as a
lodger, they could not deny the seeming advantages of the vacant
situation. There were only two pupils, and the salary offered
was fifty pounds a year. Mrs. Perkins had mentioned Elizabeth
to them, and they seemed satisfied with the description she had
given, and the Major, "who seems a quiet kind of man," Mrs.
Perkins remarked, thought that the references were very good.

So it was agreed on the following morning that Elizabeth was
to journey down to Mrs. Perkins' office in Conduit Street, to have
an interview with Major and Miss Dalziel. She felt very nervous
about going, we may be sure, but it was an opportunity not to
be lightly missed of earning an independence, for generous as
Sir John Tyrell was, Elizabeth felt that she could no longer live
on his bounty. In her deep mourning then, her crape veil
doubled over her face, she started at the appointed hour, and,
having arrived at Mrs. Perkins', was received in very kindly
fashion by that lady.

CHAPTER XXVI.
EVA DALZIEL.

THE Dalziels had not arrived when Elizabeth was first
ushered into Mrs. Perkin's office, and so she had time to look
around her, and to think of the many weary feet that had come
there before her, and of the many weary hearts that had turned
disconsolately away.

Presently, however, a hansom cab drove up to the door, and
a grey-haired, good-looking man, and a very pretty girl indeed,
entered the office.

"This is Major Dalziel and Miss Dalziel," said Mrs. Perkins, rising to receive them. "This is Miss Gordon," she added, indicating by a wave of her hand Elizabeth, who rose also, and bowed to the new-comers.

"Ah—" said the Major, "Ah—" and then he bowed, and seemed at a loss how to proceed any further with the conversation.

But Miss Dalziel (the pretty girl who accompanied him) came forward with a pleasant smile.

"Mrs. Perkins has told us about you," she said, addressing Elizabeth. "You know mamma wants a governess for my two young sisters. They are fourteen and eleven, aren't they, papa?"

"Yes, yes, I think so," responded the Major to this appeal of his daughter's.

"And mamma wants them to be taught French and music," went on Miss Dalziel, in her frank, sweet voice. "In fact just the usual things—just what we all get taught—isn't that right, papa?"

"Yes, yes, I think so," again said the Major.

"Do you think you would like to come, then?" continued Miss Eva Dalziel, smiling again. "It is a very dull place though, I ought to tell you, where we live—just a dull country village."

"Oh! I shall not mind that," answered Elizabeth. "I like a quiet place."

"You are not like me then," said pretty Miss Eva, "I hate quiet—I like to go somewhere every day, and to see lots of new people every hour of my life."

"You would soon tire of it," said Major Dalziel, looking at his daughter.

She was almost as pretty a specimen of an English maiden as it was possible to see. Her features were small and delicate, and her eyes sweet, frank, and blue. But it was her complexion that made the chief beauty of her face. Never, surely, was there another skin so fair and pure, while a perfect wild-rose tint came and went with every passing emotion on her oval cheeks. Yes, Eva Dalziel was a very pretty girl, and as sweet-tempered and charming as she looked. She was just about eighteen at this time, and had had no troubles nor cares all her young life. Her own mother had died during her childhood, and Major Dalziel's second wife made it one of the studies of her life to try to please her step-daughter, and Eva was not very difficult to please.

"So you will come then?" she said again, in her frank kind way, looking at Elizabeth.

"If—if—you think I would suit?" answered poor Elizabeth, blushing deeply.

"Oh! I am sure you will," said Eva Dalziel. "It will be so nice for me—we will walk together, and I will show you all over

our lively village. Papa, won't it be nice for me to have Miss
Gordon ? "

"Very, my dear, very," answered the Major.

"The children are very nice girls," said pretty Miss Eva,
turning her head to one side contemplatively; "but of course
they are children. You will find mamma very kind; don't you
think so, papa?"

"Yes, of course, my dear, of course," said the Major.
"And—there was something else, Eva—Oh, yes—mamma might
wish for a reference."

"Oh, never mind about that," answered Eva quickly. "I'm
sure Miss Gordon is just what we want."

"But I would rather give you a reference," said Elizabeth,
with a smile. "So if Major Dalziel will kindly write to Sir John
Tyrell, Wendell Hall, Uplandshire, I think that I can depend
upon his answer."

"Highly satisfactory," said the Major, drawing out his note-
book. "Sir John Tyrell," he inscribed in it, and then again
asked the Baronet's address.

"Then it's all settled," said Eva, "and you will come to us?
I am so pleased that you are coming," she went on, "and I hope
that you'll be happy with us. How soon do you think that you
can come ? "

"I can come as soon as your papa has heard from Sir John,"
answered Elizabeth.

"Oh, that's so nice ! We leave town, I am sorry to say,
the day after to-morrow, so will you come in a week? Papa,
you get out the guide now, and tell Miss Gordon exactly what
trains to catch We are two miles from the station, but mamma
will send her pony-chaise for you, and papa will send his cart for
your luggage."

Thus Miss Eva fixed it all. As soon as Sir John Tyrell
had replied to Major Dalziel's letter, it was settled that Miss
Dalziel would write to Miss Gordon, and as shortly afterwards as
it was convenient to her she was to proceed to Hazelhurst.

"And I hope you will like us?" again said Eva, with her
frank, bright smile, offering her hand to Elizabeth; and then,
after receiving a few directions about the trains from the Major
(who had produced his Bradshaw in obedience to his daughter's
command), the Dalziels took their departure, leaving both
Elizabeth and Mrs. Perkins highly satisfied with the result
of the interview.

"Well, Miss Gordon, I think you've got a comfortable home to
look forward to," said Mrs. Perkins, the moment after they were
gone. "It isn't many young ladies that are as pleasant-pokens
as Miss Dalziel."

"She seems very kind and bright," answered Elizabeth."

"Yes, if you saw some of my ladies you would see the difference," continued the widow "Many and many a time I've
blushed, though my blushing days are about over now, to see
the way in which some fine ladies treat other ladies, maybe
as well-born as themselves—but Miss Dalziel is not one of that
kind."

At Buckingham Palace Road, on her return there, the news
of Elizabeth's engagement was naturally received with mingled
feelings.

"You'll be a loss to us, if you're a gain to them, that's all I
can say," said Miss Jane, with a resigned sigh ; but Miss Eliza
shook her head dolefully, and, as usual, wiped a tear from her
watery eyes.

"You must look for troubles, my dear," she said, "for the
world's full of 'em, and go where you will, you'll be sure to meet
with fresh ones."

"Don't tell her that, aunt," said Miss Susy, "she may meet
with something better than troubles." And Susy nodded her
head gaily, indicating some future good luck in the way of
matrimony, which she thought was sure to happen to her favourite.

"If you mean anything about men, Susy," said the disappointed Aunt Eliza, "they bring the worst troubles of all."

"Not always," replied the youthful Susy, hopefully ; but Miss
Eliza only shook her head again and sighed, knowing from bitter
experience that her words were true.

On the afternoon of the same day Elizabeth wrote to Sir John,
and a day or two afterwards received a very kindly letter in reply.

He had heard from Major Dalziel, he informed her, and had
written to him by return of post, "saying, of course, all manner
of pretty things about you," wrote the Baronet ; and he begged
her also not to remain in her situation if she found it uncomfortable, "for you know that you can depend upon me at any time
as your banker," added Sir John. He told her also that he had
seen Robert Horton lately, who looked well, but gave a very
miserable account of his brother Richard. "In fact, my dear
young lady," Sir John concluded with, "the common report in
the neigbourhood is, that this unfortunate young man is killing
himself with drink. How far this is true I cannot personally
inform you, for he apparently never comes out of the house, but
his brother spoke of him in a very desponding manner. Write
and tell me how you get on at Hazelhurst, and believe me to
remain

"Your sincere friend,

"JOHN TYRELL."

In a postscript the Baronet added : "I wonder if your Major
Dalziel is any relation of a certain Dean Dalziel, with whom
I have a slight acquaintance ?"

Elizabeth shed some very sorrowful tears over this letter It. was dreadful, after all, to think of Dick killing himself, as apparently he was doing, in trying to drown his remorse. She remembered the days when he was a boy; when they had played together, and her kind aunt had been a mother to them all. Yet what could she do? Nothing but pray to God to pardon him—nothing but ask that some day he might find forgiveness for his crime.

A very kind letter also came from Eva Dalziel, the day after she had received Sir John's. "Papa has heard from your friend Sir John Tyrell," wrote Miss Eva, "and he says everything that is charming about you. What day will you come? I shall be so delighted to see you, and I will introduce you to all our neighbours in this interesting village. They consist of 'soldier, sailor, doctor, tailor'—no, I forgot, you must add a parson to the category. The soldier is papa, the sailor is seventy and has one leg, the doctor is fat and married! The tailor I am not acquainted with, and the parson is a prig! There, I hope you enjoy the prospect of your future society—but never mind, you must try to make the best of us, and mamma desires me to tell you that she hopes you will find your future pupils good and obedient."

Elizabeth scarcely felt as if she were going among strangers after receiving this letter. This pretty, bright, young girl she was sure would be kind to her, and this feeling added very much to the comfort of her journey down to Hazelhurst. She was glad also to leave London, and the quiet village that the girl laughingly described seemed a sort of haven of rest to her that she would gladly reach.

So, on one of the last days of February, Elizabeth took leave of her friends, the simple-hearted Miss Eliza and Miss Jane, and started on her journey. Each of the sisters gave her a little token of their regard and good-will before she left; Miss Eliza presenting her with a pair of black kid gloves, as she said that "they always came in useful." Susy's gift was not so lugubrious, for she bought Elizabeth a very gorgeous silk neck-tie, and Miss Jane presented her with a small brooch. They made her promise also that she would come to see them, and that she would write and tell them how she got on at her new home.

Elizabeth kissed all the three women before she went away They had been kind to her, and had procured her this situation even at their own loss. She slipped a little parcel also into Susy's hand, and when the girl opened it after she was gone, it was found to contain a beautifully engraved gold locket, which Elizabeth had worn in her old, bright, girlish days, and which both her aunts informed Susy was "too handsome for the like of her," and ordered her forthwith to return it. Susy, however, declined to comply with this request, and to this day wears it suspended round her neck by various tinted ribbons, to the terror of Miss Eliza, who is always prophesying that no good will come of such vanity.

It was getting dusk when Elizabeth reached the station at which she had been told by Major Dalziel that she must leave the train for Hazelhurst. But though the twilight was gathering in, it was still light enough for her to see that pretty Eva Dalziel was waiting for her on the platform.

"So you have come?" said the girl, in her blithe fresh voice, and she put out her little hand, and shook Elizabeth's warmly. "I have the pony-chaise here," she added, "and Johnnie will see after your luggage."

On this, "Johnnie," a rural-looking youth, in many buttons, advanced with a grin, and Elizabeth's new trunk, which she had purchased with part of Sir John's kind gift, was got out of the luggage-van, and her other small belongings collected; Eva ordering Johnnie to convey the small packages to the pony-chaise.

"Papa will send the cart in half-an-hour for your trunk, Miss Gordon," said Eva. "Will you get in now?" she continued, advancing towards the pony-chaise. I am the charioteer; I hope you don't think I'll upset you?"

"Oh, no," laughed Elizabeth.

"Don't be too positive about it, though," said Eva, laughing also. "You know *I did* upset mamma once, but it's a subject never mentioned in the family."

"I am anxious to see your mamma," said Elizabeth.

"Yes—well I am sure you will find her kind—yes, very kind— but she's rather a fidget. She worries herself about small things so often, that she worries other people—but still, I think you will like her. You've seen papa? He's a very dear old thing."

"He seemed very kind."

"Oh, awfully kind. He lets mamma do everything she likes, and me too. The only person that we are at all afraid of is the Dean."

"Is he a relation?"

"Oh, he's papa's brother. He's very rich you see, and we are poor, so he's the great man of the family."

"Does he live near here?"

"About fifty miles off. He's the Dean of Greyminster, but we sometimes go to stay there, and he sometimes comes to stay with us."

"Is he like your papa?"

"Oh, no. I always think that papa should have been the clergyman, and Uncle Ralph the soldier. He is just like an old general, and of very warlike temperament too, I can assure you."

"Well, perhaps I shall see him."

"Oh, you are sure to see him. He is talking of coming soon, I believe. But look," continued Eva, pointing to a poor-looking woman, who was sitting in a crouching attitude on a pile of broken stones by the road-side, "what is the matter with that woman, I wonder? Would you mind holding the reins until I get out and see?" And as Elizabeth took them in her hand, Eva sprang out of the pony-chaise, and went up to the woman's side.

"Are you ill," she said in her kind way, "that you are sitting here?"

The woman lifted up a worn, white face, when Eva thus addressed her.

"I am fairly beat, Miss," she answered. I've walked from Brocklebury to-day, and must get to Hazelhurst to-night, if I get any shelter at all, and my feet have just failed me, that's the truth."

She was quite an old woman, this poor wayfarer, and Eva's sweet nature would not allow her to leave a fellow-creature in so forlorn a condition; and the next minute she went back to the pony-chaise, and put her pretty blushing face close to Elizabeth's.

"Would you mind," she whispered, "allowing this poor creature to sit by your side as far as Hazelhurst? It is not more than a mile now, and I can walk and lead the pony?"

It was only a little incident, but it showed the girl's good heart, and Elizabeth felt almost tempted to kiss the sweet face so near to hers.

"Of course not," she said, "but let me walk."

"Indeed you shall not after your journey," answered Eva Dalziel; and in another minute or two the poor tired woman found herself being conveyed to Hazelhurst, while Eva, with the reins through her arm, walked briskly by the pony's side.

It was a sad little tale that the poor wanderer told them in that short drive—a sad and common tale of poverty and old age. Her son was a labourer at Hazelhurst, and she was tramping to his already over-crowded home, to try to find a shelter for her fast declining days. Eva led the pony close to the son's door; he lived in a small cottage in the outskirts of the village, and Elizabeth saw the girl bring out her slender purse, and put her little mite into the old woman's trembling hand before she parted with her.

"Poor soul!" said Eva, as she jumped back into her place by Elizabeth's side in the pony-chaise, "wasn't it lucky we met her?" And this was all the comment she made upon her kindly act.

CHAPTER XXVII.

HAZELHURST.

HAZELHURST, in spite of the ludicrous description that Eva had given Elizabeth of its society, is a remarkably pretty village, surrounded by pretty country, and with many natural advantages.

Major Dalziel's house stood at the upper end of it, and was a large, comfortable, family mansion, with a beautiful shady garden and orchard, sloping down at the back to the river Dill. The next house to the Dalziels was a yet larger one, and was then inhabited by the Ladons. The Ladons were rich, but they had acquired their wealth in trade, in the neighbouring town of Brocklebury, and, therefore, were not visited by Major Dalziel's family, though there was a handsome young Ladon, who was a very ardent admirer of pretty Eva Dalziel. "But it would not do, of course, " Mrs. Dalziel informed Elizabeth on many subsequent occasions; so young Mr. Ladon was obliged to restrain his sighs to his own bosom, and gaze at Eva over the garden wall in silence.

Then came the doctor's house, then the parsonage, then old Capt. Marshall's, the one-legged sailor of Eva's description. Besides these there are perhaps a score of smaller houses, all standing in one long row, with pretty green fields stretching in front of them, and their gardens and the Dill lying at the back.

It is a pretty place, but old-fashioned and out of the world; but as the houses are cheap, and the fishing good, it is not unsuitable for quiet people. "Much pleasanter for old gentlemen than young ladies, though," Eva Dalziel always declared; and there was no doubt, a great deal of truth in her remark. It was very well for the old sea captain with his one leg, to sit all day with his fishing-rod by the placid waters of the Dill, but young girls with two pretty little feet to show are not contented with such solitary enjoyment. True, when Elizabeth first went, there was young Mr. Ladon and a curate, and a doctor's assistant, still unespoused among the gentlemen of Hazelhurst, but Eva Dalziel was not permitted to form any intimacy or even acquaintance with these bachelors. She knew the curate certainly, but he was not interesting, and Eva had found Hazelhurst very dull before Elizabeth's arrival.

She was, therefore, exceedingly pleased to have got a companion, and when they reached Major Dalziel's house, she led Elizabeth up to the drawing-room and introduced her with no small pride, to her step-mother.

A short, rather good looking woman (though not pretty) rose to receive them.

"This is Miss Gordon, mamma," said Eva; and "Mamma" accordingly put out her hand very kindly, though looking at Elizabeth scrutinisingly, but rather nervously the while.

"I hope you have had a pleasant journey?" she said.

"I am sure she must be very tired, mamma," said Eva, answering for Elizabeth. "I hope dinner will be ready soon! Come. Miss Gordon, I will show you your room."

This was Elizabeth's welcome to her new home, and from the very first she found herself most kindly treated there. Mrs. Dalziel, as Eva had told Elizabeth, was a fidgety woman, and liked to interfere with every one and everything around her. But she was kind. She meant well on all occasions, though she certainly did not always do well. She wanted, in fact, tact, though she thought that she particularly excelled in that characteristic; but true tact is rarely possessed by those who have an over-weening opinion of their own qualifications.

Still, if Mrs. Dalziel had faults she had many virtues. She was a kind mother, a good manager of a limited income, and a good wife to her amiable husband. Thus the Dalziels were a very happy family, and bitter and wrangling words were rarely, if ever, known beneath the Major's house-roof. Elizabeth's pupils, Lucy and Anna, were nice girls, but not so pretty as Eva. A trace of the mother's coarser features was to be seen oddly reflected in the faces of the young daughters, and their complexions lacked the clear transparency of their half-sister's. But still, they were pretty, merry girls, and fairly attentive and obedient to Elizabeth's instructions.

She had, indeed, nothing to complain of at Hazelhurst. The Major was a gentlemanly, good-looking man, with a delicate colour, and fine features like his eldest daughter, and was one of the quietest beings in existence. He had left the Army early, married twice, and seemed content to dream away his life in this village, in the most unambitious manner possible. He read, smoked, fished, ate a good dinner, and went to bed, getting up again the next morning only to renew this placid routine.

Thus everything went on most harmoniously. Mrs. Dalziel, it is true, had occasional quarrels with the servants, and felt injured if the butcher was more attentive to the Ladons than to herself, but these small storms quickly subsided. Eva used to joke her step-mother, but Mrs. Dalziel generally took it all in good part. "I always try to please her most," she confided to Elizabeth, "because she is not my own child." And she felt perfectly satisfied with her self-abnegation, and was delighted to have the opportunity of pointing out her virtues to a stranger.

When Elizabeth had been at Hazelhurst about three weeks, a letter arrived one morning for the Major, from his brother, the Dean. The Major opened this letter, read it, and then made an awry face.

"Well, my love," said Mrs. Dalziel, addressing her husband, "and what news has your brother? Major Dalziel's brother, as perhaps you may have heard, Miss Gordon," she went on, turning to Elizabeth, "is the Dean of Greyminster—it is a very fine position—the Dean's income is very large."

"Miss Gordon will have the pleasure of seeing the Dean soon, my dear," said the Major, half-jocularly, for the men had been boys together once, though now the Dean was a great man, and the Major a small one; but still the Major remembered the early equality, and was not disposed to worship the Dean quite as much as his wife was.

"Is he coming?" asked Mrs. Dalziel, much excited.

"He proposes to come for three days," answered the Major, "his visit to commence on the 1st of March—but read his letter," and he handed his brother's letter to his wife.

Mrs. Dalziel put up her gold eye-glasses, and read it eagerly. "But what is this about a proposition he has to make?" she asked her husband as she went on.

The Major shrugged his shoulders.

"My dear, you know Ralph," he said; "perhaps he wishes me to go into the Church, and will offer to make me one of his curates."

"Now, papa, dear, do not talk in that way," answered Mrs. Dalziel. "Depend upon it the Dean has some meaning in his words. He is not a man to say anything without a meaning—what can it be? Can you guess, Eva?"

"Perhaps he is going to be married," suggested Eva, to tease her mamma.

"Oh, no! Oh, nonsense! You do not think that, dear, do you?" said Mrs. Dalziel, uneasily. "Oh, no! I do not believe that—and yet who can tell?—there are such designing women in the world."

Common report said that Mrs. Dalziel had designed to marry her husband, and had succeeded in her design after some ineffectual efforts to escape on the part of the Major; but then we know that common report is a liar, and Mrs. Dalziel always spoke with extreme horror of any such proceedings.

She, however, worked herself into the most terrible state of worry during the week that elapsed before the Dean's arrival, as to what the mysterious words in his letter could mean. She consulted her husband about them perpetually, but the Major always took refuge in a quiet shrug. Then she attacked Eva, then Elizabeth, and finally even the servants in the house knew that the Dean was expected to do or say something extraordinary when he came.

He was expected on the 1st of March, and on the 1st of March he arrived, after great preparations in his honour had taken place in his brother's house. In the first place Mrs. Dalziel considered a general cleaning necessary, and put up her summer curtains for the occasion, and drew out her white rugs, though fires were still indispensable.

"I wish he would stay away," said Miss Lucy to Elizabeth, "mamma makes such a fuss about him."

"My dear," said Eva, "allow me to imbue you with a more mercenary spirit. Unless Uncle Ralph is coming to announce his marriage, pray remember that we are his heirs, and some pretty little pickings he must have got out of the Church Militant here on earth by this time, so please be attentive to him."

"I don't care for his money," said Lucy, who was fourteen, and knew nothing of the ways of the world.

"Money is a great thing, Lucy, after all," said Elizabeth, and she sighed.

The three young ladies were walking up and down one of the smooth gravel walks in the garden at the back of the house, the day before the Dean was expected to arrive at Hazelhurst, when this conversation took place; and when Elizabeth sighed, Eva looked affectionately into her face.

"Run into the house, Lucy dear, for a garden chair," she said to her younger sister.

"Now you want to talk secrets with Miss Gordon, Eva," answered Lucy, half jealously, who was leaning on her governess's arm. "I can keep secrets too, Miss Gordon, if you will trust me," added the young girl, shyly.

"Secrets are not pleasant things, Lucy," said Elizabeth, with another sigh.

"Well, if you want to talk to Eva, I will go," said Lucy, after a minute's hesitation, and she drew her hand from Elizabeth's arm.

The moment she was gone, Eva put hers through Elizabeth's other arm, and said earnestly,

"You *have* a secret, Elizabeth? Why don't you tell me? Why do you always look so sad?"

"My life has been very sad," answered Elizabeth, with a slight quiver in her voice.

"I know it has," said Eva. "I feel it has—you have had some great grief, Elizabeth—will you tell me what it is?"

"No, dear child, no," said Elizabeth, and she put her hand into the young girl's who stooped down and kissed it.

"You are so beautiful," said Eva, "and I care for you so much. Will you promise me something, Elizabeth?"

"Well, dear Eva?"

"That we shall always be friends—that nothing shall ever change *that*? Will you promise me?"

"I hope so," said Elizabeth, sadly. "But, Eva, the dearest friends sometimes cannot be friends—the dearest friends sometimes must part."

"We won't," answered Eva, enthusiastically. "Do you know

I like everything about you, Elizabeth, but your name—I don't like Elizabeth much," she added, with a smile.

"Call me Lissa then," said Elizabeth softly, "the name my dear aunt and uncle called me—the name that those who have loved me best have always called me, Eva."

"Lissa," repeated the young girl. "Oh! I like Lissa—it is a pretty name, you shall always be Lissa now to me."

These two had grown great friends now. They walked together and read together, and sometimes went little charitable errands together, which they did not confide to any one else in the household. They had several times visited the old woman whom they had picked up on the road on the evening that Elizabeth first came to Hazelhurst, and we may be sure that the poor creature was benefited by these interviews.

"I can't preach," Eva confided to Elizabeth, "but I like to give away money, when I have it."

"You are very, very kind, Eva," answered Elizabeth.

"Oh, no—but of course it's nice to help people if you can," answered Eva. "I only wish that I were rich, and then I might do some good."

She had, indeed, very little to give, poor child, but she gave it not grudgingly. Elizabeth knew that some money that she intended to buy gloves with (and she really wanted them) was bestowed on the old woman that they had met on the road. The Major could only afford to give a very small allowance to his daughter, so Eva's charities were obliged to be paid for by sacrificing some articles of dress. The pretty generous little hand had to go shabby for the sake of the poor pensioner's pound of tea!

Mrs. Dalziel would not have approved of this if she had known it. She gave away money also, but she gave it to public charities, and loved to see her name figure in the lists. She visited the poor sometimes also, but only those who attended regularly at church. She did, indeed, everything that was proper and right to do, and had the satisfaction of thinking every day in her life what a virtuous woman she was, a pattern and example to her children and her friends.

She, however, was slightly afraid of the Dean of Greyminster, and never quite at her ease when his bright, sarcastic, black eyes were fixed upon her face. She felt, somehow, that he did not believe in her quite as much as she liked to be believed in, and as she believed in herself. But he was the Dean—a man of position and wealth, and nothing could exceed the affectionate attention that she always paid him.

He arrived as he had arranged, on the 1st of March, about dinner-time. Six o'clock was the usual hour at the Major's for that meal to be partaken of, but in honour of the Dean dinner was deferred for an hour. The Major drove to the station to meet his brother in the pony-chaise, and the ladies of the family donned their newest dresses for the occasion. Elizabeth was asked to dine with the Dean, but she declined, for she instantly recognised that Mrs. Dalziel wished her to do so, although that lady gave her the invitation herself.

She had always dined hitherto with the family. Indeed, it did not suit Mrs. Dalziel's economical plans of housekeeping to have an early and late dinner, so her two young daughters and Elizabeth had dined at six o'clock with the rest. On the day that the Dean was expected, however, Mrs. Dalziel informed Elizabeth that Lucy and Anna would dine at one o'clock.

"The Dean does not like a crowded table, you see," she said, smilingly—"but we shall be glad, Miss Gordon, if you will join us at the late dinner."

Elizabeth quite understood what she was intended to say, and she accordingly said it. She would prefer dining with her pupils during the Dean's visit, and Mrs. Dalziel approved of this arrangement.

Eva, however, was exceedingly angry when she heard of it.

"She has always dined with us," she said to her mamma, indignantly. "It is exceedingly rude—she is quite a lady, and she is my friend."

"My dear, young girls do not understand these things," said Mrs. Dalziel, soothingly.

"I hope I never shall understand them," retorted Eva, and she was anything but gracious to her mamma during the rest of the day.

Elizabeth, as we may suppose, was very indifferent about it. She heard the Dean arrive, and the bustle of the dinner being served going on downstairs, but that was all until about nine o'clock, when Eva came into the school-room and insisted on her going down to the drawing-room for tea.

"Do, Lissa, or I shall think that you do not love me," urged the young girl. "Mamma wishes Lucy and Anna to come down, and expects that you will also."

"Really I do not wish to do so," said Elizabeth.

"But to please me," pleaded Eva, and after that, what more could be said?

Elizabeth, however, did not change her dress in honour of the Dean. She always wore black now, and so in her long, sweeping black skirt she entered the drawing-room, and the great man of the occasion, who was drinking coffee near the fire-place, with his arm leaning against the mantlepiece, turned his head round at her entrance.

Full sixty years of age was the Dean of Greyminster, but erect, tall, and stalwart, as befitted the race of warriors from which he sprang, rather than the meek Churchman, the steward and minister of the grace of God. His haughty and ambitious spirit was like that of proud prelates of old, who went forth to battle in defence of their ecclesiastical territories, and trusted to their swords as well as their prayers, when dangerous or disastrous times were nigh. In these modern, peaceful, and, I fear, Dean Dalziel thought, degenerate days, his warlike spirit found vent occasionally in fierce encounters with his fellow dignitaries, who cared not often to excite the caustic sharpness of the Dean's biting acrimonious tongue. He regarded his easy-going, idle brother, the Major, with peculiar contempt. That a man could settle down to such a life was, indeed, a matter of profound astonishment to the ambitious Churchman.

"Good heaven!" he would think, "he has not even strength of character enough to rule his own wife;" and, no doubt, in the Major's household, Mrs. Dalziel was the governing power.

He was fond of his niece Eva, however, and proud of her beauty, and it was on her account that his present visit was paid to Hazelhurst.

He bowed with great courtesy to Elizabeth on being introduced to her, and at once entered into conversation with her with the practised ease of a clever and well-informed man of the world.

"Do you fish, Miss Gordon?" he inquired, for he never forgot to have a cut at his brother's occupations. "As I believe that is the only amusement Hazelhurst can boast of?"

"No, I do not fish," answered Elizabeth, smiling.

"Then what do you do?" asked the Dean, fixing his bright black eyes on Elizabeth's face.

"Ah, my dear Dean, you forget," said Mrs. Dalziel. "Where there are young people to bring up there are many duties. Miss Gordon and myself are fully occupied in educating my dear girls."

"I trust, then, that they will do your great exertions credit madam," replied the Dean, and, as usual, Mrs. Dalziel felt a little uneasy in his presence.

Her curiosity, too, remained ungratified as to the proposition that he intended to make to the family, until the following morning, and I fear that the Major's peaceful slumbers were much disturbed that night by his wife's vain attempts to unravel the mystery.

After breakfast the next day, however, he unfolded his plan. It was a fine spring morning, and after he had partaken of the luxuries that Mrs. Dalziel had prepared for his palate, the Dean rose, and opened the window of the room, through which you could pass into the garden beyond.

"Come and have a short stroll with me, Eva," he said to his favourite niece; and accordingly Eva followed him into the garden, leaving Mrs. Dalziel in a very anxious and disturbed state of mind.

"My dear Eva," began the Dean, "you have now arrived at woman's estate, and have doubtless come to a very critical period in your life."

"How do you mean, Uncle Ralph?" said Eva.

"I mean," continued the Dean, "that a woman's whole life—her whole happiness or misery—depends upon her marriage, and great responsibility therefore devolves on her relations on this account."

Eva laughed lightly, and threw back her pretty head at these words.

"Have you any one ready for me, uncle?" she said gaily. "Some long-coated curate that you have taken under your protection?"

"I should not consider a curate in a fit position to marry my niece, Eva," replied the Dean, severely; adding, after a moment's consideration, "you have not, I presume, formed any foolish attachment here?"

"Well—no—" said Eva, with pretended gravity. "There is the doctor's assistant, certainly—"

"Eva!" ejaculated the Dean.

"But all my flirtation with him," went on Eva, laughing at her uncle's horror, "consists in going to the surgery for mamma's pills. No, Uncle Ralph," she added, adroitly, as she saw wrath at her levity gathering on the Dean's brow, "I may say safely, I care for no one here—there is no one, in fact, that I could care for."

"I am pleased to hear it," said the Dean, "and now, my dear, listen to me. Your father is a man I consider utterly incapable of managing his own affairs. Your stepmother, with very good intentions, is not a person to whose management I should wish to entrust a young girl's future. There remains then of your near relations myself. What I propose to do, therefore, Eva, is this. To take a house in town this season, and introduce you to society that I consider suitable for you to associate with. An old friend of mine, Lady Curzon, who now resides at Greyminster, will act as your chaperone, and I will provide you with everything necessary; and as your personal appearance is attractive, I trust—that you will do well."

"You are very kind, uncle," said Eva, and her heart gave a great bound. Few young girls, in fact, could have heard of such a change of life without emotion, and Eva felt very much excited at the prospect before her.

CHAPTER XXVIII.

THE DEAN'S SCHEME.

IF Eva were excited by her uncle's proposal, Mrs. Dalziel was ten times more so.

"If I could only go with the dear girl," she suggested to the Dean. "You see, life has so many trials—a mother's love is such a protection—and—"

"My dear madam," interrupted the Dean, decisively, "I shall not think of depriving my brother of your agreeable society. My friend Lady Curzon is a person of position, and that is more necessary to a young girl on her introduction to the world than a step-mother's love."

Tears nearly came into Mrs. Dalziel's eyes at this unfeeling retort.

"Of course," she said meekly, "I know I'm not a titled lady— I know I'm not—"

"You are an excellent woman, my dear sister-in-law," again interrupted the Dean, "but many things are required sometimes as well as excellence. Lady Curzon understands her business, and has married her own daughters well, and I have no doubt, as Eva is such a pretty girl, that she will be equally fortunate with her."

"But," said Mrs. Dalziel, "it seems so dreadful—scheming about marriage—taking your children into the market."

"We all go to market," answered the Dean, humorously, "and the clever ones dispose the best of their goods. The man who stays at home gets nothing at the fair, and the mart that women should think most of, and do most unquestionably think most of, is the marriage one."

"I am sure," said Mrs. Dalziel, sighing, and really believing in herself at the moment, "when I was a girl I never thought of such things."

"But you cleverly made Henry think of them," replied the Dean, with a chuckle, and Mrs. Dalziel did not think it politic to pursue the discussion further.

But it was all arranged before the Dean left Hazelhurst. He intended to take a good furnished house for the season, and invite Lady Curzon, who was a baronet's widow, and who resided in Greyminster, on a somewhat limited fortune, to stay with him in town. But though Lady Curzon was not rich, she was very highly connected, and had, during her husband's lifetime, married her own two daughters so well, that the Dean justly considered her a very eligible chaperone; and Lady Curzon, who was a woman of the world, and loved pleasure still, would, he felt sure, be glad to exchange for a time her dull dower-house beneath the shadow of the cathedral towers at Greyminster, for a pleasant and lively visit to him.

So he presented Eva with a cheque for a hundred pounds before he left the village, and told her to get what was necessary. The girl was amazed at the amount of his gift, but as she knew the Dean was very rich she did not scruple to accept it.

"Write to London for what you want, Eva," advised the Dean, and Eva promised to comply with his advice. He also gave five pounds each to his younger nieces, and finally took his departure, leaving every one (except the Major) impressed with his grandeur and generosity.

The Major, however, heaved a sigh of relief as he saw the train vanish which contained his reverend and ambitious brother.

"He gets more conceited every day he lives," he confided to his wife after he had seen the last of him. "No one seems good enough company for him now but titled people. Before I would lead such a life—a man of sixty—I would see myself hanged!"

"Still, my dear, it is a great thing for Eva—being introduced, as he no doubt has the power to introduce her," said Mrs. Dalziel.

"Well, I suppose so," grumbled the Major. "She'll see a lot of fine people, but whether they may do her any good or not it is impossible to tell."

Still, though the Major spoke thus, he undoubtedly was secretly hopeful that his pretty daughter would do well in life. He had no fortune to give her, for his scanty savings out of his small yearly income all went to pay a heavy insurance on his life. Thus it was unquestionably a very advantageous offer that the Dean had made to his niece, and the next month was spent in preparing Eva for the important visit.

The girl herself began to make little jokes about it after a while.

"When I return without an admirer, won't I pity you, mamma, dear?" she said one day, merrily, in the midst of the preparations.

"Oh! Eva—" said Mrs. Dalziel, reproachfully.

"Well, I really shall," said Eva, going on with the manufacture of some finery.

"My dear, do not say such a thing," answered Mrs. Dalziel. "Of course, no one would rejoice so much as I would in any good fortune happening to you—"

"In the shape of a rich young man," suggested Eva, laughing.

"Say rather a good man, my dear—but I was not thinking of men. I am no schemer, Eva. It is your happiness, and that of my husband and two dear children, that I think of most. I trust, however, that you will be very attentive to your uncle, Eva, and seek to please him in every way. He likes agreeable things said to him, I think, so I hope you won't neglect this duty."

"Do you mean that I am to flatter him, mamma?" asked Eva, who sometimes loved to tease her step-mother.

"No, not flatter; you never hear me flatter, I am sure. But men in his position like to be told of their good qualities, and it is very easy to see good qualities in those who are kind to us, and to whom we are indebted, and you are very much indebted to your uncle Ralph."

"Very well," said Eva, "I will try to see his good qualities, and not to see his bad ones, so it will be all right."

"I hope so, I'm sure, my dear," answered Mrs. Dalziel, "I am very anxious about you, but I hope that everything will turn out for the best."

Presently the Dean wrote to say that he had engaged a house in Grosvenor Place, the owner of which had gone abroad in ill-health, and that Lady Curzon had gladly accepted his invitation to spend April, May, and June with him in town; and he further added, in this letter, that he would be pleased if his brother Henry would bring Eva up on the 7th of April, and stay a few days with him before he returned to Hazelhurst, and the "rural delights of that village."

The Major was pleased at the prospect of the little change, and the idea of looking up some of his old military acquaintances in town; but Mrs. Dalziel was exceedingly mortified that she had not been invited also.

"It is such a want of respect in your brother, Henry," she said. "I have been a good wife to you for many years, I may say without self-commendation, and for the head of your house to neglect me in such a pointed manner, I must say is very trying. I am not selfish—I do not care for my own enjoyment, but still I think he ought to have asked me; and I think if you love me as I trust I deserve, you ought not to go, just to punish your brother for his want of respect."

"My dear, it would not punish him in the least," answered the Major, who did not wish to be deprived of his treat. "Ralph has merely asked me as a convenience, as he thought that Eva could not very well travel alone."

"Then you mean to go?"

"Why should I not? I can't let the child go alone, and I'll see Ralph's grand new house into the bargain, and be able to tell you what kind of woman this Lady Curzon is."

Mrs. Dalziel only sighed deeply at this announcement, but she contrived to make her good-natured husband exceedingly uncomfortable during the time that elapsed before he and Eva started for town. Not that she absolutely meant to do this, but her vanity was very acute, though she was perfectly unconscious of its existence. She merely wished to let her husband know that she thought he was slighting her by accepting his brother's invitation, and she perfectly impressed this idea upon his mind.

But the time came at last, and pretty Eva, with her new

dresses packed in her new trunks, was ready for her journey. She had not spent all the Dean's gift on her own adornment though, for there were several poor people in Hazelhurst the richer for her new wealth. She also insisted that "Mamma" should have a dress purchased out of her uncle's money. At first, however, Mrs. Dalziel would not hear of this.

"No my dear," she said, "spend it all on yourself. My wants are small, and I must try to be contented with the humble allowance my husband is able to give me."

She ultimately relented, however, and Eva had the pleasure of presenting her mother with a dress after all—a dress which she frequently told both her husband and stepdaughter, after the Dean's invitation to the Major, that under the circumstances she had no pleasure in wearing.

In spite of all the excitement in prospect, Eva was as kind and loving as ever to Elizabeth. Nay, she declared that she would have looked forward to her visit to London with twice the pleasure if her friend had been going with her.

"You will make many friends there, Eva," said Lissa. "You will be marrying some fine gentleman, and will forget all about poor me."

"Shall I?" said Eva. "Well, you will see. I will write nearly every day, and tell you everything. Mind you are not to tell mamma; you must hint nothing to her that I tell you. You are my friend, and I shall have no secrets from you, but if I were to tell her anything, I should never hear the last of it."

"Very well," said Lissa, smiling. She was very fond of Eva, and pleased to see the young girl's excitement and joy. She remembered the time when her life also seemed all lying fair and pleasant before her, and she most earnestly trusted that pretty Eva's would not be blighted in the same cruel fashion.

To the end Mrs. Dalziel wore a slightly injured air whenever the approaching visit was mentioned, but she kissed Eva very kindly when she went away, and said she trusted it would be all for her happiness.

"Of course, of course," interrupted the Major, "but we'll lose the train if you're so long in saying good-bye."

So they went away, and the house at Hazelhurst settled down into its ordinary decorous quietude after they were gone.

"You will work more steadily at your lessons now, I trust," said Mrs. Dalziel, impressively, to her two young daughters before E'izabeth, and the governess took the hint.

Mrs. Dalziel was a little jealous, in fact, of the friendship between Elizabeth and Eva, and thought that Elizabeth should devote more time to her own daughters out of school hours. But then, had Elizabeth devoted every minute of her time to them, Mrs. Dalziel would have thought it would have been better to have given less.

The first letter from town arrived from the Major to his wife, and was brief and characteristic.

"My dear Lucy," he wrote, "We arrived all right. This is one of the smaller houses in Grosvenor Place, but well furnished, and Ralph seems inclined to do the thing in style. He has engaged two footmen and a carriage, and Lady Curzon seems a pleasant woman of the world. We have a dinner-party to-day, to which her two married daughters are coming. One is the wife of a judge—Judge Dereham—the hanging judge, I believe they call him on the circuit. The other is married to Sir James Langham, who is in the Ministry, so you see that Eva ought to get on pretty well. Lady Curzon complimented me on her beauty this morning, and she is to be presented at the first Drawing-room. That is all my news. I hope that you and the children are well. See that Johnnie gets the ground ready for the early crops of peas, etc., and believe me to remain your affectionate husband,

"HENRY DALZIEL."

Eva's first letter was to Elizabeth.

"My dearest Lissa," it began, "I feel as if I were in another world. The house here and everything is so different to what I have been accustomed to, that I can scarcely believe that I am the same person who lived eighteen, nearly nineteen, long years at poor old Hazelhurst. I was quite awe-stricken at first with the grandeur of the footmen—two tall, solemn-faced young men, who seem to anticipate your wishes at table, instead of waiting anxiously for one's turn to be helped, as we do at home. But to-day I have got quite used to be well attended upon, and I suppose I'll get used to other things in time. Lady Curzon seems very kind, but I don't know whether I shall like her or not, but I think I like her daughter, Lady Dereham, who dined here yesterday. Lord Dereham is a judge, quite an old man compared to his wife, and with such a stern face. I can imagine him *pitiless*. Lady Dereham has a sad look, but Lady Curzon tells me Lord Dereham is an excellent husband, but I know that he would frighten *me*. Who do you think dined here too? But you will never guess, so I must tell you—Sir John Tyrell, that you know, and his son! Was it not strange? I wore my white silk, and uncle gave me some lovely flowers, but I felt very nervous when the people were being announced, and kept near papa. By-and-by, two of the handsomest and most distinguished-looking men I ever saw came in, and Charles, the footman, said, 'Sir John Tyrell, and Mr. Tyrell,' and I thought of you in a moment, and wondered if he was *your* Sir John Tyrell. Well, I went down to dinner with a very stupid young man, *I thought*, but Lady Curzon whispered to me to be sure to be very agreeable to him. Then, when the gentlemen returned to the drawing-room, I saw Sir John Tyrell looking at me and speaking to Uncle Ralph, who presently brought him up to where I was sitting, and introduced him to me.

"'I have asked to be presented to you,' Sir John said, in such a courteous manner, taking the next seat to me, 'because I think you know a young friend of mine, Miss Gordon?'

"You may think how we talked about you after that. Sir John spoke of you in the highest terms, and said that family misfortunes had alone induced you to think of being a governess, and that he was so glad you had found a happy home with us (so you must have told him, dear, that you are happy at Hazelhurst), and *I am so glad*—but he said something else. Darling Lissa, I promised to tell you everything, so I will tell you this, but I thought it a strange thing of Sir John to say, and he hesitated and coloured when he did so.

"'Do you know my son?' he asked, and I said, 'No.' 'Well, then, Miss Dalziel,' he went on, smiling, 'as you probably will form Jasper's acquaintance, I am going to ask you a favour.'

"'And what is that, Sir John?' I said.

"'Not to mention that Miss Gordon is your sisters' governess to him,' he answered. 'Not, in fact, to mention Miss Gordon's name to him at all. There are reasons for this,' he added. 'Miss Gordon would not care that he—that any one, indeed, but myself, who am an old friend of her family's—should know that she has been compelled to accept a situation of this sort. Jasper, you see, is a young man,' he went on with a laugh, 'and I am an old one, and that makes all the difference how young ladies can trust us; so you must not say anything to him about her.'

"Of course, I promised, but I made up my mind that I would tell everything he said to *you*. He called his son (who is in the Navy, I believe) across the room afterwards, and introduced him, and we talked a great deal. He is amusing, and has seen lots of things. I fear he will think me a sad little ignoramus, having lived all my life in the country.

"But I must say good-bye now, my dearest, dearest Lissa. Write soon, and tell me all about Hazelhurst, and what you like about yourself.

"Your loving little friend,

"Eva."

CHAPTER XXIX.
EVA'S LOVERS.

WE can understand Elizabeth's emotion on receiving this letter. It seems so strange always to hear those who are familiar and dear to us spoken or written of as strangers; but strange, most strange, to Elizabeth, to know that Eva Dalziel knew Jasper Tyrell!

How she longed to write and ask how he looked; to ask to have repeated to her some of his careless words; to hear described the features, the little mannerisms, the very tones she knew so well !

A vague disappointment, too, grew in her heart to know that Sir John meant to keep her secret from Jasper Tyrell so well. True, she had asked him to do this—true, she knew it was far better Jasper should not know where she was living and yet—and yet—

Did the postman ever wend his slow way up the row of houses in the village without her watching him ? Had she not sometimes secretly hoped that Jasper would send her some little word or token ? Had she not thought in fact, that Sir John might have relieved in some way the natural anxiety of his son ?

But now she knew that he had not done this, and yet Jasper could go into society, and smile and talk agreeably to any young girl he met ! This letter of Eva's did not add to poor Elizabeth's happiness during the long spring days that followed its arrival; and when in about a week Major Dalziel returned to Hazelhurst, he had a word to say to Elizabeth about Jasper Tyrell also.

"I met Sir John Tyrell," he said, addressing Elizabeth, on the first evening after his arrival home, "and he spoke very highly, Miss Gordon, of you. He said you were a country neighbour of his in Uplandshire. He is a very fine-looking man."

"Yes," said Elizabeth, "and he is a very good man, too."

"He looks a good fellow," went on the Major, "and his son—the one who is in the Navy—is a handsome fellow. Little Eva seemed quite smitten with him the night he dined in Grosvenor Place. There was a great talk in the papers some two years ago about the elder son being murdered. He was found dead—at least, shot—but it was never discovered. Do you remember the circumstance ?

"Yes," again answered Elizabeth, turning away her head so that the Major should not see her face.

"Well, this one's a fine looking fellow at any rate," continued the Major, "a dark, bronzed, handsome fellow. I did not speak to him, for he seemed to be too much taken up with talking to the ladies to care to waste his time on an old fogie like me."

"And—and—did you think our dear girl—liked him, papa ? " inquired Mrs. Dalziel, anxiously.

"Oh ! nothing particular," answered the Major with a careless laugh. "There's a Sir Robert Dacre, a young north country baronet, that I believe Lady Curzon thinks admires her—but it's all nonsense trying to arrange these things."

Eva's next letter was dutifully to Mamma, and merely contained a country girl's description of all the places she had been to, and the sights she had seen. But she was enjoying herself "immensely," she wrote, and uncle Ralph was so kind, and Lady

Curzon was very kind also; and they were going to dine at her daughter's, Lady Dereham's, on Thursday, and on Friday were going somewhere else, and so on   She made no mention in this letter of either of the Tyrells, and so Elizabeth was forced to bear her anxiety on this subject as best she could. She wrote to Eva twice, however, before she received any answer, for (as Eva explained when she did write) she never had a moment of leisure to write in, "and so dearest Lissa must forgive her seeming neglect." She then proceeded to tell Elizabeth that she often saw the Tyrells now, and that she liked Sir John *so much*.   His daughters were in town also, and Lady Curzon had called upon them, and Eva had accompanied her, and now they often met. She liked Fannie the best.   Did Elizabeth know Fannie ? And did she know Mr. Tyrell well? inquired the young girl.

These were very bitter questions we may be sure for poor Elizabeth to answer, and she shed many bitter tears over Eva's innocent words. But she replied to them. She told Eva that she had known very little of the Misses Tyrell, but more of Mr. Tyrell and his unfortunate brother. She asked two or three questions about Jasper also in this letter (in her previous ones she had told Eva that it was best for her not to mention her name to Jasper, as Sir John had requested it), but she could not resist wishing to know and to hear about him, But three weeks passed, and Eva apparently had not time to write to her friend again, and only during this time indited the briefest letters home to her papa and mamma.

Then came another letter to Elizabeth, which contained some news.

It began " My dearest Lissa, I know that you must hate me by this time for not writing to you before, and I am sure that I hate myself. But every hour here seems to be occupied, and Lady Curzon scolds me if I am not always ready to go everywhere.   I must tell you, to begin with, that her ladyship and I have had a slight *fracas*. I have never described her to you, dear, but I think I must do so now. Well, she is a fine, tall, well-made woman of fifty-five or six, or seven, or eight, perhaps ! But she wears well, and dresses well, and loves the world and all the good things therein. Her son is a married man, and I believe that her own income is small, but she is well-connected, and has plenty of fine friends and companions, who all, I am sure, rather look down on poor me.

"Well, I told you that a sullen-looking young, north country baronet took me down to dinner at the first party we had here. This Sir Robert Dacre, Lady Curzon insists, is an admirer of mine, and her ladyship took me to task yesterday, if you please, about not sufficiently encouraging his attentions.

" 'But I don't think he is attentive ,' I said.

"'Nonsense, my dear,' said Lady Curzon (she patronises me on all occasions); 'I assure you *he is*. A young man of large landed property like Sir Robert would not seek you at all unless he had some serious intentions. He knows, in fact, that I should be perfectly justified in asking him what he means, and as your uncle's friend and your present chaperone, I feel that I should be so.'

"'Then I will never speak to you more if you do,' I said, in a rage, 'nor to Sir Robert either.'

"I wish you had seen her look of well-bred astonishment at this. She was silent for a moment, and then she said: 'My dear Eva, pray do not excite yourself—you should not show your country education so plainly. Your father is a half-pay officer in the Army, is he not?' she went on, 'and you are one of three daughters? Sir Robert Dacre is a man of family, and has twelve thousand a year. I must conclude,' she added, smiling, 'that since he is not acceptable to you that some one else is more so.' And with a good-natured nod, she turned away.

"But I wish I could describe the contemptuous and good-tempered pity with which she spoke of dear papa's position. He might have been a crossing-sweeper, instead of an officer and a gentleman; but then Uncle Ralph always does so too. Indeed, if it were not for *something* I do not think that I would care to stay on here much longer. Uncle Ralph is so worldly, and Lady Curzon is so worldly, and they care for nothing but great people. They never think of grand actions or noble deeds, unless they are *successful*. Sometimes, when I forget the atmosphere in which I am living, and begin to talk of higher things, as I talk to you, Lissa, Uncle Ralph will pat me good-temperedly on the shoulder.

"'Care about looking pretty, my dear,' he said the other day, 'that ought to be a woman's highest ambition; eh, Lady Curzon?'

"'She is a little rustic,' answered her Ladyship, good-naturedly, 'but after all, Dean, the smell of the wild rose is sweet;' and she laughed pleasantly at her own remark.

"So you see, Lissa, that though I am enjoying myself very, very much—sometimes I think almost too much—it is still not all roses. Uncle Ralph is so ambitious, that I am always afraid of annoying him by doing or saying something that he does not like. Indeed, I am beginning to think that I am more fitted for 'my village,' as my Uncle Ralph calls Hazelhurst, than for the great world—and yet I do not know whether I should like to come home."

This letter was written after Eva had been about two months with the Dean, and after he had been somewhat disappointed in finding that the intentions of the rich, young, north country baronet, Sir Robert Dacre, to his pretty niece had ended in nothing. As Eva had told Lissa, the leading characteristic of the Dean of Greyminster was ambition. It had not been philanthropy only, nor love for any member of his brother's family, that had induced the Dean to spend this season in town. He had ulterior motives of his own for doing so, and he knew that a pretty girl like Eva would render his house attractive, and at the same time give her an opportunity of settling herself advantageously in the world. For this season he had invited Lady Curzon; but Lady Curzon, who was a shrewd woman, and saw many things with her placid eyes (when she lifted her double gold glasses to them) that she never mentioned, soon decided in her own mind that the Dean had other designs, as well as a wealthy marriage for his niece. Nay, she became assured that his restless ambition was insatiable, and that he aspired to hold the very highest dignity that his Church could bestow. She watched him with an amused smile, making friends with great personages, and spending his wealth (for he was very rich) with judicious lavishness. The Dean, in fact, knew that a certain price must be paid for most of things, and that the chances of his success were materially enhanced by his presence amongst those who had the power to promote it.

Yet he had already far more of the world's good things than usually fall to the lot of most men. From his youth upwards he had been fortunate, and a large private fortune had been bequeathed to him by a relative, as well as the inheritance derived from his late father, General Dalziel.

The old General's will, indeed, had been most unjust, for he left nearly everything he possessed to Dean Dalziel, and only a few thousands to his brother, the Major, who had offended the irritable old General by an early and unambitious marriage with Eva's mother.

Thus from private sources, and the large revenue that accrued from his ecclesiastical appointment (the Deanery of Greyminster being one of the richest in the kingdom), Dean Dalziel was very wealthy. He did not hoard his income, however, but gave such princely sums to public and private charities that his generosity was famous, and he was a man held in high repute among all classes of society.

He especially wished, then, that his niece should marry well, both on his own account and hers, and, therefore, had indulged in such worldly talk before the young girl during the last month or so of her visit, wishing to impress upon her mind the advantages of her present position under his roof, and the social decadence she must experience if she returned unwedded, or, at least, disengaged, to her father's.

Eva, however, as we have seen by her letter to Elizabeth,

resented this. She confessed, indeed, sometimes to her own heart, that she would not now like to return to the homely mono-tony of the life at Hazelhurst; but still she would never marry for money, she always declared both to her uncle and her chaperone, that wily lady, however, not giving much heed to the young girl's assertions.

Thus, things went on and the season wore away after the usual fashion. Eva was presented, and wrote a detailed description of her dress, etc., to "Mamma," at home, who read it to the doctor, and the doctor related at each house that he called at during the morning, how Miss Dalziel had been to Court, and how elated Mrs. Dalziel seemed to be by that event.

"I wish her head mayn't be turned by such fine doings," said Mrs. Plumpton, the grocer's wife. "Well, we'll see how it all ends," suggested Mrs. Tibbits, whose husband was the landlord of the Nag's Head, the principal inn in the village. "I do not approve of people stepping out of the station to which they were called," remarked Mrs. Ladon, (the Dalziel's next door neighbour) who felt jealous on her son's account of Eva's advancement.

Yet all these good women wished the pretty girl they had known by sight since childhood no ill. They only felt it to be their duty to damp the hopes of their neighbours, and did not like to hear of any one being set up on high, without prophesying that some day they might be brought down very low.

These evil prognostications, however, were all suddenly to be disproved, for before the end of June news arrived at Hazel-hurst of Eva's engagement.

The young girl had slackened in her correspondence of late, and had only occasionally written a few hurried lines to her friend Elizabeth. In these brief notes she sometimes mentioned the Tyrells, and sometimes did not, but Elizabeth noticed that Jasper Tyrell's name rarely occurred in them, and she concluded therefore that her old lover had probably left town, and so passed away out of Eva's mind.

But one very fine summer's night, about nine o'clock, she was sitting reading in the orchard at the end of the garden, just a week before Eva was expected to return to Hazelhurst, when a letter was brought to her by one of the servants, which had just arrived by the evening post, and which she saw at once was from Eva.

With somewhat languid interest she opened it, for Eva's last letters had been full of nothing but balls, garden-parties, and other amusements, and she naturally expected that this one would be the same. The subtle influence of the world, too, Elizabeth imagined, was beginning to affect the frank, open character of Eva, and though she acknowledged that this was but natural, knowing the atmosphere in which she had been living for the last three months, still Elizabeth was disappointed, and looked now at the three note sheets, covered with Eva's careless, almost childish, handwriting with a certain amount of indifference.

Still she began to read the letter immediately, and the first lines at once riveted her attention.

It commenced even more affectionately than usual.

"My dearest, dearest Lissa," wrote Eva, "I am sure that this letter will surprise you, because I have never hinted what has been in my heart all this time ; in fact, I dared not believe in my happiness until I knew it was *true.*

"I told you about that stupid Sir Robert Dacre, that Lady Curzon and Uncle Ralph were always talking to me about. Well, though I never told them so, I believe he did just like me *a little bit ;* and perhap,s if I had not liked *somebody else,* I might have learned to have liked him a *little bit, too, in time* But I did like somebody else. Oh! so much, so much, Lissa! I dare not tell you about it, because I thought it might all end in disappointment and pain, and if I were to bear this, I felt that I could bear it best alone. But I have not to bear it, and I am the happiest girl, Lissa—yes, the very happiest girl on earth. It was only settled last night, so you see I've lost no time in telling you of my joy— but last night, at Lady Dereham's ball, Jasper told me that he loved me, and asked me to be his wife—"

Thus far Elizabeth read, and then suddenly something seemed to rush from her heart to her brain, and everything grew black and dark around her. She had, in fact, fainted, and some minutes elapsed before, with slow and deep-drawn sighs, her consciousness began to return. When she remembered where she was, and lifted up her languid eyes to the sky all glowing with the brilliant hues of eve, she could not at first recall what had happened, and put her hand with a vague and uncertain motion to her head. Then suddenly—with a rush, it all came bak. Eva was engaged to Jasper Tyrell—Eva had won her love, her life, and the exceeding bitterness of the blow seemed heavier than Elizabeth's heart could bear.

Then, as in extreme moments of pain we face the inevitable, Elizabeth again lifted Eva's letter, and with her dry, hard eyes, read the rest of the young girl's words—"but last night, at Lady Dereham's ball, Jasper told me he loved me, and asked me to be his wife." This sentence Elizabeth re-read, and then went on with the rest of the letter.

"I suppose I need not tell you my answer, for it was only one little word, but Jasper heard it and I think he needed no more.

"To-day he came and saw uncle, and it is all settled. Oh! Lissa I do not deserve this happiness—how shall I deserve it ? 'By being a good wife to Jasper,' my dear, grave Lissa will reply; but there is no merit in being what to me will be the greatest joy on earth. I think I should die now if anything parted

us, but I hope there is no fear of this. Uncle Ralph is pleased, and
Lady Curzon is pleased, and Jasper tells me that he is sure that
Sir John will be pleased also, and I suppose that dear papa and
mamma will be so, too. But *they* are not pleased at what I am
pleased at. They think that Jasper is the son of a baronet, and
that he is well off. I think only that he is *Jasper—my Jasper*, the
dearest man on earth.

"Write to me darling, and tell me how pleased *you are*, and
believe me to remain your loving, happy friend.

"EVA DALZIEL."

As Elizabeth read these words, as she pictured the girl's
innocent joy, and recalled Jasper Tyrell's passionate, and
apparently overpowering love for herself—a love for which he
had so lately been ready to sacrifice so much—it seemed to her
all like a hideous dream.

"It cannot be true!" she cried, dashing her hand impetuously
against her damp cold brow. She wanted to wake herself—it
was a nightmare—a frightful dream—it could not be real—a real,
real thing!

Alas! while she was thus struggling with emotions which were
so strong that her very senses were reeling beneath their weight,
she heard a voice calling her name which told only too plainly that
she was not dreaming—that she was really sitting in the orchard
—that Eva's letter really lay upon her knee.

It was Mrs. Dalziel who had come to seek her, and in her hand
was an open letter also.

"I have been looking everywhere for you Miss Gordon," said
that lady, now approaching Elizabeth, "but at last Jane told me
that you were here. Ah! I see you've had a letter, too, so I
suppose Eva has told you her news."

Elizabeth tried to speak, but her tongue refused its office.

"It is a great marriage, is it not?" said Mrs. Dalziel, with
elation. "Papa says that Sir John Tyrell is a rich man, and this
young gentleman is his only son. It is strange that you should
know these Tyrells, isn't it? Do tell me all about them—is there
a Lady Tyrell?"

"Yes," answered Elizabeth slowly, but in so changed a voice
that it at once attracted Mrs. Dalziel's attention.

"My dear Miss Gordon are you ill?" she said. "Dear, dear,
how strange you look! Take my arm and let me try to get you
to the house. Have you been sitting here long? I wish, I am
sure, that you may not be going to be very ill."

CHAPTER XXX.
THE BETROTHED PAIR.

ELIZABETH crept back to her own room, assisted by Mrs. Dalziel and lay down on the bed looking like one about to die. Mrs. Dalziel felt in the greatest alarm about her, and speedily procured some brandy, which she pressed Elizabeth to take.

"Drink this, my dear Miss Gordon," she said, pouring out a considerable quantity into a wine glass, and Elizabeth drank it; would have drunk anything to relieve herself from her intolerable pain.

At first a sort of warmth crept over her after she had taken the stimulant, and then a shivering fit succeeded, so that the whole bed shook beneath her form. Then her brain seemed to begin to whirl, and strange fancies took possession of her. Yet she was conscious of passing things; that the village doctor was standing beside her; that they were putting cold bandages on her forehead; that people came in and out of the room, looking at her with dismay pictured on their faces, and muttering words that she could not understand.

After, this she seemed to lose all count of time, and to be driven with irresistible swiftness, past wonderful panoramas of things that she had seen before. In these fevered hours she visited, in imagination, once more the unused store-room at Wendell, where lay hidden, amid ancient finery, the evidences of Richard Horton's crime. Then the thunder seemed to roll around her, and the lightening flash, as it did on her wedding-day; and then again she was on the hill-side, and heard the death-shot which stained her cousin's hand with his father's blood.

These things came and passed away, recurring and recurring amid a vast chaos of darkness, of grim shadows, and demon-haunted dreams. But through all—through pictures of the past, through frightful struggles with giant forms that seemed to rend her frame, or bear her along with incredible swiftness—one feeling never left her, which was a great undying sense of pain.

Many days passed thus, and many nights, and they cut off her long dark hair, and another doctor was sent for, and it was known in the Major's household that the governess was lying dangerously ill, and that brain fever had struck her down.

Mrs. Dalziel was very attentive to her, but of course could not nurse her night and day, so an old crone from the village was sent for, whose big, white cap many a time danced and whirled in Elizabeth's wild fantastic dreams.

Then came a time when she saw nothing and heard nothing, and when she lay very near to death. And then—one evening —a change came, and in wavering uncertain glimpses, Elizabeth beheld and knew again the faces of those around her.

When she first awoke to consciousness she heard someone softly crying near the bed. She tried to move to see who it was, but she could not even lift her hand, and then she heard Mrs. Dalziel's voice speaking soothingly.

"You must not grieve so, dear Eva," she said, "her life is in Higher hands than ours. We have done all we could, so whatever happens we shall always have the consolation of knowing this. You must go to bed to-night, dear. I will not have you sitting up any more—last night was the third night that you have never been in bed."

"I won't leave her," answered Eva in a very low voice. "I won't leave her with that horrid old woman, mamma, any more. I've not forgotten the night I came home and found her snoring, and Lissa on the point of death. Every moment must be watched, the doctor says, and I shall watch her myself, and trust her to no one."

"But, my dear, you will be ill."

Mamma, it's of no use talking, I mean to do it," answered Eva, and she rose softly from where she was sitting behind the curtains of Elizabeth's bed, and after drying her eyes, came forward to look at her patient, and Elizabeth smiled faintly at her as she did so

"My darling!" said Eva, almost under her breath. "Lissa, do you know me?"

"Yes," answered Elizabeth; at least her lips moved to say it, and Eva bent down and kissed her face.

"Be a good child then," she whispered, afraid even by speaking to her to scare away the look of recognition that she hailed so joyfully. "Lie quite quiet, while I give you something." And she proceeded to put spoonfuls of liquid jelly at intervals into Elizabeth's mouth, and motioned to her step-mother noiselessly to leave the room.

After this, little by little, but very slowly, Elizabeth began to recover. She was so faint and weak that though she knew things, nothing seemed very vivid to her mind, while a kind of apathy deadened her feelings, rendering her partially insensible to everything that passed around her.

Unless this had been the case she probably would never have got well, for as her bodily strength returned, so did the terrible mental pain that had struck her down, and sent her brain reeling under the sudden blow.

But she strove to conquer this. Lying there hand and hand with her sweet young nurse, who scarcely ever left her; who had watched and waited on her through many days when they had despaired of her life, and who now spent nearly the whole of her time in the sick room, poor Elizabeth tried to think it was for the best; tried to pray that Jasper might make his young wife happy;

and that the two might live on, when she was lying in her forgotten grave.

But it was very, very hard to bear. Little by little the young girl began to prattle about her lover, and to tell Elizabeth, with sweet pride shining in her eyes, of Jasper's gifts, Jasper's thoughts, Jasper's noble, generous words.

She was evidently deeply, fondly in love with him, and the thought of him coloured every action of her life. For instance, one evening, when Elizabeth urged her to go out for a walk, and to leave her post by her bedside for a little while, Eva hid her blushing face on Elizabeth's breast.

"Would I be worthy of him—of my Jasper," she whispered, "if I were to neglect you?" And with a groan Elizabeth had to listen to her words.

Eva was very anxious also to tell Jasper that Elizabeth Gordon was the "governess" that she had nursed so attentively.

"Of course I have not done so," she told Elizabeth. "You said I was not to do so, and Sir John said so, but now—Lissa, now—," and Eva blushed deeply, "I don't like to have even one litttle secret from Jasper. I wish him to know every thought of my heart."

But Elizabeth would not give the permission, fearing that some harm might come by it to this sweet child,

"Wait a little while, Eva," she said. "Jasper—Mr. Tyrell— will be coming here soon, I suppose?"

"Yes, as soon as you are better," answered Eva. "I told him that he must not come until then, because I must nurse you until you are quite well. I came home, you know, the moment that they told me you were very ill. Uncle Ralph was so cross with me for leaving, but Jasper was not, though he did not know it was a friend of his that I was going to nurse."

"I was more a friend of Sir John's," faltered Elizabeth.

"Yes, I know," answered Eva in her guileless way, "but still you knew Jasper—and his poor brother. Lissa, will you tell me all about Harry Tyrell's death, for I do not like to speak to Jasper on such a painful subject?"

But Elizabeth's irrepressible emotion at this question alarmed the young girl, and a sudden suspicion entered her mind.

"Oh! Lissa, what have I done?" she cried. She thought at that moment that Lissa had loved Harry Tyrell, and that his tragic end was the secret that had blighted Elizabeth's life.

"It is nothing," said Elizabeth, struggling with her emotion, "I knew Harry Tyrell well, that is all—it is a painful subject to me also."

So Eva never mentioned Harry's death to Elizabeth any more, but she believed that Elizabeth had loved him, and that this was the tie that bound her to Sir John. Mrs. Dalziel, however, had other uneasy thoughts about " Miss Gordon's " connections with the Tyrell family.   She had not forgotten Elizabeth's terrible look when she found her half-fainting in the orchard with Eva's letter lying on her lap. She had not forgotten either the governess's wild cries during the first period of her illness, amongst which Jasper Tyrell's name was so often heard.   True she had spoken of other things amid her ravings; of snow drifts, and the dying words of murdered men, but Jasper Tyrell's name had recurred with strange persistency, and Mrs. Dalziel, after her usual fashion, began to throw little chill doubts upon her step-daughter's bright hopes of joy.

" You should not set your heart so entirely on this marriage, Eva," she said one day. "In this world we can never tell what may happen—Mr. Tyrell may have had some previous attachment."

" What do you mean, mamma ? " said Eva, flushing deeply.

" I'm afraid to see you, my dear, wrapped up so completely in Mr. Tyrell," answered Mrs. Dalziel evasively. "I should like to see you have a little more interest in your quiet home employments—you seem to me to be utterly unsettled."

" So I am," said Eva, in her frank way. "It's quite true, mamma, that I can't think of anything but Jasper, but then I think I've a right to think—of my future husband."

" Well, I'm sure I hope it will be all right," said Mrs. Dalziel, sighing, and she would sometimes talk in this way to the Major also.

That good easy man, however, took things very calmly, and placidly remarked that he did not suppose that Mr. Tyrell would have asked Eva unless he had wanted her; and he advised his wife not to put foolish ideas into the child's head.

" I may have my reasons, papa," Mrs. Dalziel hinted darkly; but she had the good sense at least not to repeat poor Elizabeth's fevered ravings, and everything apparently went on pleasantly with the betrothed pair.

The Dean wrote a characteristic letter to his brother on the subject of the marriage, and also inviting Eva to stay at the Deanery until that ceremony was celebrated. "Hazelhurst may be very charming and salubrious, my dear Henry," wrote the proud Churchman, "but I would not recommend it as a residence for Eva at the present time.   Mr. Tyrell is accustomed to a larger establishment, and a different mode of living than that which you prefer; therefore I think that the lover's visits had better be paid to Greyminster, and I need not tell you that Eva's presence here will be agreeable to me."

The Major laughed, but rather sourly, after he had read his brother's letter, and then handed it to Eva.

" If you are ashamed of your father's roof, my dear, before your fine lover," he said. "perhaps you had better go."

"Papa!" said Eva, jumping up, and throwing her arms round his neck, and kissing him, "*I am ashamed of you.*" But when she lifted her head, tears were standing in her bright blue eyes, and the Major himself was not without some signs of emotion.

"He is not like uncle Ralph," said Eva, the next minute, proudly; and the Dean's invitation was accordingly declined.

"My little girl," wrote the Major, in answer to his brother's letter, "wishes to spend her last unmarried days at home, and I suppose if Mr. Tyrell means to marry her, that he will not be too proud to visit her here."

"If I had ever doubted the cause of my brother's want of success in life," said the Dean to his friend Lady Curzon, the day that the Major's epistle arrived at Greyminster, "this letter would explain it. Short-sighted, sentimental folly in every word it contains!"

In spite, however, of the Dean's sarcasms, Jasper Tyrell gladly accepted his first invitation to Hazelhurst, and with sweet blushing joy Eva went to tell Elizabeth that he was coming.

"He will be so astonished when he sees you, Lissa," she said. "I think that I shall tell him that he must prepare for a pleasant surprise."

With a great effort Elizabeth received the announcement of this visit without apparent emotion. She was better now, and with slow languid steps was able to walk a little in the sunny garden at the back of the house, supported by Eva's kindly arm.

But she was very miserable and unhappy. She had believed that Jasper had loved her so well; had believed that even her very flight from him would only make him respect her more; and deep down in her heart had been another scarcely permitted hope. Some day she might be free. Richard Horton's reckless life was not likely to be a long one, "and then—and then—" Elizabeth had sometimes whispered to her heart.

But it was all over now. He had forgotten her so soon, and in a fair girl's love had found consolation for the bitter self-sacrifice that she had made in giving him up. But whatever she felt, whatever sufferings she endured, she made up her mind that she must not grieve Eva.

This sweet child played beneath the suspended sword which invisibly hung over her head, in the most perfect innocence. With great glee one day she brought the thick coils of Elizabeth's hair, which had been cut off during her illness, transformed into a most fashionable chignon. She had sent it to London, she informed Elizabeth, as she was not going to allow her to wear the little cap which Elizabeth had adopted to hide her short hair, "when Jasper came."

"What matter is it?" said Elizabeth, almost bitterly.

"It is matter" persisted Eva. "I want you to look well when he comes. Jasper says it always matters how a woman looks."

So the hair was arranged, and the day was fixed, and a few days later Elizabeth sat listening in the school-room to catch the first sounds of Jasper Tyrell's arrival.

Eva had driven to the station in the pony-chaise to meet her lover, who was expected to arrive at Hazelhurst about seven o'clock in the evening, and nearly at that hour Elizabeth heard the rumble of the carriage-wheels outside, and with her hand tight clasped to her side, to still the painful beating of her heart, she waited upstairs to see what next would follow.

Another quarter of an hour then passed, during which time Mrs. Dalziel was saying agreeable things to her expected son-in-law, and making herself, she believed, very charming, while upstairs the pale governess sat alone. Then Elizabeth heard footsteps outside the school-room door, and Eva's merry laugh; and then she heard Jasper's familiar voice say jokingly—

"Don't, Eva—don't make a fool of me, there's a good child." And the next minute the door was opened, and Jasper apparently pushed in, and the door shut behind him, and as Jasper advanced smilingly into the room, he stood face to face with his old love!

Elizabeth had risen as he entered; risen pale, changed, and unconsciously reproachful; and as Jasper Tyrell met her sad dark eyes, he absolutely started back as if he had met some frightful apparition.

"Good God!" he said, "it can't be you!"

"Yes, Jasper," answered Elizabeth, and she put out her hand. But Jasper did not take it, but stood staring at her with wide open eyes.

"It was you, then," he said at length, "the sick governess that Eva nursed? What on earth induced you, Elizabeth Gordon, to come here?"

Nothing could exceed the cold sterness of his manner as he said these words, and as Elizabeth looked up in great surprise to answer him, for she had not at least expected that he would treat her thus disdainfully, the school-room door again opened, and the sweet, pretty, smiling face of Eva peeped in.

"Well," she said, "have you two found out the secret yet? Didn't I tell you, Jasper, I was going to show you an old friend? Lissa would never let me tell you that she was here before. How do you think she looks, Jasper? You know she has been so very ill."

"I am—sorry," said Jasper Tyrell, deeply embarrassed.

But Eva now saw that something had gone amiss; so after a few more words she proposed to show Jasper the garden, and the moment they had reached it Jasper said, "How did—that lady come here, Eva? How long has she been here?"

"Why, Jasper?" answered Eva, in great surprise, "you speak as if you did not know Miss Gordon, and it was your father, Sir John Tyrell, who recommended her here."

"My father!" repeated Jasper, utterly astonished.

"Yes, indeed, Jasper. He wrote to papa about her before she came, and he talked to me about her in Grosvenor Place. But it was the strangest thing—he told me not to tell you that she was here. He said that the circumstances of her family were changed, and that she did not wish any one to know that she was forced to be a governess but he. But you knew her family, Jasper; did you not?"

"Yes," answered Jasper Tyrell briefly.

"I thought it very strange of Sir John," went on Eva, "and afterwards—when I knew you would come here—I asked Lissa if I might tell you about her, but she said I had better not; it is very strange—"

"Strange, indeed," muttered Jasper Tyrell. And then, with a violent effort, he changed the conversation, and presently his young love forgot all about Elizabeth Gordon.

CHAPTER XXXI.

A SECRET MEETING.

ELIZABETH felt quite stunned and cold after Jasper Tyrell's brief visit to the school-room. She could not understand his manner with all its unmistakable resentment, its sternness, and reserve.

"He evidently wishes not to acknowledge our old acquaintance here," she thought bitterly. "What have I done that he should treat me thus?"

Then she recalled the offer that he made but a few months ago; an offer refused with such passionate tears and pain. Was this the man who was then ready to sacrifice everything for her sake —who had promised to marry her—to overcome every obstacle that stood between them?

She dreaded to meet him again, and yet was eager to hear some explanation of his conduct. He might have been angry with her, she thought, because she had not trusted herself to say good-bye to him, but now—when he was about to marry another woman—need he have treated her with such contemptuous scorn?

She scarcely knew how to act, and felt bewildered by the position in which she had found herself. Oh! how often lately she had prayed for him, trying to put self away; prayed that he and dear Eva might be happy, although she knew that her heart was breaking at the thought.

But for him to meet her thus! To reject the hand that she held towards him—the thin poor hand faded and wasted for his sake! "Oh! why did I live," she wept. "Why did they not let me die—then at least I should have been spared this bitter hour."

But she was forced to dry her tears. The happy Eva, with her glad, fresh face, came running presently up the stairs, to see after "My invalid," she said, and to extract a promise from Elizabeth that she would come down to the drawing-room to tea.

This Elizabeth tried to escape doing, but Eva would not listen to her.

"You *must* come," she said; and so pale, sick, and feeble, Elizabeth went down about nine o'clock, and in a few minutes Mrs. Dalziel and Eva joined her.

Mrs. Dalziel looked flushed and pleased.

"Well," she said to Elizabeth, "I think that I am satisfied with my future son-in-law. Of course I am very hard to please about my dear girls, but I think that I really am pleased with Mr. Tyrell.   He is handsome and very gentlemanly—my little Eva is a very fortunate young lady, don't you think?"

"Yes, indeed," answered Elizabeth, with a faint cold smile.

"What is Sir John like?" went on Mrs. Dalziel, full of maternal complacency, and forgetting all her suspicions.

"He is very noble looking," said Elizabeth.

"And the mother?"

"O mamma! Jasper told me this afternoon," said Eva quickly. "Poor Lady Tyrell is a great invalid.   She never recovered the shock of her son's death."

"The one who was murdered?" asked Mrs Dalziel.

But before Eva could reply, the voices of the Major and Jasper Tyrell were heard out-side the door, and Eva gave a warning look to her mother to end the conversation.

When the gentlemen entered the drawing-room, Mrs. Dalziel formally introduced Elizabeth to Jasper.

"I do not know whether you know Miss Gordon, Mr. Tyrell?" she said. "Your father is a friend of hers, I believe—but—" And then she hesitated.

"I have the honour of knowing Miss Gordon," answered Jasper Tyrell coldly, bowing as he spoke, "but I have already seen her since my arrival at Hazelhurst."

He spoke as if he had schooled himself to say what he was expected to say, but Mrs. Dalziel received the announcement that he had already seen Elizabeth with surprise.

"Indeed," she said, slightly elevating her eyebrows.

"Yes, I took Jasper to the school-room, as Lissa knew Sir John," said Eva; and both Jasper and Elizabeth felt grateful for these words.

But the barrier between them remained unbroken.   Again and again Elizabeth met his dark, resentful eyes fixed with almost a look of hatred on her face.   He was, indeed, furious with himself; furious that this woman exercised, in spite of all his efforts to conquer it, a fascination for him that he could not resist.   That she was unworthy, he positively believed, and he had hurried into

an engagement with Eva Dalziel for the very purpose of trying to
drive Elizabeth's memory from his heart.

Now, as he looked at her pale and altered face, he was recalling
the bitter moment when he had met Mr. Wilmot in Cambridge
Street, and heard tales about her that he could not disbelieve.
Where had she been since then? he was asking himself now.
Why and how had his father interfered to obtain her a situation
in the very family of his promised wife?

This last question he resolved at least to solve, for he determined to write to Sir John and ask how such a seemingly impossible thing occurred. With such conflicting feelings struggling
in his heart, he could not form a very agreeable guest, and once
or twice Eva wondered what made Jasper so unusually silent.
But there was no want of conversation in the room. Mrs.
Dalziel was talkative and lively, and Eva and the two young girls
had plenty to say. It was agreed that they were to take Jasper
the next day to see the beauties of the neighbourhood, and Lucy
suggested that a picnic would be highly agreeable.

"We could at least have luncheon out in the woods," said Eva.
"What do you think, Jasper?"

"Of course I shall be charmed," he answered; and after various
plans had been proposed and rejected, they settled amid much
mirth and chattering to do so.

Elizabeth, however, took no part in this arrangement.

She felt faint and sick at heart, and Mrs. Dalziel's eyes happening to fall on her face, that lady instantly exclaimed—

"My dear Miss Gordon how tired you look! I am sure you are
sitting up too long. Had you not better go to bed at once?
You see Miss Gordon has been a great invalid lately, Mr. Tyrell,"
she explained.

"I am sorry to hear it," said Jasper, in the same cold, constrained
voice in which he had first spoken to her, and while he was speaking Elizabeth rose and bid the party good night.

Jasper Tyrell opened the room door for her, but he made no
attempt to touch her hand. "Good evening," he said, as she
passed him, and that was all, and then he returned to his seat by
Eva's side.

"Dear me, how ill Miss Gordon looks!" said Mrs. Dalziel.

"I am sure when she first came I thought she was a handsome
woman, but she is dreadfully altered."

"She is a beautiful woman, I think," said Eva warmly.

"No one can look well when they are just recovering from a
fever. Don't you think she is very handsome, Jasper?"

"Yes I think her handsome," replied Jasper Tyrell, and then
the subject was dropped.

But the mirth and jesting continued. The two younger girls
were delighted with the handsome sailor, and determined that

Eva should not alone enjoy his society. They laughed and chatted therefore unceasingly, and the distant sounds of this merriment stole up at intervals to Elizabeth's bedroom ; where pale, excited, almost driven mad by what she had gone through during the day, Elizabeth was pacing backwards and forwards with hasty and uneven steps.

At last she heard the girls say good-night, and go running upstairs with their light feet. Eva came to Elizabeth's door and rapped, but as she received no answer, she concluded that her sisters' governess was asleep, and presently went away.

Jasper Tyrell had retired to smoke with the Major, and all the house was still, but the restless and unhappy Elizabeth made no attempt to prepare for bed. She had no settled purpose, and yet she felt that she must do something or die. She kept listening for Jasper's footsteps, and when she heard them slowly coming up-stairs a sudden resolution seized her, and without another thought she went out on the dark corridor, and waited for him near the school-room door.

"Jasper," she said, in a low tone, as he passed her, grasping his hand with her burning one almost before he even saw her, "why do you treat me thus? What have I done to deserve this from you?"

Jasper Tyrell was carrying his bedroom candle, and by its light he saw her pale face and flashing eyes, and put up his hand with a sudden gesture to silence her.

"Hush, for God's sake," he said, in an emphatic whisper, "Whatever you have to say you cannot say it now."

"Why not?" answered Elizabeth, almost recklessly. "Come in here, Jasper, and tell me what you mean." And she pushed open the school-room door as she spoke, and entered it; and after a moment's hesitation Jasper followed her, closing the door behind him as he went in.

The school-room was a large airy room, which looked out upon the garden below, and the window was wide open, and the moonlight shining placidly in, showing everything there quite distinctly. It showed also Elizabeth's excited face, and Jasper Tyrell's pale set one. He was furious with Elizabeth for thus waylaying him. He thought she meant to compromise him with Eva, and was indignant that under the circumstances she dare thus address him.

"What do you mean by this?" he asked, almost harshly, after he had placed his lighted candle on the school-room table.

"Nay, Jasper, what do you mean?" retorted Elizabeth, brave and fearless. "What have I done to deserve such treatment from your hands?"

"Your own conscience might tell you, I think, without asking me," answered Jasper bitterly. The very love he felt for her making him only more passionately indignant.

"If you mean that I had not courage to say what I wrote,"
said Elizabeth, with a strange pathos ringing in her voice, "why
was it, Jasper? Not to escape pain myself, but the fear of bringing
shame on you."

"Shame, indeed!" said Jasper, darkly.

"Yes, shame," went on Elizabeth, "and to spare you that I
hid myself away. As you told me I had nothing more to lose,
and you had much—and you soon forgot me, Jasper."

Unconsciouly Elizabeth said these last words reproachfully, and
they stung Jasper to a speech of open scorn.

"Forgot you!" he repeated, contemptuously. "Why should
I not forget you—you who were living with another man!"

"What!" said Elizabeth; lifting her eyes to his face full of
her perfect innocence of his accusation. "*What* do you say?"

"I say," answered Jasper Tyrell, quickly and passionately,
"that when you broke your word, and never came to meet me as
you promised, that after I had wandered more than an hour in
St. George's Square, distracted with the fear that something had
happened to you, I went to Cambridge Street—and who do you
think I found there, Elizabeth?"

"I cannot tell," said Elizabeth. "It was a disreputable house,
and Mrs. O'Shee is a disreputable woman, but I know nothing
more."

"Not of Mr. Edgar Wilmot's visits?" retorted Jasper scornfully. "I met that gentleman there, and he did me—me who
was about to give up all the world for you—the honour of informing
me of the connection that had been between you."

Elizabeth's face dyed scarlet at these words.

"And you believed him?" she said, indignantly. "You, a
gentleman, believed that the woman you professed to love was a
vile creature like this!"

"What could I believe," said Jasper gloomily, and his eyes fell,
"You had cheated me once."

"Yes, Jasper Tyrell," answered Elizabeth, her noble face
raised to his, "I did cheat you once, and so spoilt my life! But
I did so for a motive—a motive I cannot tell you now—but which,
if you knew, you would kneel down and beg my pardon on your
knees for the base words you have breathed to-night! What,"
she went on with gathering passion, "you believed this lying
stranger before *me*—me who had sacrificed everything for you—
who fled from you at last only because I knew that I loved you
too well!"

"He is an infamous scoundrel then if he told me what was
false!" said Jasper Tyrell fiercely.

"He is a scoundrel," said Elizabeth, "and forced his acquaintance on me the very night I left Wendell, watching me, tracing
me out, and covertly threatening me with exposure. For he had

learned who I was from an advertisement in the *Times*, offering a reward for my discovery, and from the lawyer he heard my whole history. But," she added vehemently, "as there is a God above us, Jasper, this man was nothing, could never be anything to me."

"But why did you not tell me about him?" said Jasper, impressed in spite of himself with the truth of her words. "Why did I never hear from you of this acquaintance until now?"

"Because I knew you were hot and quick of temper, Jasper," answered Elizabeth, "and that your blood would have boiled if you had known how this base man worried and pursued a poor woman defenceless and alone? I had no money until you came," went on Elizabeth. "I could not get any work, and so I was forced to stay on where I was; forced to endure his visits, though he only came very rarely—I do not think that altogether I saw him a dozen times—and then I met you. Oh! Jasper, you know what happened then," continued Elizabeth, a sob breaking her voice. "And—when—I knew it was right to leave you—when I knew I dare not see you any more—I wrote to your dear father and told him all. Not all about *us*, Jasper, but that I was friendless and alone; and he sent me money, and he was a reference for me, and so in the end I came here."

"Where did you go—after we parted?" asked Jasper, ashamed to be suspicious still.

"To a quiet old house, kept by two quiet old women, in Buckingham Palace Road," answered Elizabeth. "I will give you the address—they are called White, and I lived with them about six weeks—and then through them and your father (for one of them keeps a register-office for governesses) I came to the situation here."

As Elizabeth made this last explanation, Jasper Tyrell sat down on one of the school-room forms which was standing near him, and leaned his arm upon the table with a bitter sigh.

"Why did I not know all this before, Elizabeth?" he said in a low tone. "Why—not until it is too late?"

"I could not tell you, Jasper," answered Elizabeth gently, and she came near to him, "because if I had done so, you would have known where I was—and—"

"Why did you not let me know, Lissa?" said Jasper, looking up, and taking her hand. "Oh! child, child, what have you let me do? What have I done?"

These words, and the tone in which they were spoken, touched the innate nobleness and generosity of Elizabeth's heart, which had been overswept by the tide of bitter and angry passions, when she considered herself insulted and neglected by Jasper Tyrell, and she laid her hand softly on his shoulder.

"She is a sweet girl, Jasper," she said. "We—" and she

could not restrain a sigh—"could not marry. God bless you, and make you happy with your young wife."

But Jasper made no answer to this wish, which trembled and faltered unwillingly on Elizabeth's tongue. He sat there holding her hand silent and haggard-eyed. He was thinking how he loved Elizabeth—how he had always loved her, even when he tried to hate her most—and yet by his own rash deed he had put another barrier between them, which honour and every good feeling of his heart forbid him to overstep.

"I am glad at least," said Elizabeth, after a few moments of painful and oppressive silence had passed, "that I spoke to you to-night, Jasper—that you do not at least think me so unworthy now—"

As Elizabeth paused, Jasper Tyrell rose with a sudden gesture, and clasped both her hands, and stood there facing her.

"God help us, Elizabeth," he said. "God help us both !"

"I—I—prayed very hard," faltered poor Elizabeth, " for strength to leave you."

"It was a false step ; " said Jasper Tyrell, "for—Lissa, Lissa," he added in broken and passionate accents, "how can I meet you here—how can I look on your face, or you on mine ? "

"But, Jasper—"

"It can't go on," said Jasper Tyrell, in the same excited tone. "I dare not trust myself. But let me go now, Elizabeth," he added. "I will think what is best to do." And after wringing her hands, he turned and left her.

CHAPTER XXXII.
A LOVER'S QUESTION.

JASPER TYRELL went to bed, and rose the next morning a very unhappy man, after his interview with Elizabeth in the school-room. He was not, as we have seen from his conduct during the earlier period of his acquaintance with Elizabeth (when, without much regard for his unfortunate brother Harry's feelings, he had won her love), one of those who strain the code of honour to any very high or chivalrous rules. But he was a gentleman—that is, he meant his word to be his bond, and truth only to be heard from his lips. He believed himself, in fact, to be incapable of any dishonourable action, justly or unjustly thinking that a man has a right to win a woman's love if he can, unless she is bound by legal or formal ties to another.

But though he had told himself this many a time when thinking of poor Harry and Elizabeth, he had always had a sort of vague uneasy consciousness on the subject, which naturally deepened into real regret, and even remorse, after Harry's death. True, he had done his brother no wrong. Elizabeth had never been engaged to Harry Tyrell; but Jasper had known of his love, and a more chivalrous man would perhaps have left the neighbourhood, rather than un the risk of endan,ering his brother's happiness.

And now again honour and passion were opposed ; but this time there could be no delusion, and Jasper did not seek to delude himself, as he lay tossing through long hours of the night, after he had seen Elizabeth alone.

He was engaged to Eva Dalziel—engaged to a young girl whom he had wooed and won—and he felt that to retreat from that engagement would be utterly impossible. And yet, on the other hand, Elizabeth—Elizabeth loved him. Could he doubt that after he had seen her face to-night ; after he had heard her touching tender words ?

Why she had married Richard Horton, of course always remained an inexplicable mystery to Jasper Tyrell. That she had never loved her cousin he was convinced, but still the fact remained the same that she was his wife. Elizabeth had said to-night that she had sacrificed everything for Jasper. "How was this ?" thought Jasper, with painful curiosity. "What did I gain by her marriage ?" And for the first time a vague thought struck him, could it be anything connected with Harry's death ? And yet what could it be ? The cruel deceit with which Richard Horton had tricked Elizabeth, naturally could not occur to him ; so all his restless thoughts, his uneasy doubts, and bitter regrets, ended in a determination (not over-strong, perhaps) to keep his word to Eva, and to try to banish Elizabeth from his heart.

"If she had loved me as she says she does," he thought, with man-like reasoning, "she would never have left me in London as she did. I would have kept my word to her and married her, and a really loving woman would have trusted to me then."

Yet in spite of this reflection, in spite of the smile which rippled over Eva's sweet face as he entered the breakfast-room on the following morning, Jasper Tyrell felt weary and sore at heart. It was a beautiful day, and the three young girls (all fresh and fair) were planning, chattering, and laughing, but their mirth somehow jarred upon Jasper's ears. He could not forget the pale, tragic face that he had seen the night before ; the ringing voice that had told of her sorrow and her love.

"Jasper, you shall decide," said Eva, addressing her lover. " *We* want to take you to Fernside, and mamma wants to take you to Tindell Woods—so where will you go ?"

"As Fernside and Tindell Woods are alike unknown localities to me," answered Jasper, with a smile, "I shall leave it in your hands."

"Then I say Fernside," said Eva.

"But, my dear child," said Mrs. Dalziel, "as I was telling you before, the grass is so long at Fernside, and as there are no walks through the woods, I am sure, after the rain last night, I would recommend you to go to Tindell. And I am sure also," she added, looking at Jasper, "that if Mr. Tyrell knew the two places, he would think that I was advising you rightly."

"Poor Jasper! is he afraid of wet feet?" laughed Eva.

"He might be afraid of you wetting yours," said Mrs. Dalziel, with a complimentary smile at Jasper.

"You must put on thick boots, Eva," said Jasper.

"Oh! thank you," replied Eva, tossing back her pretty head.

"Then you must go to Tindell Woods," said Jasper.

"Now that's mean," cried Eva, "going over to mamma's side like that. I won't have it, sir!"

"My dear Eva, I am sure you will do whatever Mr. Tyrell wishes," said Mrs. Dalziel.

"No, he must do what I wish *now*—afterward—" And the girl stopped, her fair face dyed with blushes, and Jasper moved nervously as she paused.

"Afterwards, you will be a good wife, I hope, and obey him in everything," said Mrs. Dalziel, thinking she was saying exactly the right thing in the right place, an opinion, however, which Jasper Tyrell was far from agreeing with.

"Well, about these two places," he said, rather sharply, addressing Eva, "which are you really going to? I vote for the nearest."

"But why, Jasper?" asked Eva, looking rather disappointed.

"I dare say it will rain before long," answered Jasper, rising from the breakfast table, and going to the window. "These very bright mornings rarely last."

"Well, Tindell Woods are the nearest," said Eva.

"Let it be Tindell Woods, then," went on Jasper. "And how are we to go?"

"I thought I would drive you in the pony-chaise, if you like?" answered Eva.

"I do like. But how are you going, Mrs. Dalziel?" said Jasper.

"Oh, we have—at least we can engage—or rather procure a carriage," hesitated Mrs. Dalziel, unwilling to confess they had none but the pony-chaise, and also unwilling to say what was untrue before her daughters, to whom she always wished to appear the pattern of virtue.

"Mamma, what nonsense!" said Eva. "Jasper knows we have no carriage, but we have hired one from the Nag's Head, in the village—the only carriage, sir," she continued, laughing and looking at Jasper, "that the village of Hazelhurst can boast of."

"My dear, is it right to give Mr. Tyrell a wrong impression of your mother's character?" asked Mrs. Dalziel, in an injured tone. "Am I in the habit, Eva, of telling untruths? Do I ever say I possess luxuries that your dear papa's income would not allow?

I think I deserve a little more respect from my husband's child than your speech would lead Mr. Tyrell to think you entertained for me, Eva.''

"Mamma, I meant nothing," said Eva, good-temperedly. "You know I did not intend to offend you."

"I hope not, my love," answered Mrs. Dalziel, with a sublime air of forgiveness. "But young people do not think before they speak, do they, Mr. Tyrell?"

"I have forgotten what it is to be young," answered Jasper, "and, therefore, cannot say. At my age," he went on, with an involuntary sigh, "a man often thinks what he must not speak."

"What a sigh!" said Mrs. Dalziel, playfully. "But, my dear Lucy," she continued, turning to her own eldest daughter, "have you seen Miss Gordon this morning? It is late for her not to be down." And she looked at her watch.

"I have, mamma," said Eva, "and she seems so dreadfully ill, poor thing. She asked if we were going to a pic-nic to-day, and when I told her I thought so, she said in that case she would remain upstairs and keep quiet, for her head was aching so dreadfully."

"Dear me, dear me," said Mrs. Dalziel, shaking her head. "I fear this will never do. I have suffered the greatest anxiety, and gone through an immense amount of nursing, lately, Mr. Tyrell, with my poor governess. She has had a terrible attack of brain fever, and night and day I never left her. 1 felt it was a duty—a trying duty, certainly—but we must not shrink from our responsibilities."

"It was kind of you," said Jasper, rather huskily. "When—did the attack begin?"

"On the very day—yes, the very day," answered Mrs. Dalziel, smiling, "when that child" (and she nodded at Eva) "wrote to tell us that a certain, happy event had taken place. I mean her engagement," she continued. "Well, I went with Eva's letter in my hand, to tell Miss Gordon, and found her, poor thing, in the orchard, looking ghastly. You had written to her by the same post, had you not Eva? for she said something about it; and then I got her into the house, and that night she was taken dreadfully ill."

"She was nearly dead," said Lucy.

"Nearly dead, indeed," went on Mrs. Dalziel, "but I nursed her as if she had been my own sister. She had—though I should not say it—every attention; and then dear Eva came, and that naughty child would sit up night after night, until I thought she would be very ill too. Indeed, it was a most trying time."

"And is she better now?" said Jasper, struggling to show no signs of discomposure.

"Yes, but dreadfully altered," answered Mrs. Dalziel. "And

I'm sure—I don't wish to be unkind—I hope I never am unkind, but still it will never do to go on having an invalid governess in the house.''

"Oh! mamma!" said Eva.

"What time do you start?" asked Jasper Tyrell, sharply and impatiently. "Eva, I am going out for a quiet smoke in the garden now, so when you have completed your arrangements, you can come and tell me. Good morning to you all for the present." And with a slight bow he left the room.

"My dear," said Mrs. Dalziel, turning to Eva after he was gone, "I do not wish to say anything unpleasant, but I think you must make up your mind—you must fortify your mind with prayer and patience—to have a bad-tempered husband. If I am any judge of character, Mr. Tyrell is a passionate and hot-tempered man."

"You have no reason to say so, mamma," answered Eva quickly. "Jasper, like all men, does not care to be bothered about household arrangements, but he's not bad-tempered."

"He's an angel, of course," said Lucy. "Didn't you see his wings neatly folded up under his waiscoat, mamma? Well whatever he is, bad-tempered or good-tempered, he's handsome, and that's a great thing."

"I don't say he is an angel," answered Eva, mollified, "but he's not bad-tempered, and he's handsome—and he's—well, what I suppose most people would call *very nice*."

Meanwhile Jasper Tyrell, restless and unhappy, was walking down the garden walks towards the orchard, thinking very miserably as he went.

"Good God!" he thought. "did the very news of my engagement nearly kill this poor soul with grief—what she must have suffered—what, from a sense of honour and virtue, noble-minded creature that she is!"

Then his heart went back, with passionate longing, to the scenes at Wendell—when he had held her in his arms, and sworn that nothing should ever come between them. And now? "What shall I do?" Jasper asked himself. "Was ever a man in such miserable circumstances before?"

At the end of the orchard was a low wall covered with ivy, which served as a boundary to separate it from the green meadows, through which the Dill placidly flowed. The children in their youth had raised a mound on the orchard side of the wall, to enable them to see over it, and this had turned with time into a little grassy bank; and there Jasper now stood, leaning his elbows on the wall, and staring gloomily at the river, and at the few rustics sitting contentedly fishing by its side.

He was trying to think unselfishly; trying to weigh the position in which he found himself, without considering his own feelings in the matter; but he was trying to do what few men and women have the moral strength or courage to carry out.

He was fond of Eva; fond of the bright sunny-faced girl, that he had first admired, and then tried to love. And he did love her, undoubtedly, in a certain way; loved her as well as half the men who lead women to the altar love them, but not with the passionate and overpowering love that he felt for Elizabeth Gordon.

This love had made him hate her when he thought she had deceived him; it had made him bitter, restless, and discontented with all the world after her marriage. It had, in fact, spoilt his life. He could not be happy without Elizabeth, and in seeking Eva had only tried to forget the beautiful face that had done him, he thought, such bitter wrong.

But now he believed that Mr. Wilmot had lied to him. He remembered this man's character, to which passion had blinded him at the time. He had heard in his club of Edgar Wilmot; heard of his cool unscrupulous nature, and of his undoubtedly bad reputation where women were concerned.

And he had let this man, this scoundrel, thought Jasper, savagely, come between him and his love. If Elizabeth's story were true—and it was true, Jasper's heart told him—could he respect her less, could he love her less for hiding herself away from what she believed (foolishly believed, Jasper thought), was a deadly sin?

"Oh! my poor girl," said Jasper, half aloud, "what misery you have suffered—what misery is before you now!"

Almost as he made this last reflection, he heard a step behind him, and looking round, saw Eva in her light summer muslin dress, and her bright hair uncovered, advancing towards him.

"We have fixed the time, Jasper," she began. But something in the expression of his face—the fixed look of pain there—arrested her words before she had finished her sentence, and she added quickly, "Are you not well, Jasper? Is anything the matter?"

"No," he answered, slowly; and then he said, "Come up here, Eva, I have got something to say to you."

"What is it, Jasper?" asked the girl, wistfully, as she put her hand in his for him to help her up the little grassy mound on which he was standing.

"Do you really care for me, Eva," asked Jasper, still holding her hand, after she had come to his side on the mound, and looking steadily into her face.

"Care for you, Jasper!" repeated Eva, in astonishment.

"Yes," said Jasper, earnestly; "do you love me? Eva, is your whole life bound up in mine?"

Eva's wild-rose colour came and went on her smooth cheeks at these words, and she looked with her blue startled eyes into her lover's face.

"I can scarcely understand you," she said.

"I mean," said Jasper, "if anything were to part us—if anything came between us now, would it cause you great pain, Eva?—would you suffer very much?"

Eva's bosom heaved violently at this question, and then with a kind of cry she hid her face on Jasper's breast.

"Jasper—" she half sobbed, "if—if—anything were to part us now—I should die—I—I—could not bear the pain—"

"You shall not bear it, Eva," said Jasper, gently, and he drew her to his breast, and pressed his lips on her bright head. "I will try to make you happy, Eva—I will try at least to keep your life free from trouble as it is now."

CHAPTER XXXIII.

ANOTHER CHANGE.

THEY went to their pic-nic at Tindell Woods, and to many other pic-nics, or rather excursions in the neighbourhood, during the next few days. Jasper saw very little of Elizabeth at this time, and not a single word was exchanged between them, except in the presence of some member of the family. In fact, Elizabeth rarely appeared down stairs, her continued ill-health being the supposed cause of her seclusion. But when she did appear, and Jasper saw her face, it filled his heart with an almost intolerable sense of pain.

He recalled the bright Elizabeth that he had once known—the clever, sparkling, proud girl, with her gay, careless manner, her energetic movements, her free and noble carriage—and then he looked at the set, sharpened features, the bowed form, the too plainly written tale of suppressed sufferings, that every expression of Elizabeth's face now betrayed.

She seldom lifted her eyes to his, but when she did, the patient look of suffering in them stabbed Jasper's heart as with a knife. "Good Heavens! if I could take her in my arms!" he used to think. "If she were to die there, I could bear it better than that dreadful look of pain."

In the meantime he walked, and rode, and drove with his pretty Eva, and played the *rôle* of the betrothed lover with reasonable propriety; though he did not speak of the wedding day, nor show the eagerness to be made happy which Mrs. Dalziel thought he should have exhibited.

That good lady, indeed, became uneasy on the subject, and, as usual when she was in any anxiety, she attacked her good-tempered easy husband about it; but the Major turned a deaf ear to her insinuations.

"My dear creature, if you mean me to hurry him, or to say anything about when the wedding is to be, I may as well tell you I won't," quoth the Major. "Tyrell knows best when it would suit him to be married, and Eva's very young, and I'm in no haste to get rid of her."

"But, my dear Henry, you see it's such an anxious time for the poor child," said Mrs. Dalziel.

"She looks remarkably well, I think," replied the Major, "and uncommonly happy. You leave them alone; marriage isn't, after all, always a state of bliss." And the Major laughed.

"If you mean, Henry—" said Mrs. Dalziel, injured. "If you are insinuating—"

"I mean nothing, and I'm insinuating nothing," said the Major. "What! you silly little woman, you're not going to cry, are you?" (for Mrs. Dalziel had commenced giving premonitory symptoms of tears). "Nonsense, nonsense; here, let me give you a kiss. There! it's all right now, isn't it?"

"If I thought, Henry, that I had not made you happy—if—"

"I'm as happy as the day's long," said the Major, repeating his cure. "Come, be a good girl now, and don't be silly. What the deuce are you going on in this way for?"

"It's only out of anxiety and love for your child; you know that, Henry—and I think he should say something more definite."

"My good woman, take my advice, and let him alone," said the Major. But in spite of this matrimonial conversation Mrs. Dalziel shortly afterwards contrived to give Jasper Tyrell a hint.

"You have not settled on any future residence yet, then?" asked the proposed mother-in-law one day, when she chanced to be a few moments alone with Jasper.

"I have settled nothing yet," answered Jasper, so coldly and repressively, that Mrs. Dalziel felt the same sort of fear of him that she occasionally felt of her proud brother-in-law the Dean.

Jasper took an especial dislike to Mrs. Dalziel after this, and confided to Eva that he considered her excessively meddlesome.

"It's only mamma's way," said Eva. "She always means to be kind—but what has she been saying to vex you, Jasper?"

"Oh! nothing particular," replied Jasper Tyrell; but he perfectly understood the purport of Mrs. Dalziel's remark, and resented it accordingly.

He had been at Hazelhurst about ten days, when Mrs. Dalziel (who was always very deferential to him) asked him if he had any particular plans for the day.

"None at all," answered Jasper, "except that I think it is about time that I was thinking of changing my quarters."

But Mrs. Dalziel would not, of course, hear of such a thing. What she had been going to say, however, was that she wished Eva to drive her to the nearest town, Brocklebury, to assist her *in* making some purchases. "If, of course, *you* can spare Eva for one afternoon ?" added Mrs. Dalziel, with a smile.

"Oh! yes," said Jasper "I'll borrow the Major's fishing-rod, and try my luck in the Dill. It is all right, Mrs. Dalziel, I can take care of myself until you come back."

Jasper, indeed, f.lt glad to be free that one afternoon. He wished to speak to Elizabeth again, to ask her about her future life, and to try at least to say some words of comfort to the woman he could not help loving so well.

"I mean to act like an honourable man," he told himself, "but honour does not forbid me to do what I can for Elizabeth."

So he handed Eva and her step-mother into the pony-chaise, and saw them drive away, and then returned thoughtfully to the house, wondering how he could best contrive to see Elizabeth. He hesitated about going up to the schoolroom, for the children might be there; and it might compromise Elizabeth to do so; and yet how was he to see her? and see her he determined that he would.

While he was yet mentally arguing this question, he went into the breakfast-room to seek some of the Major's fishing flies, and happening to glance out of the window, he saw Elizabeth herself slowly walking down the garden walk, and watched her enter the orchard at the end of it. Theu, knowing that he could not miss her now, he sat deliberately down to wait a few minutes, so that it might not appear to the household as if he had followed her.

Presently (fishing-rod in hand) he also went into the garden, and entered the orchard; and there he found Elizabeth, who was sitting on the very grassy mound where a short time before he had asked Eva if she truly loved him.

The woman who sat there now, did not even hear him approach. She was half lying on the grass, one hand over her face, and the utter dejection of her attitude touched the tenderest feelings in Jasper's heart.

When he was quite close to her, she looked up and started violently.

"Elizabeth," he said, and he held out his hand, and Elizabeth rose.

"Do not rise," he said, "you look so tired. May I sit beside you, Elizabeth, for a little while ? "

"Yes," she answered, "but I thought you were out with the rest ? "

"No," said Jasper. "Eva has gone with Mrs. Dalziel to Brocklebury, and I wished to see you, Elizabeth. I intended to see you before I left Hazelhurst."

Elizabeth made no answer to this. She sat there by Jasper's side, with her head slightly turned away, but he could see her lips quiver and move, and her hands trembling on her knees.

“Dear Elizabeth!” said Jasper, in a voice of much feeling, his impetuous nature overpowering his reason, and he clasped one of her trembling hands and pressed it to his lips.

“You don’t get well,” he said. “It makes me mad, miserable, Elizabeth, to see you thus! What are you going to do? What plans have you for your future life?”

“What can I do?” answered Elizabeth. “I am homeless.”

“But,” said Jasper Tyrell eagerly, “it is about this that I wished to see you Elizabeth. Whatever we are, we are old friends?”

“Yes, Jasper.”

“And you know,” went on Jasper, his brown, handsome face colouring as he spoke, “that I am well off now. I inherited poor Harry’s fortune, as you have heard, and, besides, my father is generous to me—and, Elizabeth—Lissa—let me be your banker for a little while at least? If you had a change you might get well. Leave this place with its painful associations—so bitterly painful to us both.”

This speech hurt Elizabeth, though Jasper certainly did not intend to do so.

“I have not sought you,” she said, with some pride, while tears swelled in her dark eyes.

“Sought me!” repeated Jasper quickly; “no, you have avoided me—but, Lissa—it’s no good” (and his voice sank), “for I cannot avoid my own heart.”

“You wish me to go, then?” asked Elizabeth, a sob half choking her.

“I think it would be better for you,” said Jasper, struggling with himself; struggling with the wild wish to clasp her to his breast. “Your happiness is what I think most of now, and you never can be happy here.”

“I can be happy nowhere, Jasper.”

“Oh! do not say that!” said Jasper Tyrell, and he sprang to his feet. He had sought this interview, but he felt that he had not strength to bear it; and after a few hasty steps he came back to her, and knelt on the grass by her side.

“What can I say, Lissa?” he said, in a broken voice. “You know how I am placed—you know I love you, and yet—honour binds me to Eva?”

“Yes, I know,” said Elizabeth, and a tear fell on Jasper’s hand, which he had clasped on one of hers.

“If to give my life would save you from pain,” went on Jasper, passionately, “I would freely give it. Tell me, Elizabeth, now,” he continued; “now in this miserable hour, what was the secret that first parted us? What villainy came between us, and broke your heart and mine?”

“It was villainy,” said Elizabeth, weeping; “cruel, cruel

villainy, Jasper—but I cannot tell you now—not as long—as Richard Horton lives!''

''Did that young scoundrel dare invent some lie about me then, Lissa, or what was it?'' asked Jasper, with a fierce gleam in his dark eyes. He felt at that moment that he could have killed Richard Horton ; killed the man who had parted him from his love.

''His sin is very great, Jasper,'' said Elizabeth, and she rose and stood beside him; ''but let us leave him to God. He is my cousin—the son of the dear old man who was ever as a father to me—and I cannot, I will not, lift my hand to hurt him.''

''But have I to sit down tamely under this wrong?'' asked Jasper Tyrell, rising also, his black brows knitted, and his hands clenching in his quick anger. ''Two men have come between us, Lissa—that cursed Edgar Wilmot, and this doubly cursed young Horton, and both shall answer to me, I swear it, for what they've done!''

''We have been hardly dealt with,'' said Elizabeth gently ; ''but, Jasper (and the memory of Eva's goodness and sweetness rose reproachfully before her), ''I—I thank God—I try to thank God the misery has not fallen upon you. Eva will make you happy. After a while you will—forget—'' But here Elizabeth's voice broke and faltered.

''No, Lissa,'' said Jasper, gloomily, ''I shall never forget you. Eva is, as you say, a sweet girl, a good girl, and she deserves a better fate than she can ever have with me.''

''But she loves you, Jasper,'' said poor Elizabeth.

''To my sorrow, I believe so,'' answered Jasper Tyrell. ''If it were not for that—If I could bear the thought of seeing this girl fade, as I have seen you fade—no consideration—none, honour nor anything else, would induce me to put another bar between us, Lissa.''

''I have suffered,'' said Elizabeth, struggling to be firm, ''and now I know that I have sinned—nay, I knew that I did sin, Jasper, when I took a false oath before the altar of God. But this young girl—whose heart is so bright and pure, you must marry her, Jasper—you must never let her know the pain, the terrible pain, of losing the man she loves.''

'' You don't make it lighter to me, Elizabeth,'' said Jasper, half bitterly, ''by saying that.''

''And,'' went on Elizabeth, not heeding his interruption, ''I shall leave here. Will you go now, Jasper? very soon—and when you are away—when I get a little stronger, I will try to find another home.''

''Oh ! Lissa, Lissa,'' said Jasper Tyrell, much agitated. ''Lissa—will you give me one kiss—''

Elizabeth turned her face to him for an answer, and Jasper put his arms round her, and pressed his lips on hers.

"Oh! if I could forget," he murmured, "forget everything but this."

"Good bye, Jasper," said Elizabeth, gently releasing herself. "Good-bye, and God bless you—my dear, dear Jasper."

"When we are old, shall we meet, Elizabeth?" said Jasper, with a sort of cynicism in his voice. "When we have worn out all that would have made our lives bright and sweet, and lived in respectable misery through long years of care—shall we meet then?"

"You will not be miserable," said Elizabeth, putting her hand in his. "Good bye, Jasper." And she looked at him once more, and then turned away, proceeding straight to her room; and when she reached it, she covered her face and began weeping passionately.

"Oh! my love, my love," she said "Jasper, my only love!"

It was a terrible struggle. She knew that if she held out her hand, Jasper would throw up all—honour, the world's good name, the pure love of the girl who had promised to be his wife—all for her sake; and yet she must not make that sign. Could she forget the sweet bright face of Eva? Could she bear to see it blurred and stained with tears, and the light step turn slow and weary as hers had done?

"I pray that I may not suffer long," said Elizabeth, falling on her knees. "Oh, God! grant that my martyrdom may not last, as he said, through long years and years of care."

As she knelt thus, praying for strength, struggling to resist the tempter's voice, that kept ever whispering to her heart, a servant rapped at the room door, and, when she opened it, placed a letter in Elizabeth's hands.

One glance at the direction told Elizabeth it was from Sir John Tyrell, and with her cold, trembling hands she tore it open, and read as follows:—

"My dear Young Lady," wrote Sir John, "A sense of duty that I cannot withstand induces me to address these words to you, for I feel that it would not be right for me to withhold from you for a day the sad news that I am going to communicate. Your brother-in-law, young Robert Horton, called upon me this morning, to consult me about a letter which he had received, or rather which had come to Wendell West-house, addressed to your late poor uncle. This letter was from your father's eldest sister, Miss Gordon, and contained the news of the death of your half-brother, Malcolm Gordon, from fever, and of your own accession, therefore, to the family property in Scotland. Young Horton, naturally, was in considerable uncertainty how to act under these circumstances. You had left your home; you could not be heard of anywhere, he said, and what, therefore, should he write to Miss Gordon?—for I grieve to tell you, that he is now forced to act in the place of your late uncle, for—I do not know how to break this news to you—your unfortunate husband, Richard Horton, is pronounced to be dying.

"I did not, of course, without your leave, give the faintest hint to your cousin Robert that I knew where you were, but, at the same time, I decided in my own mind to write to you at once, and urge you to return to your home. My dear young lady, I do not know what wrong your husband did you; but I believe it must have been a very cruel one for a woman of your character to act as you did. But death is a very solemn thing— the death of a young man (for I must not shrink from the truth) who really and actually has destroyed himself by drink. I have not written this letter to you without hearing another opinion, as well as young Robert Horton's, as to his brother's condition. No sooner was your cousin gone this morning, than I despatched a messenger for the doctor, and heard from him only a sad confirmation of Robert Horton's story. After repeated and repeated attacks of delirium tremens, Richard Horton has sunk into a state of almost idiotcy, produced by softening of the brain, and the doctor's opinion is, that the end is very near. Under these sad circumstances, will you forgive me if I urge you to return to Wendell? It seems to me that this is your duty, and I am sure that when the end comes, you will feel happier for having fulfilled it. If you will write to me, I will at once communicate with your cousin Robert, and ask him to delay writing to Miss Gordon until you return, and most earnestly trusting that you will come, I remain your sincere friend,

"JOHN TYRELL."

CHAPTER XXXIV.

AT HOME ONCE MORE.

ELIZABETH read Sir John's letter through with deep emotion, and then a strange revulsion of feeling took place in her heart.

"Dick dying—the boy cousin, the unhappy, impassioned lover, driven mad by his love—driven to crime, and now, poor boy, poor boy, to death!"

Such were her thoughts; for death, as Sir John had written, is a solemn thing—a stern creditor, exacting from us a strict account of our dealings with the dead.

"I will go to him," Elizabeth decided.

"He shall not drift away unforgiven by me, at least. He shall not die without my prayers, my earnest, passionate prayers to God to pardon him."

She looked at her watch—it was just six o'clock, and when she was considering what it were best to do, she heard the pony-chaise return, and a few minutes later Eva came running upstairs, and rapped at her door.

"May I come in?" she asked; and when Elizabeth assented, she entered the room, looking bright and smiling.

"Will you take this from me?" she said, putting a little case into Elizabeth's hand. "And give me a kiss in return?"

"What is it, Eva?" asked Elizabeth.

"Only some little jet things," answered the girl, and she kissed Elizabeth's cheek. "They are not half good enough," she said; "but then you know, I'm not rich—but if you like them?"

They were a girl's gift—pretty jet ear-rings and brooch; but the way she gave them touched Elizabeth.

"My dear," she said, kissing Eva's blooming cheek, and feeling thankful that her kiss was not that of Judas, "they will be very precious coming from you." And she once more kissed Eva. Then, after a moment's silence, she said, "Eva, I have something to tell you."

"What is it, Lissa?" asked Eva.

"Some one—a near relation of mine," answered Elizabeth, trying to steady her voice, "is very ill—is, I fear, dying, Eva, at Wendell, and I must return there to-night."

"At Wendell!" repeated Eva.

"Yes," said Elizabeth; "my poor uncle's house is at Wendell; and, dear Eva, will you ask your mamma if I can see her at once?"

"Oh! yes, certainly," answered Eva. "Shall I go now!"

"Yes; please, dear. I wish to go to-night," said Elizabeth; and Eva, accordingly, at once left the room to seek her step-mother, and in a few minutes Mrs. Dalziel entered it.

"I hear," she said kindly, "that you have had bad news from home, Miss Gordon?"

"Yes," replied Elizabeth, a burning blush dyeing her face. "I—I—wish, if you will allow me, to go at once."

"Oh! yes, of course, certainly," said Mrs. Dalziel. "I have too much feeling, too much sympathy, I trust, with the sorrows of of others, to think of my own convenience in a moment like this."

"There is a train about half-past seven, I think," said Elizabeth.

"But, my dear Miss Gordon, surely you will not leave to-night? Just think—it is a quarter past six now" (and Mrs. Dalziel looked at her watch); "how can you prepare—how—"

"He may be dead if I wait," interrupted Elizabeth, and then she broke down, passionate sobs almost choking her.

"Oh! hush, my dear—my dear, hush!" said Mrs. Dalziel; and after a minute or two Elizabeth composed herself.

"I really wish to go, Mrs. Dalziel," she said, and that lady made no further objections; nay, bustled about to get tea for Elizabeth, and otherwise see after her comforts. Eva also did everything to help and assist Elizabeth, packing and arranging what she thought she would require, with the sweet consideration for others which was one of Eva's characteristics.

"Have you seen Jasper, Lissa?" asked the young girl, as she was busily helping Elizabeth. "He is not in the house, and no one appears to have seen him all the afternoon?"

"I saw him in the garden," answered Elizabeth, as calmly as she could. "He had his fishing-rod in his hand."

"Oh! then he's fishing, that's it," said Eva, with happy contentedness. "I wondered where he was, but it's all right if you've seen him. How surprised he will be when he comes in to hear you are gone! and to Wendell, too!"

"Yes," answered Elizabeth. She had thought of this too; thought "Shall I enclose Sir John's letter to him—let him know, at least, this time, where I am gone, and why?" And then she thought, "Would this be just to this sweet child?" And her heart had answered it would not. If she were free (and Elizabeth shuddered) would Jasper keep his word to Eva? And she was not free yet. "Oh! God help and pardon the poor dying sinner lying in his deadly strait," prayed Elizabeth, with all the new forgiveness and pity which had stolen into her heart when she thought of Richard Horton.

"When will you get there?" asked Eva, going on with her packing.

"Some time in the early morning," answered Elizabeth, "and I can walk from the station. I will telegraph at the station here to my cousin Robert, to say that I am coming."

"How many cousins have you, Lissa?" said Eva.

"Three," answered Elizabeth, and then she changed the conversation, and Eva asked no more questions, and presently everything was ready for Elizabeth's departure.

Mrs. Dalziel was really very kind. She went to the hall door with Elizabeth, assuring her that they would miss her greatly, but that she hoped the change would do her good, and then they would be delighted to welcome her return.

Elizabeth, however, made only very feeble answers to these parting speeches, for she knew that she would never come back to Hazelhurst, and never be a governess any more. She thought of saying something about her young brother's death having changed her position; the young brother that she had never seen, but the words died on her lips. She had not courage, in fact, to hear the mingled condolence and congratulations which she knew Mrs. Dalziel would indulge in. Better to write, she determined; and so in very kindly fashion she parted with her hostess, who wished her a pleasant journey, and then checked herself—"At least, I mean as pleasant as on such a sad occasion you can hope for," said Mrs. Dalziel, and so bid her farewell.

A more tender parting, however, took place between Eva and Elizabeth. The young girl laid her soft, blooming cheek against hers, and whispered many a loving word. She had not to forget

her—they were always to be friends—little guessing how true a
f.i nd Elizabeth had been to her that day!

"My dear," said Elizabeth, with a sort of solemnity, "God
bless you, and make you a good woman."

"Yes, God bless her," Elizabeth thought, as she was driven
away, and she looked back at Eva. standing with the evening
sun falling on her fair face, and shining on her bright and sunny
hair. "No evil has come near her," went on Elizabeth's reflections, "and none shall come through me." And she looked
upwards, praying for strength to do this child no harm.

When she reached the station, she telegraphed to Robert
Horton, and also to Sir John Tyrell. To Robert she merely
sent a message, "I will eturn to Wendell to-morrow morning;"
to Sir John, "Will you explain to Robert where I have been,
and why I am coming home?" And then, after doing this, in
a little while she started on her long journey.

We need not follow her through this. The excitement, the
strange thought that she was going home again, and would so
soon see familiar faces near her, kept her up, and prevented her
feeling the deadly fatigue which would certainly have come over
her after her recent illness, under ordinary circumstances.

"I must bear up, I must be strong," she said, resolutely;
and when, worn and pale, she approached Mitchin in the early
morning, the first person that her eyes fell upon, standing on the
platform of the station, was her cousin Robert Horton.

For a moment Robert Horton hesitated when he saw the tall
figure in black descending from a carriage, for Elizabeth's appearance was so much altered; but the next he recognized her, and
sprang forward, and caught Elizabeth in his arms.

"Lissa, dear Lissa," said Robert, much affected, and he kissed
his cousin, who looked at him with an unspoken question in her
sad dark eyes.

"He is a little better, I hope," said Robert, huskily, and he
turned his head away. This young man was generally of a
reserved and unsensational nature, but he felt strangely affected
by Elizabeth's return. Sir John had seen him at once on receiving Elizabeth's telegram, and had told him of her wanderings in
London, of her unhappiness and illness; and Robert knew more
than Sir John did, for he thought he knew why Elizabeth had
left her home.

"Why did you not trust me, Lissa?" asked Robert, in a low
tone, with some reproach in his voice, as he stood a moment by
Elizabeth's side, while the porter was seeing after her luggage.

"Dear Robert, I could not—I could trust no one," hesitated
Elizabeth.

"You might have trusted me," answered Robert, significantly;
and he looked at Elizabeth, and she knew then what she had

suspected before, that Robert guessed his unfortunate brother's secret.

In the meanwhile, Elizabeth's arrival had not been unnoticed. The station-master had known her from childhood, and knew all the gossip that her disappearance had occasioned. Robert Horton saw the curious glances that he and the porter and the few passengers on the platform were casting at his cousin, and he frowned as he did so, and drew Elizabeth's arm quickly under his, and led her to the carriage which was waiting for her outside the station.

"Get in, Lissa dear," he said; "these confounded curious fools are staring at you until they ought to be ashamed of their rudeness."

"What matter, dear Bob," answered Lissa, with her sad smile; and then she entered the carriage and was quickly driven home.

"Is—is—he very ill, Bob?" asked Elizabeth, in a faltering voice.

"Yes, very," answered Robert Horton. "O, Lissa! I've had such a time! When he awoke that morning, and found you were gone, he was like a madman. It was all that Hal and I could do to keep him from betraying himself; for Lissa, we need have no secrets now, I suppose—we both know—at least, I could not mistake Dick's wild talk—he told you that night, did he not, who shot Harry Tyrell?"

"Yes, Bob," answered Elizabeth, shuddering, and she put her hand in Robert Horton's.

"Nice thing for the family, I must say," said young Horton. "Do you know, Lissa, I've been thankful to give Dick drink until he was utterly stupefied—and he has had delirium tremens again and again, and about a week ago he took a kind of fit."

"O, Robert!" said Elizabeth.

"Yes; and he's all paralysed down one side now," went on Robert, "and his mind nearly quite gone. He remembers things sometimes, and then he forgets—he is in a frightful state. Old Pocock calls it softening of the brain, but it's nothing more nor less than drink and remorse."

"Poor, poor Dick!"

"Sometimes I feel as if I almost hated him," said Robert, sharply. "What on earth made him do such a thing? Love for you, I suppose, Lissa. But how did he ever force you to marry him?"

"I had promised to marry Jasper Tyrell," answered Elizabeth, in a broken voice, "and he made me believe—I will tell you the story afterwards, Robert, but I cannot now—but he made me believe that Jasper had killed Harry, and he swore he would betray him unless I gave up Jasper, and became his wife."

"The scoundrel!" said Robert Horton.

"It was a cruel wrong, was it not?" wept Elizabeth. "But, Bob, dear Bob, he is dying now, and we must try to forgive him."

"And you—my poor Lissa," said Robert Horton, pitifully, "you gave up Jasper Tyrell, did you, to marry this sullen, selfish brute? Don't put up your hand, Lissa, for what is he else? He has ruined your life and Jasper Tyrell's too, perhaps."

"This is not the only life, Robert," said Elizabeth, gently, "Let us pray to God to forgive poor Dick."

"That's more than I can do," answered Robert Horton. "Why, Lissa—fancy if such a thing were to come out—he might be hanged yet."

"It will never come out while Dick lives," said Elizabeth, "and afterwards—Jasper, the only one who has a right to know, will keep the secret for my sake, Robert."

"It was a disgraceful thing!"

"Yes—but oh! Robert, here we are at Wendell," and Elizabeth clasped her cousin's hand tightly; "it brings everything back—everything like a picture before me." And Elizabeth put one hand over her face, as if to shut out the familiar scene.

Robert Horton answered with some kindly and sympathetic words; and then, when the carriage stopped before the door of Wendell West-house, Harry Horton, the youngest brother, sprang forward, and kissed Elizabeth with vehement affection, and tears came into the boy's eyes when he saw the change in Elizabeth's face.

"Well, thank goodness, you've come at any rate!" he said. "I've my orders from Bob there, to ask no questions, but why you ran away, Lissa—"

"Do hold your tongue, Harry," interrupted the elder brother, "and see about getting Lissa's things out of the carriage. Come in, dear Lissa." he went on, "they will have breakfast ready for you, I expect." And Robert led the way into the house, followed by Elizabeth, and thus once more she was at home.

Everything seemed almost the same as when she left. There was the engraved silver tea-pot that she remembered so well, the mats that she had worked, the plates and cups that she had bought! Even the servants were unchanged, and received Elizabeth with respectful salutations. They had their orders also, as Harry had had, to ask Elizabeth no questions; to annoy her with no allusions to the past. But what touched Lissa most was the welcome she received from her dumb favourites of happier days. The big mastiff, Tory, blind and old, rose stiffly at the sound of her voice, and stood erect, disturbed, and expectant, and when she called its name, came forward with a whine of joy, and laid its head against her dress, lifting its almost sightless eyes to her face.

"Poor Tory knows you, you see, Lissa," said Bob. "He pined tremendously after you—but sit down, dear, and take off your hat, for you must be most awfully tired."

Elizabeth did sit down, and as she did so the black cat, that she remembered so well, emerged mysteriously and silently, as is the custom of its race, and sprang on the arm of her chair, and, with waving tail and sleek head bent down, purred its welcome.

"They are all pleased to have you back," said Bob, anxious to distract Elizabeth's mind as much as he could from the painful thoughts. "Come, dear Lissa, will you pour out the tea?"

It was her old office, but she made the effort to please her cousin; and presently Harry came in, as noisy and jolly as ever.

"Is Bob seeing after you?" he said. "And are you getting something to eat? The joy of seeing you, my dear Lissa, has increased my appetite three-fold; so pray, Bob, give me the largest chop."

"So you still have a good appetite, Harry?" said Lissa, with a smile.

"Middling, in general," replied Harry, "but to-day very good. You see we must kill the fatted calf, to celebrate our prodigal's return."

"You shut up, Harry," said Bob.

"Now, my dear Lissa, I ask you is that a proper way of teaching 'my young ideas how to shoot?'" said the incorrigible Harry, with his mouth full. "Bob, with his superior years, his sallow complexion, and grave face, should be an example, shouldn't he, of polite manners to me? yet he bids me 'shut up.'"

"Not much use bidding you do anything," growled the elder brother.

"No, it is not, Bob," said Harry, with complacency. "I am gifted, Lissa, at least in one way,"

"And what way may that be, Harry" asked Elizabeth.

"I appreciate myself," answered Harry, quite gravely, "I see the follies of others, and overlook my own."

"It is well, Harry," said Lissa, smiling.

"It is well, Lissa," said Harry; "for but for this excellent quality, I should have gone mad during the last few months We've had a precious time, haven't we, Bob?"

"No mistake about that," answered Bob.

"No, there is no mistake," went on Harry. "During them Dick has acted the madman, the drunkard, and the brute to perfection. This house has been an arena, my dear Lissa, and Bob and I gladiators, for we have had to wrestle with a wild beast."

"Hush, hush, Harry, remember how ill he is," said Elizabeth.

"I shall remember it to the last day of my life," replied Harry. And then, seeing the pain on Elizabeth's face, he rose and put his arms round her neck, like he used to do when he was a little child.

"Don't you cry about him," he said, "for he's not worth it. I'm sorry for the poor fellow now he's down," he added, "but

I'm not going to pretend that I think it wouldn't be a good thing for us all if Dick were dead."

It had come to this then—the young man who had lived but for himself, sacrificing everything to his lawless feelings, was not leaving one friend to mourn him upon earth. He was nearest and dearest to none; for evil, not good, had been the rule of his life, and his death would come as a relief to those who had the misfortune to be his kindred, and to the woman he had forced to be his wife.

Yet though this was so, his pitiable condition, when she saw him, moved Elizabeth to tears. He was lying asleep, his drawn, altered face, almost like a dead man's, so changed that Elizabeth scarcely recognized him. His left side and arm were quite powerless, and he had the strange, unmistakable look which told that the end was not far away.

Elizabeth sat and watched him, and by-and-by he began to stir, and presently he opened his dim and sunken eyes, and looked at Elizabeth. but without any recognition in them.

"How are you Dick?" said Elizabeth, bending over him, and taking hold of his cold, stiff hand.

As she spoke, a sort of gleam passed over his face, a gleam of memory.

You—you—have come back?" he said, with difficulty, for his articulation was much affected.

"Yes, and I will not leave you any more, Dick," answered Elizabeth. And she stooped over him, lifting his head higher, and smoothing and straightening the pillows for the stricken man.

CHAPTER XXXV.

THE GATE OF DEATH.

STRANGE to say, Richard Horton rallied greatly after Elizabeth's return. That is, his bodily health rallied, for his mind continued much the same, and only occasionally he understood that he was lying there face to face with death.

His terror at these moments was pitiable and extreme, for he had no Comforter to lead him through the dark valley; no stay on which to rest his parting soul.

In vain Elizabeth prayed and wept by his side. Sometimes he would pettishly forbid her to do so—memory, everything, swept away from his clouded mind; at other times he would cry out in his despair, cursing the day that he was born, and the God whose laws he had broken and defied.

Elizabeth acted very nobly during this miserable time. If this unhappy man had done her no wrong; if he had still been the dear cousin of her youth, she could not have watched and waited on him more patiently than she did. It was so terrible to see him lying there; terrible to think of his life, and approaching death; yet more terrible to think of the everlasting life beyond.

As the dreary days passed on, Elizabeth settled down, mechanically as it were, to her old place, as mistress of the household. She heard nothing of the outward scandal that her return to a scantily peopled neighbourhood like Wendell had of course created; nothing of the wondering comments that Sir John Tyrell's marked attentions to her naturally caused.

This true gentleman, whose rare nature was so far above the common average of his fellows, that he was sometimes called eccentric, though his keen good sense made him prefer to avoid that reputation, had formed a high, perhaps even a prejudicially high, opinion of Elizabeth's character.

He, therefore, not only called upon her himself at once after her return, but he requested his daughters also to do so.

"But, papa," said Miss Tyrell, whose mind was about as narrow as her father's was broad, "how can we—after the remarks?"

"What remarks, my dear?" asked Sir John, blandly.

"About—well, of course—the way she left Wendell," replied Miss Tyrell. "Some people said—"

"What, love?"

"Well—that she even ran away with some one," answered Miss Tyrell, with a blush.

"Who was the 'some one' who told you this, my dear Matilda?" asked Sir John, sarcastically.

"Well, papa—really I cannot say—common report—"

"Is proverbially a liar, my dear," went on the Baronet, as his daughter paused, "and a most horrible liar, I assure you, in this case. Mrs. Horton—I grieve even to call her by that name— left home because she could no longer endure the terrible society of the unfortunate man now lying on his death-bed."

"But why did she marry him, papa?"

"'There are more things in heaven and earth, Horatio'—or rather Matilda," quoted Sir John, "'than are dreamt of in your philosophy.' Why did she marry him? Why do many of us marry, and find out our mistakes? But this young lady may have had peculiar reasons for marrying."

"You are very mysterious, papa—certainly, poor Harry—"

"Would have married her without doubt, if he could—and so also, I believe, would Jasper."

"Oh! no. But talking of Jasper, do you know, papa, I think his marriage will be very soon now. I had a letter this morning from him, and one also from Eva Dalziel, and he wishes it to be soon. They talk of the end of this month, and Eva wishes us to go to Hazelhurst for the occasion; and, of course, as Jasper *is* going to marry her, I suppose we had better make the best of it?"

"Yes, my dear, I advise you to do so," answered Sir John,

with his quiet smile. "Remember that your brother will be the head of the family after I am canonized, and a great deal will therefore depend upon him regarding your future prospects. So I advise you to be civil to him."

Miss Tyrell looked offended.

"Really, papa, you put things in such an odd way," she said.

"My dear, the truth can be spoken between near relations, without any violation of fashionable manners," replied Sir John, again smiling. "But," he added, recurring to the object with which he had commenced this conversation, "I wish you to call on Mrs. Horton at once, Matilda; so will you oblige me by doing so ?"

"Of course, if you wish it, papa."

"I do wish it. I wish also that you will pay her every attention in your power, and thus let Mr. or Mrs. 'Someone '—your informants, in fact, of her misdeeds—see that you do not believe a word of their gossip."

Miss Tyrell made no answer to this. She was one of those who considered Sir John eccentric, but being wise in her generation, she always obeyed him when he made any particular request, knowing that the prosperity of her future life lay in a great measure in his hands. She also wrote to her brother Jasper, and to Eva Dalziel, very kindly for the same reason. She did not approve of this marriage, and Fannie Tyrell did not approve of it either. After the fashion of sisters, they considered that their brother had thrown himself away; but they knew also that it was of no more use telling Jasper this than attempting to float in the air, or do any other thing impossible to frail humanity.

So they wrote and told Jasper that they would be very glad to go to Hazelhurst for his marriage ; and Jasper read the letter when it reached him with an impatient sigh.

Yet he had settled his own fate, and what could he asy? On the very day that Elizabeth left Hazelhurst, when he returned to the house and was told that she was gone, he made up his mind. "What," thought Jasper, with almost a spasm of pain in his heart, when Mrs. Dalziel blandly communicated the fact that Miss Gordon had suddenly left them on account of the dangerous illness of a relation, "she could go so soon then, without another word? Well, she is wise—she is wise."

"Miss Gordon was not communicative about who the relation was," went on Mrs. Dalziel. "Indeed, she never spoke of her relations."

"But she is gone to Wendell, Jasper," said Eva, who was standing near.

"To Wendell !" repeated Jasper Tyrell, and his brown face grew a dusky red.

"Yes; the address she left is here—'Care of R. Horton, Esq.,

Wendell West-house, Uplandshire,'" read out Eva, from a directed envelope which was lying on the table, that Elizabeth, at Eva's request, had left.

Jasper Tyrell said not a word on receiving this piece of information, but it was a bitter blow to him. "What, she had gone back to her husband, then!" he thought, with angry jealousy. "She has truly put a bar between us," he mentally added; and he sat stroking his dark moustache and gnawing his under lip during dinner-time, from the inexpressible bitterness of the idea. Then, when that meal was over, with all the hasty passion with which we sometimes decide, when under the influence of excited feelings, Jasper Tyrell, with the privilege of a betrothed lover, asked Eva to accompany him for a stroll into the garden, and was no sooner there, than he spoke words which Eva perhaps had sometimes fondly hoped to hear before.

"Dear Eva," he said, almost abruptly, "is there any reason why we should not fix the time of our marriage day?"

Eva blushed, and hung her head down at this question, the bright, happy blush of a girl in love.

"I—I—do not know," she said.

"We should feel more settled, should we not?" went on Jasper, taking her hand, "if it were over? I want my little wife," he continued, "so when will she come to me?"

"Mamma—" began Eva hesitatingly.

"No, Eva," said Jasper Tyrell, "I want no interference of 'Mamma' between us. This is our own affair, so let us settle it."

We can easily understand how this conversation ended. Eva, with modest pride, told Mrs. Dalziel that night, before she retired to bed, that Jasper wished to be married soon now—wished to be married towards the end of the month; and Mrs. Dalziel went to her rest an elated, excited, and highly fidgety woman.

"I always said, did I not, love?" she remarked to the Major, who was very sleepy, "that darling Eva would do well? I felt sure that Mr. Tyrell—dear Jasper, I think I may call him now—would urge that their union might be soon,"

"I thought," said the Major, suppressing a yawn, "you had some anxious doubts on that point only a day or two ago."

"Henry," said Mrs. Dalziel, who was wide awake, "does anxiety about those who are dear to us show love, or does it not?"

But the Major was too drowsily inclined to enter into this delicate discussion, and merely remarked—

"Well, it is all right now—so good night, my dear." And Mrs. Dalziel was forced to lie scheming and dreaming of the wedding festivities, to the uncongenial music of the Major's snores.

But in the morning she was up and doing, and wrote at once

to her brother-in-law, the Dean, begging that he would come to Hazelhurst, to perform the ceremony of marrying "our dear child—the first that I must lose."

To this the Dean replied with characteristic brevity and sharpness:—

"My dear Sister-in-Law," he wrote, "I am glad that young Tyrell is anxious to 'complete his happiness,' as you inform me, and I shall have great pleasure in assisting him to obtain that enviable position. The expression you make use of when writing of Eva's marriage, as 'our dear child—the first that I must lose,' is, I conclude, merely a female metaphorical mode of describing your satisfaction, veiled in language of sentimental regret. At least, mothers in general are exceedingly anxious to 'lose' all their daughters, and I consider that you are losing Eva in a most gratifying manner. As you ladies, I know, think a great deal of the outward garb in which it is the fashion for you to adorn yourselves, and as it would be well that the child should enter her new family with everything necessary for her future position, I enclose a cheque for £200, and perhaps you will kindly see that she is properly dressed.

"Give my love to her, and tell her that I shall bring her a wedding present, as she has been a good child, and done her duty in 'that state of life unto which' she was called. I remain, dear sister-in-law, yours affectionately,

"RALPH DALZIEL."

"He is a strange man, uncle Ralph, is he not?" said Mrs. Dalziel, after showing this letter to her step-child. "Well, well, we must put up with the eccentricities of people in a certain position."

Thus Jasper Tyrell's wedding was all arranged and settled, a few days after Elizabeth had left Hazelhurst, and at the end of these few days Jasper received a letter from his father, Sir John. The Baronet commenced his letter by congratulating his son on his approaching marriage; but he went on to other subjects—subjects which filled Jasper Tyrell's heart with bitter pain and regret.

"You remember our beautiful neighbour, Miss Gordon, of course, dear Jasper," wrote Sir John, "whom our poor, poor Harry so frantically admired? I told you of her unaccountable marriage with her cousin Richard Horton, and of her leaving Wendell in mysterious fashion; but I did not tell you of the letter she wrote to me in London, nor of her miserable struggles there to obtain a livelihood." Sir John then proceeded to explain to his son the events that we already know—namely, how he had assisted Elizabeth, and how she had requested him to keep her secret—a request that no gentleman could refuse. He then went on to inform Jasper of the letter he had considered it

his duty to write to Elizabeth at Hazelhurst a few days back, to
recall her to her dying husband's side. "*Dying*"—as Jasper
Tyrell read that word he absolutely started, and a burning
colour flushed his brown skin. "There is no hope," continued
Sir John's letter, "that this wretched youth can live. He is
paralysed and imbecile, and is, in fact, lying on the verge of the
grave; and this noble woman is, I hear, now his devoted nurse,
though he is utterly incapable of appreciating her self-sacrifice."

Jasper Tyrell read this letter through, and then sat down sick
at heart. So this was why she had gone to Wendell—this! She
was about to be free—his Lissa, his noble girl that he had loved
so well, that he loved still. He remembered her promise too,
that when Richard Horton was dead he should know the secret
that had parted them—the secret that had spoilt his life and hers!

"Yet in three weeks—in three weeks—" muttered Jasper, and
something like a curse broke from his bitten lips.

Yes, in three weeks, Jasper Tyrell would be a married man, and
though Elizabeth might be free, he would be bound hand and
foot—was bound now by honour, from which he knew there could
be no escape.

"Good heavens!" he thought, excitedly and passionately, as
he paced the little bed-room at Hazelhurst, after reading Sir
John's letter, "what blind creatures we are—driven hither and
thither by circumstances and feelings that we can neither control
nor create! Who can say that a man acts by his own will—he
acts as he is forced to act, by the ever-shifting scenes of fate!"

So restless did Jasper Tyrell become after hearing of Richard
Horton's approaching death, that he could not even disguise the
state of his feelings from Eva's sweet, trustful eyes, and the girl
urged him once to tell her what was disturbing him.

"I wish to be your friend, you know, Jasper," she said, fondly,
"as well—as your wife; so you will tell me if you are unhappy
about anything?"

"No, no," answered Jasper Tyrell, hastily; "why should
you think I am unhappy? What nonsense, my child." And he
turned away, but Eva was not satisfied, and kept wondering to
herself what could possibly have happened to annoy Jasper.

Conscious of this, perhaps, Jasper Tyrell hastened to conclude his
already lengthened visit to Hazelhurst; and as the moth flutters
to the flame, he determined to go to Wendell before his marriage
—determined to see Elizabeth's face once more.

But we may be sure he did not leave the village until Mrs.
Dalziel had made every arrangement for his return there. She
fixed the day; talked eternally of the "happy approaching
event," and made herself (she considered) most charming to the
"young people," one of whom at least was in no mood to listen
to her common-place and unnecessary allusions.

Jasper parted with Eva outwardly as lovers part, but inwardly with a weary sense of duty, which took all charm away from the sweet kiss her blooming lips bestowed.

"Dear girl," he thought (self-convicted of ingratitude fo her tender love, and pretty, fond farewells), as he was being driven from Hazelhurst, "why is she not my sister—or rather, why did I ever see the beautiful face that seems to come between me and every pleasure and duty of my life?"

He did not travel direct to Wendell, but remained a few days in town; and though it was unlikely at this time of the year that Mr. Wilmot would be there, he endeavoured, with all the restlessness of an unhappy man, to see him. What Jasper meant to do when he sought Wilmot at his Club, he had scarcely decided. "To accuse him of his false words—perhaps strike him across his false face," thought Jasper Tyrell. At all events to ask him how he had dared to deceive him about his connection with Elizabeth, and to force him to apologize for the language he had used. But whatever were his intentions they were all abortive, for Mr. Wilmot was abroad, he was informed in answer to his inquiries, though expected shortly to return. All, therefore, that Jasper could do, he did, which was to leave his card, with a message that as soon as Mr. Wilmot returned to England he desired to see him. Then, having done this, he started for Wendell, after telegraphing to his father the train that he expected to arrive there by.

He found Sir John, on reaching the station at Mitchin, waiting for him on the platform, and with a smile the Baronet put his arm through his son's.

"Thank you for running down, my dear fellow," he said. "Shall we walk on? Roberts will see after your traps." And as Jasper moved on with his father, he could not help thinking what a noble presence he had—how superior, in fact, he was in appearance to more than half the young men that he knew.

Sir John, in truth, bore his years so well that they seemed only to add to his dignity; and the fine expression of his face, full of "the wise, sad valour," which comes only in the autumnal days of life, had a charm beyond that of youth, for it told of feelings that the young have not attained. Here was a gentleman then, mature, just, and tender, who looked on the follies of mankind with a smile, on their sins with a sigh, on their wrongs with a frown. He had been disappointed in life, for the woman that he had loved was weak of intellect and small of heart; but he blamed himself, not her, for his unfortunate choice. The lovely face of Lady Tyrell had captivated his fancy, and blinded him to her inferiority, and he therefore had been a good and kindly husband to her; but he had known no soul-friend by his domestic hearth, through the long years of his uncongenial married existence. This, however, had never embittered Sir John, and his good-natured forbearance to her was, perhaps, one of the proofs of his indifference.

But Jasper Tyrell was of a very different nature to his father. Fiery, passionate, and impulsive, he must inevitably have loved or hated the woman with whom he lived. He could not understand the placid repose of his father's mind, but, as young men will, ascribed it all to the mellowing influence of age.

"In looks he might cut out half the young fellows I know," thought Jasper Tyrell, glancing at his father's calm, fine face, "but I suppose, after all, a woman would like a young man best."

Unconscious of his son's mental comments on his appearance, they had scarcely left the station and reached the high-road, when Sir John began, with a certain inflection in his voice ; a faint agitation even, which Jasper instantly noticed, though a moment later his own overpowering emotion swept every other thought from his mind.

"Jasper," said Sir John, "I have some news for you—that unfortunate young man, Richard Horton, died this morning."

"What!" exclaimed Jasper, "dead—so soon?" And Sir John felt his son's form quiver as if he had received some desperate wound.

"Yes," answered Sir John, "he died this morning about eleven. He had another fit yesterday, I hear, and never spoke again—it is a sad end for one so young."

"Terrible!" said Jasper Tyrell, briefly, and he drew his arm from his father's ; and Sir John saw, with wonder, how pale his son had grown ; how uncontrollable was the agitation with which he received the news of Richard Horton's death.

CHAPTER XXXVI.

THE FUNERAL DAY.

THE last few days of her husband's life had been very terrible ones for Elizabeth. As is the case sometimes before death, Richard Horton's mind had cleared wonderfully, and remorse, terrible remorse, and dread had taken possession of his soul.

It was a sinner's death-bed—frighful to think of, yet more frightful to contemplate. Oh! how Elizabeth longed to cry out, "God will forgive you—God will save you!" How could she say this to one who cursed his God, to one who would not pray, would not believe, and who was drifting into the darkness with no Light to light him on his way?

She told him of the dying sinner on the cross, of the weeping Magdalene, of our Lord's gracious words to both. Alas! he would not listen, would not believe. There was no hope for him, he said ; repeating again and again, to Elizabeth's horror-stricken ears, the painful details of poor Harry Tyrell's murder—the death-cry with which the poor lad sank back into the snow, slain by an unseen hand!

Presently his mind began to wander again, and the images in his brain grew for him into grim reality, and he cried out aloud that Harry Tyrell was in the room, and then fell back in a frightful fit, after which he spoke no more. But the end did not come yet. He was speechless, but alive; and all through the hours of the night his restless eyes rolled from side to side, with so terrible an expression in them, that Elizabeth's mind almost gave way, and she kept calling to God to end his misery, to take him out of his fearful pain.

When the morning broke, his face was like the face of an old man, worn, haggard, and terrible; but just about eleven o'clock —just before the end came—a softer look stole over it, and as Elizabeth raised his head, he closed his eyes, and so died. After death he looked more as he had done in early youth, before the dark passions had swept over him which had destroyed his life.

When all was over, and his face and limbs were decently composed, Elizabeth left the room, retiring to her own, utterly worn out, her nerves shattered, and her brain throbbing with the painful scenes that she had gone through. But she could not rest. The terrible tragedy in which she had been an unconscious actor kept recurring and recurring to her mind, and at last she came downstairs and sat with Robert and Hal Horton, who did their best to soothe and comfort her; Robert gravely and quietly asking her advice as to the funeral ceremony, and about the friends who would expect to be invited to join it.

But Elizabeth would not hear of any company being asked.

"No, dear Bob," she said, "it is best to have no one."

Robert Horton looked at Elizabeth, and understood why she wished this, and yet felt unwilling, from any delicate scruples, to lose prestige among their neighbours by being considered to have acted in a niggardly manner regarding the expenses of their brother's funeral.

"Don't you think," he said, hesitatingly, "that people will think it strange—"

"It is right," said Elizabeth, decidedly, and after that nothing more was said on the subject.

On the following morning, however, a very kind, gentlemanly note arrived from Sir John Tyrell for Elizabeth, offering his company as one of the mourners to follow the young man's body to the grave.

"As his father's old friend and near neighbour," wrote Sir John, "I wish to pay him this last respect."

Elizabeth wept very bitterly when she read this note, but she answered it without even consulting her cousins, telling Sir John how much she felt his kindness, but praying him at the same time not to think of being present at Richard Horton's funeral.

"I do not wish it, dear Sir John," she added, "and I am sure you will not go when I tell you this. Some day I will tell you the reason, and many things will be clear to you then, that now you cannot understand."

Sir John read this letter very thoughtfully, and then put it gravely into Jasper's hand, for they were alone together in the library when the Baronet received it, and Jasper's eyes had already fallen jealously and uneasily on the familiar hand writing.

"There is a mystery in all this that I cannot fathom, Jasper," said Sir John. "Somehow—strange though it may seem to you for me to say it—I believe Elizabeth Gordon knew, or, at least, knows, more than we do of the secret of poor Harry's death."

"When is he to be buried?" asked Jasper, hoarsely, rising from his seat.

"To-morrow at three," answered Sir John. "I heard from one of the tenants this morning about it, and he told me that they have asked no one to attend the ceremony, and that Robert Horton had said that this was at his cousin's, or, rather, his sister-in-law's, particular request."

Jasper Tyrell made no answer to this, but stood staring gloomily out on the garden from one of the library windows.

He had as yet made no attempt to see Elizabeth, but he had sworn that the day they carried Richard Horton to his grave that he would urge her to fulfil her promise, and tell him why she had married this man—what secret had parted her life and his.

With a sort of morbid curiosity he went on the following morning to the grave-yard at Wendell, where he found two men busily engaged in digging a grave.

"Is this for young Horton?" he asked, and one of the men nodded his head, and Jasper stood by, grimly watching them throwing up spadefuls of damp soil, and thinking how he had hated and detested the coming tenant of this narrow home.

"He's young to go," said one of the men presently, looking at Jasper.

"Ay," said the other, with a chuckle, "but he liked a drop, yet it's dry work digging his grave."

Jasper took the hint, and put a couple of shillings into the grave-digger's hand, and then, with a sudden feeling of disgust and shame, he turned away.

"It makes one shudder," he thought. "What! it all ends here—youth and beauty, hope and love—all in the grave."

He felt wretchedly out of spirits, and miserable during the whole day. He knew that no good could come of seeking an interview with Elizabeth, and yet he was determined to seek one, and with restless impatience endeavoured, as best he could, to pass the time, until it was possible that he could see her.

At three o'clock the modest funeral procession that bore

Richard Horton to his untimely grave left Wendell West-house; his two brothers (by Elizabeth's especial request) being the only mourners. Old Mr. Hay, the incumbent, read the Burial Service over the body, and at four it was all over, and Richard Horton's place knew him no more. At the house, the servants upstairs took down the bed-curtains, and rolled up the carpet in the room where he had died, and from whence they had carried him away. Downstairs, his widow sat white and grave, but without the ordinary cap worn in token of woe and bereavement. When the brothers returned from the ceremony she rose up and kissed them both softly and sadly on the face, and after that nothing unusual was said or occurred, though Harry wiped away a hot tear with his hand just after Elizabeth had kissed him. Then the dinner-hour came, and the dinner was served in the ordinary fashion, and by-and-by Robert and Harry went out, and, after lighting their pipes in the hall, strolled together to the stables and outhouses, and Elizabeth was left alone—left sitting in the gathering twilight, full of solemn thoughts of the life that is present, and of the life that is to come.

Presently she rose and went to the window, and looked out at the familiar view, and as she did so (it seemed almost like a dream then, and yet it was true), Jasper Tyrell's familiar form appeared advancing up the avenue, and when Elizabeth saw him she went out to meet him, opening the hall-door, and holding out her hand.

"The boys told me that you were at the Hall," she said, as he nervously returned her greeting. "Were you coming to see me, Jasper?"

As Elizabeth asked this, the plaintive ring in her voice powerfully affected the already excited Jasper, and almost in a whisper he answered,

"Yes Elizabeth, I have come to ask you to keep your promise."

"Come in here," said Elizabeth, in the same sad voice, and she led Jasper into the dining-room, where she had been sitting, and after closing the door behind them, went up to him and took his hand.

"Jasper," she said, beseechingly, "you will not forget that he is dead?"

"No," answered Jasper, "I will try to remember that, Lissa. But you will tell me all?"

"Yes," said Elizabeth, still holding Jasper's hand, still looking with her dark, sorrowful eyes into his face; "but—he was a great sinner, Jasper—you have much to forgive."

"I do not know about forgiveness," said Jasper, sharply.

"He is dead," again almost whispered Elizabeth.

"Well?"

"Jasper," continued Elizabeth, her voice and form trembling

violently, "he whom we buried to-day—Richard Horton—was
the shedder of Harry's blood ? "

"What !" exclaimed Jasper Tyrell.

"He, and no other," said Elizabeth, was your brother's murderer."

"And yet you married him, Elizabeth!" interrupted Jasper,
with a sort of fierce cry. "How was this ? What madness induced
you to so horrible an act ? "

"Oh! my poor Jasper," went on Elizabeth, weeping, "he not
only murdered Harry's body, but your good name—he told me—
nay, he seemed to prove to me that your hand—not his—took
Harry's life."

"My God! and you believed this ? "

"What could I believe, Jasper ? " said Elizabeth. "My own
eyes saw your footprints in the snow, my own hand found the
handkerchief that I had marked for you, lying on the very spot
where Harry's murdered body was found."

"There is some hellish plot in this," said Jasper, fiercely and
excitedly.

"Yes, a wicked plot," went on Elizabeth "conceived and carried
out so subtly, Jasper, that it spoilt our lives! He had contrived
to secrete a pair of your boots," she continued, "and wore them
when he shot poor Harry from behind the hedge. And he
dragged me there—showed me the footprints in the snow; the
footprints that I knew so well, and your handkerchief lying there
—one of the handkerchiefs that I worked for you before you
went away."

"The cursed scoundrel ! "

"Hush, Jasper! you are not his Judge."

"Well, go on—tell me everything."

"It is all sin and pain," went on Elizabeth, sobbing. "He
said that this evidence would hang you, and I knew you had
quarrelled, Jasper—you and Harry—and then he asked a price if
he kept your secret."

"What price ? "

"You can guess—he forced me to marry him—and to save
you—"

"What! Oh! my God—and you made this sacrifice ? " said
Jasper Tyrell, deeply affected.

"What could I do ? You were more to me than life—I prayed
hard, but he would not spare me ! "

"Oh! Elizabeth—Lissa," said Jasper Tyrell, approaching her,
and clasping her in his arms—crushing her against his breast—
"and you did this—*for me?* "

Elizabeth's head sank upon his shoulder.

"I did this," she whispered, "more I could not do. If I could
have died, Jasper—"

"My love, this was worse than death," said Jasper Tyrell.

"'I understand it all now—my love, my Elizabeth—my noble, noble girl!"

At this moment Elizabeth forgot everything but that she was with Jasper: that her cheek was against his; that he trusted in her, and believed in her once more.

The next minute, however, Jasper himself dispelled the dream.

"Lissa," he said, lifting up his head, and speaking in the sharp quick way, which was habitual to him when he had made a sudden decision, "you gave your life for me—your honour—"

"Yes, Jasper."

"Then I will give my honour, or what the world calls honour, up for you. Eva must know this, Lissa—I will not keep my promise to her now."

At Eva's name Elizabeth started, and drew back from Jasper's embrace.

"Eva!" she repeated, and she put her hand up to her head.

"Yes," said Jasper Tyrell, "whatever the world says of me now, I will brave it—I won't marry Eva now."

"But," said Elizabeth, with a sort of quivering sigh, "it's not the world, Jasper—it's not that we must think of—but the child's heart."

Jasper was silent at this for a moment or two, and then he said, "What would you have me do?"

"It—is very near, is it not?" asked Elizabeth.

"I will not marry her," answered Jasper, with sullen doggedness.

"But, Jasper," said Elizabeth, and she came up to him, "you will not kill the child? You won't break her heart, as mine was broken?" she continued, with a sort of wild sorrow in her eyes and face. "You don't know what it is to a woman, dear, to lose the man she loves—she has no life after that—she is dead when yet alive."

"But you love me?"

"I love you, and will love no other," answered Elizabeth; "but I could not be happy with you—even as your wife, Jasper —if I won that joy by breaking Eva's heart."

This touched Jasper. His memory went back to the sweet girlish face of Eva; to her loving, simple words.

"Jasper," she had said, "if anything were to part us now, I should die—I could not bear the pain."

"You shall not bear it, Eva," Jasper had answered, and he remembered that answer now.

"What can I do?" he said, and he sat down, miserable and uncertain how to act.

"What is right," said Elizabeth, struggling with her own heart. "There is no happiness in wrong-doing, Jasper, and no good comes of it. If I had been firm—if I had not sinned by marrying when I knew my vows were false—all this misery would have been spared."

"Oh! my generous girl!" said Jasper, and he held out his hand, and Elizabeth took it, and for a moment softly pressed it to her lips.

"There is no generosity in love, Jasper," she said, "for to give is very sweet. But I have not told you all my tale," she went on. "Not how soon poor Richard's punishment came; not how heavy a price he had to pay. Oh! Jasper, he was haunted —driven mad by remorse, and one night I followed him in his sleep."

"Yes?"

"And he went to an old unused room, and there he drew out from an oaken chest which stood there, when he was still asleep, the pistol that he shot poor Harry with, and your boots. And when he awoke I charged him with the crime—charged him there, with the evidences all lying before him, and he confessed—poor, poor soul—Oh! pity him, Jasper—he confessed, and that night I fled away. You understand all now, don't you? I left Wendell, and then we saw each other in London. I could not tell you, you see, Jasper—not while Richard Horton lived."

"No," said Jasper, and he drew a long breath. He was thinking what he would have done—would he have spared his brother's murderer?

"Come with me," said Elizabeth, the next minute, "and I will show you all these things as he left them. But no, perhaps not to-night, Jasper; not the day that he has been carried to his grave."

"What was his motive?" said Jasper, slowly. "But I can guess."

"He was jealous, madly jealous of you both, he told me," answered Elizabeth. "He had seen us part that night when you went away—when we little thought—"

"Don't cry, darling—my darling, don't," said Jasper Tyrell, "or you will unman me. Ay, we little thought Lissa—" And he once more drew her to his breast.

"But we must do right," said Elizabeth, though her whole form was heaving, and her voice was choked with sobs. "Eva must never know—we must part—"

"Is it so?" said Jasper Tyrell, with a bitter sigh, and he drew away. "I remember once reading a book, Lissa," he went on, "called *Barren Honour*—it will be barren honour, won't it, child, for us—barren honour all our lives, if you and I must part?"

"Not all barren, Jasper," said Elizabeth, "if we make Eva happy."

"And what about Elizabeth?" answered Jasper, putting his hand softly against Elizabeth's wet and tear-stained cheek. "What about the woman whose heart and mine are one? Whom I have loved, and love so well?"

But here Jasper paused, and with a sudden movement Elizabeth drew quickly away from him, and seated herself in another part of the room; for just at this moment the voices of the brothers Robert and Hal Horton were distinctly to be heard talking to each other in the hall.

"Here are my cousins," said Elizabeth, and the next minute Robert Horton opened the room door and came in.

"Are you here, Lissa?" he asked, for it was now almost dark. "Why, you've let the fire go out! I'm vexed that we stayed away so long."

"I have been talking to Mr. Tyrell," answered Elizabeth, almost quietly. "I will order lights, Robert, and have the fire re-lit."

And then, before her cousin could reply, Elizabeth left the room, and Jasper Tyrell and Robert Horton were left to entertain each other as best they could.

CHAPTER XXXVII.
JASPER'S REVENGE.

THE next morning's post brought a letter for Jasper Tyrell, from Eva Dalziel—a tender, fluttering, cooing letter, such as a girl might write to the man she loved, when near her wedding day. Her pretty prattle about "the future"—the future so dark and uncertain in Jasper's mind—painfully affected him; and, with ill-concealed emotion, he rose from the breakfast-table after he had read her gentle words, leaving his sisters to comment on his unloverlike expression.

"Jasper's letter was from Eva Dalziel," said Fannie Tyrell to Matilda, "and I must say, considering that he is to be married in a fortnight, that he does not look particularly charmed to hear from her."

"Papa thinks, you know," answered Matilda, "that absolutely Jasper would have married Miss Gordon—Mrs. Horton now, I beg her pardon—at one time. Fancy, what would you say, Fannie, if he were to jilt little Eva after all, and marry the rich young widow, for since her brother's death she will be rich, in spite of all her shortcomings?"

"Oh! he never would do that—never, after all the horrid reports about her," said the younger sister.

"Men do strange things," replied Miss Tyrell; and then the conversation ceased, for Sir John entered the room, and the girls were too wise to talk in this strain before their father.

But Sir John himself grew to have uneasy doubts how his son

would act before the day was ended. These arose during an interview that he had with Jasper, when the young man, with evident agitation, placed a few lines that he had received from Elizabeth during the morning in his father's hands.

"Father," he said, I have something to tell you—something that—Elizabeth Gordon wishes you to know."

"Elizabeth Gordon?" said Sir John, with a faint inflection of surprise in his voice

"Yes, Elizabeth Gordon," repeated Jasper, "for I can think of her, can bear to think of her, by no other name. Father," he went on, "read that note, and perhaps then you will understand better what I mean."

At this Sir John drew out his double gold glasses, and placed them slowly on his high and finely-shaped nose.

"You wish me to read this, Jasper," he said, "this note—from a lady?"

"Yes," answered Jasper, in a husky and broken voice, "from one of the best and noblest ladies, father, that ever lived. Elizabeth Gordon is a woman in a thousand."

Sir John made no comment on this, but unfolded Elizabeth's letter, and read the few lines that she had written to Jasper. They were only very few, and were as follows:— "Will you come over this morning, dear Jasper, that I may show you the sad evidences of poor Richard's crime? And I think it would be well also that your dear father, Sir John, should now know the truth? It would be so painful for me to tell him, that I leave it in your hands; praying you to remember still, that he who wronged us all so cruelly has now passed away from earthly judgment. For the rest, dear Jasper, I pray God that you may be happy with one of the sweetest and best women that I have ever known."

"ELIZABETH."

Sir John read this letter, and re-read it, and then only looked up in the face of his son.

"Jasper," he said, and then he hesitated, "am I right in supposing from this—that there was once an engagement between you and Miss Gordon—and that this unhappy man, Richard Horton—"

"Was Harry's murderer," said Jasper Tyrell, as Sir John paused, while a deep flush dyed his dark skin.

"Is this so?" said Sir John, and a flush came over his face also.

"Yes," answered Jasper Tyrell, excitedly. "This scoundrel—dead though he is, I'll curse his name—not only shot Harry, but made Elizabeth, my Elizabeth then, believe that I had lifted my hand to shed my brother's blood! Was there ever such villainy on earth before, father—ever such a hellish plot?"

"What was it?" asked Sir John, with much emotion; and,

in passionate words of anger, Jasper Tyrell detailed to his father what Elizabeth had told him; while Sir John sat still, anger, regret, and an almost uncontrollable feeling of ungratified vengeance struggling for the time in his usually placid and philosophic heart.

"And this fellow died in his bed," said Jasper Tyrell, fiercely, as he ended his narrative, "after killing Harry and wronging me —as, by heavens! no man was ever wronged before."

"So—this was her secret?" said Sir John, endeavouring to be calm. "This, the reason why this fine creature did what a good woman seldom does—this, the reason, Jasper, why—"

Here Sir John paused. He was looking at his son, his only son now, who, pale and red by turns, was evidently going through some violent mental struggles. What those struggles were suddenly occurred to Sir John's clear and honourable mind.

"Jasper," he said, rising, and laying his hand lightly, but affectionately on his son's shoulder, "need I tell you what I feel for you—the sympathy that one man must feel for another, when, through no fault of his own, he loses a woman so beautiful and noble as Elizabeth Gordon—but Jasper, you must not forget the claims of your promised wife."

"But, father, you don't know all," said Jasper, as if pleading for himself; "you don't know how we loved each other—how we met in town, and how I—well, I will tell you all—begged and prayed Elizabeth to fly with me. I would have married her, father—don't frown—yes, I was ready to give up everything for her—and am now, so it's no use deceiving you!"

"Not honour, surely, Jasper?" said Sir John. "Not a gentleman's birth-right, for which he should be ever ready to cast all other considerations aside?"

"It's easy talking," muttered Jasper, almost sullenly.

"I know it is, my poor boy," answered Sir John kindly; "much easier to talk than to act, when temptation is standing in the way. But, Jasper, I must say one word, and you will forgive me? It was by your own wish, was it not, that you entered into an engagement with Miss Dalziel?"

"Of course—my wish *then*."

"Then now as a gentleman you cannot withdraw from it," went on Sir John firmly. "If this unhappy man's life had been prolonged a week or two, you would have been a married man when you learnt this sad secret, and you would not, I suppose, then have contemplated leaving your young wife?"

"No, certainly not; that is a different thing" answered Jasper, quickly.

"Not to a man of honour" said Sir John. "you have promised to marry Miss Dalziel. She is doubtless looking forward, as a loving and affectionate girl does, to the day that you will fulfil that promise; and nothing, in my own opinion, can justify you in breaking it—but, I do not doubt my son." And as Sir John said these last words, he held out his hand to Jasper, who did not certainly return his father's clasp in a very reassuring manner.

"Tell the unhappy lady," went on Sir John, not seeming to notice this, "who was Miss Gordon, that I have heard her story —a story so terrible to us all—and that I wish, as she doubtless wishes also, the grave to hide the secret, both of my poor boy's fate" (here Sir John's voice broke) "and the crime of the miserable young man who was buried yesterday. And tell her also," continued Sir John, in firmer tones, "that I respect and pity her with my whole heart; and that by-and-by, when time has softened this a little to us, that I shall trust to renew the friendship between us—a friendship which I shall ever regard as an honour to myself."

Jasper made no answer to this, and Sir John, after a few more words, left the room; but his decidedly expressed opinion was not without some influence on his son.

"So every one says the same thing," thought Jasper, bitterly; "yet I believe if this poor child but knew—"

Yet could he have the heart to tell her? That Eva loved him he was sure, and could he blight the young girl's bright love-dreams by such a cruel blow? "The future," that she wrote of so prettily, what would be her future then? "Oh! my poor Eva," thought Jasper, "poor, poor, hapless little girl!"

Yet, on the other hand, had not Elizabeth done more for him than if she had given her life? She had, indeed, given her life— all the life Jasper knew that she thought worth living for—and yet must he leave her now?

But when he saw her again; when he looked once more in the beautiful, still face, he felt somehow that the decision rested not with him, and that Elizabeth meant to do what she esteemed her duty, and had resigned all hope and claim ever to be his wife.

There was no embarrassment in the sad eyes that she raised to his face, none in the almost solemn hand-shake.

Elizabeth, indeed, had wrestled with herself—with her loving impetuous self—and had conquered in the fight. But very weary was the victor; very wistful that the days of her lonely pilgrimage would not be long.

"I suppose I am not a good woman," thought poor Elizabeth, with bitter tears. "A good woman would be happy by-and-by, in thinking that Jasper and Eva were happy—but I cannot be— I shall never be."

"But the passionate tears were all dried up before she sent for Jasper. She seemed, indeed, to him, when he first saw her after he had told her story to Sir John, almost like another person to the Elizabeth he had so ardently loved. He looked at her again and again, as she stood before him in her long black robes, **and** with the sad subdued expression on her face, and wondered at the change; following her like a man in a dream, when she led him along the deserted passage that opened into "Grandmamma's store-room;" when she unlocked the old, oak'chest, and showed him the pistol with which Richard Horton had spilt his brother's blood.

He took the boots which had once been his, in his hands when Elizabeth placed them there, and after examining them for a moment, laid them down with a sort of shudder.

"You see there are your initials, Jasper," said Elizabeth, pointing to the letters written in ink in the lining of the boots.

"I see," answered Jasper, "my servant always marked them there. But come away, Elizabeth," he added, looking round with a shiver, "this room makes me cold—I can almost fancy poor Harry is near us now."

"I thought that you had better see them," said Elizabeth, slowly; and then she replaced, one after the other, the evidences of Richard Horton's crime, back into their strange hiding place.

"They are all dead people's things," she said, as if she were thinking rather than speaking, as she put the wedding finery of a century ago on the fatal pistol and on the boots; and then, after locking the chest, with a heavy sigh, she turned away!

In silence they quitted the unused chamber, and in silence returned to the dining-room downstairs; but when they were there, Jasper, after pacing the room twice, suddenly began, in spite of Eva's letter, in spite of his father's words, and even of his own better impulses, once more to urge Elizabeth to be his wife.

"You are only preparing a life of misery for us both, Elizabeth," he said. "What! do you think a man can always act? Don't you think that Eva will learn I do not love her—that I am always thinking of, and loving you?"

"Hush, Jasper, hush;" answered Elizabeth. "Do not take my strength away—it is not great—Oh! Jasper, do not tempt me to do wrong."

"But is it wrong?" asked Jasper. "Yes," he added, his juster sense returning to him, "I admit it is wrong; but, oh! Lissa, Lissa, it is a great temptation."

"Yes—to both," said Elizabeth, and at these words the blood rushed into Jasper's face.

"I would rather die," he said. "I solemnly declare I would rather die than marry Eva Dalziel now!"

"You—will—be happy—in time," murmured Elizabeth, but a sob almost choked her utterance.

Then Jasper took her in his arms, and held her to his breast.

"I would be happy to die in your arms," he said, "to-day, to-morrow, any time, I want no better happiness than that."

They said only a few words after this—murmured words of love and parting, and then, pale and grief-stricken, they bid each other farewell.

"I will go away to-day," said Jasper. "If there is no hope for me, I will go away—but, Lissa, let me come back—let me come back to give you one kiss, before I see your face no more."

She did not refuse this, and so with heart-wrung sighs they parted; Jasper Tyrell leaving Wendell, in spite of his father's remonstrances, within an hour after his interview with Elizabeth.

"I am better away, father," he said, gloomily, and Sir John sighed uneasily, and let him go. He then proceeded direct to London, remembering, with a sort of relief, a fierce joy almost, that one man still lived who had robbed him of Elizabeth; that he could yet revenge himself on Mr. Edgar Wilmot.

That gentleman was dawdling idly through a late breakfast, in his luxuriously furnished rooms in Upper Brook Street, the day after Jasper's arrival in town, when his servant, somewhat to his annoyance (for he did not care for early or many visitors), brought in Jasper's card, accompanied by a request that Mr. Tyrell wished to see him.

"Say I'm out," said Mr. Wilmot, carelessly, after he had glanced at the card; but Jasper had followed the servant upstairs, and, as Mr. Wilmot uttered these words, he appeared at the doorway, with a very ominous frown settled on his brow.

As soon as Mr. Wilmot saw him, he at once rose courteously, and advanced towards Jasper.

"Pardon my seeming rudeness, Mr. Tyrell," he said. "I did not know that you had come upstairs, and I am very unwell this morning—unfit, in fact, to receive visitors."

"I will not intrude on you long," answered Jasper Tyrell, with a stern smile. "I have an account to settle with you, Mr. Wilmot."

"With me?" said Mr. Wilmot, and he slightly raised his eyebrows, and looked inquiringly at Jasper.

"Yes, with you," repeated Jasper. "Tell your servant to shut the door" (for the man had loitered in the room), "as what I've got to say to you needs no other listener,."

"Shut the door, Long," said Mr. Wilmot, and as the man left the room and obeyed him, Mr. Wilmot turned to Jasper once more. "Now," he said, "as we are alone, may I ask the reason of your extraordinary manner and words?"

"Do you remember our meeting in Cambridge Street, last January?" asked Jasper, sternly. "Do you remember what you said to me then of a lady—of Miss Gordon?"

"I remember perfectly the lady who called herself Miss Gordon," replied Mr. Wilmot. "I remember (pray be seated, Tyrell) that I thought I had never seen a more beautiful face—a perfect face in fact."

“I did not come here to talk about her beauty,” said Jasper, with rising passion, his face flushing deeply. “I came to tell you that you are a liar—an infamous liar!”

Mr. Wilmot’s face, too, flushed at this, and he half rose, and then, after a moment’s hesitation, sat quietly down again.

“Mr. Tyrell,” he said, slowly and deliberately, “many a man would have struck you across your face for uttering the word you have just made use of, but I will not give way to a momentary impulse. You have called me a liar—I presume then the reason you have done so is out of jealousy about—this lady?”

“No,” answered Jasper Tyrell, bitterly. “I am not jealous of you, nor any other man; but the lie—I repeat, the lie, that you then uttered, parted me from Elizabeth Gordon—”

“From Mrs. Richard Horton, you mean,” interrupted Mr. Wilmot, with a faint sneer.

But the next moment he changed the sneer into a curse; for with a fierce cry Jasper Tyrell had sprung upon him, striking him across the face with a walking-stick that he carried, and following the first blow with another that struck him sharply on the head.

“Take that, you scoundrel!” cried Jasper, “and that, and that! What, you dared to say that Elizabeth Gordon lived with you as your wife, did you! Dared to wrong the purest, the best—”

But by this time Mr. Wilmot had recovered from the first shock of the attack, and a fierce struggle ensued between them. Jasper, however, was the more powerfully made man of the two, and he had lived a different life to Mr. Wilmot, and after a few minutes he was able to fling his antagonist from him; Mr. Wilmot’s head coming in violent contact with the edge of the table as he fell, and Jasper felt, as he saw this, the stern joy of gratified revenge.

He looked at him for a moment, wondering if he were dead, and then, though the fallen man’s face was pale, except where the red weal cut across it, seeing the unmistakable signs of the Destroyer were not there, he coolly took up his stick and hat, and left the room, calling Mr. Wilmot’s servant, however, to come to him in the hall.

“Look after your master,” he said, “and when he recovers give him this address” (and he placed a card in the man’s hand). “Tell him that I shall be at the Langham for the next ten days, and that I shall be pleased to hear from him there.” And having said this, he turned and went away.

CHAPTER XXXVIII.

WEDDING DRESSES.

In the meanwhile, at Hazelhurst, the most active preparations were going on for the approaching wedding. Mrs. Dalziel worried, fretted, and sometimes even fumed, in her anxiety to spend the Dean's gift of two hundred pounds to the best advantage.

"I feel such responsibility," she said many and many a time to her easy-going husband. "Henry, how I envy you your—shall I call it—indifferent temper!"

"My dear," replied Henry, jocularly, for he also, in spite of his indifference, was rather elated about Eva's marriage, "do you mean that as a compliment or otherwise? Indifferent temper, you see, can be used in two senses."

"I mean you are so placid—so easy," answered Mrs. Dalziel, "While I am all anxiety."

"Then I might call your temper an over-anxious one," said the Major.

"That is scarcely kind, I think, Henry—as a wife and a mother—"

"My dear, you are like Martha," interrupted the Major, "'troubled about many things.' Now does that satisfy you, to be compared to a character in Scripture?"

"Martha was scarcely an amiable character, I think," said Mrs. Dalziel, a little nettled. "Well, well, Henry, when I am gone, you will not find it easy to supply my place."

"My dear, I shall never supply your place," replied the Major, solemnly; "I've too much experience for that." And Mrs. Dalziel smiled, for she did not always see the Major's little jokes.

But in spite of Mrs. Dalziel's anxiety, and in spite of some little accidents and *contretemps*, everything seemed to go on smoothly, and Eva's sweet, blooming, happy face told a tale that was very easy to understand.

She was going to marry the man she loved, and there seemed to be no shadow on her young life-path. She knew nothing, guessed nothing, of Jasper's secret, and for once Mrs. Dalziel acted wisely, and did not attempt to disturb the girl's inward peace. That lady, indeed, was almost too busy at this time to indulge in disagreeable surmises; though amid all her bustle, she had been, or affected to have been, greatly shocked when she heard that "Miss Gordon" was in reality a married woman living separate from her husband.

Elizabeth had thought it right to send this information to Hazelhurst, and she had accordingly written to Eva, and told her as much of the story as it was necessary for the Dalziels to know. She had been unhappily married to her cousin Richard Horton, she wrote, and she had on this account left her home, Sir John

Tyrell kindly acting as a referee for her when she went out into the world; and she then proceeded to tell about her young brother's death, and her own accession to the property in Scotland.

We can imagine the astonishment with which this news was received by the whole family. The Dean, indeed, when informed of it, wrote to his sister-in-law, that his idea had always been that "Miss Gordon" was no "ordinary governess," but that he seldom indulged in speculations on any subject, and therefore had kept his opinion to himself. Mrs. Dalziel then said that she also had always fancied that there was something mysterious about her, "but like your sagacious uncle, the Dean, love," she confided to Eva, "I said nothing about it."

The Major merely remarked, "Well, married or unmarried, she's a remarkably handsome woman;" on which Mrs. Dalziel (after the manner of some women) discovered various faults in her appearance.

"Oh! of course she is handsome," she said; "yes—I should say handsome. Certainly many might find fault with the darkness, almost sallowness, of her complexion at times; and then her eyes—did you admire her eyes particularly, papa?"

"My dear, it does not do for married men to be looking too closely into ladies' eyes," answered the discreet Major.

"Oh! absurd papa! Well," Mrs. Dalziel went on, "I have heard people say her eyes are not comfortable eyes—they are so large, and have such a very melancholy expression in them."

"No wonder, poor darling," said Eva, "when she had such a bad husband." And Eva blushed.

"Still, my love, was it doing her duty to leave him?" asked Mrs. Dalziel. "However bad the husband is (and we have no proof that this Mr. Horton was very bad), should not his wife cling to him? My dear Eva, remember 'those whom God hath joined'—these are solemn words, love—words you soon will hear, and may they never be forgotten by you in any trials that lie before you."

"But Jasper will be good to me, not bad!" said Eva, energetically, blushing deeper still.

"We hope so," answered Mrs. Dalziel, "we pray so, we trust so, love, but who can foresee the future? Be prepared, therefore, my dear Eva, never to ignore the duties of a wife—remember it is for better or for *worse.*"

"I fear no worse," said Eva, proudly; and she did, indeed, fear nothing, so strong was her faith and trust in Jasper's love.

Mrs. Dalziel no sooner heard that Jasper Tyrell was in town, than she became exceedingly anxious to go up for a few days, accompanied by Eva, to choose some of the wedding dresses; and Eva, not unwilling to see the beloved face a little earlier than she had expected, was also very anxious to go. She therefore wrote to Jasper shortly after his encounter with Mr. Wilmot, to tell him on what day and by what train they expected to arrive, and Jasper received this information with anything but a gladdened heart.

He had heard nothing from Mr. Wilmot; indeed, what could he hear, for Mr. Wilmot was lying in bed dangerously ill? A slight concussion of the brain had been brought on by the blow on his head, and perfect quiet had been enjoined by the doctor who attended him. But this the enraged and furious man could hardly attain. Proud, self-satisfied, and vicious, Edgar Wilmot could scarcely realise the disgrace that had befallen him. He had been horse-whipped—struck like a dog—and here he was lying helpless, vowing the bitterest vengeance, however, on Jasper Tyrell (which he was quite capable of carrying out) when he was once more able to lift his hand to hurt him.

As for Jasper Tyrell, he felt so reckless and unhappy, that had this man called him out, he would gladly have gone abroad to fight him, and risk his life to avenge Elizabeth's wrong. But he heard nothing from him; nothing, in fact, of the affair at all, for Mr. Wilmot's valet, with commendable prudence, had kept it to himself, merely sending at once for his master's medical attendant, when he found him lying all but insensible on the floor. The doctor, of course, had followed his example, and we may be sure Mr. Wilmot himself was only too anxious for it to be kept quiet. His revenge would keep, he told himself, and he lay for hours daily, planning how he could best punish Jasper Tyrell.

Thus Eva, when she came to town, was in perfect innocence that her lover had placed himself within the clutches of the law. Still at once she recognised, with the subtle instincts of love, that Jasper was greatly changed. He tried in vain to hide his depression, and the intense weariness of everything that had stolen over him; and for the first time since her engagement, anxious doubts and fears took possession of her mind.

It was not a happy visit, though Mrs. Dalziel, immersed at first in silks and laces, did not quickly perceive that all was not as usual with the betrothed pair. But a speech that Jasper made about the wedding dresses struck her as very remarkable.

Mrs. Dalziel had been planning and arranging as usual. She wished Jasper to meet them at this shop, and to accompany them to that, and so on.

"Good heavens!" said Jasper, "what weary work seeing about these dresses is!" And he gave an unmistakable yawn.

"Do you not think," said Mrs. Dalziel, "that it is very important that a young lady should appear to advantage when she first enters her husband's family?"

"I think that it matters very little," answered Jasper, and

Eva, who was standing near, heard this conversation, and gave a low, quick sigh.

"Is Jasper not well, do you think?" asked Mrs. Dalziel, of her step-child during the same evening. "For he certainly seems in a very depressed state."

"He does not look very well, I think," replied Eva, gently; but a sharp pang darted into her heart at her stepmother's words.

Still Jasper said nothing. He was going to accept the fate which his own hand had carved out for him, and his sense of right and justice told him that the young girl he had asked to be his wife, while labouring under an error about the woman he loved, was in no way to blame for the position in which he found himself. He knew that Eva was a good girl, and a sweet girl, and as such he honoured and liked her; but he knew also that he did not love her as he should love her, and that the life he had to look forward to seemed to him to be a dreary waste.

But he tried to be very kind to Eva, and bought her presents, and went about with her, as a lover so near his marriage naturally might be expected to do. Yet in her heart Eva was not happy. She missed something that she cared for more than his lavish gifts. When she looked into his face for sympathy and love, his eyes met hers kindly, not tenderly—sometimes she even thought compassionately. Yes, Jasper pitied Eva, "for I cannot love the child," he often thought, "as she should be loved, as she deserves to be loved, and some day she will be sure to find it out."

So this visit to London was not a happy one, and Eva returned to Hazelhurst, just seven days before the day which was to be her wedding one, with some uneasy doubts and uncertainty in her heart. She had been so happy before, *so sure*. Now, what was it that had come between them? Alas, in Jasper's case it was the certain knowledge of Elizabeth's devoted love, and of his own passionate and over-powering feelings. Parted from Elizabeth, everything seemed wearisome to him, and, try as he might, he could not quite hide this from the girl he was about to wed.

But in spite of some secret cares and inward misgivings, the days passed quickly away, and the preparations grew more and more complete for the approaching marriage.

It was arranged that the Dean should arrive at Hazelhurst on the 28th of the month, and Jasper on the 29th, and the 30th was to be Eva's wedding-day. It was to be a very quiet ceremony, in the village church, both by the wish of the bridegroom and the bride; Jasper's two sisters and Eva's half-sisters being the only bride's-maids. The Dean also had concurred in this arrangement, as Eva had declined to be married in state from the Deanery.

"The child shows good taste in this," he informed his sister-in-law in a letter, in reply to some regrets on Mrs. Dalziel's part that Eva wished no one else to be invited. "You have not the means of doing things well at Hazelhurst, therefore it is best to attempt nothing."

Sir John Tyrell was asked, but he declined. "My poor wife's daily increasing ill-health must form my excuse," he wrote to Mrs. Dalziel, "but I shall be pleased to welcome my new daughter to Wendell." He wrote to Eva also, accompanying his letter with a very valuable wedding present.

Eva, indeed, got many presents; presents from friends she scarcely knew, and from distantly related connections, who would not probably have remembered her so kindly, unless she had been going to make a good marriage. But one friend that she had truly loved sent her none, and Eva could not help wondering why Lissa, as she still called her, had not given her some little token of affection.

That unhappy woman, whose misery seemed to grow greater than she could bear, as the days passed swiftly away—the days before Jasper was to wed—had found it beyond her strength to write an ordinary letter of congratulation, or to send an ordinary marriage gift to her innocent rival. She could not grow reconciled to the idea. She would not wrong Eva, but, struggle as she might, pray as she did, the thought of his marriage with another woman was absolute torture to her heart.

She heard all about it: all the details of the wedding dresses, and the wedding gifts. There are some women who take pleasure in inflicting little stabs to other women, and among these female matadores, I am sorry to say, the Misses Tyrell might be counted.

They were annoyed at their father requesting them to call on Elizabeth, and though they yielded to his wish, they were pleased to have the opportunity of telling her what their penetration induced them to believe would be painful to her, and during their visit "dear Eva's" name was very often on their lips.

Yes, she was "dear Eva" now, for in a few days was she not to become their brother's wife? Their brother's wife, the future Lady Tyrell, was, of course, rather an important personage in their eyes, and so they accordingly began to love her beforehand.

"She is so lovely, and Jasper is so devoted," said Matilda Tyrell, her placid eyes fixed on Elizabeth's changing face the while.

"Yes, it is quite a love match," chimed in Fannie. "Of course, Jasper might have married better in a worldly point of view, but he is so deeply attached to her, that he is sure to be happy."

Elizabeth made no answer to this. She did not say "I hope so," or "I trust so," but she sat pale, with her hands tightly clasped, and a great throbbing and burning pain in her heart. It wanted but a few days now, and yet Jasper had not come to

say farewell—to take the last kiss from the lips that he was to
see no more!

"We start to-morrow," said Miss Tyrell. "I wish that papa
could have gone too, but poor mamma's health is so very uncertain."

"I heard that she was worse," answered Elizabeth.

"She is weaker, the doctors say," said Miss Tyrell, "and papa
therefore says that we cannot all leave her; and as dear Eva
naturally wishes her new sisters-in-law to be her bride's-maids,
we decided that papa had better remain at home, though I am
sure he regrets that he cannot be present at Jasper's wedding."

"He has sent her such lovely diamond earrings," said Fannie
Tyrell. "I declare I felt quite envious of them."   And she gave
a little laugh.

So Elizabeth knew all about it, and had to sit still and listen
while these girls went on with their insipid talk.   Not insipid to
Elizabeth though, for each idle word they uttered added a pang
to her already breaking heart.

The Misses Tyrell paid their visit to Elizabeth on Monday, the
27th, and on Tuesday, the 28th, they had arranged to start for
Hazelhurst, being expected to arrive there the same day as the
Dean. "Jasper joins us on the 29th," said Miss Tyrell, with a
smile, " and Thursday, the 30th, is the wedding-day."

Thus Elizabeth knew that if Jasper meant to keep his promise
and come to say good-bye, he could only come on the 28th, and
with a sick feeling of despair, she waited and watched for him
through the day.

It was a blinding storm of wind and rain; one of those days of
autumn which give us warning of the coming winter, and Elizabeth stood hour after hour by the rain-beaten panes, watching
the flowers dashed to the ground, the tall hollyhocks levelled,
and their yellow and rose-coloured blossoms befouled in the wet
soil.   The pink leaves of the last fragile roses of summer came
floating past the windows, and the trees shook their branches
with melancholy moans.

It was a dismal day, in fact, but it suited better the mood of
the watcher than the sunshine would have done, for all hope was
crushed now out of Elizabeth's heart.

Patient and gentle in general, to-day she could not even bear
to hear her cousins' voices, and under the excuse of a severe
head-ache, she had asked to be left quite alone.   She was very
wretched.   She had tried to do right, but peace had not come to
her; and she felt again and again as she had done in London,
that her burden was greater than she could bear.

Slowly the day dragged on its weary length, and still Jasper
came not.   Reader, have you ever counted the hours, the half-
hours, the minutes even, in times of intolerable suspense? Tick,
tick, tick, went on the clock in the hall, throbbing went on

Elizabeth's beating passionate heart. Then the night came, and the mysterious, dusky mantle from on high fell on the earth, but still no Jasper!

"He will not come," said Elizabeth, half-aloud, with a sort of wail of despair, and she covered her face, for she could watch no more. What did she expect from this last farewell—this last sad parting? Nothing, nothing, and yet that Jasper had failed to keep his tryst seemed to add inexpressible sharpness to her sorrow, and with an "exceeding bitter cry" she turned away.

But even as she did so, she heard a quick step on the gravel below, and the next moment the house-door bell rang; and as Elizabeth went hastily to the door of the room, Jasper Tyrell, wet and travel-stained, was admitted by a servant into the hall.

Then Elizabeth went forward, and took his hand.

"Come in here," she said, and she led him into the breakfast-room that she had just left, which was dimly lighted by a fire burning low and red in the grate; and Jasper followed her, closing the door behind them, and they two were alone.

"Well, I have come," he said, and he put his arm round her, and Elizabeth's head fell upon his breast.

"It is such a storm," she whispered, thinking, woman-like, even then of his comforts, "and you are wet and weary, Jasper."

"It is no matter," he said; "but I have come a long way—for this—"

But let us draw a veil over this last parting, for there are scenes, are there not, of which it is too painful to write or to read? Not many words passed between these two—what words could pass—for there was no comfort nor hope, either to give or to take? To Elizabeth it was more bitter than death, more cruel than the grave; and after Jasper had pressed his last kiss on her cold lips, and left her, she fell on her knees, covering her face, and crying out in the extreme anguish of her soul.

"Oh! God, take us," she cried; "God take us both—for I cannot bear the pain."

CHAPTER XXXIX.
THE WEDDING DAY.

THE Misses Tyrell arrived at Hazelhurst on the 28th, in perfect safety and comfort, for the Dean had despatched one of his own carriages a few days previously to his brother's residence, as he was not partial to "hired conveyances," he informed his sister-in-law, and this carriage was accordingly waiting for the sisters on their arrival at the railway station nearest to Hazelhurst.

The Major also came to meet them, and they were welcomed with great cordiality when they reached the village by Mrs. Dalziel, and with sweet smiles by the bride-elect. Eva was nervous and excited, but she tried now to forget all her fears

and doubts of the week before. "Jasper was to come to-morrow
—when she was his wife he would tell her all his troubles,"
thought the young girl; and so the last few days Eva's heart
had grown light again, and she looked very happy and pretty as
she kissed her future sisters-in-law.

The Dean arrived the same day by a later train, and the
haughty but courteous old man exerted himself to be agreeable
to the Misses Tyrell. They were not a little shocked, however,
at the style of the house, though it was larger than the one they
had inhabited before their father succeeded his cousin Sir Henry,
and became proprietor of Wendell Hall. Mrs. Dalziel was
also a little startling, but they had come determined to make the
best of the situation, and they accordingly did so; and the
dinner, which had cost Mrs. Dalziel much mental anxiety beforehand, passed off very satisfactorily.

Mrs. Dalziel had engaged a professional cook when she was in
town for a week, not daring to trust her ordinary domestic's
culinary powers at such a time of festivity; and to her great
relief this person knew her duty, and successfully performed
it. The Dean even condescended to compliment his sister-
in-law on her soup, and gave her the most sincere pleasure
by doing so.

"You have arranged everything very well, considering," said
the great man, and Mrs. Dalziel was charmed by the compliment.
The Major, however, looked rather rueful when these arrangements were mentioned, and he had certainly good reason for
doing so, as Mrs. Dalziel had insisted on his vacating the comfortable bedroom where he had reposed for twenty years, to make
room for her visitors.

"Well, my dear," he said, "as I luckily have but three daughters
remember I shall only do this twice more." And so he meekly
resigned himself, shaving at a minute glass that had hitherto
done duty in the children's room, and putting up as best he
might with all other inconveniences.

On the following morning—the morning of the 29th, the day
that Jasper Tyrell was expected to arrive at Hazelhurst, the
Dean proposed to take the ladies out for a drive before lunch, to
see some of the neighbourhood, and the Misses Tyrell were very
glad to go. Eva had received a few lines from Jasper on the
morning of the 28th—just a few lines—to tell her that he
had arranged to be at Hazelhurst by dinner-time on Wednesday
the 29th, and, fluttered and nervous, the girl awaited her bridegroom's arrival.

All the morning, when the Tyrells were out with her uncle
was spent in packing her dresses, in preparation for the bridal
tour. After lunch, the three girls sat chattering and laughing
together, and then, at Matilda Tyrell's proposal, went out for a

little stroll in the village, until it was time for them to drive to the station to meet Jasper.

How strange it seemed to Eva, as she went down the familiar street, where she had lived since she was a little child, to think that before to-morrow at this time she would be far away from it, and that her new life would have then begun! Dull as this village was, it was her home, and the girl looked with her sweet, wistful eyes around her, with a strange timidity and humility in her heart. Was she worthy of Jasper? she was thinking, and then she gave a little gentle smile. "I must try to be worthy," she resolved; and with such tender thoughts she wiled away the afternoon, while the Tyrells talked and planned about visits, garden parties, and all sorts of gaieties, that must take place when she and Jasper came to Wendell.

She did not go with his sisters to the station to meet her lover, but, after chatting a little while with her stepmother, went upstairs to dress for dinner, before his arrival. She remembered a certain dress that he had admired before their engagement had taken place, and with sweet, modest blushes she donned it now. Then, when she was dressed, she went down into the drawing-room, and presently she heard the carriage drive up and stop before the house door, and the next minute the two Tyrell girls came together hastily into the room.

"Fancy! Jasper has not come," said Matilda. "Is it not annoying? He must have missed the train—I never knew anything so vexing."

Eva did not speak. She was so much disappointed, that for a moment she could not; and then, after Fannie Tyrell had made some stupid remark, she said hesitatingly and nervously—

"Can he come to-night?"

"That's the worst of it," replied Matilda, "he can't come now until the night train, and won't reach the station here, they told us there, until about two o'clock in the morning. I can't imagine how he could do such a stupid thing—so unlike Jasper."

Eva felt very cold and sick. She sat down and turned so pale that the Tyrells were almost alarmed.

"Don't be so put out about it, you dear child," said Matilda, going up to her and kissing her. "Ah, Miss Eva, we must tell Jasper that you nearly fainted because he had missed the train!"

But Eva could not jest about it. It was so strange and unaccountable, she thought; and presently, when Mrs. Dalziel came in and heard the news, she added to the girl's agitation.

"I hope nothing can have happened," she said, "no accident?"

"Madam," said the Dean sharply, who had overheard this inopportune remark, "you amaze me! What accident can have happened, but the very common accident of losing a train? If anything had happened do you for a moment suppose it would not have been telegraphed to us at once? No, Miss Eva will have to wait until two in the morning to see her lover, that is all."

But even her uncle's consoling words did not bring the colour back to Eva's pale face. She could not touch, did not even pretend to touch, the well-cooked dinner that was presently spread before her, and her evident anxiety and uneasiness unconsciously affected the others, the Dean alone preserving his wonted, sarcastic calmness.

"Ladies," he said to Miss Tyrell, "are wonderful creatures. Their imaginative and creative powers are so great, that for them to invent is one of the greatest pleasures in their existence. I account for the enormous mass of female writers that we rejoice in now-a-days, entirely to this propensity. You all love fiction better than fact."

"But, my dear Dean," said Mrs. Dalziel, who had got over his little rebuke before dinner by this time, "do you not allow us to have quicker instincts than you gentlemen in matters of feeling, now?—I always seem to foresee misfortunes."

"A charming gift, doubtless, my dear sister-in-law," replied the Dean, "but one trying to all but the possessor. Though I fear it will be painful to you, pray suppress your prognostications for the future."

"Well, I only know, Dean, before little Anna had scarlatina, I dreamt—"

"So did I, my good madam. last night," interrupted the Dean, "but I will not record my midnight experiences. Eva, I have two little commissions which I wish you to execute for me in Paris; but as they are both presents for ladies, I must whisper what I want in your ear."

"Very well, uncle Ralph," said Eva, in a low tone, but not all her uncle's well-meant attempts could scare her fears away.

When the ladies returned to the drawing-room, her restlessness was painful to see. She took up a book and laid it down; she went hither and thither; she looked through the window-blinds, and answered vaguely, almost as if she did not understand the kindly-meant attempts that were made to distract her attention from her absorbing thought.

When the Major came into the drawing-room, he went up to her and laid his hand on her shoulder.

"I have ordered Johnnie," he said (this was their own boy) to have the pony-chaise at the station to meet the two train, for I fully expect Jasper will come by that; and I dare not venture to tell your uncle's coachman to go in the middle of the night." And the Major gave a kind, little, reassuring smile to his daughter.

"Thank you, papa," answered Eva, and she looked piteously into her father's face.

"My little girl," said the Major, "don't get nervous. If anything had happened to Tyrell, we should have heard by this time—your uncle is quite right there. Come, Eva, come and play a game of besique with your old dad for the last time, for a long, long time eh?"

The poor child complied with her father's request, but the Major had not the heart to ask her to play a second game. She could not, indeed, remember what she was doing. She started at imaginary rings at the door bell. She was thinking all the while, "Oh! what has become of Jasper?—what can have happened to him?—what shall I do?"

She did not attempt to go to bed, though she made a pretence of doing so, retiring to her room when the other ladies went to theirs, only, however, to hold a dreary vigil there. She heard one o'clock strike, and then counted the minutes by the pretty jewelled watch that Jasper had given her, until it was thirty minutes past. It took about half-an-hour to drive to the station; and a few minutes after the half-hour, she heard the pony-chaise start, which was going to meet Jasper. The Major (though he did not tell his daughter so) went in it, and minute after minute Eva waited and listened on. The quarter chimed in the hall clock below, and then slowly, slowly, the next fifteen minutes passed away. Then two struck, and then came another half-hour of almost intolerable suspense, and then, with a start and half cry, she heard the sound of the wheels of the pony-chaise again.

She could not contain her anxiety this time, but ran down to the house door only to reach it as the Major entered it alone.

"Papa—" broke from Eva's white lips.

"He has not come, dear. It is very odd" said the Major, trying to speak reassuringly. "But there is a train from the South passes at eight—and Horrocks, the station-master you know, thinks that he is sure to come by that. Don't look so white, darling, it will be all right yet."

Eva made no reply to this, but sat down with almost a moan, in one of the hall chairs. Other anxious listeners, too, had heard the pony-chaise return, for Mrs. Dalziel, in her dressing-gown, now appeared upon the scene.

"What!" she said, "has he not come?" But her husband gave her a warning glance to say no more.

"Come, little Eva, get to bed," went on the kind Major, who felt, indeed, anything but easy in his own mind. "What will Tyrell say when he comes in the morning, if he sees such a pale face?"

"Come, darling, to bed," said Mrs. Dalziel, and she put her arm round Eva's waist, and led the poor girl upstairs.

"Mamma," said Eva, when she got to her own room, in an awe-struck whisper, "something has happened—something is happening to Jasper now."

"If so, darling, we must try to bear it," said Mrs. Dalziel, who could not resist a homily. "I always told you, did I not, love, not to set your affections entirely on any earthly thing ?" But, with an impatient gesture, Eva pushed her step-mother away.

"Leave me alone, mamma; don't talk to me, please," she said, "I cannot bear it now."

"Well, my dear love, good-night, then," said Mrs. Dalziel. And she kissed her step-daughter, retiring to her own room, where she relieved her mind by uttering the most gloomy apprehensions to the unhappy Major.

"Depend upon it, Henry," she said, "he has either committed suicide or been murdered; most likely, when I reflect, murdered by some woman, for we know what these officers are."

"Thank you, my dear," meekly put in the Major, even amid his own secret alarm.

"I do not say *all*, Henry," said Mrs. Dalziel. "I hope, I pray, I trust, that I did not marry a profligate; but what can we tell —what do we know of the antecedents of Jasper Tyrell ? Depend upon it, there is some woman in the case."

"If I thought," said the Major, energetically, putting on his white, cotton night-cap, and with some of his brother's war-like spirit sparkling in his eyes, "that this fellow means to behave badly to the child, I would—yes, by jove !—I would shoot him like a dog." And he flung off his night-cap again in his wrath.

"Is that Christian-like, Henry ?" answered Mrs. Dalziel. "Should you forget that you have other children—and must I, need I remind you, a devoted wife ? Oh ! Henry," she went on, embracing the irate Major, "if this unhappy man is lying foully murdered—"

"Don't believe it," interrupted the Major; "believe if he's done anything he's bolted. Remember very well when the 18th were in Ireland in '57, Jackson of ours got entangled with a girl, and the day was fixed and everything, and he bolted—off to Australia, I believe—we never heard of him any more."

"But, Henry, *entangled*—what word is that I hear ? Did our child—I call her our child, although she was born before I saw you—still ours by love, although her mother was another woman. Did *our child* then entangle this young man, I ask you that ?"

"Nonsense," replied the Major, in a rage " don't pull a fellow up like that at every word he utters ! You know well enough what I mean, but I'm not going to talk any more to-night—but I say," added the Major, waxing furious, as he pulled the blankets over his nose, "I say if he's behaved badly to the child he shall repent it, that's all!"

While this matrimonial discussion was going on between the Major and his wife, Eva was lying quite prostrate on her bed. She was parted from Jasper—she was not going to be a bride or his wife now. The poor child lay there tearless, cold and shuddering, and as the morning hours wore on, she fell into an uneasy slumber, only however to be recalled to sad reality by hearing the sound of carriage wheels once more start for the station.

The Major, in fact, had ordered the pony-chaise to be ready again at half-past seven o'clock, and such was his anxiety on his young daughter's account, that he was up and prepared long before the hour to drive to the station.

The eight o'clock train from the South came in, but no Jasper Tyrell was among the travellers, and the Major, accordingly, before he left the station, telegraphed to the Langham Hotel, where he knew that Jasper had been staying last in town. He telegraphed both to Jasper and to the manager of the hotel, and then, in a most unhappy mood, returned to Hazelhurst.

As he neared his own home, he saw Eva's pale face watching him from the window, and his wife also was gazing anxiously out, waiting for his return. He threw the reins to the boy, and ran at once to Eva's room, who turned round a face so white and ghastly to greet him that the Major fairly broke down.

"My darling," he said, folding his little girl in his arms, "he has not come, but I have telegraphed. In a couple of hours we shall hear some news at least. Keep up your heart, my darling —if this scoundrel has behaved badly to you, you have a father to avenge your wrongs."

" He has not behaved badly, papa," said Eva, in a sharp, changed voice. "I think he is dead !" And she also gave way, sobbing and weeping as if her heart would break, in her father's arms.

The next few hours were very miserable ones. Matilda and Fannie Tyrell cried too, and Mrs. Dalziel was in a most distracted state of mind. The Dean tried to be hopeful, and conduct himself with the composure that a high church dignity should (according to his ideas) under any circumstances of life; but the proud, old man's hands trembled a little as he pretended to eat a good breakfast, and his tongue had lost some of its usual caustic sharpness as he endeavoured in various ways to account for Jasper's absence.

At ten o'clock (the hour fixed for the marriage) a telegram arrived for the Major, from the manager of the Langham.

"Mr. Tyrell had left in time to catch the mid-day train north," the manager telegraphed, "on the morning of the 28th; since then the manager had heard nothing, and received no directions from Mr. Tyrell."

The wedding-guests looked at each other blankly, after reading this. Eva, exhausted with weeping, said no word, but shivered and shuddered, listening, as if in a dream, to the consoling words that fell trembling from the lips of those around her. The Dean was the first to rouse himself, saying almost calmly—

"Henry, order the carriage.   I will go to the station and
telegraph to Sir John Tyrell. Young ladies," (this was to Matilda
and Fannie Tyrell) "have you any message for your father?"

"Only—" faltered Matilda.

"That we are all very anxious," said the Dean, and in a few
minutes he had started in his own carriage for the station,
sending from thence a very pressing message to Sir John.

But all the day passed, and no answer came.   Not one word
from Sir John; not one word from Jasper Tyrell, on the day that
was to have been his wedding day.

CHAPTER XL.
NEWS OF JASPER.

On the evening of the 28th, after Jasper Tyrell had parted with
Elizabeth, she felt as if she were going mad.   Her brain seemed
absolutely reeling, and so terrible were her sensations, that at
last she went to her cousin Robert Horton, and entreated him
to go to the doctor, and procure her a powerful sleeping draught;
and Robert Horton was so alarmed by her looks and manner,
that he not only at once went for the doctor, but requested him
to accompany him back to Wendell West-house.

"Ah," said little Dr. Pocock, shaking his head, as usual,
when Robert had described her symptoms as best he could,
"worry, worry, Mr. Bob—that is doubtless what ails your cousin.
Your poor brother's sad death, and my old friend, Horton's,
were sure to tell.   Sensitive women can only bear a certain
amount of mental trouble, after that the pressure is too strong."

He accordingly went with Robert Horton back to the homestead, armed with a powerful sedative, and this he administered
to Elizabeth, who, under its influence, sank into a temporary
insensibility of her misery.   All the next day its half-stupefying
effects remained, accompanied by a dull, heavy pain in her head,
which rendered her almost incapable of lifting it from the pillow.
She seemed to care for nothing more; fate had done its worst
for her, and her only wish was to lie quiet there until
she died.

Yet, with a sharper pang of pain in her heart than that which
now seemed always there, she awoke, or rather aroused herself
to fuller consciousness on the morning of the 30th, when she
remembered that this was Jasper Tyrell's wedding day.   With a
miserable cry of despair, she "turned her face to the wall."   Her
Jasper—*hers*—Oh! bitter mockery!   She seemed to see the church
at Hazelhurst; the simple, country church, with the whitewashed
walls she knew so well, and the bride's fair face, and *Jasper's*—
"Till death us do part."—Oh! she had heard these words and
uttered them, and again she seemed to hear them now, coming
from Jasper's lips—coming like a whisper to her distracted soul!

She could not lie in bed, but, ill in body and mind, she rose; and scarcely had the clock struck eight, when she heard the house-door bell ring, and presently one of the maids came upstairs, and rapped quietly at her door.

"Come in," said Elizabeth, and she opened the door, and the servant half-started back, for she had not expected to see her up and dressed at this early hour.

"Oh! you're up, ma'am," she said, "I hope you're better? I came to tell you, ma'am, that Sir John Tyrell is here, and he has sent up this, and if he can see you, he would like to very much."

Elizabeth glanced at the card which the servant had placed in her hand, on which Sir John had written "They tell me you are very ill; but still can I see you? It is a matter of life and death."

"I will see him," said Elizabeth; and, pale and trembling, she followed the servant down-stairs, and in the breakfast-room Sir John was standing.

He took her hand in silence, pressed it, and then turned away with a heavy sigh.

"What is it, Sir John?" gasped out Elizabeth, shaking in every limb.

"Jasper—" said Sir John, with a sort of sob. "My poor Jasper—" And then he paused, quite overcome with his emotions.

"What!" cried Elizabeth, in the sharp voice of despair.

"There has been a terrible railway accident." said Sir John, struggling for composure. "On the night of the 28th, the South express was run into, and it seems—I cannot understand it, for I believed that Jasper was in town at the Langham—but it seems that he was in it—and he is terribly, mortally injured."

"O God! O God!" cried Elizabeth, and she fell on her knees, burying her face in her hands.

"My poor girl!" said Sir John, compassionately, and he laid his hand on Elizabeth's shoulder.

"Go on—tell me all," moaned Elizabeth; "go on."

"He was insensible all yesterday, it seems," continued Sir John, "but during the night he recovered consciousness, and was able to tell who he was, and to desire the doctor to telegraph to me He also sent a private telegram," faltered Sir John, and then he paused.

"What is it?" said Elizabeth, looking up.

"It is here," answered Sir John, and he placed the thin pink paper in Elizabeth's hand, on which was written :—

"Come to me, father, and bring Elizabeth Gordon. I wish to see her before I die."

Elizabeth read this, and then rose and stood before Sir John.

"Come," she said, wildly, "let us go to him before he dies."

"Yes," said Sir John, and he looked away. "My dear young

lady," he asked the next moment, taking her hand, "it is useless in this miserable hour to disguise the past—was Jasper here on the night of the accident—on the 28th?"

"Yes," answered Elizabeth, "he came to say good-bye--he came to—"

"To see, I fear, the woman that he deeply loves," went on Sir John, as Elizabeth paused, utterly unable to complete her sentence. "There is a fatality in this—my poor boys—both my poor boys!"

"Sir John!" said Elizabeth, her voice ringing with passionate pathos, "he went away because honour bid him. We parted—we who loved too well, because Jasper could not break his word! But it broke our hearts—both our hearts."

"I pity you, sincerely pity you," said Sir John.

"I prayed to die," went on Elizabeth, "to die before he married —and now—O God! be merciful—O God! be merciful to us all!"

"Will—you go?" said Sir John, wiping away the tears that filled his eyes.

"To Jasper?" asked Elizabeth, as if in surprise at the question. "O! yes, yes, I am ready now—come at once Sir John; do not let us delay a single moment now."

"But, my dear," said Sir John, "you must have your bonnet and cloak on before you go," for Elizabeth had turned as if to leave the house. "Where is your maid? Let me tell your cousins you are going. We can catch the ten train at Mitchin." And Sir John looked at his watch.

"Be sure and do not miss it," said Elizabeth, with fevered restlessness. "I shall be ready—I will tell the boys."

"It is only half-past eight now," said Sir John, "so we have plenty of time. If you are ready in an hour—"

"I cannot wait an hour," said Elizabeth, wringing her hands. "Oh! come now, Sir John! We may miss the train—fancy if we miss the train!"

"We shall not miss the train," answered Sir John, soothingly. "Come, my dear young lady, try to compose yourself. Remember you have a journey before you."

"I will try," said Elizabeth, and she put her hand to her head. "I can't think," she went on piteously. "but we are going to Jasper?—say that again, Sir John—we are going to Jasper before he dies?"

Sir John made no answer. "Was this poor soul distracted with grief?" he thought. "Had he driven Jasper away, and severed two lives that could not live apart?" "Would that I had never spoken," half groaned the Baronet, and Elizabeth looked at him with her wild, wide open eyes.

"Did you speak?" she said.

"It—it—is a grievous affair," faltered Sir John.

"Grievous, grievous," repeated Elizabeth. And then, as if that word had touched the fountain of her tears, she broke into a wild passion of sobs and weeping.

"Hush, hush, my dear," said Sir John; "hush, Elizabeth."

"Let me go on!" cried Elizabeth, putting her hand to her spasm-racked throat. "Let me go on—or my heart and head will burst!"

Sir John rang the bell violently for assistance, urging Elizabeth to drink some wine that the servants brought in.

"Drink this," he said, "it will compose you—it will enable you to travel. Think, Elizabeth—for poor Jasper's sake."

"Yes, for Jasper's sake," she repeated, amid her sobs. And then with a great effort she endeavoured to be calm.

"I am better now," she said. "I can think now—I will be very quiet, Sir John—do not fear me."

"Yes, I am sure you will," said Sir John, kindly. "And now," he continued, addressing one of the maids who had brought in the wine, and who was standing near them, "pack some necessaries for your mistress. She is going in the ten train South with me, and so you must have everything ready for her."

"But she is so ill," said the girl.

"I will take care of her," said Sir John. "Where is Mr. Horton, Mr. Robert Horton? I wish to speak to him."

In a few minutes Sir John had settled it all, though Robert Horton looked anything but pleased when he heard from the Baronet that Elizabeth was going to accompany him to what was supposed to be Jasper's death-bed.

"It is a strange business, I think," he said, with some of the sullen air that used to characterise the unfortunate Richard Horton. "It does not seem to me to be Elizabeth's place."

"It is my son's wish," answered Sir John, with just a touch of haughtiness, and the youth dared say no more; and in another half-hour or so Elizabeth had started on her journey with Sir John.

But few words were exchanged between them as they travelled on their dismal way. It seemed to Sir John as if a fatality pursued his sons, and that Elizabeth's beautiful face had been a curse to them both. But he was too just and too generous to blame Elizabeth for this, and with grave and gentle courtesy he endeavoured to show his sympathy for her, and to hide, as best he could, the grief that filled his own heart.

It was about four o'clock in the afternoon when they neared the scene of the accident, shown only too plainly by the broken débris, and an engine and three or four overturned and crushed carriages lying a little off the line.

The fatal catastrophe, which had occurred near a small station called Annerley, had happened, it was afterwards ascertained, by a mistake of the pointsman. At the point where it took place there are two lines of rails, with sidings on to both up and down lines. A coal train was shunted out of the down siding, and as the points had by some means been left open, it went into the main line, instead of into the up siding. At this moment the express came at full speed, the signals being open for it, and dashed into the rear of the coal train as it was going back to get on to its proper line of rails.

The collision that ensued was of extreme violence. Three of the unfortunate passengers in the express train were killed on the spot, while about fifteen others were more or less (some fatally) injured.

The very bad cases, amongst which was Jasper Tyrell's, were conveyed as soon as possible into the nearest station-house at Annerley, and as Elizabeth and Sir John approached it, they found themselves among other melancholy seekers for the wounded and the dead.

It was, indeed, a terrible sight. On the floor, in the first-class waiting-room, lay the bodies of three dead men, lying there to be identified and claimed by those whom they had probably parted from, little dreaming that they would see them alive no more.

Upstairs, in two or three decently furnished bedrooms, which the station-master's family had given up to their unfortunate guests, lay the desperately injured and the dying. Those who could bear the journey had been taken to the hospital of the nearest town, which is about three miles distant from the scene of the accident; but it was amongst the desperately injured that Elizabeth and Sir John had come to seek Jasper Tyrell.

Elizabeth glanced at the bodies decently covered, and yet visible in the outlines, as she passed them, and a shudder ran through her frame. Sir John pressed her arm, which was resting in his, protectingly, and then gave his card to a policeman standing near.

"My son," he said, "Mr. Tyrell, is among the injured. I wish to see him."

The policeman touched his hat, and ran for the doctor. They were expecting Sir John Tyrell at the station, and a whisper quickly ran through the groups collected near the fatal spot, that this was the father of one of the dying passengers; and in a few minutes a clever-looking, gentlemanly, young man came up to Sir John and Elizabeth.

"You are Sir John Tyrell I understand?" he said, "I am Dr. Spencer, of the Mortaindale Hospital. Your son. Mr. Tyrell, is among those unfortunately injured in this accident."

"You telegraphed to me?" said Sir John. rather huskily.

"Yes, by Mr. Tyrell's wish," replied Dr. Spencer. "At first, we could not distinctly, in the confusion, ascertain his identity, for he had no letters about him to prove it.   But last night he partially revived, and now he is quite conscious."

"Is—is—he very ill?" faltered Sir John.

The doctor shook his head.

"He is most severely injured," he said; "the most severely now alive of the sufferers.   Of course, we cannot tell—but—" •And the doctor paused, leaving his ominous sentence unfinished.

"Tell him that we are here," said Sir John, much affected. "His father—and the lady that he wished to see."

"He already knows it," answered Dr. Spencer, with some feeling.   "I was with him when your card was brought up to me.   If you will follow me, I will take you to his room."

"In a moment," said Elizabeth, with a sort of gasp, and then the doctor looked at her attentively.

"If you will allow me," he said, courteously addressing her, "I will give you a little sal-volatile and water before you go to Mr. Tyrell.   Of course, you must be prepared for a great change."

Elizabeth took what the doctor gave her, and then, trembling in every limb, and with a damp, white, though resolute face, she followed him upstairs, and into a neat little bedroom, in which stood a small, white-curtained bed, and on which a ghastly figure was lying.

Was this Jasper? This bandaged, crushed, and shattered form? Yes, for the dark eyes—the dark eyes which still were visible—lit up with a sudden gleam of joy as Elizabeth entered the room; and the next moment she had knelt down by the bedside, and pressed her lips on what had been the handsome face of Jasper Tyrell.

Alas, now crushed so terribly that no one could have recognised them, were the fine features that Elizabeth knew so well. When he was dragged from beneath the broken carriages where he was found after the accident, it was at first, indeed, believed that Jasper Tyrell was among the dead.   His injuries were of a frightful nature, but he feebly endeavoured to acknowledge Elizabeth's inarticulate words, as she laid her head beside his crushed and broken figure.

Sir John and the doctor turned away for a moment or two, after they had entered the room; and then Sir John went up to the side of his son.

"My—dear—Jasper," he said, and that was all.   But tears filled his eyes, as Jasper looked up into his father's face and smiled.

"You have brought her," he said.   "I thank you, father."

"We—we started at once," faltered Sir John, trying to suppress the shocked feelings that his son's terribly altered appearance naturally caused.

"You know I've got my 'quietus'?" went on Jasper. "We won't part now, Lissa—I shall die where I wished," (and then he whispered low, so that she only who knelt by his side could hear) "in my darling's arms."

CHAPTER XLI.

POOR EVA!

FROM this moment Elizabeth never left Jasper Tyrell. She nursed him, dressed his injuries, and waited on him as if she were his wife.

Some one asked Sir John during the day if she were so, and Sir John answered, after a moment's hesitation, "She was engaged to him," and after this it seemed only natural to the sympathizing station-master's family and the doctor that she should be constantly by his side.

This question, however, which was asked on the night of the 30th (the day Sir John and Elizabeth went to Jasper), recalled to Sir John's mind what, in the sudden shock of the sad news of his son's dangerous condition, had passed completely out of his memory. "Did Eva Dalziel know?" thought Sir John. "Did the bride, on her intended bridal day, know that he who was to have been her husband lay desperately injured and about to die?" Yet what could Sir John say? Could he recall what the dying man seemed to have forgotten? Could he go in and breathe another woman's name before the one who sat holding his son's crushed hand, or lifting his mangled form so tenderly in her arms?

Strange as it may seem, Elizabeth, also, never remembered Eva Dalziel. In that room, the simple room with the white bed on which lay Jasper, but one thought seemed to fill her whole being. She was with Jasper—with her darling. Nothing could part them now. She would be with him at the end of his life, and at the end of hers she would be with him again. No cold shadow of another now came between them. The dying cannot marry, and Elizabeth believed from the first that Jasper was dying.

He, too, partly stupefied perhaps by his great pain, seemed to have forgotten that this was to have been his wedding day. He would never marry now, he thought; he would die with his Lissa near him; and so, half unconsciously, the hours passed on—the hours of miserable suspense to her whom he had promised to make his wife. The next day, however, by the early post, the Dean's telegram to Sir John was forwarded to him from Wendell Hall, and no sooner had Sir John received it, than he saw that it was his imperative duty at once to inform Eva's family of the miserable accident that had happened to the promised bridegroom.

With sorrow and hesitation he approached the subject to Jasper, who looked surprised and pained as he did so.

"They know," he said, "they must know—why, this happened days ago!"

"But, my dear Jasper," went on Sir John, "you forget that all Wednesday you were insensible, and unable to tell the people here who you were. And yesterday—of course—"

"Poor little Eva!" said Jasper Tyrell. "Why, father, surely you have let her know that I am dying. She is better without me—tell her that—thank God I have no one with me but Lissa now."

After this it seemed cruelty to Sir John to enter into any more particulars with his son. He evidently thought that Eva knew; evidently imagined that approaching death relieved him from all further claims, and Sir John had no heart to tell him that probably the poor girl had spent the whole previous day in a state of pitiable suspense.

He beckoned to Elizabeth to come to him, and for a moment to leave Jasper, and when she did so, he said sadly—

"My dear, we all seem to have forgotten one thing—the poor girl Jasper was to marry."

At these words a sudden flush passed over Elizabeth's pale face.

"He cannot marry now," she said quickly.

"I know that too well," answered Sir John "but not the less should we have remembered what she must have felt yesterday."

"She must know," interrupted Elizabeth, in a sharp voice of pain.

"How can she know?" went on Sir John. "We only knew yesterday—the telegram was to us—none went to her."

Elizabeth covered her face at these words. She had forgotten this also. In the distracted state of her mind she had forgotten everything but that Jasper could not marry Eva now.

"It is my duty—" continued Sir John.

"Not to bring her here!" said Elizabeth, with sudden fear. "Don't say that, Sir John! We want no one here—no one to come between me and Jasper now."

"She shall not come here," said Sir John, gravely. "I will go and see her to-day. I will tell her the truth—it is better and kinder to do so, and not let the poor girl go on mourning for a man who gave her no love."

"He—tried to do his duty," said Elizabeth. "Poor Eva!"

"Poor girl indeed!" said Sir John, whose sympathy for Eva was now fairly roused after receiving the Dean's anxious telegram. "Conceive what she must have suffered Poor Jasper seems to have forgotten—to have forgotten everything but you."

"I was to have been his wife once too," said Elizabeth, looking up into Sir John's face with a sort of reproach. "I was his wife

in my heart always, and shall be his wife still when they lay me
in my grave.''

''My dear,'' answered Sir John, gently, ''do not think that I
do not feel for you. You have acted well and nobly all through
a most unhappy, trying life—but—''

''She will forget him, she will marry some one else now,'' said
Elizabeth, as Sir John paused, for a strange jealousy of Jasper's
last few days had rushed into her heart during this conversation
with Sir John. She had to give him up to death, she thought,
but while he lived no other should come between them, and she
felt as if it were cruel of Sir John even to mention Eva's name.

''I trust that she will forget him,'' said Sir John, ''and that
she will marry some one else ; but, in the meanwhile, I am bound
by honour, however painful the office may be, to tell her the
exact truth, and I shall do so this very day.''

''You will do what is right I am sure,'' answered Elizabeth ;
''but don't bring her here, Sir John, that is all I ask, don't disturb
Jasper's last hours—don't inflict this useless torture on us both.''

''I will not bring her here,'' said Sir John, and with this
promise Elizabeth seemed satisfied ; but Sir John turned away,
thinking how selfish grief makes us all.

He started half-an-hour after he had parted with Elizabeth
for Hazelhurst, but in the meantime some explanation of Jasper's
disappearance had been received there through the public papers.

The Dean had seen the account of the accident that had happened to the South express on the night of the 28th, in the
Times, on the evening of the 30th ; but as he never imagined that
Jasper Tyrell, who was supposed to be in town, would be travelling by it, he said nothing on the subject, even during the miserable uncertainty they were all feeling, thinking that by so doing
he would only probably increase the anxiety of the unhappy
household.

But on the morning of the 31st (the day after the one which
should have been Eva's wedding day) a more detailed account of
the accident appeared in the papers, and among the unfortunate
sufferers' names was Jasper Tyrell's.

The Dean turned a little pale, just a little pale as he read the
paragraph. Mr. Tyrell, R. N., the only son of Sir John Tyrell
of Wendell Hall, it informed him, was supposed to be fatally
injured, and Sir John Tyrell had arrived at the scene of the
catastrophe, and was in close attendance on his unfortunate son.

The Dean read this, and then rose from the breakfast table,
looking significantly at his brother, the Major, as he did so ; and
having done this he left the room, carrying the paper that
contained the news away with him.

There were present at the table when he left it, the Major,
Mrs. Dalziel, and Matilda and Fannie Tyrell. Eva was too ill to

appear. The poor girl had fainted twice du·ing the previous day, and was in a state of extreme nervous depression. The two Tyrells also were very unhappy. They had written the most urgent letters to their father the day before, when Jasper had failed to appear at Hazelhurst, and had hoped some answer and explanation would arrive by this morning's post. But none had come, and their uncertainty and anxiety were very great.

When the Dean rose and left the room, not only the Major had seen his brother's look, but the three ladies also; and as the Major followed the Dean out, they looked at each other with sudden fear.

"There is something in that paper," said Matilda, who was the first to speak.

"I think so too," said Mrs. Dalziel, now rising also. "And I will go and see."

In a few minutes it was all known. The weeping sisters read the paragraph, and she who was to have been the injured man's bride had the news broken to her as gently as her good father could do it.

"Let me tell the child," he said to his wife; and although Mrs. Dalziel dissolved in floods of tears at the slight cast upon her judgment and delicacy of feeling as she called it, the Major had his own way, and went up to Eva's bedroom with his grievous story.

"My little girl," he said, "I've sad news for you—God help and comfort you, my darling child."

"Jasper is dead, papa?" asked Eva, fixing her eyes, that were weary with weeping, with a wild inquiring gaze on her father's face.

"Not dead, my darling," answered the Major, in a faltering voice; "but I fear, dying. A great grief has come to you, Eva, and you must let us all try to help and comfort you in this miserable hour."

Then he told how it had happened; how, as far at least as he knew, from the papers, that it had happened, and the poor child wept on her father's breast.

"I would like to go to him, papa," she said. "I would like to see him before he dies!"

"Well, darling, we shall see," said the Major, soothingly. If he could he would spare the child, he thought, any painful sight; any useless aggravation of her misery now.

On the whole she bore it better than he had even dared to hope for. The miserable suspense, at all events, was over, and she knew now why Jasper had not come.

"Papa, take me to him," she pleaded. "Papa, he will want to see me now."

Alas! poor child, he of whom she thought so tenderly had

forgotten her. He saw only one face in the darkened room where he lay in his pain—one grand, beautiful face, full of unutterable passionate love for him.

In these hours—hours in which were condensed the emotions of years—Elizabeth told Jasper all. Told him of the struggles and temptations through which her fervid, wayward heart had passed, and how the inspired preacher's voice in the church at Eaton Square had called her back from the brink on which she stood.

Jasper Tyrell had lived as most men live, though he had never led an immoral or disgraceful life. But when we lie near the verge of the grave, one life behind, the other before, we see things nearer and clearer than we do in the soul-blindng glow of youth and prime. These two lovers, then, with hand clasped in hand, spoke much in the little room where Jasper Tyrell believed he was to die, of the still bright world above, where the storms and troubles of earth would never come.

Sometimes he would look sorrowfully back though. Had this been, or the other been, he would say. He was so young and Elizabeth so beautiful; and let people say what they will, beauty is one of God's best gifts, winning, if not retaining, His sweetest one of love. So when the young man looked on the lovely face he thought he was to leave, who can blame him if some regretful feelings rose unbidden in his poor human heart?

"But, my love," answered Elizabeth, in reply to some words which told her what was passing in his mind, "we must have parted you know at the last just like this. Suppose, dear, we were old—old, old people, who had lived seventy or eighty years, still one of us must have died the first?"

"Yes," said Jasper, "if we had but lived our lives."

"But it would seem the same then as now," said Elizabeth. "It would be all over then, just as it is now, Jasper, except our love, which can never die."

"And will you never marry, Elizabeth?" said Jasper, with a touch of the old jealous love. "Will you come to me, loving me as you do now?"

"I will never marry," answered Elizabeth; "and whether I die this year, Jasper, or next year, or twenty years after this, I will come to you the same as if God permitted me to go with you now. I have loved you too well to change."

In the meantime, while these two talked thus, trying to reconcile themselves to what they believed to be inevitable, Sir John was going through one of the most painful interviews of his life, with Eva Dalziel.

The poor girl had risen, after her father had told her of the dangerous condition of Jasper Tyrell, with the fullest intention of proceeding to his bedside. But before anything could be arranged, a telegram was received from Sir John, informing them that he was on his way to Hazelhurst; and when he arrived, about noon, Eva was ready waiting to see him.

He was much touched by her appearance. All the sweet rose bloom of her cheeks was gone, and her large, blue eyes had a wistful look of pain in them that told of long-endured anxiety and heart-felt grief. Sir John's tender, manly heart swelled at the sight of this childish, suffering face; at the thought that he was about to inflict a fresh pang on this gentle breast.

He had already gone through a very painful meeting with his daughters, and when the Major led him to the room where Eva was, for a moment he could not speak for emotion, when she put her little, cold, fluttering hand into his.

"Is—there no hope Sir John?" she asked, in pathetic accents.

"I fear none," answered Sir John, much affected. "The doctors say he will probably linger a few days—and then—"

"O, Jasper!—poor Jasper!" said Eva, covering her face, while tears rolled heavily down her cheeks.

"But you will take me to him Sir John?" went on Eva, after a few moments' silence. "You will take me with you to-day, won't you? Papa I am sure will let me go."

"My dear child—" began Sir John, and then he paused.

"What is it?" she asked, looking up into his face with her sad eyes.

"Cruel wrong has been done to you," said Sir John, trying to speak composedly; "cruel, I think shameful wrong. Eva, my dear Eva, you must not regret my son—he is unworthy—I must say it—of your love."

"What do you mean, Sir John?" said Eva, and a faint colour flew to her pale face.

"He meant to marry you," went on Sir John, "but an unhappy attachment—an attachment begun long before he ever saw you —prevented him feeling towards you as a man should feel to the girl about to be his wife."

"Do you mean he did not love me?" asked Eva, as Sir John paused.

"He thought he did, I believe, when he asked you to marry him," replied Sir John; but this former affection—this affection for Elizabeth Gordon—"

"For Elizabeth Gordon!" repeated Eva, in utter amazement.

"Yes," said Sir John, "for Elizabeth Gordon—for a woman whose tragic history, interwoven as it is with the lives of both my unhappy sons, I now consider it my duty to tell you. Sit down, my poor child, while I repeat this painful story."

So Eva sat and listened while Sir John told the sad tale that we already know; told of his young son's murder, and the shameful fraud by which Elizabeth Gordon and Jasper were parted. Then he related Elizabeth's unhappy marriage, and her discovery of her husband's crime, and her midnight flight from her uncongenial home.

Without a word Eva heard all this. Pale, mute, and still, she sat, as the life of her unhappy rival was laid bare before her. But when Sir John went on to tell her of Elizabeth's struggles in London, of her meeting with Jasper there, and how, for the sake of his passionate love for her, he would have given up all the world, and yet she left him, Eva gave a heavy sigh.

"Poor Elizabeth!" she said, "poor Lissa! I understand it all now."

Then Sir John told her of the deceit Mr. Wilmot had practised upon Jasper, and how, with a bitter, angry, jealous heart, he had determined to marry, and forget Elizabeth.

"And then," went on Sir John, "he saw your sweet face, and I would, my dear, for your sake, and his, that you had been his first love, for I feel sure that nothing then would ever have come between you."

Eva did not speak for a moment, and then with another sigh, and with some womanly dignity, she said—

"They should have told me. Did Jasper think, did Elizabeth think, I would wish to marry a man who loved another?"

"He was bound by honour to keep his promise to you," answered Sir John.

"Not when he did not keep his faith," said Eva, with deepening colour, and then she was silent. Suddenly, however, there rushed into her generous heart the remembrance of Jasper's grievous condition, of Elizabeth's long-suffering and pain.

"Forgive me," she said, with a grave sweetness of manner that completely won Sir John's heart, "if I have spoken selfishly— nay, I know that I have done so, for I have been thinking of myself—instead of poor, poor Jasper—and Elizabeth."

"You seem to forget yourself," said Sir John quickly.

"I think I should now," answered Eva; "but it is very difficult. I—I—loved Jasper very much, Sir John, if—he did not love me!"

"I am sure you did," said Sir John. "You are not a girl to marry a man unless you loved him."

"So you undertand," went on Eva, "that I must feel all this very deeply. But do not tell Jasper—do not grieve him now by a single word."

"You are a good, good girl. Eva."

"I'm afraid not—but now we must all think of him most. Tell him from me that I would like to see him, but perhaps—"

"No, dear child, no," said Sir John, a flush passing over his fine skin, you had better not go, you must not go."

"What! is *she* there?" asked Eva, with quickened breath.

"Yes," answered Sir John, turning away his head.

"And he sent for *her?*" said Eva, with a deep drawn sigh. "He—must love her well."

"I fear too well."

Again Eva sighed as Sir John said this, and then, after a little struggle, a little painful effort to conquer the bitter feelings that would rise in her bruised and tender heart, she said, gently—

"Tell *them* then, that I shall pray night and day for them both. Tell Jasper I do not wonder that he loved Elizabeth, she is so beautiful, and—and tell Elizabeth I hope—she will love me still."

Eva's voice faltered and broke as she uttered these last few words, and Sir John was also much affected.

"And—now I think I will say good-bye, Sir John," went on Eva, after a moment. "I—I—am a little tired—and all this sad news—"

"God bless you," said Sir John, taking her outstretched hand in his, and pressing it to his lips. "You have acted to-day as few women would have done—nay, as no other woman I know would have done."

"Oh, no," said Eva; and then she added, "Give him my love— tell him I pray God will comfort him, and be very near him now."

"I will tell him," said Sir John, turning away his head to hide the tears that dimmed his eyes; and when he looked around again, Eva was gone.

Could Sir John have seen into her little chamber during the next few minutes, he would have seen the poor child on her knees. She we praying for Jasper—asking God to spare him— or, at least, spare him some of the cruel pain she feared he must be suffering now, the very thought of which wrung her tender and forgiving heart.

CHAPTER XLII.
LIFE OR DEATH.

SIR JOHN did not return to his son's bedside at once on leaving Hazelhurst, for his daughters begged that he would take them home before he did so. At first the girls were very anxious to go to Jasper with their father; but when, with faltering tongue, Sir John was forced to explain to them that Elizabeth was there with him, Miss Tyrell, even amid her grief, drew back.

"Let us go home then, papa," she said. "We cannot stay here another day."

To this Sir John agreed; telegraphing to Elizabeth that he would join her on the following day; and then a tearful parting took place between the Tyrells and Eva, and about two hours after Sir John's arrival in the village, all the long-looked for wedding guests were gone.

The Dean had an interview with Eva also before he went away, and the proud old man kissed her white cheek with some feeling, and a strange moisture for a moment dimmed his bright, black eyes.

"This has been a grievous affair, my dear," he said; "but, Eva, you will get over it—you are young and handsome—a happy life I trust is before you still."

"Thank you, uncle Ralph," said Eva, gently and sorrowfully.

"You must not remain here," went on the Dean, decisively. "I have given your father a cheque, and he has promised me before another week is over that you shall be on your way to Italy. See all that is worth seeing there, my child, and when your father wants a fresh supply of money, write to me. Have no delicacy about this, Eva. I can afford to give it to you, and it will please me to do so, and to welcome back my pretty niece when she is once more looking and feeling well."

"I fear that will never be, uncle Ralph," said poor Eva.

"You think so now, my dear," answered the Dean, "and it is but natural that you should think so, but in youth our feelings quickly change Before a year is over, I trust that the memory of this unhappy young man will have completely died out of your mind, and I believe that such will be the case."

But Eva only shook her head sadly at this, and then her uncle once more kissed her and bade her good-bye, his last words to his brother when he parted with him at the station being to urge him to take Eva immediately abroad.

"Get her away at once, my dear fellow," said the Dean, "and thus spare her as much as possible the condolences of your amiable wife."

"It is a miserable affair," answered the Major, gloomily.

"Talking about it won't mend it," said the Dean, "Get the child away, and she will do well yet." And then the great man entered the railway carriage, and waved his hand as a parting salutation to his brother, who was standing on the platform, as the train left, in a very dejected attitude.

It was, indeed, a miserable home that he had to return to. Mrs. Dalziel was quite overcome by the blow, and her sighs had a most oppressive effect on the unhappy Major. But even her sighs were easier for the kind-hearted man to bear than the sad little attempts at smiles with which poor Eva greeted him. The poor girl was struggling with her grief, with her wounded affections and bitter disappointment, for her dear father's sake.

"We will go away together, darling," said the Major, putting his arm round his little girl's waist on his return from the station, and Eva laid her head wearily on her father's shoulder.

"Yes, dear papa," she said, "but wait—a little while."

"But why wait, darling?" urged the Major.

"I cannot go, papa—quite yet," answered Eva, with quivering lips; and so for the present the Major said no more.

But he did to his wife.

"Lucy, I've got a word to say to you," he said, addressing her kindly, but gravely, "a word about Eva."

"Well, poor love, what about her?" sighed Mrs. Dalziel, more dolefully than ever.

"Simply, don't mention this unhappy affair to her at all," went on the Major. "Ralph has given me the money, and as soon as she will go, I will take her abroad—in the meantime—"

"What, Henry?" asked Mrs. Dalziel, in a tone of deep reproach.

"Don't say anything to her about it," said the Major. "Don't condole with her, or sigh in that way, for heaven's sake!"

"May I not sigh?" said Mrs. Dalziel, looking upwards. "May I not relieve my overcharged heart by a sigh then? Oh, Henry! what have I done," continued Mrs. Dalziel, bursting into tears, "that you have thus utterly lost confidence in me?"

"Nonsense, nonsense," said the Major. "Come, come, my dear, don't be silly. I've not lost confidence in you—I only wish to spare the child."

"Do you think I wish to hurt her?" asked Mrs. Dalziel, drying her eyes tragically. "Did I upset the train, Henry, and hurry this unfortunate young man to his untimely grave? Did I not prophesy rather what was really true? Did I not warn Eva, as a mother should, not to set her heart too much on anything so unstable as a man?"

"Well, well, never mind," said the Major, soothingly, afraid now of the storm that he had provoked. "Come, Lucy, try to make the best of it, for poor Eva's sake."

"I will never mention his name," said Mrs. Dalziel firmly. "I will never seek to console your child by one single word of comfort from a mother's lips. I will watch her, and attend upon her, when she falls into consumption, and dies of a broken heart, as I've no doubt she will, but it shall be in silence. Henry, you have wounded me more deeply than I can express!"

"I meant to do nothing of the kind," replied the Major.

"But you have. Do you think I do not feel this? Do you think I have not seen Mrs. Ladon sneering out of the back windows, and can I disguise from myself that every one in the village is talking about us?"

"What matter! Let them talk," said the Major; and he walked hastily out of the room, fairly roused out of his usual apathy by the grief of his little girl.

While all this was happening at Hazelhurst, in the little station-house at Annerley Jasper Tyrell and Elizabeth were speaking and thinking of Eva too.

Scarcely, indeed, had Sir John started on his painful mission to the village, when Elizabeth's conscience smote her for her forgetfulness of Eva's feelings, and for the quick jealousy that had sprung up in her heart and that had hardened her to the sufferings which she now remembered that the poor girl was certain to endure.

She was sitting watching Jasper when this mental conflict took place; watching the broken and uneasy slumber into which he constantly fell, and even as the last thought struck her, his lips began to murmur.

"Poor Eva," he said, "poor child!"

Tears sprang into Elizabeth's eyes at these words, and she laid her head down on Jasper's hand, and that slight touch awokehim.

"Lissa—darling," he said, in a feebler voice than usual, "I was dreaming, I think—dreaming of poor little Eva Dalziel."

"And I was thinking of her," answered Elizabeth, softly. "Jasper—dear love, you talked this morning of your will?"

"Yes," said Jasper Tyrell, rousing himself. "I wish to make a will; I wish to leave you what I can. Poor Harry's money, you know—some twenty thousand pounds, I believe, was left after all his bills were paid—and this is mine. And I wish to leave everything to you."

"Don't leave it to me, dear Jasper," said Elizabeth, kneeling down by the bedside, and laying her face close to his. "I have enough, far more than enough; for what shall I want with money —when I am alone—"

Jasper moved his face slightly on the pillow at these words, so that it touched Elizabeth's.

"You are crying, my darling," he said, tenderly "Don't, my Lissa, don't—"

"What I mean," said Elizabeth, trying to speak composedly, "is this, Jasper. I don't want any money—no money can do me any good now; but it could and would do good to—Eva Dalziel."

"You think then—" said Jasper.

"I think that you should leave her some. They are not rich, you know, Jasper, and if you left Eva a fortune—it would atone—"

"You wish this, Lissa?"

"I earnestly wish it. As time goes on she will probably marry —and you see, Jasper, money makes things easier—a girl with money has more choice, and I am sure you wish little Eva to be happy."

Strange, subtle, human hearts! Elizabeth thought at that moment, "I wish her to be happy—I wish her to be happy with some one else—to forget Jasper—to leave his memory alone to me."

Jasper did not speak for a moment after this, and then he said, with a restless sigh—

"I wonder how dying people feel, Lissa? I wonder what it feels like to die?"

"O, Jasper!" sighed Elizabeth.

"Because," went on Jasper, "I feel somehow as if I had life in me still. I feel somehow—that I can't leave you yet, Elizabeth."

Elizabeth looked quickly up at these words, and for the first time since his accident a gleam of hope stole into her heart.

"What do you feel, dear Jasper?" she said, trying to speak calmly.

"Horribly enough—all pain—but still not dying. I wonder if that fellow, the doctor, understands the case, Elizabeth?"

"My dear," answered Elizabeth, and she rose up from the bedside, pale and steadfast, "if—if you think there is any hope—if God will mercifully spare you to us one day more, I will telegraph to London at once, and summon the first doctors there?"

"I think I would like to see some one else," said Jasper. "I dare say it will be no use—still—"

"I will send the message now," said Elizabeth, almost calmly, and she left the room; going at once to the station-master, who telegraphed, at her desire, to Sir H—— T——, and to Dr. J—— H——, two of the most famous surgeons in London. Then, after the message went, she crept back to a little room adjoining Jasper's, which had been given up to her, and fell down on her knees in passionate entreaty for his life.

"Oh! spare him—my Father, spare him!" she asked. "Spare him, O God; spare him!"

She could say no more. It was her one cry. Until now she had no hope,—they had told her there was none—and Jasper had talked as the dying talk; and Sir John had spoken of him as we speak of those about to leave us. But now? "Oh! if he could but live," thought poor Elizabeth, "live for one year—even one month."

So for this boon of life she prayed with passionate earnestness; prayed with her whole heart and soul. Jasper lying in the next room heard her voice lifted up in fervent entreaty, and when she went back to his side, he whispered as she knelt down by him—

"Were you praying for me, Lissa?"

"Yes, Jasper," said Elizabeth, "yes my darling. Oh! try to live, Jasper—try, for my sake!"

"Perhaps God will spare me," answered Jasper, gravely.

"Let us pray," said Elizabeth, "pray together." And so, with hands tight clasped, they prayed for Jasper's life—prayed that the young man might live, even if it were only for a little time.

A few hours later in the day, Sir H—— T—— and Dr. J—— H—— arrived, and a prolonged and painful examination of Jasper's injuries then took place.

In the little dressing-room adjoining, while the surgeons were with Jasper, Elizabeth stood pale and tearless, enduring the terrible ordeal of suspense. Then she heard Sir H—— T—— say to Jasper, "Is the lady who left the room your wife?"

"If I live she will be," replied Jasper's faint voice, for he was much exhausted; and then Elizabeth went to the door of the dressing-room, and beckoned the famous surgeon to come in.

"Is there—" she asked hoarsely, but she could not complete the sentence.

"Any hope?" said Sir H—— T——, kindly. "I trust so. His constitution must have been splendid, and his rallying powers great, to have so long survived the shock, for he is desperately injured—but if no fatal change occurs—"

"There is hope?" gasped Elizabeth, with her clammy lips.

"I repeat, I trust so," answered the great surgeon. "Remember, it is but a chance; but he is young, and has much in his favour, and with skilled attention and nursing—"

"Come every day," said Elizabeth, grasping Sir H—— T——'s hand. "Don't think of the expense; it is nothing. I am rich, he is rich. Only save him and everything I have may be yours."

Sir H—— T—— smiled a somewhat stately smile.

"My dear young lady," he said, "I shall do my best for him. Of course, he will never be what he has been. His face will remain disfigured, and his injuries are too severe for him ever entirely to recover from them—but he may live."

"If he lives, nothing else matters," said Elizabeth; and after making arrangements for Sir H—— T——'s return, she hurried back to Jasper's side, who opened his eyes with a moan of pain when he heard her come.

"Has he told you?" she asked, in an excited whisper.

"What?" said Jasper, and a shade passed over his face, for he thought he was about to hear his coming doom.

"You will live!" said Elizabeth, "you will live!" And she fell down by Jasper, and laid her lips on his.

"Is it so, darling?" said Jasper, after a few moments of grateful joy. "Then you will never leave me, Lissa—promise me that?"

"I will never leave you," answered Elizabeth, " as long as we both shall live."

CHAPTER XLIII.
EVA'S LETTER.

So when Sir John returned the next day to the station-house at Annerley, he had news to hear that he had little hoped for.

"Jasper was rallying. Sir H—— T—— said there was *hope*." Elizabeth could scarcely get the words out fast enough, as she clasped tight Sir John's hand, her cheeks flushed, and her eyes sparkled with her new joy.

Then Sir John went up to his son, and stood beside him; beside the handsome son of whom he had been so proud, now lying so strangely changed.

Jasper was asleep when his father went in, but by-and-by he

awoke, and looked up, and met his father's kindly, thoughtful gaze.

"Father!" said Jasper, and he smiled.

"My dear boy," said Sir John, much affected. "So God has been very merciful to us—Elizabeth tells me you are better, Jasper?"

"Yes," said Jasper, and he smiled again; "they say I have a chance now."

"You have a good nurse," said Sir John, looking at Elizabeth kindly, who was standing near.

"Yes," answered Jasper, "and she has promised never to leave me, father—never to leave me, do you hear, any more?"

"I do not wish her to do so," said Sir John, and he held out his hand to Elizabeth.

"And Eva, father?" asked Jasper, presently, for his mind was clearer now. "She knows everything now, I hope?"

"Yes, Jasper," answered Sir John, gravely, "she knows everything now—and bore it better," he added considerately, "than I almost hoped for. She sent her love to you both," he went on, with a somewhat sad smile.

"She is a dear girl," said Elizabeth, softly, her heart reproaching her as she spoke.

"She is more like an angel, I think," said Sir John, in a low tone, and he turned away his head; the sweet, childish, grief-stricken face of Eva having left a very deep and painful impression on his mind.

But though there might be hope for Jasper, his life for many weeks after this hung on a thread. Such were the extent of his injuries, that at any moment, the surgeons warned both Elizabeth and Sir John, a fatal change might take place. Many a time Elizabeth's heart died within her as she watched the cruel suffering which at times racked his frame with almost intolerable pain. But she never left him. Night and day, except a few hours in the day when Sir John watched him, Elizabeth was at her post by his side. He could sleep best when she had hold of his hand, and so, hand-clasped, hour after hour, she used to kneel beside him.

Sir John wrote to Eva after his return to the station-house at Annerley, to tell her that Sir H—— T—— had pronounced there was now a faint hope that his son's life might be spared, and the poor girl sent him a few touching lines in reply.

Eva wrote to Elizabeth also, and her letter was blotted by many self-reproachful tears, which fell from Elizabeth's eyes as she read Eva's gentle words.

"My dear Elizabeth," her letter began, "Sir John tells me that there is now hope that Jasper may recover from his dreadful injuries, and I need not, I suppose, tell you that I pray God that

it may be so. Dear Lissa, this has been very sad for us both;
but though I know he meant it kindly, I think Jasper should
have told me the truth. I would not have married him if I had
known that he loved you, and what would it have been if I had
found it out afterwards? Tell him I hope he will live to be
happy with you, and that all this sorrow will pass away. Uncle
Ralph has given papa the money, and we (just papa and I) are
going abroad very soon. I cannot write a long letter to you to-
day, but I will write to you afterwards—when I hear that you
and Jasper are married—and I trust that God, dear Lissa, will
bless you both. You are sure to be happy, because he loves you
so much, and I know you will always be good to him. God
bless you both.

"Your affectionate friend,
"Eva Dalziel."

Elizabeth did not show this letter to Jasper—she could not.
"I could not have written it," she thought, almost jealously.
"She is a thousand, thousand times better than I am. Oh! dear,
little Eva, what would I give to see you happy—to see you a
happy wife."

Eva had shed many tears before she could write to Elizabeth,
bitter, bitter tears; but her sweet, unselfish nature was about as
little tainted with the evil passions "which so easily beset us,"
as it was almost possible for a human soul to be. After, however, she heard that Jasper was better, and likely to live, she felt
anxious to go away, and the very night she received Sir John's
letter she went behind her papa's chair, and put her arms round
his neck, and whispered in his ear.

"Papa, dear," she said, "shall we go now? I should like to go
now."

"You mean abroad, darling?" said the Major, looking round.
"I'll go with you to-morrow, if you will go?"

So Eva and her father went away, and Mrs. Dalziel was left to
indulge in her sighs in private, and to groan over the uncertainty
of all human events.

"I will never believe in anything until it happens, again," she
frequently said; and her letters to the Major were always of so
desponding a nature that he invariably hid them away from his
little girl.

Thus the autumn passed away, and the early winter began,
but before the end of November Elizabeth and Jasper
were married. It was a very solemn ceremony which
took place in the little station-house at Annerley, when the bride
plighted herself to the bridegroom "till death us do part," for
death did not seem to be very far away. But it was Jasper's
wish, and neither Sir John nor Elizabeth cared to refuse his
earnest request.

Sir H—— T—— wished him to go up to town, so that he might more frequently see him; and as Jasper would not go without Elizabeth, it was agreed that Elizabeth had better go with him as his wife.

So by special license one dull, grey, November morning, Jasper and Elizabeth were wedded. The bridegroom was propped up in bed to go through the ceremony, and his crushed hand refused its office to put the ring on Elizabeth's dear finger; but his father placed it there for him, and thus in solemn fashion the two who had loved each other so well were made man and wife.

The marriage festivities took place downstairs in the station-master's family, and were provided for in the most lavish manner by Sir John. Upstairs Elizabeth sat with her sweet, grave face, holding Jasper's hand, while their health and happiness were drunk in many a flowing bumper of champagne. Sir John went down among the wedding-party for a short while, winning, as he always did, universal admiration by his gentle and courteous bearing; and as the distant sound of merriment stole to the sick-room, Jasper looked at Elizabeth with a faint smile.

"Do you hear?" he said, and then, seeing the grave expression of Elizabeth's face, he added, quickly. "You don't regret this, do you, darling?"

"Regret what, Jasper?" she asked, as if in surprise.

"Marrying a poor cripple like me," answered Jasper, with a half-impatient sigh.

At these words Elizabeth looked at him with such deep love and tenderness shining in her eyes, that Jasper said, the next moment,

"No, no, I know you don't, darling. Kiss me Lissa."

"Do you know what I was thinking?" said his wife, as she pressed her lips to his.

"No; what, dear?"

"That we can never be like other people," answered Elizabeth. "God has given you to me, Jasper, as if from death, and what is called the world can now never be anything to *us*. My whole world is here."

And once more she kissed her husband's lips.

"Well, I am content," said Jasper.

"And as time goes on," continued Elizabeth, in her sweet, ringing voice, "and you get stronger, dear, let us live as those live whose hopes of happiness end not with the grave. I think we shall always be like quite old people, Jasper," she added, with a smile; "we have gone through so much, that we shall be like an old grave couple going down together hand in hand, happy to the end."

"What a strange fancy, Lissa! It's all very well for me— but you—"

"'As the husband is, the wife is,'" said Lissa, softly; and with such gentle, tender words she wiled away the wedding-day.

They went up to London a few days after this, where Sir John had taken a good furnished house for them in Belgrave Road. Here, everything that surgical aid and skill could do for Jasper was done, and gradually, little by little, he began to recover. But it was a slow and painful process, and Jasper's handsome face was marred and changed for evermore. Not in Elizabeth's eyes though. The scarred visage to her was more beautiful even than the young lover's had been, who had wooed her beneath the woods at Wendell, before their cruel separation had begun, and her devotion to him was complete.

His sisters wrote to Elizabeth after she became their brother's wife, and Sir John often stayed with them. During one of these visits, just a few days before the second anniversary of Harry Tyrell's death, the poor mother of the murdered youth passed quietly away.

Lady Tyrell had got weaker and weaker, but so gradually that it was scarcely noticed in the household; but one morning, just as the sun was rising, the end suddenly came. Her usual attendant was engaged making her some tea by the fire, when a slight noise attracted her attention to the invalid, and turning quickly round she saw Lady Tyrell had half-raised herself up in bed, with a new, strange, and wondrous expression on her face.

"What is it, my lady?" asked the nurse, approaching the bed.

But Lady Tyrell did not answer this question, but with her eyes fixed beyond the woman, softly uttered one word.

"Harry!" she said, "Harry!" and then fell back and died, even as her dead son's name faltered on her parting lips.

Sir John was sincerely and deeply affected when the news reached him. He went up to his own room and sat down, thinking gravely and sadly of the past. Had he been always kind to her? he thought. Had he tried to share her heavy burden, and comfort her as best he could? Alas! "the dimly lighted soul," that had flickered and gone out, had been beyond the reach, since her grievous loss, of his kindly care. But we think of many things, when we stand face to face with the ashen hues of death, that do not strike us when the life-blood is flowing through the veins. Sir John at least had no unkind word, no unkind deed, to haunt him as he looked on his dead wife's face. He had not loved her. How could this noble-minded gentleman love the narrow-heart that had never beat in unison with his own? But he had been kind to her, kind, considerate, and faithful, and had in truth, no reason to reproach himself as he looked on her lying in her last, calm sleep.

In very gorgeous fashion she was carried to her grave. Si

John did not care for these things, disliking parade on all occasions, and mostly so when connected with the services for the
dead.   But his daughters wished it, and the very fact that Sir
John felt that he was not mourning this poor woman as he thought
he should mourn her, made him prefer to be guided by their
wishes rather than his own.   So in the family vault at Wendell,
with much pomp and ceremony, Lady Tyrell was laid by her dead
son's side.   It was a sad ending to a sad drama, and with pale
face and quivering lips Sir John returned to his stately home after
all was over.

> "Leaves have their time to fall,
> And flowers to wither at the north wind's breath,
> And stars to set; but all—
> Thou hast all seasons for thine own, O Death!"

CHAPTER XLIV.
"A GENEROUS FRIENDSHIP."

THE New Year found Jasper and Elizabeth still in town.   Jasper's
improvement was gradual, but very slow, and as he required
constant medical attendance, they both thought it wiser to stay,
and, therefore, had declined Sir John's repeated and pressing
invitation to visit him at Wendell.

When Jasper became well enough for Elizabeth to leave him
for a short time without anxiety, she did not forget her friends,
the kind old maids in Buckingham Palace Road.   Great excitement was created in that quiet family by her first visit there; and
when Elizabeth announced that she was actually married to the
son of the very Sir John Tyrell who had acted as a reference for
her, the Misses White lifted up their hands in astonishment to
hear of her good fortune.   Miss Eliza was, indeed, a little reconciled to the idea, when she heard that Mr. Tyrell had been nearly
killed by a railway accident, and was now barely able to cross the
room with the aid of crutches.

"There's always something," she said to Elizabeth, wiping her
watery eyes.   "Ah—well, I suppose, troubles are good for us."

The young girl, Susy, was overjoyed at Elizabeth's good luck.

"Didn't I always tell you, Aunt Eliza," she said, with no small
pride at her discernment, "that Miss Gordon would be sure to
have lovers?   Didn't I now?"

"Ah, Susy," answered Aunt Eliza, shaking her head, "don't
forget that men are snares."

"Then I wouldn't mind being caught by one!" replied the
thoughtless Susy, and Aunt Eliza nearly fell off her chair in
horror at her niece's indiscretion.

But even poor Eliza's faded eyes brightened when one day
Elizabeth took Susy with her to Gorringe's tempting shop in
Buckingham Palace Road, and there, among other purchases
bought Aunt Eliza such a jacket and bonnet, that a glow of pride

nay, I fear of vanity, passed through the old lady's disappointed heart.

Susy had always been an enthusiastic admirer of Elizabeth's, but now (not unnaturally) her admiration increased three-fold. The young girl could not find words to express her gratitude for the pretty costumes and thoughtful gifts that Elizabeth's lavish hand showered upon her. Nothing pleased Elizabeth so much as to give pleasure, and Susy's delight was so heartfelt and sincere that it was real enjoyment to Elizabeth to watch her. Often and often in these day Elizabeth thought of another young girl, whose sweet hopes of happiness she felt (though not intentionally) she had blighted. It was the shadow that lay over her life, and sometimes she fancied that Jasper too thought of Eva now with much self-reproach and pain. But it was a subject they never mentioned. Deeply as they loved each other, and closely as their hearts were knit, they never alluded to it. But often Elizabeth thought of the fair, almost childish, face of Eva, that she had last seen with the evening sun falling upon it, the night when she left Hazelhurst, and the bright, soft, trustful eyes then raised to hers, who was fated afterwards to cause her such cruel pain !

Eva had not written again as she had promised to Elizabeth, and thus Elizabeth had no means of knowing where she was, nor of hearing of her welfare. She concluded therefore that Eva and her father were still abroad, but she would have given much (she scarcely acknowledged to herself how much) to know that Eva was well and happy.

Sometimes she would walk round the quiet square where she used to meet Jasper, while a strange and solemn thankfulness glowed in her heart. "Last year at this time," she would think, "last year!"   A great change had, indeed, happened to her, for God had given her her heart's desire.   But as she had told Jasper on their wedding day, her youth seemed to have died in the dark struggles that had passed over her soul, and a grave, sweet serenity, such as should come in the decline of life, had taken the place of the quick, warm feelings of her girlhood.

In one of her rambles with Susy, for nothing gave the young girl so much pleasure as to be allowed to go for a walk with "Mrs Tyrell," curiosity prompted Elizabeth to pass down Cambridge Street, to see once more the house where she had spent such miserable days.

As they neared Mrs. O'Shee's door, Elizabeth was surprised to see around it the unmistakable crowd that indicated that a sale was going on within.

"Some one's being sold off there," remarked Susy, and, indeed, there was no mistake about the matter, for just as they approached the house a feather bed was carried out of it by two men, followed by Mrs. O'Shee herself, who was clinging to the bed in a most frantic manner imaginable.

"Me feather bed!" exclaimed the miserable little Irishwoman, whose hair and whole appearance was in the most dishevelled condition, "on which me own father died, to go for one pound ten! "Ye're robbers, ivery one of ye! I won't let it go, I won't, I say!"

And she held with her bony hands on the bed, amid the derisive laughter of the spectators.

"Come, my good woman, it's no use, let it go," said one of the men, trying to push her away.

Just at this moment a clock was carried out, and at the sight of it Mrs. O'Shee set up a perfect shriek of despair.

"What did it go for?" she cried. "Oh! ye villians! ye villians!" And she left the bed to make a vain rush to rescue the clock.

Elizabeth could not help feeling sorry. After all, the poor soul had, doubtless, had to struggle with the grim clutches of poverty, and her household furniture being thus sold would probably reduce her to complete beggary. She looked so miserable too. Her little, blue, pinched face was soiled and stained, and here and there a tear had made a small rivulet, as it were, through the dust on her skin, which added not a little to her deplorable appearance.

Elizabeth drew out her purse, and was actually considering how she could best relieve the woman, who, at one time, had acted as a spy on her actions, and whose pilfering fingers had taken money from her, when money had been of the most vital consequence. But at this moment Mrs. O'Shee's eyes fell on her face, and the next instant, with a cry of recognition, the little Irishwoman had darted through the crowd, and caught Elizabeth by the hand.

"Me young friend!" she exclaimed, "where have ye come from? What d'ye think of this?" she continued, theatrically pointing to her departing goods. "Me furniture, and ye know how good it was, sold off to pay a paltry twenty pounds!"

"Is that really all, Mrs. O'Shee?" asked Elizabeth.

"On me soul, if I have one," swore the Irishwoman, falling on her knees in the street, "I don't owe another ha'penny in all the wide world! And if ye could—Oh! the dear, if ye would—advance this troifle, I'll kneel down night and day before ye, except when I get up to endeavour by my exertions to make the money to refund ye!"

Elizabeth hesitated. She had a sum of money with her, which she had intended taking as a gift to a certain hospital in the neighbourhood; but the Irishwoman's miserable condition touched her, and, perhaps, she also remembered "If thine enemy hunger, feed him; if he thirst, give him drink" At all events Mrs.

O'Shee's sharp eyes read compliance with her modest petition on Elizabeth's relenting face, and she instantly sprang to her feet.

"Stop!" she cried, "I command ye!" to the broker's men who were in the act of conveying her feather bed away on a hand-barrow. "Me young friend here will pay ye the money. And tell the villian that employed ye I'll take me custom away from him this very day!"

Mrs O'Shee's goods, in fact, had been seized by a general dealer in the neighbourhood, who had distrained for the amount of his bill, which Elizabeth found really to be slightly under twenty pounds. She therefore settled this, amid such protestations of gratitude, and entreaties to know where she was "resoiding," that Elizabeth was glad again to escape out of the house.

In voluble language Mrs. O'Shee related Mr. Wilmot's regret and anger when he found that Elizabeth had left Cambridge Street, and she tried to insist on telling the old story that Elizabeth knew too well. How "another foine young gintleman" had come, and how Mr. Wilmot and he had quarrelled "about ye," and how this, and how that. But Elizabeth would not stay to listen. She had relieved Mrs. O'Shee's necessities, and that was enough; and in spite of all the little Irishwoman's questions, she declined to tell her where she was living, or with whom she had been since she left Cambridge Street. Indeed, when she related this adventure to Jasper, the first frown that she had ever seen since their marriage, contracted his brow.

"My dear Elizabeth!" he said.

"Are you angry with me, Jasper?" asked Elizabeth, "for giving this money?"

"I think you had much better have given her in charge of a policeman instead," answered Jasper, with some sharpness.

But Elizabeth went up to him and took his hand.

"My dear," she said, and she looked up into his face, "she did not part us." And Jasper could not resist her tender words.

"But she might have done so, you silly little woman," he said, pushing back Elizabeth's dark hair from her fine brow.

"She is very poor, Jasper," answered Elizabeth, "and we are very happy—I can't feel angry to any one *now*."

This appeared to be a convincing argument to Jasper, for he did not continue to frown, and Elizabeth, like a good wife, respected her husband's wish, and never went near Mrs. O'Shee any more. So whether she keeps her head above water still, or whether the stream has swept over her, carrying her meagre little body and soul away to yet deeper depths, Elizabeth does not know, and does not care to inquire. Miss Susy, indeed, told her that some six months after Elizabeth had given Mrs. O'Shee the twenty pounds, that she saw that No.—— Cambridge Street was to be let, and that the house was evidently uninhabited. Where,

however, this erring member of the vast human family has found
refuge is unknown, and will probably continue to be unknown,
to the Tyrells. She has drifted away, and is lost amid the ever-
moving crowd.

But the spring-time brought another familiar face to Elizabeth
—the sweet, lovely face of Eva Dalziel. Jasper was better now;
that is, he could go out, and supported by a crutch and Elizabeth's
arm, would sometimes walk in the quiet squares in the neighbourhood. Sir John happened to be in town towards the end of
April, and one fine afternoon the Baronet and Jasper and Elizabeth had gone out for a short stroll up Belgrave Road, and just
as they were returning, near their own house, a hansom cab
passed them and then stopped.

Elizabeth looked carelessly up, but the next moment a cry of
recognition faltered on her lips, for the light, girlish figure of Eva
Dalziel sprang out of the cab, followed by the grayhaired Major,
and with out-stretched hand Eva advanced towards them.

"Elizabeth! Lissa!" she said, and that was all. In fact, she
was too much agitated for many words.

Not one of those present was unmoved at this meeting. Jasper's
pale face dyed a dusky red, while Elizabeth's rich colouring faded,
and a flush passed over both Sir John's handsome, aristocratic
face, and the Major's fine, delicately-tinted skin.

Sir John was the first to recover himself, and courteously addressing the Major, made some inquiries about their journey and
their return to England, to which, however, the Major was apparently unable to give any very articulate replies.

In the meanwhile, Eva, for the first time, had looked in her old
lover's face, and a little startled shocked look came over her own
sweet one, when, she saw how greatly Jasper was changed.

"Jasper," she said, and she put out a little fluttering hand,
"are you better?"

"Yes, but only a poor cripple, as you see, still," answered
Jasper, nervously.

"Will you come in, Eva?" said Elizabeth, endeavouring to
speak composedly. "We live close here. Do come in and have
some tea?"

To this Eva assented, and the Major, after a moment's hesitation,
made no demur, but followed his daughter into Jasper's and
Elizabeth's house.

The Major, indeed, did not blame Jasper, for he and his little
girl had had no secrets between them during their long foreign
tour.

With her hand in her dear father's, Eva had told him Elizabeth's tragic history: told him what Sir John had told her; and
the Major was too just a man to have any ill-feeling towards
Jasper in consequence. Nay, he thought that he had behaved

as a man of honour, believing that he would have kept his promise to Eva, but for the unfortunate accident, which had so nearly destroyed his life. So he made no objection to the renewal of their acquaintance, and even offered his arm to assist Jasper upstairs, when they entered the house. But this was Elizabeth's office, for she knew best how to help Jasper, and everything gave way in her eyes to this duty.

Before she even rang for tea, Jasper was assisted to his usual couch by her careful hands, and a restorative administered to him and while Elizabeth was thus employed, Sir John approached Eva whose eyes were fixed pityingly on her old lover's altered form.

"How ill he looks," she said to Sir John; almost under her breath.

"Do you think so?" said Sir John, glancing round at his son. "We think he looks wonderfully well now. He has had, indeed, a narrow escape."

"Poor Jasper!" said Eva, in the same tone; and Sir John looked at her curiously, wondering if the old feeling lived still, or had died in the young girl's heart.

But with easy tact he changed the conversation, and presently, in her pretty, frank way, Eva was telling Sir John about their foreign tour, and how "papa" had liked this place, and she had liked that. By-and-by, a little laugh rang through the room from the girl's lips at some remark of Sir John's, and when Jasper heard it, he looked at Elizabeth and smiled.

Yet both Elizabeth and Jasper had noted the change on the sweet face; the almost nameless change which told of endured, though it might be conquered pain. Eva was prettier perhaps even than ever, but her wild-rose colour did not come and go so quickly as it did a year ago, and her manner was a little, just a little, more gentle and subdued.

But she chatted and talked quite cheerfully during the tea-drinking that followed, speaking once or twice to Jasper, but mostly to Sir John, who was charmed with her whole appearance. After tea was over, Elizabeth asked her if she would like to see the house, and Eva accepted this invitation, and followed Elizabeth to her room. Then, when they were alone, the two women looked into each other's faces, and the next moment Eva had flung herself on Elizabeth's breast, putting her arms round her neck, and sobbing like a little child.

"My dear, my dear!" said Elizabeth, much affected, and so they wept in each other's arms.

But Eva was the first to dry her tears.

"I should not be so silly," she said, "but seeing you again Elizabeth—"

"I did not mean to hurt you, Eva," wept Elizabeth. "God knows I did not mean to hurt you!"

"I know, dear," said Eva gently, and then she kissed Elizabeth. "You were very good and noble. It is all for the best, Elizabeth—God took my idol away—for I think once I loved Jasper too much."

As Eva made this simple confession, Elizabeth clasped her closer in her arms.

"And now?" she said, "now, Eva?"

"Now, he is your husband," answered Eva, bravely. "And besides," she added, while a little sad smile stole round her pretty lips, "he is so changed, Lissa—he scarcely seems to me to be the same Jasper—I used to know."

"And you are not unhappy now," asked Elizabeth.

"Oh! no. dear—I am happy now," answered Eva, though for a moment the last words faltered on her generous lips.

"Thank God that it is so!" said Elizabeth.

"I am not going home quite yet," went on Eva. "Uncle Ralph has invited me for a long visit to Greyminster, and papa will take me there before he returns to Hazelhurst. Uncle Ralph has been so good to me, Lissa. He sent us more money even than we could spend abroad, and you know travelling costs a great deal." Thus in this tender fashion the two renewed their friendship, and not one bitter or jealous thought sprang up between them. When they returned to the drawing-room, Eva went up to the couch on which Jasper was lying, and spoke to him very kindly.

"I hope you will soon get stronger, Jasper?" she said.

"Thanks, I hope so," answered Jasper. "But you know, Eva," he added, fixing his dark eyes on her face, "I shall never be the same any more."

______

CHAPTER XLV.
"THE INAUDIBLE AND NOISELESS FOOT OF TIME."

THE next day Sir John went to call on the Major at his hotel, and brought Eva back to lunch at Belgrave Road. Elizabeth was very pleased to see her, and kissed her with fond affection when the girl came into the room. The husband and wife had broken through the one barrier that had been between their hearts the night before, after the Major and Eva had left, and Elizabeth had told Jasper all Eva's generous words. All, except—Oh! poor Elizabeth, she was very human after all—she did not tell him that Eva had said that God had taken her idol away—that she had once loved Jasper too much. Perhaps this was wise. Jasper was high-minded enough only to have felt pain if he had heard it, and to repeat it could have now done Eva no possible good. It might have even created fresh embarrassment between them, which for both their sakes it was much better to avoid. As it was, Eva met Jasper on this second visit with quiet friendliness, with which was mingled a little womanly dignity and pride.

Her manner to Jasper, in fact, completely won Sir John's heart. He could understand so well the fine feelings that dictated her considerate gentle words.

"She is perfect," he whispered to Elizabeth; and Elizabeth smiled good-naturedly at his unqualified praise.

Eva had expressed a wish to see the Art School of Needle-work, now located at South Kensington, and Sir John pleasantly offered to escort the ladies there during the afternoon. He was, indeed, pleased to amuse Eva in any way, and made such lavish purchases at the Art School that he was a most welcome visitor to that establishment.

He bought Elizabeth and Eva several things. In fact, they might have had what they fancied, and he also purchased a very elaborate table-cover, which, when they returned to Belgrave Road, he presented to Eva, with a smile.

"Will you give this to your mamma, from me? "he said, and Eva, in her sweet, pretty way, accepted the gift. Nay, knowing that by doing so she would give sincere pleasure to her step-mother, she forwarded the table-cover to Hazelhurst the very next day; and when Mrs. Dalziel received it, for the first time since Eva's engagement was ended, she felt a little gratified.

Nothing, indeed, could exceed the mortification that Mrs. Dalziel had felt about the unfortunate affair that had dashed her own pride and poor Eva's hopes so low. She had kept her word, and, after the Major had spoken to her on the subject, had never uttered Jasper Tyrell's name to Eva during the short time she was at home after his accident. But she had done this with the air of a martyr. Eva knew very well that her father must have ordered her step-mother to avoid the subject; and, indeed, when they were abroad together, the Major confessed, in confidence, to his daughter that this was the case.

"Your mother, you know, is an excellent woman, my dear," said the Major, "but sometimes I think she says things that are best unsaid—but then we all have our faults."

On the occasion of receiving the table-cover, however, Mrs. Dalziel being obliged to mention the Tyrells' name, took the opportunity of enlarging considerably on the subject. After thanking Sir John for remembering "my humble name, and the hospitality which I endeavoured to show his daughters, during the most trying period of my life," Mrs. Dalziel proceeded to inform Eva, in her letter, that she had heard from papa with "pious gratitude," that Eva's health and spirits had survived a shock which she herself had been prepared to find fatal. "Be thankful, therefore, my dearest Eva," Mrs. Dalziel continued, "for the *placidity* of your temperament, which you have doubtless inherited from papa; for had you possessed *my* feelings, I do not doubt that now you would have been lying in an early grave. I am glad to hear also that the unfortunate young man, though hopelessly disfigured and irreparably crippled, *still lives*. I will say nothing further. Nothing of the indecency of a woman, who had only lost her husband a fortnight, going to the bedside of another man, even though that other man was supposed to be dying, which it turned out he was not! Your papa informs me that you met Mrs. *Jasper Tyrell* in the *most friendly manner*. I can only repeat that I *envy* you the easy nature which made this possible to you; and I must endeavour to subdue the too impulsive feelings of my heart, which rendered me (apparently) an unsuitable companion for my husband and step-daughter, during days which I should have considered of *crushing sorrow*."

Eva read this letter first with a sigh, and then with a smile "It is so like mamma;" she thought, and then she quietly put Mrs. Dalziel's epistle in the fire, and tried to forget all about it. Yet it left a sting. This sweet child had tried hard to bear her pain bravely, and for her dear father's sake, when they were abroad, had often seemed amused and happy, when her heart felt very sore and sad within.

But she was better now. Better, strange to say, after she had seen Jasper. They were not forced smiles which rippled over her sweet face, when, day after day, Sir John planned some fresh amusement for the Major and his pretty daughter. Eva had all a young girl's fondness for seeing "sights" still, and Sir John was only too pleased to escort her to the various exhibitions and picture galleries, and to explain with his fluent tongue, and cultivated taste, the artistic work of which he was so excellent a judge.

Elizabeth rarely accompanied them, for Jasper, of course, could not endure the fatigue of sight-seeing. But the patient Major made no complaint, being only too glad to see his little girl looking amused and happy once more, and, catalogue in hand, placidly followed Sir John and Eva from picture to picture, though often, it must be admitted, he would turn aside to yawn!

Before Eva left town for Greyminster, she had received (at their father's request) a kind invitation from the Misses Tyrell, to visit them at Wendell. Eva showed this to Elizabeth, and Elizabeth pressed her to accept it.

"Do go, Eva," she said, "and then you will see my old home, and my cousins."

"What are your cousins like?" asked Eva.

"Robert is a handsome young man," answered Elizabeth smiling; "and Master Hal is a very nice, but, I must add, a very impudent boy."

"I would like to go," said Eva, hesitatingly, "and yet—"

"Why yet, Eva?" asked Elizabeth "Jasper and I have fixed to go to West-house in June, and it would be so pleasant if you were at the Hall at the same time that we are at Wendell."

Sir John also was very pressing that Eva should accept this invitation, and it was finally arranged that she should do so. She was to pay her visit to the Dean first, at Greyminster, and then to proceed towards the end of June to Wendell. "And you will stay with us until you are tired of us, I hope?" said Sir John. And Jasper, who overheard this speech, looked with rather an amused smile at Elizabeth, after his father had left the room to escort Eva to the hotel.

"He can't be thinking of her, surely?" he said. "Why, he's fifty, and she's only a child to him!"

"I think he is very fond of her," answered Elizabeth, thoughtfully.

"Oh! I suppose as a father, and that kind of thing," said Jasper, carelessly. "But if she goes to Wendell, Lissa, what do you say to Robert Horton? Do you think he would suit her, eh?"

"I think, dear, these things are best left alone," said Elizabeth "But I think Robert is a nice fellow, and if a girl liked him, she might do worse than marry Bob."

CHAPTER XLVI.

EVA'S VISIT.

It was quite the latter end of June before Eva arrived at Wendell-hall. Elizabeth and Jasper had been nearly a month at Wendell West-house before she came, and Jasper was decidedly better for the change. Bob Horton and Harry were delighted to have Elizabeth back again, and soon became great friends with Jasper Tyrell. These young fellows (Harry especially) helped to amuse Jasper, and to wile away the weary hours of weakness and pain which he still was forced often to endure. But he bore it all bravely. He might well bear it, when the woman he loved so well was so entirely devoted to him.

His sisters, too, often came to see him, and Sir John, looking handsomer than ever, was a constant visitor at the homestead.

It was a happy family party, then, that Eva joined, and we may be sure her sweet face brought no gloom to it. She was, indeed, delighted with the farm, and had never seen a dairy, nor had the pleasure of nursing young ducks and chickens before. Bob broke in for her, and presented her with, a very handsome little pony, and in return was allowed the honour of teaching her to ride. She used to go every day to see Elizabeth, though it must be confessed the Misses Tyrell did not quite approve of this arrangement, and Sir John once or twice looked grave when Eva did not return to dinner at the Hall.

"She is so childish," said Miss Tyrell, on one of these occasions.

"I believe she is never so happy as when she is nursing some pet or other that she has picked up."

"She has a beautiful nature," said Sir John. "A loving, tender nature, which makes her sympathise with all God's creature's, however small they are."

Miss Tyrell shrugged her shoulder at this; and then presently, after dinner was over, when Sir John put on his hat and strolled out in the direction of West-house, she said, with some anxiety in her tone, to her sister—

"Fannie, did you hear what papa said of Eva Dalziel?"

"Of course I heard," said Fannie.

"He can't, surely, be thinking of her?" went on Matilda "No, it's impossible; she is a mere child."

"She is a very pretty child though," answered Fannie, "and there is no doubt that papa is very fond of her. But I suppose, as you say, he looks upon her as a child, and, besides, I think he is very sorry for her about Jasper."

"Well, she has quite got over that, at any rate," said the elder sister.

"Still, one can't help being sorry for her," said Fannie. "I shall never forget her face in those dreadful days at Hazelhurst, when Jasper did not come."

In the meanwhile, Sir John was walking thoughtfully through the fields which part the Hall from the homestead. He was thinking of a painful subject—of the years which had passed over his head, and left him now, in middle age, a lonely, solitary man. His daughters would marry, he reflected, his son was already married, and then he would be alone.

Suddenly the sound of laughter was borne to his ears by the summer evening's breeze, of a young man's laughter and a girl's—and Sir John stopped when he heard it, and gave rather a heavy sigh.

"It is but natural," he thought, "youth turns to youth; how could I expect that a man of my years could win a young girl's love."

Presently Robert Horton and Eva (Robert leading Eva's pony) appeared in sight, and when they saw Sir John they came up to him.

"Just fancy, Sir John!" cried Eva, laughing. "Robin" (this was the pony) "has run away with me."

"Robin," who decidedly looked a scampish pony, shook his head, and rolled his eyes back at this, rather as if he meditated running away again.

"Oh! you wicked little Robin!" said Eva, stroking the pony's glossy head. "I'm sure he knows what we are saying, Sir John."

"You should take care, Eva," said Sir John, also stroking Robin's head.

"Oh! there's no danger," said Robert Horton, rather jealously. "Miss Eva likes the fun of being run away with, I think."

"Well, take care of her," said Sir John, quietly; and then after touching his hat to Eva, he moved on towards West-house

He found Jasper and Elizabeth in the dining-room, when he reached it This was one of Jasper's bad days; days when the terrible shock that his constitution had received brought on severe nervous pains, rendering him for the time in a very prostrate condition. He was lying on a couch near the window, and Elizabeth was bathing his brow with eau-de-Cologne and water when Sir John entered the room, but Jasper had always a smile ready to greet his father.

"He is suffering very much to-day," said Elizabeth, gently, to Sir John.

"Are you, my dear boy!" said Sir John, and he drew a chair, and sat down beside his son.

By-and-bye he said, addressing Elizabeth, "I met young Horton and Eva as I came across the fields."

"Oh! Bob is quite devoted," said Jasper, with a little laugh.

"Well, she is a sweet girl," went on Sir John, suppressing another sigh, and seems quite happy again now."

"Thank God for that!" said Elizabeth.

"Yes, indeed," replied Sir John, and then the conversation changed, but Elizabeth noticed that Sir John was not in his usual calm, philosophic state of mind.

Yet when Eva came into the room, with her fair face flushed with exercise, Sir John told himself again, as he glanced at her in the soft twilight, that to think of wooing this sweet child would be an act of madness on his part.

"She will make some young man happy," thought Sir John, "and I must learn to be content with my lonely lot."

But though he made this decision, he reflected almost at the same time that Robert Horton was not a fit husband for Eva Dalziel, and he determined, when he had an opportunity, to speak to Elizabeth on the subject.

"The young man may be very well," thought the baronet, with an unconscious touch of pride, "but, independently of station, I would not like to see Eva married to a brother of the unhappy youth who did us all such dreadful wrong, and I cannot conceive how Jasper can seem so indifferent about it."

So, just before they left West-house, when Robert Horton (who had now also entered the room) said, "Shall I bring the pony for you to-morrow morning, Miss Eva?" Sir John answered for her, and declined this offer.

"Not to-morrow, I think, Eva," he said. "I heard Matilda say that she wished you to pay some visits with her to-morrow."

"Not in the morning, surely?" said Robert Horton, who did not like the Baronet's interference.

"Oh! some other day will do for Robin,' said Eva, smiling to

Robert; and then the party separated, Sir John gravely offering his arm to Eva, as soon as they were in the open air.

It was a tranquil, moonlight night, calm and still, and as Eva glanced at Sir John's face, she thought it wore a look of sadness which was not usual to it, and imagining that perhaps he was thinking of his son, she said, timidly—

"Jasper looked ill to-day, did he not, Sir John?"

"Yes," replied Sir John, "but he is subject to these changes, and will be so for years, the doctors told us in town. It is a sad change, is it not, Eva?" And Sir John looked down at the sweet girlish face by his side.

"Yes," said Eva; and then she added, quickly and nervously, "but he is happy, Sir John; happier than if this had not happened to him."

"You think so?" said Sir John, still looking at the delicate profile of Eva's face, for the girl had turned her head slightly away as she said the last few words.

"I do think so," answered Eva, and her colour deepened. "I think Jasper is happier with Elizabeth than he could have been—with any one else."

"It is generous of you to say so," said Sir John.

"Not now," said Eva, and her breath came quickly, "for now I see it was all for the best, Sir John—Elizabeth suits Jasper better than I should have done."

"And you don't regret it?" asked Sir John, slowly.

"No, certainly not," answered Eva quickly. "I am glad now that Elizabeth and Jasper are married."

"Thank God that it is so, my child," said Sir John, and he put his hand on Eva's which was resting on his arm; and as he did so, he felt it flutter and tremble beneath his touch.

They were close to the rustic gateway in the holly hedge at the end of the Hall grounds at this moment—the little gateway through which Harry Tyrell's murderer had crept to commit his cruel deed, and through which the miserable man had dragged Elizabeth on the fatal morning when he falsely accused Jasper of the crime; and as they passed it, Eva clung closer to Sir John.

"It was here, was it not?" she asked, in an awe-struck whisper.

"Yes," said Sir John, and he paused. "Here my light-hearted boy was called to go in a moment 'we know not where.' But," he added, kindly, moving onward again, as he felt the girl's arm tremble on his, "you are not afraid, surely, Eva?"

"I think I am rather," answered Eva, nervously.

"Perhaps it is natural," said Sir John, "for the young to fear death—but when a man comes to my age—" And Sir John sighed.

"But you are not old, Sir John!" said Eva, quickly, almost

forgetting her fears. "You should not talk as if you were an old man."

"Should I not, my child?" said Sir John, with rather a sad smile. "Well, then, when a man comes to middle age, Eva—"

"Yes?" said Eva, as Sir John paused.

"He looks on all things naturally," continued the Baronet, "with different eyes to the young. He knows then, Eva, that life must ever be a mingled skein, where good and evil will cross and recross each other in the strange, entangled web, through which every human soul must pass."

"But some people seem always very happy," said Eva modestly.

"We do not see behind the scenes, Eva," answered Sir John. "But the old, or the middle aged—if you like that better—know, or guess too well what is being enacted there."

"And you think—"

"I think," went on the Baronet, "that every man who has ever lived, unless he is wrapped in the fool's vain garments, learns, as he advances on the path of life, lessons which teach him its true value, and which prepare him to regard its inevitable end as by no means an unmixed evil. But I weary you with this dry talk, my child?"

"No, no," said Eva, "you never weary me." And after she had retired to her own room that night, she thought, almost impatiently, "He thinks of me as a child—he only regards me as a child."

In the meanwhile, however, Sir John was standing at one of his library windows, through which the moon was shining, his thoughtful face even more thoughtful than usual, and his ordinarily calm temperament strangely moved.

"What is it about this child that charms me so?" he was thinking. "It is not her beauty, surely—not the fleeting charms which in my youth attracted me to poor Eleanor? No, I am too old for this. It is the beauty of her mind, the truth, the purity, the sweet truthfulness of her unsoiled heart, that has made me, a man—well, of middle age, as she calls it—as stupid and foolish about her as any love-sick boy. But it is a vain folly," went on the Baronet's reflections: "She will marry some young man—she will never know that she has been the one perfect ideal of womanhood to me."

But in spite of Sir John's decision that Eva would marry a young man, he made it a point of duty to go across to West-house on the following afternoon, to represent to Elizabeth the impropriety of allowing Eva to be so constantly with Robert Horton.

Yet he felt exceedingly embarrassed to begin this conversation, remembering that Robert was Elizabeth's own cousin, and naturally unwilling to allude to the painful objection of his relationship to the miserable man who had caused them all such bitter pain.

Elizabeth could not understand Sir John's manner (usually so courteous and so calm) when he first arrived at West-house on his unpalatable errand. He began a subject and wandered from it. He went to talk to Jasper, who was lying on a couch, basking in the sun in the garden, and then he came back to Elizabeth, who was busy in her drawing-room, arranging some household accounts.

At last he began. "Elizabeth," he said, "I wish to say a few words to you, if it is not disturbing all this serious business." And he pointed to Elizabeth's accounts, which were lying on the table beside her, with rather an uneasy smile.

"Not in the least,' said Elizabeth, pushing her papers aside. "I was merely going through them this afternoon because Jasper has got a book which interests him, and so he does not need me to talk to him.'

"You are a good little wife, Elizabeth," said Sir John, still uneasily.

"Well," answered Elizabeth, smiling, I accept the compliment. And now tell me what it is you wish to say?"

Sir John took a turn across the room, and then he once more came behind Elizabeth's chair.

"I think, my dear," he said, "you will understand that I mean no disrespect to your cousin—but still—don't you think, Elizabeth, that as you and I are at present acting as guardians, or chaperons (or whatever you ladies call it) to Eva Dalziel, that you throw her too much with Robert Horton?"

"I don't think I throw them together, Sir John," answered Elizabeth, with a smile, for she thought she guessed now the cause of Sir John's nervousness.

"But at least you allow them to be constantly together," went on Sir John, "and I scarcely think that Major Dalziel—" And here Sir John made an expressive pause.

"Well, I do not think that Major Dalziel, or Dean Dalziel rather, for the Major is not ambitious," said Elizabeth still smiling, "need be afraid of Eva falling in love with poor Bob."

"But—it is only natural, Elizabeth," said Sir John with a sigh.

"Perhaps, so," went on Elizabeth. "But in my opinion," she added, looking pleasantly round at the Baronet, "there is much more danger of Eva falling in love with some one else."

"Whom do you mean, Elizabeth?" asked Sir John, quickly.

"I mean a certain Sir John Tyrell," answered Elizabeth, with some playfulness. "A certain Sir John Tyrell, who seems to forget that he is much more with Eva than my poor cousin Bob."

"But, my dear girl, what nonsense! I am old enough to be her father." And Sir John sighed again as he made this last remark.

"But then you are so handsome, Sir John!" said Elizabeth.

"Nonsense, nonsense!" cried Sir John; but the man was human, and he coloured, and a pleased smile stole over his fine face.

"But it is a fact!" went on Elizabeth, laughing. "And really, without joking," she added, more seriously, and she rose and took Sir John's hand, "I believe that Eva cares for you. She is a girl, you know," continued Elizabeth, "peculiarly fitted to marry a man older than herself, for it is her nature to cling to some one stronger than she is. She is a dear, loving, tender-hearted child, and I feel sure, Sir John, she will bring sunshine and happiness to your home, if you will ask her to remain there."

"If I were twenty years younger—" said Sir John, hesitatingly.

"Well," answered Elizabeth, smiling, "I cannot take away the twenty years, nor do I, as a rule, approve of marriages where there is a great difference of age. But you know there are not many Sir Johns."

"My dear, you flatter me outrageously!" said Sir John; but though he might say this, Elizabeth's words were not without balm and pleasantness to his soul.

Nay, so strongly did they influence him, that as he recrossed the fields towards the Hall, he made up his mind to ask Eva to be his wife. "It is a vain man only who fears rejection," he thought; "and Eva will not marry me, I feel sure of that, unless she feels she can love me as she ought."

Yet, as ill-luck would have it, Eva had never looked more childish than she did on this very day, when Sir John was contemplating taking so serious a step. A young gentleman of the neighbourhood, and a supposed admirer of one of the Miss Tyrells, chanced to be dining at the Hall, and Eva had arrayed herself in some airy, white fabric which added to the extreme youthfulness of her appearance. But when she put her little hand on Sir John's arm, and looked with her sweet, trustful eyes into his face, all doubts vanished from the Baronet's mind. "I will try to make her love me," he thought, "I will try to win her love."

He watched her as she moved about the room; noting that if anything were said that touched or moved her sympathies, she looked at him, as if she knew that he would understand her thoughts. This was true. Though the difference of age was so great between them, they had much in common, and Sir John's fine and delicate instincts recognized this fact. No mean word or contemptible idea had ever stained this fair girl's lips, and of Sir John it might truly be said—

> "And thus he bore without abuse
> The grand old name of gentleman."

None of the Tyrells were like their father. Jasper, the most high-minded and generous-hearted of them, yet lacked the almost chivalrous nobleness of character that distinguished Sir John.

Jasper was too fiery and passionate to reach the calm heights to which his father's larger and more elevated mind had soared. But few understood this; few saw beyond the placid pleasantness of manner that made Sir John always an agreeable companion, and hid away from those whom he did not care to interest, the finer and tenderer emotions of his heart.

And now, in middle age, a strange longing for sympathy—a longing which, through the years of his uncongenial married existence, he had never dared to hope for—had come over him. This feeling had arisen at a young girl's trustful glance; in the belief that he understood and appreciated the gentle nobleness (of which Eva herself was quite unaware) which had made her act so sweet and womanly a part in her connection with his son.

Jasper had never appreciated Eva, Sir John thought. He had regarded her as a dear, pretty girl, who would make a good wife, and that was all. But to Sir John she seemed far beyond this, and each day increased his admiration of her character.

But though it may not be a very difficult thing for a man to make up his mind to ask a woman to marry him, when he likes and admires her as much as Sir John liked and admired Eva, it is sometimes a very difficult thing to accomplish. Sir John, at least, found it so. For the first time almost in his life, he could not find words or courage to say what he wished. A sort of shyness, too, came over Eva; a shyness which a vainer man would not have found it very difficult to understand.

Things went on thus for a few days after Elizabeth had spoken to Sir John about Eva, and then an incident occurred which settled the matter. Eva had been spending the day with Elizabeth, and it was agreed that in the evening Sir John should go across to West-house to bring Eva back to the Hall, and he had told himself many times during the day that he must find words and opportunity to ask the momentous question this night.

When he reached West-house, he found the whole of the party out of doors, and he accordingly went into the garden to seek them. He saw nothing of them at first, for Jasper and Elizabeth had strolled into some of the adjoining fields. As, however, he neared a little rustic summer-house in the grounds, which the young Hortons had erected when they were boys, and which is now thickly covered with ivy, he heard distinctly, in the clear air, the sound of a woman's voice speaking in tones of great agitation. For a moment Sir John paused, and his cheek grew pale; the next he passed on with his stately step, and as he did so, he heard Eva say—

"It is unjust and ungenerous of you to say such things. Miss Tyrell is incapable of saying anything so mean !"

"Well, I'm only telling you what I've heard, though I cannot believe it," said Robert Horton, in rather sullen tones. Then he suddenly stopped, for they both now saw and heard Sir John passing the summer-house.

But Sir John (on Eva's account) affected to have no knowledge of their near vicinity. He passed the summer-house, walked slowly out of the garden, and returned to the house, and waited there until Jasper and Elizabeth came in. Presently Eva passed the windows, and also came into the house, but she did not go into the room where Sir John, Elizabeth, and Jasper were, but went upstairs, and sat down there in a very agitated and unhappy frame of mind.

The truth was that, during the evening, while they were in the summer-house, Robert Horton had made a proposal of marriage. This Eva had gently, but firmly, declined. Then, with some temper and surprise, perhaps, Robert Horton had asked her the reason.

"I—I—do not think you have quite a right to ask, Mr. Robert," said Eva, hesitatingly.

"People say, you know," said Robert, forgetting himself in his disappointment and anger, "that you actually think of marrying Sir John—that Miss Tyrell says you think of it."

Then Eva had answered the words that Sir John had overheard, and Robert made the reply which had also reached the Baronet's ears.   At this moment Sir John's step passing the summer-house had startled them both, and with burning blushes Eva looked indignantly at Robert.

"Sir John must have heard you!" she said. "What shall I do? I can never look in his face again!"

"Nonsense! an old man like that! What matter is it?" answered Robert Horton, who, however, really was anything but pleased at the idea that Sir John should have overheard his ungentlemanly speech to Eva. "Besides, he added, "he didn't seem to know we were here."

"He is too gentlemanly to do so," said Eva, still indignantly. And not all Robert's apologies (who began to see into what rudeness his temper had betrayed him) could make poor Eva forget his unkind words.

By-and-by (as Eva did not come downstairs) Sir John asked Elizabeth to enquire if she were ready to return to the Hall with him. He did this so nervously, that Elizabeth guessed at once that something had occurred in her absence, and when she went upstairs to seek Eva, she found her sitting, poor child, crying in the dark.

"My dear, what has happened?" asked Elizabeth putting her arms round Eva's neck.

"Mr. Robert has said something to me so rude—so unkind," sobbed Eva, "that I shall leave Wendell."

"Robert!" repeated Elizabeth, in astonishment, "why, my dear, he thinks no one is like you!"

"It was about Sir John," said Eva, drying her eyes.

"Oh!" said Elizabeth, who began to see how it was. "Well, never mind, dear. Youths of Robert's age, when they are jealous, sometimes forget themselves. Come, dear Eva, bathe your eyes and smooth your hair, and come downstairs. Sir John sent me to inquire if you were ready to walk home with him."

"I'm afraid he overheard what Mr. Robert said," answered Eva.

"If he did, Sir John is not a man to care for a stupid youth's speech," said Elizabeth, with a smile, kissing Eva.

Eva, accordingly, did bathe her eyes, and did come downstairs at Elizabeth's bidding, and when she did so, Sir John rose at once to leave.

"I think we had better go now, Eva," he said, and Eva made no objection; hoping in her heart that Sir John had not overheard, or, at least, understood, what Robert Horton had said.

But scarcely had they left the West-house, when all doubt in her mind was over on this subject.

"Eva," began Sir John, before they had quitted the avenue, "I must tell you something. I must tell you that I overheard a few words that you said to-night in the summer-house to young Horton—and as I heard my daughter's name—" And Sir John hesitated.

"It was some impertinent folly," said Eva, quickly and hotly. "Something that Mr. Horton had no right to say to me!"

"Then," said Sir John, gently, "you do not care for this young man, Eva?"

"Certainly not," answered Eva, with energy. "He is Elizabeth's cousin—that is the only reason—"

"Of your being friendly with him?" asked Sir John, as Eva paused.

"Yes, the only reason," said Eva.

"In that case," went on Sir John, in his grave, sweet manner, "may I say something to you, Eva?" And he took her trembling hand in his. "May I tell you something that I have thought of, almost ever since you have been here?"

"Oh! Sir John," said Eva, with a nervous little start.

"I am so much older than you," continued Sir John, "that I scarcely know how to shape the question that I wish so much to ask, lest you should think it too preposterous, too absurd. But, Eva—if you could learn to care for me—my whole future life would be devoted to repay you for your love?"

For a moment Eva did not answer. Then, falteringly and sweetly, she said—

"I—I—cannot *learn* to care for you, Sir John—for—"

"What, dear child?" asked Sir John, eagerly, as Eva paused, looking quickly down into the fair and blushing face so near his.

"*For I do*," whispered Eva, and the next moment Sir John ha
clasped her to his breast.

"My dearest little girl!" he said.   "God grant that I ma
make you happy—as happy as I wish my darling wife to be!"

CHAPTER XLVII, AND LAST.
A BRIDAL PARTY.

EVA would not allow any one to be told of her engagement t
Sir John, until her dear father knew of it.   The Major accord
ingly received a very pressing and urgent letter from the Barone
inviting him to come at once to Wendell, and Eva wrote to hin
also by the same post.

"I have *something* very particular to tell you, dear papa," sh
informed the Major; and Mrs. Dalziel immediately decided tha
it was an offer of marriage from Robert Horton.

"Take my word for it, Henry," she said, shaking her head
"for it is what I have always feared.   I was not consulted abou
this visit to Wendell Hall.   In my opinion it was indelicate o
Eva to go, and I felt certain from the first that no good woul
come of it—and you see my words are true."

"We had better wait to hear what she has got to tell us, befor
we decide whether it is bad or good news, said the Major, wh
had his own private opinion on the subject.

"You would not consider this Mr. Robert Horton a goo
marriage for Eva, even after her disappointment, I suppose?'
asked Mrs. Dalziel.

"No; certainly not," answered the Major, quickly.

"Then you will see," said Mrs. Dalziel, gloomily.   But th
Major declined to continue the discussion, and on the following
day started for Wendell, leaving his wife to break her apprehensions gradually to her two young daughters, of Eva having
formed an unsuitable engagement.

"It is sad for you, my dears," she said, "but we could expec
nothing else after Eva's first unfortunate affair."

As soon as the Major reached Wendell, he had an interview
with his daughter; and when, with faltering tongue and many
blushes, Eva proceeded to tell her papa the news, the Major pul
on rather a comical smile."

"Aren't you surprised, papa?   Aren't you very much surprised?" asked Eva.

"Not very much, my dear," answered the Major; "for I ofter
walked behind you and Sir John in town."   And the Major gave
a little laugh as he made the reply.

He, however, felt a truly thankful and happy man when he
looked on his young daughter's face.   Eva really liked Sir John,
and was not a little proud of having been chosen by so superioi
a man.   "The only thing is," she told him, with the sweet humil-

rty of her nature, "that I am not half good enough for you."
But Sir John answered with a smile, "I am quite content, my
child," and Eva knew in her heart that his words were true.

The Major, therefore, had only to give his consent, and to
listen with agreeable astonishment to the very handsome settlement with which Sir John proposed to endow his bride.   Sir John,
indeed, was a rich man, and could please himself, and it was no
small satisfaction to the Major to know that his favourite child
was thus amply provided for.

Eva took her papa across to West-house to see Elizabeth the
first day that he was at Wendell, and while the Major was
talking to Jasper, she drew Elizabeth aside and whispered a word
in her ear.   What that word was we can understand, for a glad
smile came over Elizabeth's face as she stooped down and kissed
Eva's blooming cheek.

"And you are content?   You are happy?" she said quickly.

"Yes," said Eva "I am content and happy," and Elizabeth's
heart too felt content and happy at her words.

When Jasper was told of it, he first exclaimed "By Jove!"
And then rather a harsh little laugh broke from his lips. "We need
not have distressed ourselves so much, need we, Elizabeth,
about her?" he said, and he held out his hand to his wife.

"Yes, dear," answered Elizabeth, looking fondly into his face,
"for I am sure she suffered very, very much.   But there are
natures, you know, whose wounds mercifully heal quickly, and
thank God that dear little Eva's is one of these."

"Dear old boy!" went on Jasper. the next moment, thinking
of his father, of whom he was very fond.   "Well I hope and
trust he may be happy."

"I have no fear," said Elizabeth.   "As years go on, Eva will
cling more and more to Sir John.   His wife is sure to love him."

"My dear," laughed Jasper, "I shall begin to be jealous."

"And Jasper's wife is sure to love him always too," half
whispered Elizabeth, and Jasper answered with some tender
word.

Everything thus was soon settled amicably at Wendell.   The
Misses Tyrell, when told of their father's engagement, were too
wise to make any open objections, and indeed consoled themselves with the idea that sooner or later he was sure to have
married "some one."

But Mrs. Dalziel's congratulations were the most profuse.
When the Major, with some timidity in his heart, it must be confessed, wrote to inform her of the news, and began his letter by
breaking it gradually (he expected) by telling her that he had
noticed Sir John's attentions to Eva in the Spring, but that he
had thought it wiser not to mention anything about them, Mrs.
Dalziel replied to the letter in the following terms :—

"My dear Henry,—Had you treated me with the confidence that as a devoted wife I think I deserve, you would have spared me *months* of cruel anxiety about our beloved Eva. You never (as you say in your letter) *hinted* to me the brilliant prospects that were opening before her, but allowed me to endure an *immense* amount of mental disquietude at the idea that she might form some unsuitable engagement. But I will say no more. Luckily for me, amid all the trials of my life, I endeavour by pious meditation to fortify myself to bear them; and now in this moment of apparently unqualified joy, I must try not to allow too sanguine expectations of the future to arise in my heart. Still I offer you (and I shall write also to our dearest child) my *cordial congratulations.* You speak of Sir John as being a little old for Eva, but I cannot call a man in the *prime* of life *old*. His position also, and the very handsome settlement that he proposes to make, are, I think, everything to be desired; and with love and forgiveness for all the anxiety you have *unnecessarily* caused me,

"I remain your devoted wife,
"Lucy Dalziel.

"P. S. I think we may now reasonably hope that our dear Anna and Lucy may also make good marriages."

Mrs. Dalziel's letter to Eva was equally characteristic. She assured her that she prayed night and day for the happiness of "my beloved child," and trusted that "nothing *this time*" would interfere with the happy prospects before her. She also wrote to Sir John, but Sir John read the letter in private with a smile, and then, without any comment on it, even to Eva, put it quietly into the fire. The Dean also wrote, accompanying his congratulations with an invitation to Eva to stay at the Deanery until the time of her marriage.

This, after a little consideration—a little shrinking, perhaps, at the idea of returning to Hazelhurst, where she had borne such cruel pain—she determined to accept. Both by Sir John's wishes and her own it was agreed that the marriage was not to take place until after the anniversary of poor Lady Tyrell's death was over. This had occurred early in the December of the previous year, and so Sir John and Eva decided on January as the month in which they were to be married.

Eva left Wendell with her father, and Sir John also accompanied her to Greyminster, and paid many visits there during the autumn and early winter to his young betrothed. At each of these visits he grew more and more attached to Eva; and Eva, in the sweet, pretty way which was natural to her, trusted and confided in Sir John, all her heart's pure hopes. The Dean was sincerely pleased at the marriage his pretty niece was about to form, and exerted himself to make Sir John's visits to Greyminster highly agreeable.

Then, when the chill days of January set in, he began to prepare for the wedding festivities. The Dean knew how to do things well, and he did them well. He chose his guests on this occasion from among the most distinguished of his acquaintances; not necessarily for their wealth nor their rank, but for the estimation in which they were regarded in the circles in which the proud Churchman had chosen to form his friends.

It was a real trial to him, therefore, to know that he would be obliged to invite his brother and his wife. The quiet Major might have passed, thought the Dean, "but *that woman!*"

"I suppose;" he said, hesitatingly, to Eva, "your step-mother will expect to. be asked?"

"Oh! yes, Uncle Ralph," laughed Eva,; "I think mamma would die if you were to leave her out."

"Well, I hope, without wishing her any serious ill, my dear, that she may take an opportune attack of influenza, which is a common ailment of hers, isn't it?" said the Dean, smiling rather sourly. "I must impress upon her in my letter, I think, that the Deanery is damp."

"O, Uncle Ralph!"

"At least I hope if she does come," went on the Dean, "that she will keep herself quiet. I suppose it will be etiquette for Sir John to take her in to dinner on the 18th?" The 18th being the day before Eva's marriage was to take place, when all the wedding guests would be assembled at Greyminster.

Alas, poor Dean! Mrs. Dalziel came to the Deanery on the 18th, determined to show every one there that, as the bride elect's mother, she ought to be considered a person of considerable consequence. She talked of her "dear brother-in-law the Dean," until the Dean nearly forgot dignity and hospitality alike; and she was absolutely coquettish with her future son-in-law, telling him playfully many interesting anecdotes of "darling Eva's" infancy and youth. Sir John, however, bore it all manfully. He took Mrs. Dalziel in to dinner, and demeaned himself to her with kindness and courtesy. Once, however—nay, twice—he thought he heard her call him "*John,*" though not in a very firm or assured tone of voice. The third time he was certain he was not mistaken.

"John," said Mrs. Dalziel, hesitatingly, meaning to address her future son-in-law the Baronet.

"John," said the Baronet, authoritatively, calling to one of the footmen in attendance; "Mrs. Dalziel is speaking to you." And Mrs. Dalziel, covered with confusion, asked the man for a spoon.

But she did not venture on the familiarity again, and rather subsided after this episode. She, however, of course, made various inopportune remarks with happy unconsciousness, and

Sir John could not help feeling thankful that Hazelhurst and Wendell lay very wide apart.

He was too wise a man though to allow Mrs. Dalziel to ruffle his equanimity.   His pretty Eva was opposite to him, and when he looked on her sweet face, he was quite willing to pay the penalty of having Mrs. Dalziel for a mother-in-law.   Lady Curzon, too, goodnaturedly undertook to amuse Mrs. Dalziel after dinner, and on the whole the Dean alone suffered much from her presence. Mrs. Dalziel, however, retired to bed in the highest spirits.

"This day has repaid me, Henry," she said to the Major, "for the years of anxiety and devoted love that I have bestowed on your darling child.   When you asked me to marry you, I made a solemn resolution.   I said *his* child shall be my first care, and I thank Heaven during various trials I have never broken it."

"Very well, my dear," said the Major, mildly.

"Is it not true, Henry?" said Mrs. Dalziel, surveying herself with gratification in one of the Dean's cheval-glasses.   "Have I done my duty to dear Eva, or have I not?"

"Certainly, my dear, certainly," replied the Major, and Mrs. Dalziel therefore commenced removing her finery in a contented state of mind.

The marriage the next day passed off very well.   The Dean read the service, and the Major gave his little girl away, feeling as he did so that some of the brightness of his own home went with her.   Then followed the wedding breakfast, the display of the presents, and the congratulations of the guests.   Among the most beautiful presents that Eva received, and one which was was most universally admired, was a very splendid diamond and ruby pendant from Elizabeth and Jasper.   They had been invited to the wedding, but had declined.   Jasper's health, Elizabeth wrote, prevented his joining in any gaiety, and every one felt that under the circumstances they were better away.

But it was a very tender letter that Elizabeth wrote to the bride, and the bride answered it in very loving words.   "I would just like to see you dressed for a minute," Elizabeth had written, and Eva replied by promising when she came home to Wendell that she would don her wedding dress a second time for Elizabeth's benefit.

The sun was shining when Eva was married, and as the old saying runs, the sun never shone on a fairer bride.   Sir John might well look with pride as well as love on the graceful, white-robed girl that he swore to love and cherish; and Eva did look with pride on the grave and handsome gentleman, to whom she plighted her troth.

When it was all over, and the bride and bridegroom had left, the Major lit a cigar, and strolled out rather pensively beneath the cathedral tower of Greyminster.   After all, he thought, his little girl was gone from him. But when he hinted something of this feeling to his brother the Dean, during the afternoon, the Dean smiled rather grimly.

"My dear Henry," he said, "do you remember the quotation? 'How blessings brighten as they take their flight!' I recall to my recollection at this moment how I left you apparently in absolute despair at Hazelhurst, now a little more than a year ago, because your 'blessing' or your 'little girl,' or whatever name you choose to designate Eva by, was then left unexpectedly on your hands." And the Major laughed good-naturedly, and admitted that the Dean's words were true.

But if her papa felt a little sad at losing Eva, Mrs. Dalziel's elation knew no bounds. When she first returned to Hazelhurst, indeed, she was almost unbearable. She sent for her friend the doctor, and boasted until even the doctor grew weary. As for the old one-legged sailor, Captain Marshall, after she had informed him during a visit that he paid her, that Sir John Tyrell had said this, and that Sir John Tyrell had said the other, at least twenty times, the old sea-captain rose almost with a roar.

"Madam," he said, seizing his hat; "I've been Sir John Tyrelled enough for one day!" And he accordingly marched out of the house, stumping down his wooden leg with extraordinary vigour, and leaving Mrs. Dalziel certainly feeling rather uncomfortable.

To write to Eva also, was a subject of endless complacency to her. No one ever called upon Mrs. Dalziel now, that she had not just heard from, or was just going to write to, my dear child, Lady Tyrell." Little Eva, in her wanderings abroad with her husband, received so many letters from "Mamma," that at last Sir John, with rather a comical smile, asked Eva what they were all about?

"I cannot tell you," answered Eva, laughing, "but if you would like to read them—"

"Not for the world!" cried Sir John, with such genuine alarm on his face that Eva could not contain her mirth.

It was quite the spring before Sir John and Eva returned from their wedding tour. By this time Elizabeth and Jasper were settled in London, Jasper preferring to be in town, both on account of his health, and also because, being unable to join in country sports, he found more amusement and society there. There were changes at Wendell West-house, too, by this time. Robert Horton had got over his disappointment about Eva, and become engaged to a really nice girl in the neighbourhood; and Harry (to Elizabeth's great regret) insisted on being a soldier, and had left the homestead, and gone to Sandhurst.

"My dear," said the boy, on Elizabeth remonstrating with him on taking this step, "you see you are a swell now, and I do **not** wish you to be ashamed of me, if you are called upon to weep over my untimely grave. As Ensign or Lieutenant Horton, perhaps you might pay me this attention without disgrace; but if I were a lawyer's clerk, or a doctor's apprentice, I could not reasonably expect it."

"You foolish boy!" said Elizabeth. But for all that, Master Hal had his own way and left Wendell, paying frequent visits to Jasper and Elizabeth in town, whenever he had the opportunity.

Sir John and Eva came to Elizabeth's house at once on their return to England. Eva looked radiantly pretty, and whispered, as she flung her arms round Elizabeth's neck, "He is so good to me. He quite spoils me." And, indeed, the little lady was so daintily dressed, and altogether had such an air of lavish expenditure on her adornment, that Elizabeth thought there must be some truth in her words.

"But it is an excellent fault in a husband, my dear," answered Elizabeth, laughing, and Eva laughed also pleasantly at Elizabeth's reply.

Eva was very anxious that Elizabeth should go sometimes to places of amusement with herself and Sir John, but as Jasper was unable to accompany them, Elizabeth declined. On one occasion, however, Jasper interfered, and insisted that Elizabeth should go, and when she came down dressed to do so, he looked at her with great pride.

"My handsome girl!" he said, "Why don't you go out oftener, dressed as you are now? Every one would admire you, Lissa."

"I only care for one admirer, Sir," answered Elizabeth, with some of her old liveliness of manner, "and if I can keep him, I am content." And Jasper took her in his arms, while for a moment a strange moisture dimmed his eyes.

But if Elizabeth is a rare visitor among the rich and great, she is a very frequent one among the poor and needy. To darkened sick rooms, along the dreary wards of hospitals, she goes, a beautiful and welcome guest.

"God has been very good to me," she once said softly to some one who was wondering at her life; and so among the sick and sorrowing she chiefly spends her wealth and time.

THE END.